BY KATHERINE PATERSON

CONTENTS

HARPERCOLLINS*PUBLISHERS*

Bridge to Terabithia

By the Author

The Sign of the Chrysanthemum

Of Nightingales That Weep

The Master Puppeteer

Bridge to Terabithia

The Great Gilly Hopkins

Angels and Other Strangers

Jacob Have I Loved

Bridge to Terabithia

KATHERINE PATERSON

Illustrated by Donna Diamond

HARPERCOLLINS*PUBLISHERS*

Bridge to Terabithia

Printed in the United States of America. For information address HarperCollins Children's Books, a division of HarperCollins Publishers, 10 East 53rd Street, New York, NY 10022.

Library of Congress Cataloging-in-Publication Data
Paterson, Katherine.
Bridge to Terabithia.
Summary: The life of a ten-year-old boy in rural Virginia expands when he becomes friends with a newcomer who subsequently meets an untimely death trying to reach their hideaway, Terabithia, during a storm.
[1. Friendship—Fiction. 2. Death—Fiction.]
I. Diamond, Donna, ill. II. Title.
PZ7.P273Br [Fic] 77-2221
ISBN 0-690-01359-0
ISBN 0-690-04635-9 (lib. bdg.)
ISBN 0-06-440184-7 (pbk.)

First Harper Trophy edition, 1987

I wrote this book
for my son
David Lord Paterson,
but after he read it
he asked me to put Lisa's name
on this page as well,
and so I do.
For
David Paterson and Lisa Hill,
banzai

Contents

Bridge to Terabithia

ONE

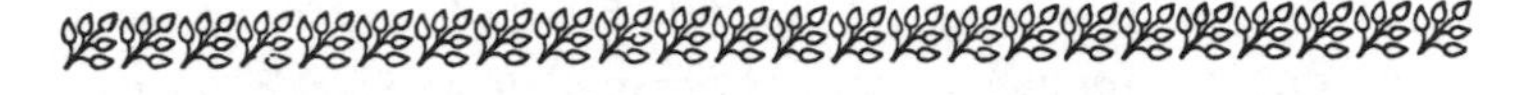

Jesse Oliver Aarons, Jr.

Ba-room, ba-room, ba-room, baripity, baripity, baripity, baripity—Good. His dad had the pickup going. He could get up now. Jess slid out of bed and into his overalls. He didn't worry about a shirt because once he began running he would be hot as popping grease even if the morning air was chill, or shoes because the bottoms of his feet were by now as tough as his worn-out sneakers.

"Where you going, Jess?" May Belle lifted herself up sleepily from the double bed where she and Joyce Ann slept.

"*Sh.*" He warned. The walls were thin. Momma would be mad as flies in a fruit jar if they woke her up this time of day.

He patted May Belle's hair and yanked the twisted sheet up to her small chin. "Just over the cow field," he whispered. May Belle smiled and snuggled down under the sheet.

"Gonna run?"

"Maybe."

Of course he was going to run. He had gotten up early every day all summer to run. He figured if he worked at it—and Lord, had he worked—he could be the fastest runner in the fifth grade when school opened up. He had to be the fastest—not one of the fastest or next to the fastest, but *the* fastest. The very best.

He tiptoed out of the house. The place was so rattly that it screeched whenever you put your foot down, but Jess had found that if you tiptoed, it gave only a low moan, and he could usually get outdoors without waking Momma or Ellie or Brenda or Joyce Ann. May Belle was another matter. She was going on seven, and she worshiped him, which was OK sometimes. When you were the only boy smashed between four sisters, and the older two had despised you ever since you stopped letting them dress you up and wheel you around in their rusty old doll carriage, and the littlest one cried if you looked at her cross-eyed, it was nice to have somebody who worshiped you. Even if it got unhandy sometimes.

He began to trot across the yard. His breath was coming out in little puffs—cold for August. But it was early yet. By noontime when his mom would have him out working, it would be hot enough.

Miss Bessie stared at him sleepily as he climbed across the scrap heap, over the fence, and into the cow field. "*Moo—oo,*" she said, looking for all the world like another May Belle with her big, brown droopy eyes.

"Hey, Miss Bessie," Jess said soothingly. "Just go on back to sleep."

Miss Bessie strolled over to a greenish patch—most of the field was brown and dry—and yanked up a mouthful.

"That'a girl. Just eat your breakfast. Don't pay me no mind."

He always started at the northwest corner of the field, crouched over like the runners he had seen on *Wide World of Sports*.

"Bang," he said, and took off flying around the cow field. Miss Bessie strolled toward the center, still following him with her droopy eyes, chewing slowly. She didn't look very smart, even for a cow, but she was plenty bright enough to get out of Jess's way.

His straw-colored hair flapped hard against his forehead, and his arms and legs flew out every which way. He had never learned to run properly, but he was long-legged for a ten-year-old, and no one had more grit than he.

Lark Creek Elementary was short on everything, especially athletic equipment, so all the balls went to the upper grades at recess time after lunch. Even if a fifth grader started out the period with a ball, it was sure to be in the hands of a sixth or seventh grader before the hour was half over. The older boys always took the dry center of the upper field for their ball games, while the girls claimed the small top section for hopscotch and jump rope and hanging around talking. So the lower-grade boys had started this running thing. They would all line up on the far side of the lower field, where it was either muddy or deep crusty ruts. Earle Watson who was no good at running, but had a big mouth, would yell "Bang!" and they'd race to a line they'd toed across at the other end.

One time last year Jesse had won. Not just the first heat but the whole shebang. Only once. But it had put into his mouth a taste for winning. Ever since he'd been in first grade he'd been that "crazy little kid that draws all the time." But one day—April the twenty-second, a drizzly Monday, it had been—he ran ahead of them all, the red mud slooching up through the holes in the bottom of his sneakers.

For the rest of that day, and until after lunch on the next, he had been "the fastest kid in the third, fourth, *and* fifth grades," and he only a fourth grader. On Tuesday, Wayne Pettis had won again as usual. But this year Wayne Pettis would be in the sixth grade. He'd play football until Christmas and baseball until June with the rest of the big guys. Anybody had a chance to be the fastest runner, and by Miss Bessie, this year it was going to be Jesse Oliver Aarons, Jr.

Jess pumped his arms harder and bent his head for the distant fence. He could hear the third-grade boys screaming him on. They would follow him around like a country-music star. And May Belle would pop her buttons. *Her brother* was the fastest, the best. That ought to give the rest of the first grade something to chew their cuds on.

Even his dad would be proud. Jess rounded the corner. He couldn't keep going quite so fast, but he continued running for a while—it would build him up. May Belle would tell Daddy, so it wouldn't look as though he, Jess, was a bragger.

Maybe Dad would be so proud he'd forget all about how tired he was from the long drive back and forth to Washington and the digging and hauling all day. He would get right down on the floor and wrestle, the way they used to. Old Dad would be surprised at how strong he'd gotten in the last couple of years.

His body was begging him to quit, but Jess pushed it on. He had to let that puny chest of his know who was boss.

"Jess." It was May Belle yelling from the other side of the scrap heap. "Momma says you gotta come in and eat now. Leave the milking til later."

Oh, crud. He'd run too long. Now everyone would know he'd been out and start in on him.

"Yeah, OK." He turned, still running, and headed for the scrap heap. Without breaking his rhythm, he climbed over the fence, scrambled across the scrap heap, thumped May Belle on the head ("Owww!"), and trotted on to the house.

"We-ell, look at the big O-lympic star," said Ellie, banging two cups onto the table, so that the strong, black coffee sloshed out. "Sweating like a knock-kneed mule."

Jess pushed his damp hair out of his face and plunked down on the wooden bench. He dumped two spoonfuls of sugar into his cup and slurped to keep the hot coffee from scalding his mouth.

"*Oooo*, Momma, he stinks." Brenda pinched her nose with her pinky crooked delicately. "Make him wash."

"Get over here to the sink and wash yourself," his mother said without raising her eyes from the stove. "And step on it. These grits are scorching the bottom of the pot already."

"Momma! Not again," Brenda whined.

Lord, he was tired. There wasn't a muscle in his body that didn't ache.

"You heard what Momma said," Ellie yelled at his back.

"I can't stand it, Momma!" Brenda again. "Make him get his smelly self off this bench."

Jess put his cheek down on the bare wood of the tabletop.

"Jess-*see*!" His mother was looking now. "And put on a shirt."

"Yes'm." He dragged himself to the sink. The water he flipped on his face and up his arms pricked like ice. His hot skin crawled under the cold drops.

May Belle was standing in the kitchen door watching him.

"Get me a shirt, May Belle."

She looked as if her mouth was set to say no, but instead she said, "You shouldn't ought to beat me in the head," and went off obediently to fetch his T-shirt. Good old May Belle. Joyce Ann would have been screaming yet from that little tap. Four-year-olds were a pure pain.

"I got plenty of chores needs doing around here this morning," his mother announced as they were finishing the grits and red gravy. His mother was from Georgia and still cooked like it.

"Oh, *Momma*!" Ellie and Brenda squawked in concert. Those girls could get out of work faster than grasshoppers could slip through your fingers.

"Momma, you promised me and Brenda we could go to Millsburg for school shopping."

"You ain't got no money for school shopping!"

"*Momma.* We're just going to look around." Lord, he wished Brenda would stop whining so. "*Christmas*! You don't want us to have no fun at all."

"*Any* fun," Ellie corrected her primly.

"Oh, shuttup."

Ellie ignored her. "Miz Timmons is coming by to pick us up. I told Lollie Sunday you said it was OK. I feel dumb calling her and saying you changed your mind."

"Oh, all right. But I ain't got no money to give you."

Any money, something whispered inside Jess's head.

"I know, Momma. We'll just take the five dollars Daddy promised us. No more'n that."

"What five dollars?"

"Oh, Momma, you *remember*." Ellie's voice was sweeter than a melted Mars Bar. "Daddy said last week we girls were going to have to have *something* for school."

"Oh, take it," his mother said angrily, reaching for her cracked vinyl purse on the shelf above the stove. She counted out five wrinkled bills.

"Momma"—Brenda was starting again—"can't we have just one more? So it'll be three each?"

"No!"

"Momma, you can't buy nothing for two fifty. Just one little pack of notebook paper's gone up to . . ."

"No!"

Ellie got up noisily and began to clear the table. "Your turn to wash, Brenda," she said loudly.

"*Awww*, Ellie."

Ellie jabbed her with a spoon. Jesse saw that look. Brenda shut up her whine halfway out of her Rose Lustre lipsticked mouth. She wasn't as smart as Ellie, but even she knew not to push Momma too far.

Which left Jess to do the work as usual. Momma never sent the babies out to help, although if he worked it right he could usually get May Belle to do something. He put his head down on the table. The running had done him in this morning. Through his top ear came the sound of the Timmonses' old Buick—"Wants oil," his dad would say—and the happy buzz of voices outside the screen door as Ellie and Brenda squashed in among the seven Timmonses.

"All right, Jesse. Get your lazy self off that bench. Miss

Bessie's bag is probably dragging ground by now. And you still got beans to pick."

Lazy. *He* was the lazy one. He gave his poor deadweight of a head one minute more on the tabletop.

"Jess-*see*!"

"OK, Momma. I'm *going*."

It was May Belle who came to tell him in the bean patch that people were moving into the old Perkins place down on the next farm. Jess wiped his hair out of his eyes and squinted. Sure enough. A U-Haul was parked right by the door. One of those big jointed ones. These people had a lot of junk. But they wouldn't last. The Perkins place was one of those ratty old country houses you moved into because you had no decent place to go and moved out of as quickly as you could. He thought later how peculiar it was that here was probably the biggest thing in his life, and he had shrugged it off as nothing.

The flies were buzzing around his sweating face and shoulders. He dropped the beans into the bucket and swatted with both hands. "Get me my shirt, May Belle." The flies were more important than any U-Haul.

May Belle jogged to the end of the row and picked up his T-shirt from where it had been discarded earlier. She walked back holding it with two fingers way out in front of her. "*Oooo*, it stinks," she said, just as Brenda would have.

"Shuttup," he said and grabbed the shirt away from her.

TWO

Leslie Burke

Ellie and Brenda weren't back by seven. Jess had finished all the picking and helped his mother can the beans. She never canned except when it was scalding hot anyhow, and all the boiling turned the kitchen into some kind of hellhole. Of course, her temper had been terrible, and she had screamed at Jess all afternoon and was now too tired to fix any supper.

Jess made peanut-butter sandwiches for the little girls and himself, and because the kitchen was still hot and almost nauseatingly full of bean smell, the three of them went outside to eat.

The U-Haul was still out by the Perkins place. He couldn't see anybody moving outside, so they must have finished unloading.

"I hope they have a girl, six or seven," said May Belle. "I need somebody to play with."

"You got Joyce Ann."

"I hate Joyce Ann. She's nothing but a baby."

Joyce Ann's lip went out. They both watched it tremble. Then her pudgy body shuddered, and she let out a great cry.

"Who's teasing the baby?" his mother yelled out the screen door.

Jess sighed and poked the last of his sandwich into Joyce Ann's open mouth. Her eyes went wide, and she clamped her jaws down on the unexpected gift. Now maybe he could have some peace.

He closed the screen door gently as he entered and slipped past his mother, who was rocking herself in the kitchen chair watching TV. In the room he shared with the little ones, he dug under his mattress and pulled out his pad and pencils. Then, stomach down on the bed, he began to draw.

Jess drew the way some people drink whiskey. The peace would start at the top of his muddled brain and seep down through his tired and tensed-up body. Lord, he loved to draw. Animals, mostly. Not regular animals like Miss Bessie or the chickens, but crazy animals with problems—for some reason he liked to put his beasts into impossible fixes. This one was a hippopotamus just leaving the edge of the cliff, turning over and over—you could tell by the curving lines—in the air toward the sea below where surprised fish were leaping goggle-eyed out of the water. There was a balloon over the hippopotamus—where his head should have been but his bottom actually was—"Oh!" it was saying. "I seem to have forgot my glasses."

Jesse began to smile. If he decided to show it to May Belle, he would have to explain the joke, but once he did, she would laugh like a live audience on TV.

He would like to show his drawings to his dad, but he didn't dare. When he was in first grade, he had told his dad that he

wanted to be an artist when he grew up. He'd thought his dad would be pleased. He wasn't. "What are they teaching in that damn school?" he had asked. "Bunch of old ladies turning my only son into some kind of a—" He had stopped on the word, but Jess had gotten the message. It was one you didn't forget, even after four years.

The devil of it was that none of his regular teachers ever liked his drawings. When they'd catch him scribbling, they'd screech about waste—wasted time, wasted paper, wasted ability. Except Miss Edmunds, the music teacher. She was the only one he dared show anything to, and she'd only been at school one year, and then only on Fridays.

Miss Edmunds was one of his secrets. He was in love with her. Not the kind of silly stuff Ellie and Brenda giggled about on the telephone. This was too real and too deep to talk about, even to think about very much. Her long swishy black hair and blue, blue eyes. She could play the guitar like a regular recording star, and she had this soft floaty voice that made Jess squish inside. Lord, she was gorgeous. And she liked him, too.

One day last winter he had given her one of his pictures. Just shoved it into her hand after class and run. The next Friday she had asked him to stay a minute after class. She said he was "unusually talented," and she hoped he wouldn't let anything discourage him, but would "keep it up." That meant, Jess believed, that she thought he was the best. It was not the kind of best that counted either at school or at home, but it was a genuine kind of best. He kept the knowledge of it buried inside himself like a pirate treasure. He was rich, very rich, but no one could know about it for now except his fellow outlaw, Julia Edmunds.

"Sounds like some kinda hippie," his mother had said

when Brenda, who had been in seventh grade last year, described Miss Edmunds to her.

She probably was. Jess wouldn't argue that, but he saw her as a beautiful wild creature who had been caught for a moment in that dirty old cage of a schoolhouse, perhaps by mistake. But he hoped, he prayed, she'd never get loose and fly away. He managed to endure the whole boring week of school for that one half hour on Friday afternoons when they'd sit on the worn-out rug on the floor of the teachers' room (there was no place else in the building for Miss Edmunds to spread out all her stuff) and sing songs like "My Beautiful Balloon," "This Land Is Your Land," "Free to Be You and Me," "Blowing in the Wind," and because Mr. Turner, the principal, insisted, "God Bless America."

Miss Edmunds would play her guitar and let the kids take turns on the autoharp, the triangles, cymbals, tambourines, and bongo drum. Lord, could they ever make a racket! All the teachers hated Fridays. And a lot of the kids pretended to.

But Jess knew what fakes they were. Sniffing "hippie" and "peacenik," even though the Vietnam War was over and it was supposed to be OK again to like peace, the kids would make fun of Miss Edmunds' lack of lipstick or the cut of her jeans. She was, of course, the only female teacher anyone had ever seen in Lark Creek Elementary wearing pants. In Washington and its fancy suburbs, even in Millsburg, that was OK, but Lark Creek was the backwash of fashion. It took them a long time to accept there what everyone could see by their TV's was OK anywhere else.

So the students of Lark Creek Elementary sat at their desks all Friday, their hearts thumping with anticipation as they listened to the joyful pandemonium pouring out from the teachers' room, spent their allotted half hours with Miss Edmunds under the spell of her wild beauty and in the snare of her enthusiasms, and then went out and pretended that they couldn't be suckered by some hippie in tight jeans with make-up all over her eyes but none on her mouth.

Jess just kept his mouth shut. It wouldn't help to try to defend Miss Edmunds against their unjust and hypocritical attacks. Besides, she was beyond such stupid behavior. It couldn't touch her. But whenever possible, he stole a few minutes on Friday just to stand close to her and hear her voice, soft and smooth as suede, assuring him that he was a "neat kid."

We're alike, Jess would tell himself, me and Miss Edmunds. Beautiful Julia. The syllables rolled through his head like a ripple of guitar chords. We don't belong at Lark Creek, Julia and me. "You're the proverbial diamond in the rough," she'd said to him once, touching his nose lightly with the tip of her electrifying finger. But it was she who was the diamond, sparkling out of that muddy, grassless, dirty-brick setting.

"Jess-*see*!"

Jess shoved the pad and pencils under his mattress and lay down flat, his heart thumping against the quilt.

His mother was at the door. "You milk yet?"

He jumped off the bed. "Just going to." He dodged around her and out, grabbing the pail from beside the sink and the stool from beside the door, before she could ask him what he had been up to.

Lights were winking out from all three floors of the old Perkins place. It was nearly dark. Miss Bessie's bag was tight, and she was fidgeting with discomfort. She should have been milked a couple of hours ago. He eased himself onto the stool and began to tug; the warm milk pinged into the pail. Down on the road an occasional truck passed by with its dimmers on.

His dad would be home soon, and so would those cagey girls who managed somehow to have all the fun and leave him and their mother with all the work. He wondered what they had bought with all their money. Lord, what he wouldn't give for a new pad of real art paper and a set of those marking pens—color pouring out onto the page as fast as you could think it. Not like stubby school crayons you had to press down on till somebody bitched about your breaking them.

A car was turning in. It was the Timmonses'. The girls had beat Dad home. Jess could hear their happy calls as the car doors slammed. Momma would fix them supper, and when he went in with the milk, he'd find them all laughing and chattering. Momma'd even forget she was tired and mad. He was the only onc who had to take that stuff. Sometimes he felt so lonely among all these females—even the one rooster had died, and they hadn't yet gotten another. With his father gone from sunup until well past dark, who was there to know how he felt? Weekends weren't any better. His dad was so tired from the wear and tear of the week and trying to catch up around the place that when he wasn't actually working, he was sleeping in front of the TV.

"Hey, Jesse." May Belle. The dumb kid wouldn't even let you think privately.

"What do you want now?"

He watched her shrink two sizes. "I got something to tell you." She hung her head.

"You ought to be in bed," he said huffily, mad at himself for cutting her down.

"Ellie and Brenda come home."

"Came. Came home." Why couldn't he quit picking on her?

But her news was too delicious to let him stop her sharing it. "Ellie bought herself a see-through blouse, and Momma's throwing a fit!"

Good, he thought. "That ain't nothing to cheer about," he said.

Baripity, baripity, baripity.

"Daddy!" May Belle screamed with delight and started running for the road. Jess watched his dad stop the truck, lean over to unlatch the door, so May Belle could climb in. He turned away. Durn lucky kid. She could run after him and grab him and kiss him. It made Jess ache inside to watch his dad grab the little ones to his shoulder, or lean down and hug them. It seemed to him that he had been thought too big for that since the day he was born.

When the pail was full, he gave Miss Bessie a pat to move her away. Putting the stool under his left arm, he carried the heavy pail carefully, so none of the milk would slop out.

"Mighty late with the milking, aren't you, son?" It was the only thing his father said directly to him all evening.

The next morning he almost didn't get up at the sound of the pickup. He could feel, even before he came fully awake, how tired he still was. But May Belle was grinning at him, propped up on one elbow. "Ain't 'cha gonna run?" she asked.

"No," he said, shoving the sheet away. "I'm gonna fly."

Because he was more tired than usual, he had to push himself harder. He pretended that Wayne Pettis was there, just ahead of him, and he had to keep up. His feet pounded the uneven ground, and he thrashed his arms harder and harder. He'd catch him. "Watch out, Wayne Pettis," he said between his teeth. "I'll get you. You can't beat me."

"If you're so afraid of the cow," the voice said, "why don't you just climb the fence?"

He paused in midair like a stop-action TV shot and turned,

almost losing his balance, to face the questioner, who was sitting on the fence nearest the old Perkins place, dangling bare brown legs. The person had jaggedy brown hair cut close to its face and wore one of those blue undershirtlike tops with faded jeans cut off above the knees. He couldn't honestly tell whether it was a girl or a boy.

"Hi," he or she said, jerking his or her head toward the Perkins place. "We just moved in."

Jess stood where he was, staring.

The person slid off the fence and came toward him. "I thought we might as well be friends," it said. "There's no one else close by."

Girl, he decided. Definitely a girl, but he couldn't have said why he was suddenly sure. She was about his height—not quite though, he was pleased to realize as she came nearer.

"My name's Leslie Burke."

She even had one of those dumb names that could go either way, but he was sure now that he was right.

"What's the matter?"

"Huh?"

"Is something the matter?"

"Yeah. No." He pointed his thumb in the direction of his own house, and then wiped his hair off his forehead. "Jess Aarons." Too bad May Belle's girl came in the wrong size. "Well—well." He nodded at her. "See you." He turned toward the house. No use trying to run any more this morning. Might as well milk Miss Bessie and get that out of the way.

"Hey!" Leslie was standing in the middle of the cow field, her head tilted and her hands on her hips. "Where you going?"

"I got work to do," he called back over his shoulder. When he came out later with the pail and stool, she was gone.

THREE

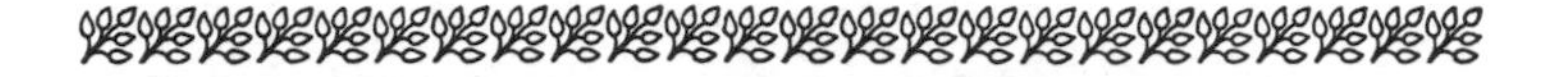

The Fastest Kid in the Fifth Grade

Jess didn't see Leslie Burke again except from a distance until the first day of school, the following Tuesday, when Mr. Turner brought her down to Mrs. Myers' fifth-grade class at Lark Creek Elementary.

Leslie was still dressed in the faded cutoffs and the blue undershirt. She had sneakers on her feet but no socks. Surprise swooshed up from the class like steam from a released radiator cap. They were all sitting there primly dressed in their spring Sunday best. Even Jess wore his one pair of corduroys and an ironed shirt.

The reaction didn't seem to bother her. She stood there in front, her eyes saying, "OK, friends, here I am," in answer to their open-mouthed stares while Mrs. Myers fluttered about trying to figure where to put the extra desk. The room was a small basement one, and five rows of six desks already filled it more than comfortably.

"Thirty-one," Mrs. Myers kept mumbling over her double

chin, "thirty-one. No one else has more than twenty-nine." She finally decided to put the desk up against the side wall near the front. "Just there for now—uh—Leslie. It's the best we can do—for now. This is a very crowded classroom." She swung a pointed glance at Mr. Turner's retreating form.

Leslie waited quietly until the seventh-grade boy who'd been sent down with the extra desk scraped it into position hard against the radiator and under the first window. Without making any noise, she pulled it a few inches forward from the radiator and settled herself into it. Then she turned once more to gaze at the rest of the class.

Thirty pairs of eyes were suddenly focused on desk-top scratches. Jess ran his forefinger around the heart with two pairs of initials, BR + SK, trying to figure out whose desk he had inherited. Probably Sally Koch's. Girls did more of the heart stuff in fifth grade than boys. Besides BR must be Billy Rudd, and Billy was known to favor Myrna Hauser last spring. Of course, these initials might have been here longer than that, in which case . . .

"Jesse Aarons. Bobby Greggs. Pass out the arithmetic books. Please." On the last word, Mrs. Myers flashed her famous first-day-of-school smile. It was said in the upper grades that Mrs. Myers had never been seen to smile except on the first and the last day of school.

Jess roused himself and went to the front. As he passed Leslie's desk, she grinned and rippled her fingers low in a kind of wave. He jerked a nod. He couldn't help feeling sorry for her. It must be embarrassing to sit in front when you find yourself dressed funny on the first day of school. And you don't know anybody.

He slapped the books down as Mrs. Myers directed. Gary Fulcher grabbed his arm as he went by. "Gonna run today?"

Jess nodded. Gary smirked. *He thinks he can beat me, the dumbhead.* At the thought, something jiggled inside Jess. He knew he was better than he had been last spring. Fulcher might think he was going to be the best, now that Wayne Pettis was in sixth, but he, Jess, planned to give old Fulcher a *le-etle* surprise come noon. It was as though he had swallowed grasshoppers. He could hardly wait.

Mrs. Myers handed out books almost as though she were President of the United States, dragging the distribution process out in senseless signings and ceremonies. It occurred to Jess that she, too, wished to postpone regular school as long as possible. When it wasn't his turn to pass out books, Jess sneaked out a piece of notebook paper and drew. He was toying with the idea of doing a whole book of drawings. He ought to choose one chief character and do a story about it. He scribbled several animals and tried to think of a name. A good title would get him started. *The Haunted Hippo*? He liked the ring of it. *Herby the Haunted Hippo*? Even better. *The Case of the Crooked Crocodile*. Not bad.

"Whatcha drawing?" Gary Fulcher was leaning way over his desk.

Jess covered the page with his arm. "Nothing."

"Ah, c'mon. Lemme see."

Jess shook his head.

Gary reached down and tried to pull Jess's hand away from the paper. "The Case of the Crooked—c'mon, Jess," he whispered hoarsely. "I ain't gonna hurt nothing." He yanked at Jess's thumb.

Jess put both arms over the paper and brought his sneaker heel crashing down on Gary Fulcher's toe.

"*Ye-ow*!"

"Boys!" Mrs. Myers' face had lost its lemon-pie smile.

"He stomped my toe."

"Take your seat, Gary."

"But he—"

"Sit down!"

"Jesse Aarons. One more peep from your direction and you can spend recess in here. Copying the dictionary."

Jess's face was burning hot. He slid the notebook paper back under his desk top and put his head down. A whole year of this. Eight more years of this. He wasn't sure he could stand it.

The children ate lunch at their desks. The county had been promising Lark Creek a lunchroom for twenty years, but there never seemed to be enough money. Jess had been so careful not to lose his recess time that even now he chewed his bologna sandwich with his lips tight shut and his eyes on the initialed heart. Around him conversations buzzed. They were not supposed to talk during lunch, but it was the first day and even Monster-Mouth Myers shot fewer flames on the first day.

"She's eating clabber." Two seats up from where he sat, Mary Lou Peoples was at work being the second snottiest girl in the fifth grade.

"Yogurt, stupid. Don't you watch TV?" This from Wanda Kay Moore, the snottiest, who sat immediately in front of Jess.

"Yuk."

Lord, why couldn't they leave people in peace? Why shouldn't Leslie Burke eat anything she durn pleased?

He forgot that he was trying to eat carefully and took a loud slurp of his milk.

Wanda Moore turned around, all priss-face. "Jesse Aarons. That noise is pure repulsive."

He glared at her hard and gave another slurp.

"You are disgusting."

Brrrrring. The recess bell. With a yelp, the boys were pushing for first place at the door.

"The boys will all sit down." Oh, Lord. "While the girls line up to go out to the playground. Ladies first."

The boys quivered on the edges of their seats like moths fighting to be freed of cocoons. Would she never let them go?

"All right, now if you boys . . ." They didn't give her a chance to change her mind. They were halfway to the end of the field before she could finish her sentence.

The first two out began dragging their toes to make the finish line. The ground was rutted from past rains, but had hardened in the late summer drought, so they had to give up on sneaker toes and draw the line with a stick. The fifth-grade boys, bursting with new importance, ordered the fourth graders this way and that, while the smaller boys tried to include themselves without being conspicuous.

"How many you guys gonna run?" Gary Fulcher demanded.

"Me—me—me." Everyone yelled.

"That's too many. No first, second, *or* third graders—except maybe the Butcher cousins and Timmy Vaughn. The rest of you will just be in the way."

Shoulders sagged, but the little boys backed away obediently.

"OK. That leaves twenty-six, twenty-seven—stand still—twenty-eight. You get twenty-eight, Greg?" Fulcher asked Greg Williams, his shadow.

"Right. Twenty-eight."

"OK. Now. We'll have eliminations like always. Count off by fours. Then we'll run all the ones together, then the twos—"

"We know. We know." Everyone was impatient with Gary, who was trying for all the world to sound like this year's Wayne Pettis.

Jess was a four, which suited him well enough. He was impatient to run, but he really didn't mind having a chance to see how the others were doing since spring. Fulcher was a one, of course, having started everything with himself. Jess grinned at Fulcher's back and stuck his hands into the pockets of his corduroys, wriggling his right forefinger through the hole.

Gary won the first heat easily and had plenty of breath left to boss the organizing of the second. A few of the younger boys drifted off to play King of the Mountain on the slope between the upper and lower fields. Out of the corner of his eye, Jess saw someone coming down from the upper field. He turned his back and pretended to concentrate on Fulcher's high-pitched commands.

"Hi." Leslie Burke had come up beside him.

He shifted slightly away. "Umph."

"Aren't you running?"

"Later." Maybe if he didn't look at her, she would go back to the upper field where she belonged.

Gary told Earle Watson to bang the start. Jess watched. Nobody with much speed in that crowd. He kept his eyes on the shirttails and bent backs.

A fight broke out at the finish line between Jimmy Mitchell and Clyde Deal. Everyone rushed to see. Jess was aware that Leslie Burke stayed at his elbow, but he was careful not to look her way.

"Clyde." Gary Fulcher made his declaration. "It was Clyde."

"It was a tie, Fulcher," a fourth grader protested. "I was standing right here."

"Clyde Deal."

Jimmy Mitchell's jaw was set. "I won, Fulcher. You couldn't even see from way back there."

"It was Deal." Gary ignored the protests. "We're wasting time. All threes line up. Right now."

Jimmy's fists went up. "Ain't fair, Fulcher."

Gary turned his back and headed for the starting line.

"Oh, let 'em both run in the finals. What's it gonna hurt?" Jess said loudly.

Gary stopped walking and wheeled to face him. Fulcher glared first at Jess and then at Leslie Burke. "Next thing," he said, his voice dripping with sarcasm, "next thing you're gonna want to let some *girl* run."

Jess's face went hot. "Sure," he said recklessly. "Why not?" He turned deliberately toward Leslie. "Wanna run?" he asked.

"Sure." She was grinning. "Why not?"

"You ain't scared to let a girl race are you, Fulcher?"

For a minute he thought Gary was going to sock him, and he stiffened. He mustn't let Fulcher suspect that he was scared of a little belt in the mouth. But instead Gary broke into a trot and started bossing the threes into line for their heat.

"You can run with the fours, Leslie." He said it loudly enough to make sure Fulcher could hear him and then concentrated on the runners. See, he told himself, you can stand up to a creep like Fulcher. No sweat.

Bobby Miller won the threes easily. He was the best of the fourth graders, almost as fast as Fulcher. *But not as good as me,* Jess thought. He was beginning to get really excited now. There wasn't anybody in the fours who could give him much of a race. Still it would be better to give Fulcher a scare by running well in the heat.

Leslie lined up beside him on the right. He moved a tiny bit to the left, but she didn't seem to notice.

At the bang Jess shot forward. It felt good—even the rough ground against the bottom of his worn sneakers. He was pumping good. He could almost smell Gary Fulcher's surprise at his improvement. The crowd was noisier than they'd been during the other heats. Maybe they were all noticing. He wanted to look back and see where the others were, but he resisted the temptation. It would seem conceited to look back. He concentrated on the line ahead. It was nearing with every step. "Oh, Miss Bessie, if you could see me now."

He felt it before he saw it. Someone was moving up. He automatically pumped harder. Then the shape was there in his sideways vision. Then suddenly pulling ahead. He forced himself now. His breath was choking him, and the sweat was in his eyes. But he saw the figure anyhow. The faded cutoffs crossed the line a full three feet ahead of him.

Leslie turned to face him with a wide smile on her tanned face. He stumbled and without a word began half walking, half trotting over to the starting line. This was the day he was going to be champion—the best runner of the fourth and fifth grades, and he hadn't even won his heat. There was no cheering at either end of the field. The rest of the boys seemed as stunned as he. The teasing would come later, he felt sure, but at least for the moment none of them were talking.

"OK." Fulcher took over. He tried to appear very much in charge. "OK, you guys. You can line up for the finals." He walked over to Leslie. "OK, you had your fun. You can run on up to the hopscotch now."

"But I won the heat," she said.

Gary lowered his head like a bull. "Girls aren't supposed to play on the lower field. Better get up there before one of the teachers sees you."

"I want to run," she said quietly.

"You already did."

"Whatsa matter, Fulcher?" All Jess's anger was bubbling out. He couldn't seem to stop the flow. "Whatsa matter? Scared to race her?"

Fulcher's fist went up. But Jess walked away from it. Fulcher would have to let her run now, he knew. And Fulcher did, angrily and grudgingly.

She beat him. She came in first and turned her large shining eyes on a bunch of dumb sweating-mad faces. The bell rang. Jess started across the lower field, his hands still deep in his pockets. She caught up with him. He took his hands out and began to trot toward the hill. She'd got him into enough trouble. She speeded up and refused to be shaken off.

"Thanks," she said.

"Yeah?" For what? he was thinking.

"You're the only kid in this whole durned school who's worth shooting." He wasn't sure, he thought her voice was quivering, but he wasn't going to start feeling sorry for her again.

"So shoot me," he said.

On the bus that afternoon he did something he had never thought he would do. He sat down beside May Belle. It was the only way he could make sure that he wouldn't have Leslie plunking herself down beside him. Lord, the girl had no notion of what you did and didn't do. He stared out the window, but he knew she had come and was sitting across the aisle from them.

He heard her say "Jess" once, but the bus was noisy enough that he could pretend he hadn't heard. When they came to the stop, he grabbed May Belle's hand and dragged her off, conscious that Leslie was right behind them. But she didn't try to speak to him again, nor did she follow them. She just took off running to the old Perkins place. He couldn't help turning to watch. She ran as though it was her nature. It reminded him of the flight of wild ducks in the autumn. So smooth. The word "beautiful" came to his mind, but he shook it away and hurried up toward the house.

FOUR

Rulers of Terabithia

Because school had started on the first Tuesday after Labor Day, it was a short week. It was a good thing because each day was worse than the one before. Leslie continued to join the boys at recess, and every day she won. By Friday a number of the fourth- and fifth-grade boys had already drifted away to play King of the Mountain on the slope between the two fields. Since there were only a handful left, they didn't even have to have heats, which took away a lot of the suspense. Running wasn't fun anymore. And it was all Leslie's fault.

Jess knew now that he would never be the best runner of the fourth and fifth grades, and his only consolation was that neither would Gary Fulcher. They went through the motions of the contest on Friday, but when it was over and Leslie had won again, everyone sort of knew without saying so that it was the end of the races.

At least it was Friday, and Miss Edmunds was back. The

fifth grade had music right after recess. Jess had passed Miss Edmunds in the hall earlier in the day, and she had stopped him and made a fuss over him. "Did you keep drawing this summer?"

"Yes'm."

"May I see your pictures or are they private?"

Jess shoved his hair off his red forehead. "I'll show you 'um."

She smiled her beautiful even-toothed smile and shook her shining black hair back off her shoulders. "Great!" she said. "See you."

He nodded and smiled back. Even his toes had felt warm and tingly.

Now as he sat on the rug in the teachers' room the same warm feeling swept through him at the sound of her voice. Even her ordinary speaking voice bubbled up from inside her, rich and melodic.

Miss Edmunds fiddled a minute with her guitar, talking as she tightened the strings to the jingling of her bracelets and the thrumming of chords. She was in her jeans as usual and sat there cross-legged in front of them as though that was the way teachers always did. She asked a few of the kids how they were and how their summer had been. They kind of mumbled back. She didn't speak directly to Jess, but she gave him a look with those blue eyes of hers that made him zing like one of the strings she was strumming.

She took note of Leslie and asked for an introduction, which one of the girls prissily gave. Then she smiled at Leslie, and Leslie smiled back—the first time Jess could remember seeing Leslie smile since she won the race on Tuesday. "What do you like to sing, Leslie?"

"Oh, anything."

Miss Edmunds picked a few odd chords and then began to sing, more quietly than usual for that particular song:

> *"I see a land bright and clear*
> *And the time's coming near*
> *When we'll live in this land*
> *You and me, hand in hand . . ."*

People began to join in, quietly at first to match her mood, but as the song built up at the end, their voices did as well, so that by the time they got to the final "Free to be you and me," the whole school could hear them. Caught in the pure delight of it, Jess turned and his eyes met Leslie's. He smiled at her. What the heck? There wasn't any reason he couldn't. What was he scared of anyhow? Lord. Sometimes he acted like the original yellow-bellied sapsucker. He nodded and smiled again. She smiled back. He felt there in the teachers' room that it was the beginning of a new season in his life, and he chose deliberately to make it so.

He did not have to make any announcement to Leslie that he had changed his mind about her. She already knew it. She plunked herself down beside him on the bus and squeezed over closer to him to make room for May Belle on the same seat. She talked about Arlington, about the huge suburban school she used to go to with its gorgeous music room but not a single teacher in it as beautiful or as nice as Miss Edmunds.

"You had a gym?"

"Yeah. I think all the schools did. Or most of them anyway." She sighed. "I really miss it. I'm pretty good at gymnastics."

"I guess you hate it here."

"Yeah."

She was quiet for a moment, thinking, Jess decided, about

her former school, which he saw as bright and new with a gleaming gymnasium larger than the one at the consolidated high school.

"I guess you had a lot of friends there, too."

"Yeah."

"Why'd you come here?"

"My parents are reassessing their value structure."

"Huh?"

"They decided they were too hooked on money and success, so they bought that old farm and they're going to farm it and think about what's important."

Jess was staring at her with his mouth open. He knew it, and he couldn't help himself. It was the most ridiculous thing he had ever heard.

"But you're the one that's gotta pay."

"Yeah."

"Why don't they think about you?"

"We talked it over," she explained patiently. "I wanted to come, too." She looked past him out the window. "You never know ahead of time what something's really going to be like."

The bus had stopped. Leslie took May Belle's hand and led her off. Jess followed, still trying to figure out why two grown people and a smart girl like Leslie wanted to leave a comfortable life in the suburbs for a place like this.

They watched the bus roar off.

"You can't make a go of a farm nowadays, you know," he said finally. "My dad has to go to Washington to work, or we wouldn't have enough money . . ."

"Money is not the problem."

"Sure it's the problem."

"I mean," she said stiffly, "not for us."

It took him a minute to catch on. He did not know people

for whom money was not the problem. "Oh." He tried to remember not to talk about money with her after that.

But Leslie had other problems at Lark Creek that caused more of a rumpus than lack of money. There was the matter of television.

It started with Mrs. Myers reading out loud a composition that Leslie had written about her hobby. Everyone had had to write a paper about his or her favorite hobby. Jess had written about football, which he really hated, but he had enough brains to know that if he said drawing, everyone would laugh at him. Most of the boys swore that watching the Washington Redskins on TV was their favorite hobby. The girls were divided: those who didn't care much about what Mrs. Myers thought chose watching game shows on TV, and those like Wanda Kay Moore who were still aiming for A's chose reading Good Books. But Mrs. Myers didn't read anyone's paper out loud except Leslie's.

"I want to read this composition aloud. For two reasons. One, it is *beautifully* written. And two, it tells about an unusual hobby—for a girl." Mrs. Myers beamed her first-day smile at Leslie. Leslie stared at her desk. Being Mrs. Myers' pet was pure poison at Lark Creek. " 'Scuba Diving' by Leslie Burke."

Mrs. Myers' sharp voice cut Leslie's sentences into funny little phrases, but even so, the power of Leslie's words drew Jess with her under the dark water. Suddenly he could hardly breathe. Suppose you went under and your mask filled all up with water and you couldn't get to the top in time? He was choking and sweating. He tried to push down his panic. This was Leslie Burke's favorite hobby. Nobody would make up scuba diving to be their favorite hobby if it wasn't so. That meant Leslie did it a lot. That she wasn't scared of going deep,

deep down in a world of no air and little light. Lord, he was such a coward. How could he be all in a tremble just listening to Mrs. Myers read about it? He was worse a baby than Joyce Ann. His dad expected him to be a man. And here he was letting some girl who wasn't even ten yet scare the liver out of him by just telling what it was like to sight-see under water. Dumb, dumb, dumb.

"I am sure," Mrs. Myers was saying, "that all of you were as impressed as I was with Leslie's exciting essay."

Impressed. Lord. He'd nearly drowned.

In the classroom there was a shuffling of feet and papers. "Now I want to give you a homework assignment"—muffled groans—"that I'm sure you'll enjoy."—mumblings of unbelief—"Tonight on Channel 7 at 8 P.M. there is going to be a special about a famous underwater explorer—Jacques Cousteau. I want everyone to watch. Then write one page telling what you learned."

"A whole page?"

"Yes."

"Does spelling count?"

"Doesn't spelling always count, Gary?"

"Both sides of the paper?"

"One side will be enough, Wanda Kay. But I will give extra credit to those who do extra work."

Wanda Kay smiled primly. You could already see ten pages taking shape in her pointy head.

"Mrs. Myers."

"Yes, Leslie." Lord, Mrs. Myers was liable to crack her face if she kept up smiling like that.

"What if you can't watch the program?"

"You inform your parents that it is a homework assignment. I am sure they will not object."

"What if"—Leslie's voice faltered; then she shook her head

and cleared her throat so the words came out stronger—"what if you don't have a television set?"

Lord, Leslie. Don't say that. You can always watch on mine. But it was too late to save her. The hissing sounds of disbelief were already building into a rumbling of contempt.

Mrs. Myers blinked her eyes. "Well. Well." She blinked some more. You could tell she was trying to figure out how to save Leslie, too. "Well. In that case one could write a one-page composition on something else. Couldn't one, Leslie?" She tried to smile across the classroom upheaval to Leslie, but it was no use. "Class! Class! *Class*!" Her Leslie smile shifted suddenly and ominously into a scowl that silenced the storm.

She handed out dittoed sheets of arithmetic problems. Jess stole a look at Leslie. Her face, bent low over the math sheet, was red and fierce.

At recess time when he was playing King of the Mountain, he could see that Leslie was surrounded by a group of girls led by Wanda Kay. He couldn't hear what they were saying, but he could tell by the proud way Leslie was throwing her head back that the others were making fun of her. Greg Williams grabbed him then, and while they wrestled, Leslie disappeared. It was none of his business, really, but he threw Greg down the hill as hard as he could and yelled to no one in particular, "Gotta go."

He stationed himself across from the girls' room. Leslie came out in a few minutes. He could tell she had been crying.

"Hey, Leslie," he called softly.

"Go away!" She turned abruptly and headed the other way in a fast walk. With an eye on the office door, he ran after her. Nobody was supposed to be in the halls during recess. "Leslie. Whatsa matter?"

"You know perfectly well what's the matter, Jess Aarons."

"Yeah." He rubbed his hair. "If you'd justa kept your mouth shut. You can always watch at my . . ."

But she had wheeled around again, and was zooming down the hall. Before he could finish the sentence and catch up with her, she was swinging the door to the girls' room right at his nose. Jess slunk out of the building. He couldn't risk Mr. Turner catching him hanging around the girls' room as though he was some kind of pervert or something.

After school Leslie got on the bus before he did and went straight to the corner of the long back seat—right to the seventh graders' seat. He jerked his head at her to warn her to come farther up front, but she wouldn't even look at him. He could see the seventh graders headed for the bus—the huge bossy bosomy girls and the mean, skinny, narrow-eyed boys. They'd kill her for sitting in their territory. He jumped up and ran to the back and grabbed Leslie by the arm. "You gotta come up to your regular seat, Leslie."

Even as he spoke, he could feel the bigger kids pushing up behind him down the narrow aisle. Indeed, Janice Avery, who among all the seventh graders was the one person who devoted her entire life to scaring the wits out of anyone smaller than she, was right behind him. "Move, kid," she said.

He planted his body as firmly as he could, although his heart was knocking at his Adam's apple. "C'mon, Leslie," he said, and then he made himself turn and give Janice Avery one of those look-overs from frizz blond hair, past too tight blouse and broad-beamed jeans, to gigantic sneakers. When he finished, he swallowed, stared straight up into her scowling face, and said, almost steadily, "Don't look like there'll be room across the back here for you *and* Janice Avery."

Somebody hooted. "Weight Watchers is waiting for you, Janice!"

Janice's eyes were hate-mad, but she moved aside for Jess and Leslie to make their way past her to their regular seat.

Leslie glanced back as they sat down, and then leaned over. "She's going to get you for that, Jess. Boy, she is mad."

Jess warmed to the tone of respect in Leslie's voice, but he didn't dare look back. "Heck," he said. "You think I'm going to let some dumb cow like that scare me?"

By the time they got off the bus, he could finally send a swallow past his Adam's apple without choking. He even gave a little wave at the back seat as the bus pulled off.

Leslie was grinning at him over May Belle's head.

"Well," he said happily. "See you."

"Hey, do you think we could do something this afternoon?"

"Me, too! I wanna do something, too," May Belle shrilled.

Jess looked at Leslie. No was in her eyes. "Not this time, May Belle. Leslie and I got something we gotta do just by ourselves today. You can carry my books home and tell Momma I'm over at Burkes'. OK?"

"You ain't got nothing to do. You ain't even planned nothing."

Leslie came and leaned over May Belle, putting her hand on the little girl's thin shoulder. "May Belle, would you like some new paper dolls?"

May Belle slid her eyes around suspiciously. "What kind?"

"Life in Colonial America."

May Belle shook her head. "I want Bride or Miss America."

"You can pretend these are bride paper dolls. They have lots of beautiful long dresses."

"Whatsa matter with 'um?"

"Nothing. They're brand-new."

"How come you don't want 'um if they're so great?"

"When you're my age"—Leslie gave a little sigh—"you just

don't play with paper dolls anymore. My grandmother sent me these. You know how it is, grandmothers just forget you're growing up."

May Belle's one living grandmother was in Georgia and never sent her anything. "You already punched 'um out?"

"No, honestly. And all the clothes punch out, too. You don't have to use scissors."

They could see she was weakening. "How about," Jess began, "you coming down and taking a look at 'um, and if they suit you, you could take 'um along home when you go tell Momma where I am?"

After they had watched May Belle tearing up the hill, clutching her new treasure, Jess and Leslie turned and ran up over the empty field behind the old Perkins place and down to the dry creek bed that separated farmland from the woods. There was an old crab apple tree there, just at the bank of the creek bed, from which someone long forgotten had hung a rope.

They took turns swinging across the gully on the rope. It was a glorious autumn day, and if you looked up as you swung, it gave you the feeling of floating. Jess leaned back and drank in the rich, clear color of the sky. He was drifting, drifting like a fat white lazy cloud back and forth across the blue.

"Do you know what we need?" Leslie called to him. Intoxicated as he was with the heavens, he couldn't imagine needing anything on earth.

"We need a place," she said, "just for us. It would be so secret that we would never tell anyone in the whole world about it." Jess came swinging back and dragged his feet to stop. She lowered her voice almost to a whisper. "It might be a whole secret country," she continued, "and you and I would be the rulers of it."

Her words stirred inside of him. He'd like to be a ruler of something. Even something that wasn't real. "OK," he said. "Where could we have it?"

"Over there in the woods where nobody would come and mess it up."

There were parts of the woods that Jess did not like. Dark places where it was almost like being under water, but he didn't say so.

"I know"—she was getting excited—"it could be a magic country like Narnia, and the only way you can get in is by swinging across on this enchanted rope." Her eyes were bright. She grabbed the rope. "Come on," she said. "Let's find a place to build our castle stronghold."

They had gone only a few yards into the woods beyond the creek bed when Leslie stopped.

"How about right here?" she asked.

"Sure," Jess agreed quickly, relieved that there was no need to plunge deeper into the woods. He would take her there, of course, for he wasn't such a coward that he would mind a little exploring now and then farther in amongst the ever-darkening columns of the tall pines. But as a regular thing, as a permanent place, this was where he would choose to be—here where the dogwood and redbud played hide and seek between the oaks and evergreens, and the sun flung itself in golden streams through the trees to splash warmly at their feet.

"Sure," he repeated himself, nodding vigorously. The underbrush was dry and would be easy to clear away. The ground was almost level. "This'll be a good place to build."

Leslie named their secret land "Terabithia," and she loaned

Jess all of her books about Narnia, so he would know how things went in a magic kingdom—how the animals and the trees must be protected and how a ruler must behave. That was the hard part. When Leslie spoke, the words rolling out so regally, you knew she was a proper queen. He could hardly manage English, much less the poetic language of a king.

But he could make stuff. They dragged boards and other materials down from the scrap heap by Miss Bessie's pasture and built their castle stronghold in the place they had found in the woods. Leslie filled a three-pound coffee can with crackers and dried fruit and a one-pound can with strings and nails. They found five old Pepsi bottles which they washed and filled with water, in case, as Leslie said, "of siege."

Like God in the Bible, they looked at what they had made and found it very good.

"You should draw a picture of Terabithia for us to hang in the castle," Leslie said.

"I can't." How could he explain it in a way Leslie would understand, how he yearned to reach out and capture the quivering life about him and how when he tried, it slipped past his fingertips, leaving a dry fossil upon the page? "I just can't get the poetry of the trees," he said.

She nodded. "Don't worry," she said. "You will someday."

He believed her because there in the shadowy light of the stronghold everything seemed possible. Between the two of them they owned the world and no enemy, Gary Fulcher, Wanda Kay Moore, Janice Avery, Jess's own fears and insufficiencies, nor any of the foes whom Leslie imagined attacking Terabithia, could ever really defeat them.

A few days after they finished the castle, Janice Avery fell down in the school bus and yelled that Jess had tripped her as she went past. She made such a fuss that Mrs. Prentice, the driver, ordered Jess off the bus, and he had to walk the three miles home.

When Jess finally got to Terabithia, Leslie was huddled next to one of the cracks below the roof trying to get enough light to read. There was a picture on the cover which showed a killer whale attacking a dolphin.

"Whatcha doing?" He came in and sat beside her on the ground.

"Reading. I had to do something. That girl!" Her anger came rocketing to the surface.

"It don't matter. I don't mind walking all that much." What was a little hike compared to what Janice Avery might have chosen to do?

"It's the *principle* of the thing, Jess. That's what you've got to understand. You have to stop people like that. Otherwise they turn into tyrants and dictators."

He reached over and took the whale book from her hands, pretending to study the bloody picture on the jacket. "Getting any good ideas?"

"What?"

"I thought you was getting some ideas on how to stop Janice Avery."

"No, stupid. We're trying to *save* the whales. They might become extinct."

He gave her back the book. "You save the whales and shoot the people, huh?"

She grinned finally. "Something like that, I guess. Say, did you ever hear the story about Moby Dick?"

"Who's that?"

"Well, there was once this huge white whale named Moby Dick. . . ." And Leslie began to spin out a wonderful story about a whale and a crazy sea captain who was bent on killing it. His fingers itched to try to draw it on paper. Maybe if he had some proper paints, he could do it. There ought to be a way of making the whale shimmering white against the dark water.

At first they avoided each other during school hours, but by October they grew careless about their friendship. Gary Fulcher, like Brenda, took great pleasure in teasing Jess about his "*girl* friend." It hardly bothered Jess. He knew that a *girl* friend was somebody who chased you on the playground and tried to grab you and kiss you. He could no more imagine Leslie chasing a boy than he could imagine Mrs. Double-Chinned Myers shinnying up the flagpole. Gary Fulcher could go to you-know-where and warm his toes.

There was really no free time at school except recess, and now that there were no races, Jess and Leslie usually looked for a quiet place on the field, and sat and talked. Except for the magic half hour on Fridays, recess was all that Jess looked forward to at school. Leslie could always come up with something funny that made the long days bearable. Often the joke was on Mrs. Myers. Leslie was one of those people who sat quietly at her desk, never whispering or daydreaming or chewing gum, doing beautiful schoolwork, and yet her brain was so full of mischief that if the teacher could have once seen through that mask of perfection, she would have thrown her out in horror.

Jess could hardly keep a straight face in class just trying to imagine what might be going on behind that angelic look of

Leslie's. One whole morning, as Leslie had related it at recess, she had spent imagining Mrs. Myers on one of those fat farms down in Arizona. In her fantasy, Mrs. Myers was one of the foodaholics who would hide bits of candy bars in odd places —up the hot water faucet!—only to be found out and publicly humiliated before all the other fat ladies. That afternoon Jess kept having visions of Mrs. Myers dressed only in a pink corset being weighed in. "You've been cheating again, Gussie!" the tall skinny directoress was saying. Mrs. Myers was on the verge of tears.

"Jesse Aarons!" The teacher's sharp voice punctured his daydream. He couldn't look Mrs. Myers straight in her pudgy face. He'd crack up. He set his sight on her uneven hemline.

"Yes'm." He was going to have to get coaching from Leslie. Mrs. Myers always caught him when his mind was on vacation, but she never seemed to suspect Leslie of not paying attention. He sneaked a glance up that way. Leslie was totally absorbed in her geography book, or so it would appear to anyone who didn't know.

Terabithia was cold in November. They didn't dare build a fire in the castle, though sometimes they would build one outside and huddle around it. For a while Leslie had been able to keep two sleeping bags in the stronghold, but around the first of December her father noticed their absence, and she had to take them back. Actually, Jess made her take them back. It was not that he was afraid of the Burkes exactly. Leslie's parents were young, with straight white teeth and lots of hair—both of them. Leslie called them Judy and Bill, which bothered Jess more than he wanted it to. It was none of his business what Leslie called her parents. But he just couldn't get used to it.

Both of the Burkes were writers. Mrs. Burke wrote novels and, according to Leslie, was more famous than Mr. Burke, who wrote about politics. It was really something to see the shelf that had their books on it. Mrs. Burke was "Judith Hancock" on the cover, which threw you at first, but then if you looked on the back, there was her picture looking very young and serious. Mr. Burke was going back and forth to Washington to finish a book he was working on with someone else, but he had promised Leslie that after Christmas he would stay home and fix up the house and plant his garden and listen to music and read books out loud and write only in his spare time.

They didn't look like Jess's idea of rich, but even he could tell that the jeans they wore had not come off the counter at Newberry's. There was no TV at the Burkes', but there were mountains of records and a stereo set that looked like something off *Star Trek*. And although their car was small and dusty, it was Italian and looked expensive, too.

They were always nice to Jess when he went over, but then they would suddenly begin talking about French politics or string quartets (which he at first thought was a square box made out of string), or how to save the timber wolves or redwoods or singing whales, and he was scared to open his mouth and show once and for all how dumb he was.

He wasn't comfortable having Leslie at his house either. Joyce Ann would stare, her index finger pulling down her mouth and making her drool. Brenda and Ellie always managed some remark about "*girl* friend." His mother acted stiff and funny just the way she did when she had to go up to school about something. Later she would refer to Leslie's "tacky" clothes. Leslie always wore pants, even to school. Her hair was "shorter than a boy's." Her parents were "hardly more than hippies." May Belle either tried to push in with him and Leslie or sulked at being left out. His father had seen Leslie only a few times and had nodded to show that he had noticed her, but his mother said that she was sure he was fretting that his only son did nothing but play with girls, and they both were worried about what would become of it.

Jess didn't concern himself with what would "become of it." For the first time in his life he got up every morning with something to look forward to. Leslie was more than his friend. She was his other, more exciting self—his way to Terabithia and all the worlds beyond.

Terabithia was their secret, which was a good thing, for how could Jess have ever explained it to an outsider? Just walking down the hill toward the woods made something warm and liquid steal through his body. The closer he came to the dry creek bed and the crab apple tree rope the more he could feel the beating of his heart. He grabbed the end of the rope and swung out toward the other bank with a kind of wild exhilaration and landed gently on his feet, taller and stronger and wiser in that mysterious land.

Leslie's favorite place besides the castle stronghold was the pine forest. There the trees grew so thick at the top that the sunshine was veiled. No low bush or grass could grow in that dim light, so the ground was carpeted with golden needles.

"I used to think this place was haunted," Jess had confessed to Leslie the first afternoon he had revved up his courage to bring her there.

"Oh, but it is," she said. "But you don't have to be scared. It's not haunted with evil things."

"How do you know?"

"You can just feel it. Listen."

At first he heard only the stillness. It was the stillness that had always frightened him before, but this time it was like the moment after Miss Edmunds finished a song, just after the chords hummed down to silence. Leslie was right. They stood there, not moving, not wanting the swish of dry needles beneath their feet to break the spell. Far away from their former world came the cry of geese heading southward.

Leslie took a deep breath. "This is not an ordinary place," she whispered. "Even the rulers of Terabithia come into it only at times of greatest sorrow or of greatest joy. We must strive to keep it sacred. It would not do to disturb the Spirits."

He nodded, and without speaking, they went back to the creek bank where they shared together a solemn meal of crackers and dried fruit.

FIVE

The Giant Killers

Leslie liked to make up stories about the giants that threatened the peace of Terabithia, but they both knew that the real giant in their lives was Janice Avery. Of course, it wasn't only Jess and Leslie that she was after. She had two friends, Wilma Dean and Bobby Sue Henshaw, who were almost as big as she was, and the three of them would roam the playground, grabbing up hopscotch rocks, running through jump ropes, and laughing while second graders screamed. They would even stand outside the girls' room first thing every morning and make the little girls give them their milk money before they'd let them go to the bathroom.

May Belle, unfortunately, was a slow learner. Her daddy had brought her a package of Twinkies, and she was so proud that as soon as she got on the bus she forgot everything she knew and yelled to another first grader, "Guess what I got in my lunch today, Billy Jean?"

"What?"

"Twinkies!" she shouted so loud you could have heard her in the back seat even if you were deaf in both ears. Out of the corner of his eye, Jess thought he saw Janice Avery perk up.

When they sat down, May Belle was still screeching about her dadgum Twinkies over the roar of the motor. "My daddy brung 'um to me from Washington!"

Jess threw another look at the back seat. "You better shut up about those dang Twinkies," he said in her ear.

"You just jealous 'cause Daddy didn't bring you none."

"OK." He shrugged across her head at Leslie to say *I warned her, didn't I*? and Leslie nodded back.

Neither of them was too surprised to see May Belle come screaming toward them at recess time.

"She stole my Twinkies!"

Jess sighed. "May Belle, didn't I tell you?"

"You gotta kill Janice Avery. Kill her! Kill her! Kill her!"

"*Shhh*," Leslie said, stroking May Belle's head, but May Belle didn't want comfort, she wanted revenge.

"You gotta beat her up into a million pieces!"

He'd sooner tangle with Mrs. Godzilla herself. "Fighting ain't gonna get back nothing, May Belle. Them Twinkies is well on the way to padding Janice Avery's bottom by now."

Leslie snickered, but May Belle was not to be distracted. "You're just yeller, Jesse Aarons. If you wasn't yeller, you'd beat somebody up if they took your little sister's Twinkies." She broke into a fresh round of sobbing.

Jess stiffened. He avoided Leslie's eyes. Lord, there was no escape. He'd have to fight the female gorilla now.

"Look, May Belle," Leslie was saying. "If Jess picks a fight with Janice Avery, you know perfectly well what will happen."

May Belle wiped her nose on the back of her hand. "She'll beat him up."

"Noooo. *He'll* get kicked out of school for fighting a girl. You know how Mr. Turner is about boys who pick on girls."

"She stole my Twinkies."

"I know she did, May Belle. And Jess and I are going to figure out a way to pay her back for it. Aren't we Jess?"

He nodded vigorously. Anything was better than promising to fight Janice Avery.

"Whatcha gonna do?"

"I don't know yet. We'll have to plan it out very carefully, but I promise you, May Belle, we'll get her."

"Cross-your-heart-and-hope-to-die?"

Leslie solemnly crossed her heart. May Belle turned expectantly to Jess, so he crossed his, too, trying hard not to feel like a fool, crossing his heart to a first grader in the middle of the playground.

May Belle snuffled loudly. "It ain't as good as seeing her beat to a million pieces."

"No," said Leslie, "I'm sure it isn't, but with Mr. Turner running this school, it's the best we can do, right, Jess?"

"Right."

That afternoon, crouched in the stronghold of Terabithia, they held a council of war. How to get Janice Avery without ending up squashed or suspended—that was their problem.

"Maybe we could get her caught doing something." Leslie was trying out another idea after they had both rejected putting honey on her bus seat and glue in her hand lotion. "You know she smokes in the girls' room. If we could just get Mr. Turner to walk past while the smoke is pouring out—"

Jess shook his head hopelessly. "It wouldn't take her five minutes to find out who squawked." There was a moment of silence while they both considered what Janice Avery might do to anyone who reported her to the principal. "We gotta get her without her knowing who done it."

"Yeah." Leslie chewed away at a dried apricot. "You know what girls like Janice hate most?"

"What?"

"Being made a fool of."

Jess remembered how Janice had looked that day he'd made everyone laugh at her on the bus. Leslie was right. There was a crack in the old hippo hide. "Yeah." He nodded, beginning to smile. "Yeah. Do we get her about being fat?"

"How about," Leslie began slowly, "how about boys? Who's she stuck on?"

"Willard Hughes, I reckon. Every girl in the seventh grade slides to the ground when he walks by."

"Yeah." Leslie's eyes were shining. The plan came all in a rush. "We write her a note, you see, and pretend it's from Willard."

Jess was already getting a pencil from the can and yanking a piece of notebook paper out from under a rock. He handed them to Leslie.

"No, you write. My handwriting is too good for Willard Hughes."

He got set and waited.

"OK," she said. "Um. 'Dear Janice.' No. 'Dearest Janice.' "

Jess hesitated, doubtful.

"Believe me, Jess. She'll eat it up. OK. 'Dearest Janice.' Don't worry about punctuation or anything. We have to make it look as if Willard Hughes really wrote it. OK. 'Dearest Janice, Maybe you won't believe me, but I love you.' "

"You think she'll . . . ?" he asked as he wrote it down.

"I told you, she'll eat it up. Girls like Janice Avery believe just what they want to in this kind of situation. OK, now. 'If you say you do not love me, it will break my heart. So please don't. If you love me as much as I love you, my darling—' "

"Hold it. I can't write that fast."

Leslie waited, and when he looked up, she continued in a moony voice, " 'Meet me behind the school this afternoon after school. Do not worry about missing your bus. I want to walk home with you and talk about US'—put 'us' in capitals —'my darling. Love and kisses, Willard Hughes.' "

"Kisses?"

"Yeah, kisses. Put a little row of x's in there, too." She paused, looking over his shoulder while he finished. "Oh, yes. Put 'P.S.' "

He did.

"Um. 'Don't tell any—don't tell *no*body. Let our love be a secret for only us two right now.' "

"Why'cha put that in?"

"So she'll be sure to tell somebody, stupid." Leslie reread the note, nodding approval. "Good. You misspelled 'believe' and 'two.' " She studied it a minute longer. "Gee, I'm pretty good at this."

"Sure. You probably had some big secret love down in Arlington."

"Jess Aarons, I'm going to kill you."

"Hey, girl, you kill the king of Terabithia, and you're in trouble."

"Regicide," she said proudly.

"Regi-what?"

"Did I ever tell you the story of Hamlet?"

He rolled over on his back. "Not yet," he said happily. Lord, he loved Leslie's stories. Someday, when he was good enough, he would ask her to write them in a book and let him do all the pictures.

"Well," she began, "there was once a prince of Denmark, named Hamlet. . . ."

In his head he drew the shadowy castle with the tortured prince pacing the parapets. How could you make a ghost come out of the fog? Crayons wouldn't do, of course, but with paints you could put one thin color on top of another so that you would begin to see a pale figure moving from deep inside the paper. He began to shiver. He knew he could do it if Leslie would let him use her paints.

The hardest part of the plan to get Janice Avery was to plant the note. They sneaked into the building the next morning before the first bell. Leslie went several yards ahead so that if they were caught, no one would think they were together. Mr. Turner was death on boys and girls he caught sneaking around the halls together. She got to the door of the seventh-grade classroom and peeked in. Then she signaled Jess to come ahead. The hairs prickled up his neck. Lord.

"How'll I find her desk?"

"I thought you knew where she sat."

He shook his head.

"I guess you'll have to look in every one until you find it. Hurry. I'll be lookout for you." She closed the door quietly and left him shuffling through each desk, trying to be careful not to make a mess, but his stupid hands were shaking so much he could hardly pull anything out to look for names.

Suddenly he heard Leslie's voice. "Oh, *Mrs. Pierce*, I've just been standing here *waiting* for you."

Lord. The seventh-grade teacher was right out there in the hall, heading for this room. He stood frozen. He couldn't hear what Mrs. Pierce was saying back to Leslie through the closed door.

"Yes, ma'am. There is a very interesting nest on the south end of the building, and since"—Leslie raised her voice even louder—"you know so much about science, I was hoping you could take a minute *to look at it with me* and tell me what built it."

There was the mumble of a reply.

"Oh, *thank you*, Mrs. Pierce"—Leslie was practically screaming—"It won't take but a *minute*, and it would mean so much to me!"

As soon as he heard their retreating footsteps, he flew around the remaining desks until, oh, joy, he found one with a composition book that had Janice Avery's name on it. He stuffed the note on top of everything else inside the desk and raced out of the room to the boys' room, where he hid in one of the stalls until the bell rang to go to homeroom.

At recess time Janice Avery was in a tight huddle with Wilma and Bobby Sue. Then, instead of teasing the little girls, the three of them wandered off arm in arm to watch the big boys' football. As the trio passed them, Jess could see Janice's face all pink and prideful. He rolled his eyes at Leslie, and she rolled hers back at him.

As the bus was about to pull out that afternoon, one of the seventh-grade boys, Billy Morris, yelled up to Mrs. Prentice that Janice Avery wasn't on the bus yet.

"It's OK, Miz Prentice," Wilma Dean called up. "She ain't riding this evening." Then in a loud whisper, "Reckon you all know that Janice has a heavy date with you know who."

"Who?" asked Billy.

"Willard Hughes. He's so crazy about her he can't hardly stand it. He's even walking her all the way home."

"Yeah? Well the 304 just pulled out with Willard Hughes on the back seat. If he's got a big date, he don't seem to know much about it."

"You lie, Billy Morris!"

Billy yelled a cuss word, and the entire back seat plunged into a heated discussion as to whether Janice Avery and Willard Hughes were or were not in love and were or were not seeing each other secretly.

As Billy got off the bus, he hollered to Wilma, "You just better tell Janice that Willard is gonna be mad when he hears what she's spreading all over the school!"

Wilma's face was crimson as she screamed out the window, "OK, you dummy! You talk to Willard. You'll see. Just ask him about that letter! You'll see!"

"Poor old Janice Avery," Jess said as they sat in the castle later.

"Poor old Janice? She deserves everything she gets and then some!"

"I reckon." He sighed. "But, still—"

Leslie looked stricken. "You're not sorry we did it, are you?"

"No. I reckon we had to do it, but still—"

"Still what?"

He grinned. "Maybe I got this thing for Janice like you got this thing for killer whales."

She punched him in the shoulder. "Let's go out and find some giants or walking dead to fight. I'm sick of Janice Avery."

The next day Janice Avery stomped onto the bus, her eyes daring everyone in sight to say a word. Leslie nudged May Belle.

May Belle's eyes went wide. "Did 'cha—?"

"*Shhh*. Yes."

May Belle turned completely around and stared at the back seat; then she turned back and poked Jess. "You made her *that* mad?"

Jess nodded, trying to move his head as little as possible as he did so.

"We wrote that letter," Leslie whispered. "But you mustn't tell anyone, or she'll kill us."

"I know," said May Belle, her eyes shining. "I know."

SIX

The Coming of Prince Terrien

Christmas was almost a month away, but at Jess's house the girls were already obsessed with it. This year Ellie and Brenda both had boyfriends at the consolidated high school and the problem of what to give them and what to expect from them was cause of endless speculation and fights. Fights, because as usual, their mother was complaining that there was hardly enough money to give the little girls something from Santa Claus, let alone a surplus to buy record albums or shirts for a pair of boys she'd never set eyes on.

"What are you giving your girl friend, Jess?" Brenda screwed her face up in that ugly way she had. He tried to ignore her. He was reading one of Leslie's books, and the adventures of an assistant pig keeper were far more important to him than Brenda's sauce.

"Don't you know, Brenda?" Ellie joined in. "Jess ain't got no *girl* friend."

"Well, you're right for once. Nobody with any sense would call that stick a *girl.*" Brenda pushed her face right into his and grinned the word "girl" through her big painted lips. Something huge and hot swelled right up inside of him, and if he hadn't jumped out of the chair and walked away, he would have smacked her.

He tried to figure out later what had made him so angry. Partly, of course, it made him furious that anyone as dumb as Brenda would think she could make fun of Leslie. Lord, it hurt his guts to realize that it was Brenda who was his blood sister, and that really, from anyone else's point of view, he and Leslie were not related at all. Maybe, he thought, I was a foundling, like in the stories. Way back when the creek had water in it, I came floating down it in a wicker basket waterproofed with pitch. My dad found me and brought me here because he'd always wanted a son and just had stupid daughters. My real parents and brothers and sisters live far away—farther away than West Virginia or even Ohio. Somewhere I have a family who have rooms filled with nothing but books and who still grieve for their baby who was stolen.

He shook himself back to the source of his anger. He was angry, too, because it would soon be Christmas and he had nothing to give Leslie. It was not that she would expect something expensive; it was that he needed to give her something as much as he needed to eat when he was hungry.

He thought about making her a book of his drawings. He even stole paper and crayons from school to do it with. But nothing he drew seemed good enough, and he would end up scrawling across the half-finished page and poking it into the stove to burn up.

By the last week of school before the holiday, he was growing desperate. There was no one he could ask for help or advice. His dad had told him he would give him a dollar for each member of the family, but even if he cheated on the family presents, there was no way he could get from that enough to buy Leslie anything worth giving her. Besides, May Belle had her heart set on a Barbie doll, and he had already promised to pool his money with Ellie and Brenda for that. Then the price had gone up, and he found he would have to go over into every one else's dollar to make up the full amount for May Belle. Somehow this year May Belle needed something special. She was always moping around. He and Leslie couldn't include her in their activities, but that was hard to explain to someone like May Belle. Why didn't she play with Joyce Ann? He couldn't be expected to entertain her all the time. Still—still, she ought to have the Barbie.

So there was no money, and he seemed paralyzed in his efforts to make anything for Leslie. She wouldn't be like Brenda or Ellie. She wouldn't laugh at him no matter what he gave her. But for his own sake he had to give her something that he could be proud of.

If he had the money, he'd buy her a TV. One of those tiny Japanese ones that she could keep in her own room without bothering Judy and Bill. It didn't seem fair with all their money that they'd gotten rid of the TV. It wasn't as if Leslie would watch the way Brenda did—with her mouth open and her eyes bulging like a goldfish, hour after hour. But every once in a while, a person liked to watch. At least if she had one, it would be one less thing for the kids at school to sneer about. But, of course, there was no way that he could buy her a TV. It was pretty stupid of him even to think about it.

Lord, he was stupid. He gazed miserably out the window of the school bus. It was a wonder someone like Leslie would even give him the time of day. It was because there was no one else. If she had found anyone else at that dumb school—he was so stupid he had almost gone straight past the sign without catching on. But something in a corner of his head clicked, and he jumped up, pushing past Leslie and May Belle.

"See you later," he mumbled, and shoved his way up the aisle through pair after pair of sprawling legs.

"Lemme off here, Miz Prentice, will you?"

"This ain't your stop."

"Gotta do an errand for my mother," he lied.

" 'Long as you don't get me into trouble." She eased the brakes.

"No'm. Thanks."

He swung off the bus before it had really stopped and ran back toward the sign.

"Puppies," it said. "Free."

Jess told Leslie to meet him at the castle stronghold on Christmas Eve afternoon. The rest of his family had gone to the Millsburg Plaza for last-minute shopping, but he stayed behind. The dog was a little brown-and-black thing with great brown eyes. Jess stole a ribbon from Brenda's drawer, and hurried across the field and down the hill with the puppy squirming in his arms. Before he got to the creek bed, it had licked his face raw and sent a stream down his jacket front, but he couldn't be mad. He tucked it tightly under his arm and swung across the creek as gently as he could. He could have walked through the gully. It would have been easier, but he couldn't escape the feeling that one must enter Terabithia only by the prescribed entrance. He couldn't let the puppy break the rules. It might mean bad luck for both of them.

At the stronghold he tied the ribbon around the puppy's

neck, laughing as it backed out of the loop and chewed at the ends of the ribbon. It was a clever, lively little thing—a present Jess could be proud of.

There was no mistaking the delight in Leslie's eyes. She dropped to her knees on the cold ground, picked the puppy up, and held it close to her face.

"Watch it," Jess cautioned. "It sprays worse'n a water pistol."

Leslie moved it out a little way. "Is it male or female?"

Once in a rare while there was something he could teach Leslie. "Boy," he said happily.

"Then we'll name him Prince Terrien and make him the guardian of Terabithia."

She put the puppy down and got to her feet.

"Where you going?"

"To the grove of the pines," she answered. "This is a time of greatest joy."

Later that afternoon Leslie gave Jess his present. It was a

box of watercolors with twenty-four tubes of color and three brushes and a pad of heavy art paper.

"Lord," he said. "Thank you." He tried to think of a better way to say it, but he couldn't. "Thank you," he repeated.

"It's not a great present like yours," she said humbly, "but I hope you'll like it."

He wanted to tell her how proud and good she made him feel, that the rest of Christmas didn't matter because today had been so good, but the words he needed weren't there. "Oh, yeah, yeah," he said, and then got up on his knees and began to bark at Prince Terrien. The puppy raced around him in circles, yelping with delight.

Leslie began to laugh. It egged Jess on. Everything the dog did, he imitated, flopping down at last with his tongue lolling out. Leslie was laughing so hard she had trouble getting the words out. "You—you're crazy. How will we teach him to be a noble guardian? You're turning him into a clown."

"*R-r-r-oof*," wailed Prince Terrien, rolling his eyes skyward. Jess and Leslie both collapsed. They were in pain from the laughter.

"Maybe," said Leslie at last. "We'd better make him court jester."

"What about his name?"

"Oh, we'll let him keep his name. Even a prince"—this in her most Terabithian voice—"even a prince may be a fool."

That night the glow of the afternoon stayed with him. Even his sisters' squabbling about when presents were to be opened did not touch him. He helped May Belle wrap her wretched little gifts and even sang "Santa Claus Is Coming to Town" with her and Joyce Ann. Then Joyce Ann cried because they had no fireplace and Santa wouldn't be able to find the way, and suddenly he felt sorry for her going to Millsburg Plaza and seeing all those things and hoping that some guy in a red suit would give her all her dreams. May Belle at six was already too wise. She was just hoping for that stupid Barbie. He was glad he'd splurged on it. Joyce Ann wouldn't care that he only had a hair clip for her. She would blame Santa, not him, for being cheap.

He put his arm awkwardly around Joyce Ann. "C'mon Joyce Ann. Don't cry. Old Santa knows the way. He don't need a chimney, does he, May Belle?" May Belle was watching him with her big, solemn eyes. Jess gave her a knowing wink over Joyce Ann's head. It melted her.

"Naw, Joyce Ann. He knows the way. He knows everything." She squenched up her right cheek in a vain effort to return his wink. She was a good kid. He really liked old May Belle.

The next morning he helped her dress and undress her Barbie at least thirty times. Slithering the skinny dress over the doll's head and arms and snapping the tiny fasteners was more than her chubby six-year-old fingers could manage.

He had received a racing-car set, which he tried to run to please his father. It wasn't one of those big sets that they advertised on TV, but it was electric, and he knew his dad had put more money into it than he should have. But the silly cars kept falling off at the curves until his father was cursing at them with impatience. Jess wanted it to be OK. He wanted so much for his dad to be proud of his present, the way he, Jess, had been proud of the puppy.

"It's really great. Really. I just ain't got the hang of it yet." His face was red, and he kept shoving his hair back out of his eyes as he leaned over the plastic figure-eight track.

"Cheap junk." His father kicked at the floor dangerously near the track. "Don't get nothing for your money these days."

Joyce Ann was lying on her bed screaming because she had yanked the string out of her talking doll and it was no longer talking. Brenda had her lip stuck out because Ellie had gotten a pair of panty hose in her Christmas stocking and she had only bobby socks. Ellie wasn't helping matters, prancing around in her new hose, making a big show of helping Momma with the ham and sweet potatoes for dinner. Lord, sometimes Ellie was as snotty as Wanda Kay Moore.

"Jesse Oliver Aarons, Jr., if you can stop playing with those fool cars long enough to milk the cow, I'd be most appreciative. Miss Bessie don't take no holiday, even if you do."

Jess jumped up, pleased for an excuse to leave the track which he couldn't make work to his dad's satisfaction. His mother seemed not to notice the promptness of his response but went on in a complaining voice, "I don't know what I'd do without Ellie. She's the only one of you kids ever cares whether I live or die." Ellie smiled like a plastic angel first at Jess and then at Brenda, who glared back.

Leslie must have been watching for him because as soon as he started across the yard he could see her running out of the old Perkins place, the puppy half tripping her as it chased circles around her.

They met at Miss Bessie's shed. "I thought you'd never come out this morning."

"Yeah, well, Christmas, you know."

Prince Terrien began to snap at Miss Bessie's hooves. She stamped in annoyance. Leslie picked him up, so Jess could milk. The puppy squirmed and licked, making it almost impossible for her to talk. She giggled happily. "Dumb dog," she said proudly.

"Yeah." It felt like Christmas again.

SEVEN

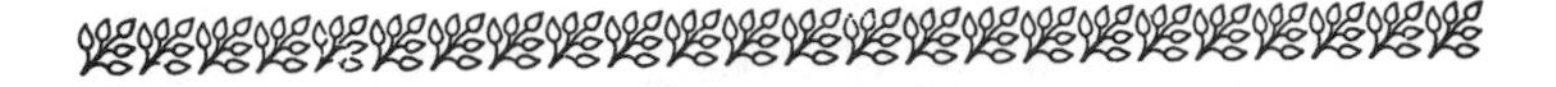

The Golden Room

Mr. Burke had begun to repair the old Perkins place. After Christmas, Mrs. Burke was right in the middle of writing a book, so she wasn't available to help, which left Leslie the jobs of hunting and fetching. For all his smartness with politics and music, Mr. Burke was inclined to be absent-minded. He would put down the hammer to pick up the "How to" book and then lose the hammer between there and the project he was working on. Leslie was good at finding things for him, and he liked her company as well. When she came home from school and on the weekends, he wanted her around. Leslie explained all this to Jess.

Jess tried going to Terabithia alone, but it was no good. It needed Leslie to make the magic. He was afraid he would destroy everything by trying to force the magic on his own, when it was plain that the magic was reluctant to come for him.

If he went home, either his mother was after him to do

some chore or May Belle wanted him to play Barbie. Lord, he wished a million times he'd never helped buy that stupid doll. He'd no more than lie down on the floor to paint than May Belle would be after him to put an arm back on or snap up a dress. Joyce Ann was worse. She got a devilish delight out of sitting smack down on his rump when he was stretched out working. If he yelled at her to get the heck off him, she'd stick her index finger in the corner of her mouth and holler. Which would, of course, crank up his mother.

"Jesse Oliver! You leave that baby alone. Whatcha mean lying there in the middle of the floor doing nothing anyway? Didn't I tell you I couldn't cook supper before you chopped wood for the stove?"

Sometimes he would sneak down to the old Perkins place and find Prince Terrien crying on the porch, where Mr. Burke had exiled him. You couldn't blame the man. No one could get anything done with that animal grabbing his hand or jumping up to lick his face. He'd take P. T. for a romp in the Burkes' upper field. If it was a mild day, Miss Bessie would be mooing nervously from across the fence. She couldn't seem to get used to the yipping and snapping. Or maybe it was the time of year—the last dregs of winter spoiling the taste of everything. Nobody, human or animal, seemed happy.

Except Leslie. She was crazy about fixing up that broken-down old wreck of a house. She loved being needed by her father. Half the time they were supposed to be working they were just yakking away. She was learning, she related glowingly at recess, to "understand" her father. It had never occurred to Jess that parents were meant to be understood any more than the safe at the Millsburg First National was sitting around begging him to crack it. Parents were what they were; it wasn't up to you to try to puzzle them out. There was something weird about a grown man wanting to be friends with his own child. He ought to have friends his own age and let her have hers.

Jess's feelings about Leslie's father poked up like a canker sore. You keep biting it, and it gets bigger and worse instead of better. You spend a lot of time trying to keep your teeth away from it. Then sure as Christmas you forget the silly thing and chomp right down on it. Lord, that man got in his way. It even poisoned what time he did have with Leslie. She'd be sittting there bubbling away at recess, and it would be almost like the old times; then without warning, she'd say, "Bill thinks so and so." Chomp. Right down on the old sore.

Finally, finally she noticed. It took her until February, and for a girl as smart as Leslie that was a long, long time.

"Why don't you like Bill?"

"Who said I didn't?"

"Jess Aarons. How stupid do you think I am?"

Pretty stupid—sometimes. But what he actually said was, "What makes you think I don't like him?"

"Well, you never come to the house any more. At first I thought it was something I'd done. But it's not that. You still talk to me at school. Lots of times I see you in the field, playing with P. T., but you don't even come near the door."

"You're always busy." He was uncomfortably aware of how much he sounded like Brenda when he said this.

"Well, for spaghetti sauce! You could offer to help, you know."

It was like all the lights coming back on after an electrical storm. Lord, who was the stupid one?

Still, it took him a few days to feel comfortable around Leslie's father. Part of the problem was he didn't know what to call him. "Hey," he'd say, and both Leslie and her father would turn around. "Uh, Mr. Burke?"

"I wish you'd call me Bill, Jess."

"Yeah." He fumbled around with the name for a couple more days, but it came more easily with practice. It also helped to know some things that Bill for all his brains and books didn't know. Jess found he was really useful to him, not a nuisance to be tolerated or set out on the porch like P. T.

"You're amazing," Bill would say. "Where did you learn that, Jess?" Jess never quite knew how he knew things, so he'd shrug and let Bill and Leslie praise him to each other—though the work itself was praise enough.

First they ripped out the boards that covered the ancient fireplace, coming upon the rusty bricks like prospectors upon the mother lode. Next they got the old wallpaper off the living-room wall—all five garish layers of it. Sometimes as they lovingly patched and painted, they listened to Bill's records or sang, Leslie and Jess teaching Bill some of Miss Edmunds' songs and Bill teaching them some he knew. At other times they would talk. Jess listened wonderingly as Bill explained things that were going on in the world. If Momma could hear him, she'd swear he was another Walter Cronkite instead of "some hippie." All the Burkes were smart. Not smart, maybe, about fixing things or growing things, but smart in a way Jess had never known real live people to be. Like one day while they were working, Judy came down and read out loud to them, mostly poetry and some of it in Italian which, of course, Jess couldn't understand, but he buried his head in the rich sound of the words and let himself be wrapped warmly around in the feel of the Burkes' brilliance.

They painted the living room gold. Leslie and Jess had wanted blue, but Bill held out for gold, which turned out to be so beautiful that they were glad they had given in. The sun would slant in from the west in the late afternoon until the room was brimful of light.

Finally Bill rented a sander from Millsburg Plaza, and they took off the black floor paint down to the wide oak boards and refinished them.

"No rugs," Bill said.

"No," agreed Judy. "It would be like putting a veil on the Mona Lisa."

When Bill and the children had finished razor-blading the last bits of paint off the windows and washed the panes, they called Judy down from her upstairs study to come and see. The four of them sat down on the floor and gazed around. It was gorgeous.

Leslie gave a deep satisfied sigh. "I love this room," she said. "Don't you feel the golden enchantment of it? It is worthy to be"—Jess looked up in sudden alarm—"in a palace." Relief. In such a mood, a person might even let a sworn secret slip. But she hadn't, not even to Bill and Judy, and he knew how she felt about her parents. She must have seen his anxiety because she winked at him across Bill and Judy just as he sometimes winked at May Belle over Joyce Ann's head. Terabithia was still just for the two of them.

The next afternoon they called P. T. and headed for Terabithia. It had been more than a month since they had been there together, and as they neared the creek bed, they slowed down. Jess wasn't sure he still remembered how to be a king.

"We've been away for many years," Leslie was whispering. "How do you suppose the kingdom has fared in our absence?"

"Where've we been?"

"Conquering the hostile savages on our northern borders," she answered. "But the lines of communication have been broken, and thus we do not have tidings of our beloved homeland for many a full moon." How was that for regular queen talk? Jess wished he could match it. "You think anything bad has happened?"

"We must have courage, my king. It may indeed be so."

They swung silently across the creek bed. On the farther bank, Leslie picked up two sticks. "Thy sword, sire," she whispered.

Jess nodded. They hunched down and crept toward the stronghold like police detectives on TV.

"Hey, queen! Watch out! Behind you!"

Leslie whirled and began to duel the imaginary foe. Then more came rushing upon them and the shouts of the battle rang through Terabithia. The guardian of the realm raced about in happy puppy circles, too young as yet to comprehend the danger that surrounded them all.

"They have sounded the retreat!" the brave queen cried.

"Yey!"

"Drive them out utterly, so they may never return and prey upon our people."

"Out you go! Out! Out!" All the way to the creek bed, they forced the enemy back, sweating under their winter jackets.

"At last. Terabithia is free once more."

The king sat down on a log and wiped his face, but the queen did not let him rest long. "Sire, we must go at once to the grove of the pines and give thanks for our victory."

Jess followed her into the grove, where they stood silently in the dim light.

"Who do we thank?" he whispered.

The question flickered across her face. "O God," she began. She was more at home with magic than religion. "O Spirits of the Grove."

"Thy right arm hast given us the victory." He couldn't remember where he'd heard that one, but it seemed to fit. Leslie gave him a look of approval.

She took up the words. "Now grant protection to Terabithia, to all its people, and to us its rulers."

"*Aroooo.*"

Jess tried hard not to smile. "And to its puppy dog."

"And to Prince Terrien, its guardian and jester. Amen."

"Amen."

They both managed somehow to keep the giggles buttoned in until they got out of the sacred place.

A few days after the encounter with the enemies of Terabithia, they had an encounter of a different sort at school. Leslie came out at recess to tell Jess that she had started into the girls' room only to be stopped by the sound of crying from one of the stalls. She lowered her voice. "This sounds crazy," she said. "But from the feet, I'm sure it's Janice Avery in there."

"You're kidding." The picture of Janice Avery crying on the toilet seat was too much for Jess to imagine.

"Well, she's the only one in school that has Willard Hughes's name crossed out on her sneakers. Besides, the smoke is so thick in there you need a gas mask."

"Are you sure she was crying?"

"Jess Aarons, I can tell if somebody's crying or not."

Lord, what was the matter with him? Janice Avery had given him nothing but trouble, and now he was feeling responsible for her—like one of the Burkes' timber wolves or beached whales. "She didn't even cry when kids teased her 'bout Willard after the note."

"Yeah. I know."

He looked at her. "Well," he said. "What should we do?"

"Do?" she asked. "What do you mean what should we do?"

How could he explain it to her? "Leslie. If she was an *animal* predator, we'd be obliged to try to help her."

Leslie gave him a funny look.

"Well, you're the one who's always telling me I gotta care," he said.

"But Janice Avery?"

"If she's crying, there gotta be something really wrong."

"Well, what are you planning to do?"

He flushed. "I can't go into no girls' room."

"Oh, I get it. You're going to send me into the shark's jaws. No, thank you, Mr. Aarons."

"Leslie, I swear—I'd go in there if I could." He really thought he would, too. "You ain't scared of her, are you, Leslie?" He didn't mean it in a daring way, he was just dumbfounded by the idea of Leslie being scared.

She flashed her eyes at him and tossed her head back in that proud way she had. "OK, I'm going in. But I want you to know, Jess Aarons, I think it's the dumbest idea you ever had in your life."

He crept down the hall after her and hid behind the nearest alcove to the girls' room door. He ought at least to be there to catch her when Janice kicked her out.

There was a quiet minute after the door swung shut behind Leslie. Then he heard Leslie saying something to Janice. Next a string of cuss words which were too loud to be blurred by the closed door. This was followed by some loud sobbing, not Leslie's, thank the Lord, and some sobbing and talking mixed up and—the bell.

He couldn't be caught staring at the door of the girls' room, but how could he leave? He'd be deserting in the line of fire. The rush of kids into the building settled it. He let himself be caught up in the stream and made his way to the basement steps, his brains still swirling with the sounds of cussing and sobbing.

Back in the fifth-grade classroom, he kept his eye glued on

the door for Leslie. He half expected to see her come through flattened straight out like the coyote on *Road Runner*. But she came in smiling without so much as a black eye. She waltzed over to Mrs. Myers and whispered her excuse for being late, and Mrs. Myers beamed at her with what was becoming known as the "Leslie Burke special."

How was he supposed to find out what had happened? If he tried to pass a note, the other kids would read it. Leslie sat way up in the front corner nowhere near the waste basket or pencil sharpener, so there was no way he could pretend to be heading somewhere else and sneak a word with her. And she wasn't moving in his direction. That was for sure. She was sitting straight up in her seat, looking as pleased with herself as a motorcycle rider who's just made it over fourteen trucks.

Leslie smirked clear through the afternoon and right on to the bus where Janice Avery gave her a little crooked smile on the way to the back seat, and Leslie looked over at Jess as if to say, "See!" He was going crazy wanting to know. She even put him off after the bus pulled away, pointing her head at May Belle as if to say, "We shouldn't discuss it in front of the children."

Finally, finally in the safe darkness of the stronghold she told him.

"Do you know why she was crying?"

"How'm I supposed to know? Lord, Leslie, will you tell me? What in the heck was going on in there?"

"Janice Avery is a very unfortunate person. Do you realize that?"

"What was she crying about, for heaven's sake?"

"It's a very complicated situation. I can understand now why Janice has so many problems relating to people."

"Will you tell me what happened before I have a hernia?"

"Did you know her father beats her?"

"Lots of kids' fathers beat 'um." *Will you get on with it?*

"No, I mean really beats her. The kind of beatings they take people to jail for in Arlington." She shook her head in disbelief. "You can't imagine. . . ."

"Is that why she was crying? Just 'cause her father beats her?"

"Oh, no. She gets beaten up all the time. She wouldn't cry at school about that."

"Then what *was* she crying for?"

"Well—" Lord, Leslie was loving this. She'd string him out forever. "Well, today she was so mad at her father that she told her so-called friends Wilma and Bobby Sue about it."

"Yeah?"

"And those two—two—" She looked for a word vile enough to describe Janice Avery's friends and found none. "Those two girls blabbed it all over the seventh grade."

Pity for Janice Avery swept across him.

"Even the teacher knows about it."

"Boy." The word came out like a sigh. There was a rule at Lark Creek, more important than anything Mr. Turner made up and fussed about. That was the rule that you never mixed up troubles at home with life at school. When parents were poor or ignorant or mean, or even just didn't believe in having a TV set, it was up to their kids to protect them. By tomorrow every kid and teacher in Lark Creek Elementary would be talking in half snickers about Janice Avery's daddy. It didn't matter if their own fathers were in the state hospital or the federal prison, they hadn't betrayed theirs, and Janice had.

"Do you know what else?"

"What?"

"I told Janice about not having a TV and everyone laughing.

I told her I understood what it was like to have everyone think I was weird."

"What'd she say to that?"

"She knew I was telling the truth. She even asked me for advice as if I was Dear Abby."

"Yeah?"

"I told her just to pretend she didn't know what on earth Wilma and Bobby Sue had said or where they had got such a crazy story and everybody would forget about it in a week." She leaned forward, suddenly anxious. "Do you think that was good advice?"

"Lord, how should I know? Make her feel better?"

"I think so. She seemed to feel a lot better."

"Well, it was great advice then."

She leaned back, happy and relaxed. "Know what, Jess?"

"What?"

"Thanks to you, I think I now have one and one-half friends at Lark Creek School."

It hurt him for it to mean so much to Leslie to have friends. When would she learn they weren't worth her trouble? "Oh, you got more friends than that."

"Nope. One and one-half. Monster Mouth Myers doesn't count."

There in their secret place, his feelings bubbled inside him like a stew on the back of the stove—some sad for her in her lonesomeness, but chunks of happiness, too. To be able to be Leslie's one whole friend in the world as she was his—he couldn't help being satisfied about that.

That night as he started to get into bed, leaving the light off so as not to wake the little girls, he was surprised by May Belle's shrill little "Jess."

"How come you still awake?"

"Jess. I know where you and Leslie go to hide."

"What d'you mean?"

"I followed ya."

He was at her bedside in one leap. "You ain't supposed to follow me!"

"How come?" Her voice was sassy.

He grabbed her shoulders and made her look him in the face. She blinked in the dim light like a startled chicken.

"You listen here, May Belle Aarons," he whispered fiercely, "I catch you following me again, your life ain't worth nothing."

"OK, OK."—she slid back into the bed—"Boy, you're mean. I oughta tell Momma on you."

"Look, May Belle, you can't do that. You can't tell Momma 'bout where me and Leslie go."

She answered with a little sniffing sound.

He grabbed her shoulders again. He was desperate. "I mean it, May Belle. You can't tell nobody nothing!" He let her go. "Now, I don't want to hear about you following me *or* squealing to Momma ever again, you hear?"

"Why not?"

" 'Cause if you do—I'm gonna tell Billy Jean Edwards you still wet the bed sometimes."

"You wouldn't!"

"Boy, girl, you just better not try me."

He made her swear on the Bible never to tell and never to follow, but still he lay awake a long time. How could he trust everything that mattered to him to a sassy six-year-old? Sometimes it seemed to him that his life was delicate as a dandelion. One little puff from any direction, and it was blown to bits.

EIGHT

Easter

Even though it was nearly Easter, there were still very few nights that it was warm enough to leave Miss Bessie out. And then there was the rain. All March it poured. For the first time in many years the creek bed held water, not just a trickle either, enough so that when they swung across, it was a little scary looking down at the rushing water below. Jess took Prince Terrien across inside his jacket, but the puppy was growing so fast he might pop the zipper any time and fall into the water and drown.

Ellie and Brenda were already fighting about what they were going to wear to church. Since Momma got mad at the preacher three years back, Easter was the only time in the year that the Aarons went to church and it was a big deal. His mother always cried poor, but she put a lot of thought and as much money as she could scrape together into making sure she wouldn't be embarrassed by how her family looked. But the day before she planned to take them all over to Millsburg Plaza for new clothes, his dad came home from Washington early. He'd been laid off. No new clothes this year.

A wail went up from Ellie and Brenda like two sirens going to a fire. "You can't make me go to church," Brenda said. "I ain't got nothing to wear, and you know it."

"Just 'cause you're too fat," May Belle muttered.

"Did you hear what she said, Momma? I'm gonna kill that kid."

"Brenda, will you shut your mouth?" his mother said sharply; then more wearily, "We got lot more than Easter clothes to worry about."

His dad got up noisily and poured himself a cup of black coffee from the pot on the back of the stove.

"Why can't we charge some things?" Ellie said in her wheedling voice.

Brenda burst in. "Do you know what some people do? They charge something and wear it, and then take it back and say it didn't fit or something. The stores don't give 'em no trouble."

Her father turned in a kind of roar. "I never heard such a fool thing in my life. Didn't you hear your mother tell you to shut your mouth, girl!"

Brenda stopped talking, but she popped her gum as loudly as she could just to prove she wasn't going to be put down.

Jess was glad to escape to the shed and the complacent company of Miss Bessie. There was a knock. "Jess?"

"Leslie. Come on in."

She looked first and then sat on the floor near his stool. "What's new?"

"Lord, don't ask." He tugged the teats rhythmically and listened to the *plink*, *plink*, *plink*, in the bottom of the pail.

"That bad, huh?"

"My dad's got laid off, and Brenda and Ellie are fit to fry 'cause they can't have new clothes for Easter."

"Gee, I'm sorry. About your dad, I mean."

Jess grinned. "Yeah. I ain't too worried about those girls. If I know them, they'll trick new clothes out of somebody. It would make you throw up to see how those girls make a spectacle of themselves in church."

"I never knew you went to church."

"Just Easter." He concentrated on the warm udders. "I guess you think that's dumb or something."

She didn't answer for a minute. "I was thinking I'd like to go."

He stopped milking. "I don't understand you sometimes, Leslie."

"Well, I've never been to a church before. It would be a new experience for me."

He went back to work. "You'd hate it."

"Why?"

"It's boring."

"Well, I'd just like to see for myself. Do you think your parents would let me go with you?"

"You can't wear pants."

"I've got some dresses, Jess Aarons." Would wonders never cease?

"Here," he said. "Open your mouth."

"Why?"

"Just open your mouth." For once she obeyed. He sent a stream of warm milk straight into it.

"Jess Aarons!" The name was garbled and the milk dribbled down her chin as she spoke.

"Don't open your mouth now. You're wasting good milk."

Leslie started to giggle, choking and coughing.

"Now if I could just learn to pitch a baseball that straight. Lemme try again."

Leslie controlled her giggle, closed her eyes, and solemnly opened her mouth.

But now Jess was giggling, so that he couldn't keep his hand steady.

"You dunce! You got me right in the ear." Leslie hunched up her shoulder and rubbed her ear with the sleeve of her sweat shirt. She collapsed into giggles again.

"I'd be obliged if you'd finish milking and come on back to the house." His dad was standing right there at the door.

"I guess I'd better go," said Leslie quietly. She got up and went to the door. "Excuse me." His dad moved aside to let her pass. Jess waited for him to say something more, but he just stood there for a few minutes and then turned and went out.

Ellie said she would go to church if Momma would let her wear the see-through blouse, and Brenda would go if she at least got a new skirt. In the end everyone got something new except Jess and his dad, neither of whom cared, but Jess got the idea it might give him a little bargaining power with his mother.

"Since I ain't getting anything new, could Leslie go to church with us?"

"That girl?" He could see his mother rooting around in her head for a good reason to say no. "She don't dress right."

"Momma!"—his voice sounded as prissy as Ellie's—"Leslie's got dresses. She got hundreds of 'um."

His mother's thin face drooped. She bit the outside of her bottom lip in a way Joyce Ann sometimes did and spoke so softly Jess could hardly hear her. "I don't want no one poking up their nose at my family."

Jess wanted to put his arm around her the way he put it around May Belle when she was in need of comfort. "She don't poke her nose up at you, Momma. Honest."

His mother sighed. "Well, if she'll look decent. . . ."

Leslie looked decent. Her hair was kind of slicked down, and she wore a navy-blue jumper over a blouse with tiny old-fashioned-looking flowers. At the bottom of her red knee socks were a pair of shiny brown leather shoes that Jess had never seen before as Leslie always wore sneakers like the rest of the kids in Lark Creek. Even her manner was decent. Her usual sparkle was toned way down, and she said "Yes'm" and "No'm" to his mother just as though she were aware of Mrs. Aaron's dread of disrespect. Jess knew how hard Leslie must be trying, for Leslie didn't say "ma'am" naturally.

In comparison to Leslie, Brenda and Ellie looked like a

pair of peacocks with fake tail feathers. They both insisted on riding in the front of the pickup with their parents, which was some kind of a squeeze with Brenda's shape to consider. Jess and Leslie and the little girls climbed happily into the back and sat down on the old sacks his dad had put against the cab.

The sun wasn't exactly shining, but it was the first day in so long that the rain wasn't actually coming down that they sang "O Lord, What a Morning," "Ah, Lovely Meadows," and "Sing! Sing a Song" that Miss Edmunds had taught them, and even "Jingle Bells" for Joyce Ann. The wind carried their voices away from them. It made the music seem mysterious, which filled Jess with a feeling of power over the hills rolling out from behind the truck. The ride was much too short, especially for Joyce Ann, who began to cry because the arrival interrupted the first verse of "Santa Claus Is Coming to Town," which after "Jingle Bells" was her favorite song. Jess tickled her to get her giggling again, so that when the four of them clambered down over the tail gate, they were flushed-faced and happy once more.

They were a little late, which didn't bother Ellie and Brenda for it meant that they got to flounce down the entire length of the aisle to the first pew, making sure that every eye in the church was on them, and every expression of every eye a jealous one. Lord, they were disgusting. And his mother had been scared Leslie might embarrass her. Jess hunched his shoulders and slunk into the pew after the string of womenfolks and just before his dad.

Church always seemed the same. Jess could tune it out the same way he tuned out school, with his body standing up and sitting down in unison with the rest of the congregation but his mind numb and floating, not really thinking or dreaming but at least free.

Once or twice he was aware of being on his feet with the loud not really tuneful singing all around him. At the edge of his consciousness he could hear Leslie singing along and drowsily wondered why she bothered.

The preacher had one of those tricky voices. It would buzz along for several minutes quite comfortably, then bang! he was screaming at you. Each time Jess would jump, and it would take another couple of minutes to relax again. Because he wasn't listening to the words, the man's red face with sweat pouring down seemed strangely out of place in the dull sanctuary. It was like Brenda throwing a tantrum over Joyce Ann touching her lipstick.

It took a while to get Ellie and Brenda pulled away from the front yard of the church. Jess and Leslie went ahead and put the little girls in the back and settled down to wait.

"Gee, I'm really glad I came."

Jess turned to Leslie in unbelief.

"It was better than a movie."

"You're kidding."

"No, I'm not." And she wasn't. He could tell by her face. "That whole Jesus thing is really interesting, isn't it?"

"What d'you mean?"

"All those people wanting to kill him when he hadn't done anything to hurt them." She hesitated. "It's really kind of a beautiful story—like Abraham Lincoln or Socrates—or Aslan."

"It ain't beautiful," May Belle broke in. "It's scary. Nailing holes right through somebody's hand."

"May Belle's right." Jess reached down into the deepest pit of his mind. "It's because we're all vile sinners God made Jesus die."

"Do you think that's true?"

He was shocked. "It's in the Bible, Leslie."

She looked at him as if she were going to argue, then seemed to change her mind. "It's crazy, isn't it?" She shook her head. "You have to believe it, but you hate it. I don't have to believe it, and I think it's beautiful." She shook her head again. "It's crazy."

May Belle had her eyes all squinched as though Leslie was some strange creature in a zoo. "You gotta believe the Bible, Leslie."

"Why?" It was a genuine question. Leslie wasn't being smarty.

" 'Cause if you don't believe the Bible"—May Belle's eyes were huge—"God'll damn you to hell when you die."

"Where'd she ever hear a thing like that?" Leslie turned on Jess as though she were about to accuse him of some wrong he had committed against his sister. He felt hot and caught by her voice and words.

He dropped his gaze to the gunnysack and began to fiddle with the raveled edge.

"That's right, ain't it, Jess?" May Belle's shrill voice demanded. "Don't God damn you to hell if you don't believe the Bible?

Jess pushed his hair out of his face. "I reckon," he muttered.

"I don't believe it," Leslie said. "I don't even think you've read the Bible."

"I read most of it." Jess said, still fingering the sack. "S'bout the only book we got around our place." He looked up at Leslie and half grinned.

She smiled. "OK," she said. "But I still don't think God goes around damning people to hell."

They smiled at each other trying to ignore May Belle's anxious little voice. "But Leslie," she insisted. "What if you *die*? What's going to happen to you if you *die*?"

NINE

The Evil Spell

On Easter Monday the rain began again in earnest. It was as though the elements were conspiring to ruin their short week of freedom. Jess and Leslie sat cross-legged on the porch at the Burkes', watching the wheels of a passing truck shoot huge sprays of muddy water to its rear.

"That ain't no fifty-five miles per hour," Jess muttered.

Just then something came out of the window of the cab. Leslie jumped to her feet. "Litterbug!" she screamed after the already disappearing taillights.

Jess stood up, too. "What d'ya want to do?"

"What I want to do is go to Terabithia," she said, looking out mournfully at the pouring rain.

"Heck, let's go," he said.

"OK," she said, suddenly brightening. "Why not?"

She got her boots and raincoat and considered the umbrella. "D'ya think we could swing across holding the umbrella?"

He shook his head. "Nah."

"We better stop by your house and get your boots and things."

He shrugged. "I don't have nothing that fits. I'll just go like this."

"I'll get you an old coat of Bill's." She started up the stairs. Judy appeared in the hallway.

"What are you kids doing?" It was the same words that Jess's mother might have used, but it didn't come out the same way. Judy's eyes were kind of fuzzed over as she spoke, and her voice sounded as though it were being broadcast from miles away.

"We didn't mean to bother you, Judy."

"That's all right, I'm stuck right now. I might as well stop. Have you had any lunch?"

"S'all right, Judy. We can get something ourselves."

Judy's eyes focused slightly. "You've got your boots on."

Leslie looked down at her feet. "Oh, yeah," she said, as though she were just noticing them herself. "We thought we'd go out for a while."

"Is it raining again?"

"Yeah."

"I used to like to walk in the rain." Judy smiled the kind of smile May Belle did in her sleep. "Well, if you two can manage. . . ."

"Sure."

"Is Bill back yet?"

"No. He said he wouldn't be back until late, not to worry."

"Fine," she said. "Oh," she said suddenly, and her eyes popped wide open. "Oh!" She almost ran back to her room, and the plinkety-plink of the typewriter began at once.

Leslie was grinning. "She came unstuck."

He wondered what it would be like to have a mother whose stories were inside her head instead of marching across the television screen all day long. He followed Leslie up the hall to where she was pulling things out of a closet. She handed him a beige raincoat and a peculiar round black woolly hat.

"No boots." Her voice was coming out of the depths of the closet and was muffled by a line of overcoats. "How about a pair of clumps?"

"A pair of what?"

She stuck her head out between the coats. "Cleats. Cleats." She produced them. They looked like size twelves.

"Naw. I'd lose 'em in the mud. I'll just go barefoot."

"Hey," she said, emerging completely. "Me, too."

The ground was cold. The icy mud sent little thrills of pain up their legs, so they ran, splashing through the puddles and slushing in the mud. P. T. bounded ahead, leaping fishlike from one brown sea to the next, then turning back to herd the two of them forward, nipping at their heels and further splashing their already sopping jeans.

When they got to the bank of the creek, they stopped. It was an awesome sight. Like in *The Ten Commandments* on TV when the water came rushing into the dry path Moses had made and swept all the Egyptians away, the long dry bed of the creek was a roaring eight-foot-wide sea, sweeping before it great branches of trees, logs, and trash, swirling them about like so many Egyptian chariots, the hungry waters licking and sometimes leaping the banks, daring them to try to confine it.

"Wow." Leslie's voice was respectful.

"Yeah." Jess looked up at the rope. It was still twisted around the branch of the crab apple tree. His stomach felt cold. "Maybe we ought to forget it today."

"C'mon, Jess. We can make it." The hood of Leslie's raincoat had fallen back, and her hair lay plastered to her forehead. She wiped her cheeks and eyes with her hand and then untwisted the rope. She unsnapped the top of her coat with her left hand. "Here," she said. "Stick P. T. in here for me."

"I'll carry him, Leslie."

"With that raincoat, he'll slip right out the bottom." She was impatient to be gone, so Jess scooped up the sodden dog and shoved him rear-first into the cave of Leslie's raincoat.

"You gotta hold his rear with your left arm and swing with your right, you know."

"I know. I know." She moved backward to get a running start.

"Hold tight."

"Good gosh, Jess."

He shut his mouth. He wanted to shut his eyes, too. But he forced himself to watch her run back, race for the bank, leap, swing, and jump off, landing gracefully on her feet on the far side.

"Catch!"

He stuck his hand out, but he was watching Leslie and P. T. and not concentrating on the rope, which slipped off the end of his fingertips and swung in a large arc out of his reach. He jumped and grabbed it, and shutting his mind to the sound and sight of the water, he ran back and then speeded forward. The cold stream lapped his bare heels momentarily, but then he was into the air above it and falling awkwardly and landing on his bottom. P. T. was on him immediately, muddy paws all over the beige raincoat, and pink tongue sandpapering Jess's wet face.

Leslie's eyes were sparkling. "Arise"—she barely swallowed a giggle—"arise, king of Terabithia, and let us proceed into our kingdom."

The king of Terabithia snuffled and wiped his face on the

back of his hand. "I will arise," he replied with dignity, "when thou removes this fool dog off my gut."

They went to Terabithia on Tuesday and again on Wednesday. The rain continued sporadically, so that by Wednesday the creek had swollen to the trunk of the crab apple and they were running through ankle-deep water to make their flight into Terabithia. And on the opposite bank Jess was more careful to land on his feet. Sitting in cold wet britches for an hour was no fun even in a magic kingdom.

For Jess the fear of the crossing rose with the height of the creek. Leslie never seemed to hesitate, so Jess could not hang back. But even though he could force his body to follow after, his mind hung back, wanting to cling to the crab apple tree the way Joyce Ann might cling to Momma's skirt.

While they were sitting in the castle on Wednesday, it began suddenly to rain so hard that water came through the top of the shack in icy streams. Jess tried to huddle away from the worst of them, but there was no escaping the miserable invaders.

"Dost know what is in my mind, O king?" Leslie dumped the contents of one coffee can on the ground and put the can under the worst leak.

"What?"

"Methinks some evil being has put a curse on our beloved kingdom.

"Damn weather bureau." In the dim light he could see Leslie's face freeze into its most queenly pose—the kind of expression she usually reserved for vanquished enemies. She didn't want to kid. He instantly repented his unkingly manner.

Leslie chose to ignore it. "Let us go even up into the sacred grove and inquire of the Spirits what this evil might be and how we must combat it. For of a truth I perceive that this is no ordinary rain that is falling upon our kingdom."

"Right, queen," Jess mumbled and crawled out of the low entrance of the castle stronghold.

Under the pines even the rain lost its driving power. Without the filtered light of the sun it was almost dark, and the sound of the rain hitting the pine branches high above their heads filled the grove with a weird, tuneless music. Dread lay on Jess's stomach like a hunk of cold, undigested doughnut.

Leslie lifted her arms and face up toward the dark green canopy. "O Spirits of the grove," she began solemnly. "We are come on behalf of our beloved kingdom which lies even now under the spell of some evil, unknown force. Give us, we beseech thee, wisdom to discern this evil, and power to overcome it." She nudged Jess with her elbow.

He raised his arms. "Um. Uh." He felt the point of her sharp elbow again. "Um. Yes. Please listen, thou Spirits."

She seemed satisfied. At least she didn't poke him again. She just stood there quietly as if she was listening respectfully to someone talking to her. Jess was shivering, whether from the cold or the place, he didn't know. But he was glad when she turned to leave the grove. All he could think of was dry clothes and a cup of hot coffee and maybe just plunking down in front of the TV for a couple of hours. He was obviously not worthy to be king of Terabithia. Whoever heard of a king who was scared of tall trees and a little bit of water?

He swung across the creek almost too disgusted with himself to be afraid. Halfway across he looked down and stuck his tongue out at the roaring below. *Who's afraid of the big bad wolf? Tra-la-la-la-la,* he said to himself, then quickly looked up again toward the crab apple tree.

Plodding up the hill through the mud and beaten-down grasses, he slammed his bare feet down hard. *Left, left,* he

addressed them inside his head. *Left my wife and forty-nine children without any gingerbread, think I did right? Right. Right by my . . .*

"Why don't we change our clothes and watch TV or something over at your house?"

He felt like hugging her. "I'll make us some coffee," he said joyfully.

"Yuk," she said smiling and began to run for the old Perkins place, that beautiful, graceful run of hers that neither mud nor water could defeat.

It had seemed to Jess when he went to bed Wednesday night that he could relax, that everything was going to be all right, but he awoke in the middle of the night with the horrible realization that it was still raining. He would just have to tell Leslie that he wouldn't go to Terabithia. After all, she had told him that when she was working on the house with Bill. And he hadn't questioned her. It wasn't so much that he minded telling Leslie that he was afraid to go; it was that he minded being afraid. It was as though he had been made with a great piece missing—one of May Belle's puzzles with this huge gap where somebody's eye and cheek and jaw should have been. Lord, it would be better to be born without an arm than to go through life with no guts. He hardly slept the rest of the night, listening to the horrid rain and knowing that no matter how high the creek came, Leslie would still want to cross it.

TEN

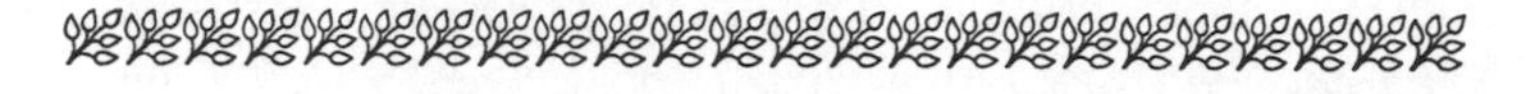

The Perfect Day

He heard his dad start the pickup. Even though there was no job to go to, he left every morning early to look. Sometimes he just hung around all day at the unemployment office; on lucky days he got picked up to unload furniture or do cleaning.

Jess was awake. He might as well get up. He could milk and feed Miss Bessie, and get that over with. He pulled on a T-shirt and overalls over the underwear he slept in.

"Where you going?"

"Go back to sleep, May Belle."

"I can't. The rain makes too much noise."

"Well, get up then."

"Why are you so mean to me?"

"Will you shut up, May Belle? You'll have everyone in the whole house woke up with that big mouth of yours."

Joyce Ann would have screamed, but May Belle made a face.

"Oh, c'mon," he said. "I'm just gonna milk Miss Bessie. Then maybe we can watch cartoons if we keep the sound real low."

May Belle was as scrawny as Brenda was fat. She stood a moment in the middle of the floor in her underwear, her skin white and goose-bumpy. Her eyes were still drooped from sleep, and her pale brown hair stuck up all over her head like a squirrel's nest on a winter branch. That's got to be the world's ugliest kid, he thought, looking her over with genuine affection.

She threw her jeans into his face. "I'm gonna tell Momma."

He threw the jeans back at her. "Tell Momma what?"

"How you just stand there staring at me when I ain't got my clothes on."

Lord. She thought he was enjoying it. "Yeah, well," he said, heading for the door so she wouldn't throw anything else at him. "Pretty girl like you. Can't hardly help myself." He could hear her giggling as he crossed the kitchen.

The shed was filled with Miss Bessie's familiar smell. He clucked her gently over and set his stool at her flank and the pail beneath her speckled udder. The rain pounded the metal roof of the shed so that the plink of milk in the pail set up a counter-rhythm. If only it would stop raining. He pressed his forehead against Miss Bessie's warm hide. He wondered idly if cows were ever scared—really scared. He had seen Miss Bessie jitter away from P.T., but that was different. A yapping puppy at your heels is an immediate threat, but the difference between him and Miss Bessie was that when there was no P. T. in sight she was perfectly content, sleepily chewing her cud. She wasn't staring down at the old Perkins place, wondering and worrying. She wasn't standing there on her tippytoes while anxiety ate holes through all her stomachs.

He stroked his forehead across her flank and sighed. If there was still water in the creek come summer, he'd ask Leslie to teach him how to swim. How's that? he said to himself. I'll just grab that old terror by the shoulders and shake the daylights out of it. Maybe I'll even learn scuba diving. He shuddered. He may not have been born with guts, but he didn't have to die without them. Hey, maybe you could go down to the Medical College and get a gut transplant. No, Doc, I got me a perfectly good heart. What I need is a *gut* transplant. How 'bout it? He smiled. He'd have to tell Leslie about wanting a gut transplant. It was the kind of nonsense she appreciated. Of course—he broke the rhythm of the milking long enough to shove his hair out of his face—of course what I really need is a brain transplant. I know Leslie. I know she's not going to bite my head off or make fun of me if I say I don't want to go across again till the creek's down. All I gotta do is say "Leslie, I don't wanta go over there today." Just like that. Easy as pie. "Leslie, I don't want to go over there today." "How come?" "How come. Because, because, well because. . . ."

"I called ya three times already." May Belle was imitating Ellie's prissiest manner.

"Called me for what?"

"Some lady wants you on the telephone. I had to get dressed to come get you."

He never got phone calls. Leslie had called him exactly once, and Brenda had gone into such a song and dance with her about Jess's getting a call from his *sweetheart* that Leslie had decided it was simpler to come to the house and get him when she wanted to talk.

"Sounds kinda like Miss Edmunds."

It was Miss Edmunds. "Jess?" her voice flowed through the receiver. "Miserable weather, isn't it?"

"Yes'm." He was scared to say more for fear she'd hear the shake.

"I was thinking of driving down to Washington—maybe go to the Smithsonian or the National Gallery. How would you like to keep me company?"

He broke out in a cold sweat.

"Jess?"

He licked his lips and shoved his hair off his face.

"You still there, Jess?"

"Yes'm." He tried to get a deep breath so he could keep talking.

"Would you like to go with me?"

Lord. "Yes'm."

"Do you need to get permission?" she asked gently.

"Yes—yes'm." He had somehow managed to twist himself up in the phone cord. "Yes'm. Just—just a minute." He untangled himself, put the phone down quietly, and tiptoed into his parents' room. His mother's back made a long hump under the cotton blanket. He shook her shoulder very gently. "Momma?" he was almost whispering. He wanted to ask her without really waking her up. She was likely to say no if she woke up and thought about it.

She jumped at the sound but relaxed again, not fully awake.

"Teacher wants me to go to Washington to the Smithsonian."

"Washington?" The syllables were blurred.

"Yeah. Something for school." He stroked her upper arm. "Be back before too late. OK?"

"Umm."

"Don't worry. I done milking."

"Umm." She pulled the blanket to her ears and turned on her stomach.

Jess crept back to the phone. "It's OK, Miss Edmunds. I can go."

"Great. I'll pick you up in twenty minutes. Just tell me how to get to your house."

As soon as he saw her car turn in, Jess raced out the kitchen door through the rain and met her halfway up the drive. His mother could find out the details from May Belle after he was safely up the road. He was glad May Belle was absorbed in the TV. He didn't want her waking Momma up before he got away. He was scared to look back even after he was in the car and on the main road for fear he'd see his mother screaming after him.

It didn't occur to him until the car was past Millsburg that he might have asked Miss Edmunds if Leslie could have come, too. When he thought about it, he couldn't suppress a secret pleasure at being alone in this small cozy car with Miss Edmunds. She drove intently, both hands gripping the top of the wheel, peering forward. The wheels hummed and the windshield wipers slicked a merry rhythm. The car was warm and filled with the smell of Miss Edmunds. Jess sat with his hands clasped between his knees, the seat belt tight across his chest.

"Damn rain," she said. "I was going stir crazy."

"Yes'm," he said happily.

"You, too, huh?" She gave him a quick smile.

He felt dizzy from the closeness. He nodded.

"Have you ever been to the National Gallery?"

"No, ma'am." He had never even been to Washington before, but he hoped she wouldn't ask him that.

She smiled at him again. "Is this your first trip to an art gallery?"

"Yes'm."

"Great," she said. "My life has been worthwhile after all." He didn't understand her, but he didn't care. He knew she was happy to be with him, and that was enough to know.

Even in the rain he could make out the landmarks, looking surprisingly the way the books had pictured them—the Lee Mansion high on the hill, the bridge, and twice around the circle, so he could get a good look at Abraham Lincoln looking out across the city, the White House and the Monument and at the other end the Capitol. Leslie had seen all these places a million times. She had even gone to school with a girl whose father was a congressman. He thought he might tell Miss Edmunds later that Leslie was a personal friend of a real congressman. Miss Edmunds had always liked Leslie.

Entering the gallery was like stepping inside the pine grove—the huge vaulted marble, the cool splash of the fountain, and the green growing all around. Two little children had pulled away from their mothers and were running about, screaming to each other. It was all Jess could do not to grab them and tell them how to behave in so obviously a sacred place.

And then the pictures—room after room, floor after floor. He was drunk with color and form and hugeness—and with the voice and perfume of Miss Edmunds always beside him. She would bend her head down close to his face to give some explanation or ask him a question, her black hair falling across her shoulders. Men would stare at her instead of the pictures, and Jess felt they must be jealous of him for being with her.

They ate a late lunch in the cafeteria. When she mentioned lunch, he realized with horror that he would need money, and he didn't know how to tell her that he hadn't brought any—didn't have any to bring, for that matter. But before he had time to figure anything out, she said, "Now I'm not going to have any argument about whose paying. I'm a liberated woman, Jess Aarons. When I invite a man out, I pay."

He tried to think of some way to protest without ending up with the bill, but couldn't, and found himself getting a three-dollar meal, which was far more than he had meant to have her spend on him. Tomorrow he would check out with Leslie how he should have handled things.

After lunch, they trotted through the drizzle to the Smithsonian to see the dinosaurs and the Indians. There they came upon a display case holding a miniature scene of Indians disguised in buffalo skins scaring a herd of buffalo into stampeding over a cliff to their death with more Indians waiting below to butcher and skin them. It was a three-dimensional nightmare version of some of his own drawings. He felt a frightening sense of kinship with it.

"Fascinating, isn't it?" Miss Edmunds said, her hair brushing his cheek as she leaned over to look at it.

He touched his cheek. "Yes'm." To himself he said, *I don't think I like it*, but he could hardly pull himself away.

When they came out of the building, it was into brilliant

spring sunshine. Jess blinked his eyes against the glare and the glisten.

"Wow!" Miss Edmunds said. "A miracle! Behold the sun! I was beginning to think she had gone into a cave and vowed never to return, like the Japanese myth."

He felt good again. All the way home in the sunshine Miss Edmunds told funny stories about going to college one year in Japan, where all the boys had been shorter than she, and she hadn't known how to use the toilets.

He relaxed. He had so much to tell Leslie and ask her. It didn't matter how angry his mother was. She'd get over it. And it was worth it. This one perfect day of his life was worth anything he had to pay.

One dip in the road before the old Perkins place, he said, "Just let me out at the road, Miss Edmunds. Don't try to turn in. You might get stuck in the mud."

"OK, Jess," she said. She pulled over at his road. "Thank you for a beautiful day."

The western sun danced on the windshield dazzling his eyes. He turned and looked Miss Edmunds full in the face. "No, ma'am." His voice sounded squeaky and strange. He cleared his throat. "No ma'am, thank *you*. Well—" He hated to leave without being able to really thank her, but the words were not coming for him now. Later, of course, they would, when he was lying in bed or sitting in the castle. "Well—" He opened the door and got out. "See you next Friday."

She nodded, smiling. "See you."

He watched the car go out of sight and then turned and ran with all his might to the house, the joy jiggling inside of him so hard that he wouldn't have been surprised if his feet had just taken off from the ground the way they sometimes did in dreams and floated him right over the roof.

He was all the way into the kitchen before he realized that

something was wrong. His dad's pickup had been outside the door, but he hadn't taken it in until he came into the room and found them all sitting there: his parents and the little girls at the kitchen table and Ellie and Brenda on the couch. Not eating. There was no food on the table. Not watching TV. It wasn't even turned on. He stood unmoving for a second while they stared at him.

Suddenly his mother let out a great shuddering sob. "O my God. O my God." She said it over and over, her head down on her arms. His father moved to put his arm around her awkwardly, but he didn't take his eyes off Jess.

"I tolja he just gone off somewhere," May Belle said quietly and stubbornly as though she had repeated it often and no one had believed her.

He squinted his eyes as though trying to peer down a dark drain pipe. He didn't even know what question to ask them. "What—?" he tried to begin.

Brenda's pouting voice broke in, "Your girl friend's dead, and Momma thought you was dead, too."

ELEVEN

No!

Something whirled around inside Jess's head. He opened his mouth, but it was dry and no words came out. He jerked his head from one face to the next for someone to help him.

Finally his father spoke, his big rough hand stroking his wife's hair and his eyes downcast watching the motion. "They found the Burke girl this morning down in the creek."

"No," he said, finding his voice. "Leslie wouldn't drown. She could swim real good."

"That old rope you kids been swinging on broke." His father went quietly and relentlessly on. "They think she musta hit her head on something when she fell."

"No." He shook his head. "No."

His father looked up. "I'm real sorry, boy."

"No!" Jess was yelling now. "I don't believe you. You're

lying to me!" He looked around again wildly for someone to agree. But they all had their heads down except May Belle, whose eyes were wide with terror. *But, Leslie, what if you die?*

"No," he said straight at May Belle. "It's a lie. Leslie ain't dead." He turned around and ran out the door, letting the screen bang sharply against the house. He ran down the gravel to the main road and then started running west away from Washington and Millsburg—and the old Perkins place. An approaching car beeped and swerved and beeped again, but he hardly noticed.

Leslie—dead—girl friend—rope—broke—fell—you—you—you. The words exploded in his head like corn against the sides of the popper. *God—dead—you—Leslie—dead—you.* He ran until he was stumbling but he kept on, afraid to stop. Knowing somehow that running was the only thing that could keep Leslie from being dead. It was up to him. He had to keep going.

Behind him came the *baripity* of the pickup, but he couldn't turn around. He tried to run faster, but his father passed him and stopped the pickup just ahead, then jumped out and ran back. He picked Jess up in his arms as though he were a baby. For the first few seconds Jess kicked and struggled against the strong arms. Then Jess gave himself over to the numbness that was buzzing to be let out from a corner of his brain.

He leaned his weight upon the door of the pickup and let his head thud-thud against the window. His father drove stiffly without speaking, though once he cleared his throat as though he were going to say something, but he glanced at Jess and closed his mouth.

When they pulled up at his house, his father sat quietly, and Jess could feel the man's uncertainty, so he opened the

door and got out, and with the numbness flooding through him, went in and lay down on his bed.

He was awake, jerked suddenly into consciousness in the black stillness of the house. He sat up, stiff and shivering, although he was fully dressed from his windbreaker down to his sneakers. He could hear the breathing of the little girls in the next bed, strangely loud and uneven in the quiet. Some dream must have awakened him, but he could not remember it. He could only remember the mood of dread it had brought with it. Through the curtainless window he could see the lopsided moon with hundreds of stars dancing in bright attendance.

It came into his mind that someone had told him that Leslie was dead. But he knew now that that had been part of the dreadful dream. Leslie could not die any more than he himself could die. But the words turned over uneasily in his mind like leaves stirred up by a cold wind. If he got up now and went down to the old Perkins place and knocked on the door, Leslie would come to open it, P. T. jumping at her heels like a star around the moon. It was a beautiful night. Perhaps they could run over the hill and across the fields to the stream and swing themselves into Terabithia.

They had never been there in the dark. But there was enough moon for them to find their way into the castle, and he could tell her about his day in Washington. And apologize. It had been so dumb of him not to ask if Leslie could go, too. He and Leslie and Miss Edmunds could have had a wonderful day—different, of course, from the day he and Miss Edmunds had had, but still good, still perfect. Miss Edmunds and Leslie liked each other a lot. It would have been fun to have Leslie along. *I'm really sorry, Leslie.* He took off his jacket and sneakers, and crawled under the covers. *I was dumb not to think of asking.*

S'OK, Leslie would say. *I've been to Washington thousands of times.*

Did you ever see the buffalo hunt?

Somehow it was the one thing in all Washington that Leslie had never seen, and so he could tell her about it, describing the tiny beasts hurtling to destruction.

His stomach felt suddenly cold. It had something to do with the buffalo, with falling, with death. With the reason he had not remembered to ask if Leslie could go with them to Washington today.

You know something weird?

What? Leslie asked.

I was scared to come to Terabithia this morning.

The coldness threatened to spread up from his stomach. He turned over and lay on it. Perhaps it would be better not to think about Leslie right now. He would go to see her the first thing in the morning and explain everything. He could explain it better in the daytime when he had shaken off the effects of his unremembered nightmare.

He put his mind to remembering the day in Washington, working on details of pictures and statues, dredging up the sound of Miss Edmunds' voice, recalling his own exact words and her exact answers. Occasionally into the corner of his mind's vision would come a sensation of falling, but he pushed it away with the view of another picture or the sound of another conversation. Tomorrow he must share it all with Leslie.

The next thing he was aware of was the sun streaming through the window. The little girls' bed was only rumpled covers, and there was movement and quiet talking from the kitchen.

Lord! Poor Miss Bessie. He'd forgotten all about her last night, and now it must be late. He felt for his sneakers and shoved his feet over the heels without tying the laces.

His mother looked up quickly from the stove at the sound of him. Her face was set for a question, but she just nodded her head at him.

The coldness began to come back. "I forgot Miss Bessie."

"Your daddy's milking her."

"I forgot last night, too."

She kept nodding her head. "Your daddy did it for you." But it wasn't an accusation. "You feel like some breakfast?"

Maybe that was why his stomach felt so odd. He hadn't had anything to eat since the ice cream Miss Edmunds had bought them at Millsburg on the way home. Brenda and Ellie stared up at him from the table. The little girls turned from their cartoon show at the TV to look at him and then turned quickly back.

He sat down on the bench. His mother put a plateful of pancakes in front of him. He couldn't remember the last time she had made pancakes. He doused them with syrup and began to eat. They tasted marvelous.

"You don't even care. Do you?" Brenda was watching him from across the table.

He looked at her puzzled, his mouth full.

"If Jimmy Dicks died, I wouldn't be able to eat a bite."

The coldness curled up inside of him and flopped over.

"Will you shut your mouth, Brenda Aarons?" His mother sprang forward, the pancake turner held threateningly high.

"Well, Momma, he's just sitting there eating pancakes like nothing happened. I'd be crying my eyes out."

Ellie was looking first at Mrs. Aarons and then at Brenda. "Boys ain't supposed to cry at times like this. Are they, Momma?"

"Well, it don't seem right for him to be sitting there eating like a brood sow."

"I'm telling you, Brenda, if you don't shut your mouth. . . ."

He could hear them talking but they were farther away than the memory of the dream. He ate and he chewed and he swallowed, and when his mother put three more pancakes on his plate, he ate them, too.

His father came in with the milk. He poured it carefully into the empty cider jugs and put them into the refrigerator. Then he washed his hands at the sink and came to the table. As he passed Jess, he put his hand lightly on the boy's shoulder. He wasn't angry about the milking.

Jess was only dimly aware that his parents were looking at each other and then at him. Mrs. Aarons gave Brenda a hard look and gave Mr. Aarons a look which was to say that Brenda was to be kept quiet, but Jess was only thinking of how good the pancakes had been and hoping his mother would put down some more in front of him. He knew somehow that he shouldn't ask for more, but he was disappointed that she didn't give him any. He thought, then, that he should get up and leave the table, but he wasn't sure where he was supposed to go or what he was supposed to do.

"Your mother and I thought we ought to go down to the neighbors and pay respects." His father cleared his throat. "I think it would be fitting for you to come, too." He stopped again. "Seeing's you was the one that really knowed the little girl."

Jess tried to understand what his father was saying to him, but he felt stupid. "What little girl?" He mumbled it, knowing it was the wrong thing to ask. Ellie and Brenda both gasped.

His father leaned down the table and put his big hand on top of Jess's hand. He gave his wife a quick, troubled look. But she just stood there, her eyes full of pain, saying nothing.

"Your friend Leslie is dead, Jesse. You need to understand that."

Jess slid his hand out from under his father's. He got up from the table.

"I know it ain't a easy thing—" Jess could hear his father speaking as he went into the bedroom. He came back out with his windbreaker on.

"You ready to go now?" His father got up quickly. His mother took off her apron and patted her hair.

May Belle jumped up from the rug. "I wanta go, too," she said. "I never seen a dead person before."

"No!" May Belle sat down again as though slapped down by her mother's voice.

"We don't even know where she's laid out at, May Belle," Mr. Aarons said more gently.

TWELVE

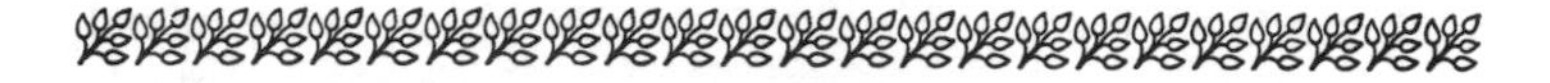

Stranded

They walked slowly across the field and down the hill to the old Perkins place. There were four or five cars parked outside. His father raised the knocker. Jess could hear P. T. barking from the back of the house and rushing to the door.

"Hush, P. T.," a voice which Jess did not know said. "Down." The door was opened by a man who was half leaning over to hold the dog back. At the sight of Jess, P. T. snatched himself loose and leapt joyfully upon the boy. Jess picked him up and rubbed the back of the dog's neck as he used to when P. T. was a tiny puppy.

"I see he knows you," the strange man said with a funny half smile on his face. "Come in, won't you." He stood back for the three of them to enter.

They went into the golden room, and it was just the same, except more beautiful because the sun was pouring through the south windows. Four or five people Jess had never seen before were sitting about, whispering some, but mostly not talking at all. There was no place to sit down, but the strange man was bringing chairs from the dining room. The three of them sat down stiffly and waited, not knowing what to wait for.

An older woman got up slowly from the couch and came over to Jess's mother. Her eyes were red under her perfectly white hair. "I'm Leslie's grandmother," she said, putting out her hand.

His mother took it awkwardly. "Miz Aarons," she said in a low voice. "From up the hill."

Leslie's grandmother shook his mother's and then his father's hands. "Thank you for coming," she said. Then she turned to Jess. "You must be Jess," she said. Jess nodded. "Leslie—" Her eyes filled up with tears. "Leslie told me about you."

For a minute Jess thought she was going to say something else. He didn't want to look at her, so he gave himself over to rubbing P. T., who was hanging across his lap. "I'm sorry—" Her voice broke. "I can't bear it." The man who had opened the door came up and put his arm around her. As he was leading her out of the room, Jess could hear her crying.

He was glad she was gone. There was something weird about a woman like that crying. It was as if the lady who talked about Polident on TV had suddenly burst into tears. It didn't fit. He looked around at the room full of red-eyed adults. *Look at me*, he wanted to say to them. *I'm not crying.* A part of him stepped back and examined this thought. He was the only person his age he knew whose best friend had died. It made him important. The kids at school Monday would probably whisper around him and treat him with respect—the way they'd all treated Billy Joe Weems last year after his father had been killed in a car crash. He wouldn't have to talk to anybody if he didn't want to, and all the teachers would be especially nice to him. Momma would even make the girls be nice to him.

He had a sudden desire to see Leslie laid out. He wondered if she were back in the library or in Millsburg at one of the funeral parlors. Would they bury her in blue jeans? Or maybe that blue jumper and the flowery blouse she'd worn Easter. That would be nice. People might snicker at the blue jeans, and he didn't want anyone to snicker at Leslie when she was dead.

Bill came into the room. P. T. slid off Jess's lap and went to him. The man leaned down and rubbed the dog's back. Jess stood up.

"Jess." Bill came over to him and put his arms around him as though he had been Leslie instead of himself. Bill held him close, so that a button on his sweater was pressing painfully into Jess's forehead, but as uncomfortable as he was, Jess didn't move. He could feel Bill's body shaking, and he was afraid that if he looked up he would see Bill crying, too. He didn't want to see Bill crying. He wanted to get out of this house. It was smothering him. Why wasn't Leslie here to help him out of this? Why didn't she come running in and make everyone laugh again? *You think it's so great to die and make everyone cry and carry on. Well, it ain't.*

"She loved you, you know." He could tell from Bill's voice that he was crying. "She told me once that if it weren't for you . . ." His voice broke completely. "Thank you," he said a moment later. "Thank you for being such a wonderful friend to her."

Bill didn't sound like himself. He sounded like someone in an old mushy movie. The kind of person Leslie and Jess would laugh at and imitate later. *Boo-hooooooo, you were such a wonderful friend to her.* He couldn't help moving back, just enough to get his forehead off the stupid button. To his relief, Bill let go. He heard his father ask Bill quietly over his head about "the service."

And Bill answering quietly almost in his regular voice that they had decided to have the body cremated and were going to take the ashes to his family home in Pennsylvania tomorrow.

Cremated. Something clicked inside Jess's head. That meant Leslie was gone. Turned to ashes. He would never see her again. Not even dead. Never. How could they dare? Leslie belonged to him. More to him than anyone in the world. No one had even asked him. No one had even told him. And now he was never going to see her again, and all they could do was cry. Not for Leslie. They weren't crying for Leslie. They were crying for themselves. Just themselves. If they'd cared at all for Leslie, they would have never brought her to this rotten place. He had to hold tightly to his hands for fear he might sock Bill in the face.

He, Jess, was the only one who really cared for Leslie. But Leslie had failed him. She went and died just when he needed her the most. She went and left him. She went swinging on that rope just to show him that she was no coward. *So there, Jess Aarons.* She was probably somewhere right now laughing at him. Making fun of him like he was Mrs. Myers. She had tricked him. She had made him leave his old self behind and come into her world, and then before he was really at home in it but too late to go back, she had left him stranded there—like an astronaut wandering about on the moon. Alone.

He was never sure later just when he left the old Perkins place, but he remembered running up the hill toward his own house with angry tears streaming down his face. He banged through the door. May Belle was standing there, her brown eyes wide. "Did you see her?" she asked excitedly. "Did you see her laid out?"

He hit her. In the face. As hard as he had ever hit anything in his life. She stumbled backward from him with a little yelp. He went into the bedroom and felt under the mattress until he retrieved all his paper and the paints that Leslie had given him at Christmastime.

Ellie was standing in the bedroom door fussing at him. He pushed past her. From the couch Brenda, too, was complaining, but the only sound that really entered his head was that of May Belle whimpering.

He ran out the kitchen door and down the field all the way to the stream without looking back. The stream was a little lower than it had been when he had seen it last. Above from the crab apple tree the frayed end of the rope swung gently. *I am now the fastest runner in the fifth grade.*

He screamed something without words and flung the papers and paints into the dirty brown water. The paints floated on top, riding the current like a boat, but the papers swirled about, soaking in the muddy water, being sucked down, around, and down. He watched them all disappear. Gradually his breath quieted, and his heart slowed from its wild pace. The ground was still muddy from the rains, but he sat down anyway. There was nowhere to go. Nowhere. Ever again. He put his head down on his knee.

"That was a damn fool thing to do." His father sat down on the dirt beside him.

"I don't care. I don't care." He was crying now, crying so hard he could barely breathe.

His father pulled Jess over on his lap as though he were

Joyce Ann. "There. There," he said, patting his head. "*Shhh. Shhh.*"

"I hate her," Jess said through his sobs. "I hate her. I wish I'd never seen her in my whole life."

His father stroked his hair without speaking. Jess grew quiet. They both watched the water.

Finally his father said, "Hell, ain't it?" It was the kind of thing Jess could hear his father saying to another man. He found it strangely comforting, and it made him bold.

"Do you believe people go to hell, really go to hell, I mean?"

"You ain't worrying about Leslie Burke?"

It did seem peculiar, but still— "Well, May Belle said . . . ."

"May Belle? May Belle ain't God."

"Yeah, but how do you know what God does?"

"Lord, boy, don't be a fool. God ain't gonna send any little girls to hell."

He had never in his life thought of Leslie Burke as a little girl, but still God was sure to. She wouldn't have been eleven until November. They got up and began to walk up the hill. "I didn't mean that about hating her," he said. "I don't know what made me say that." His father nodded to show he understood.

Everyone, even Brenda, was gentle to him. Everyone except May Belle, who hung back as though afraid to have anything to do with him. He wanted to tell her he was sorry, but he couldn't. He was too tired. He couldn't just say the words. He had to make it up to her, and he was too tired to figure out how.

That afternoon Bill came up to the house. They were about to leave for Pennsylvania, and he wondered if Jess would take care of the dog until they got back.

"Sure." He was glad Bill wanted him to help. He was afraid he had hurt Bill by running away this morning. He wanted, too, to know that Bill didn't blame him for anything. But it was not the kind of question he could put into words.

He held P. T. and waved as the dusty little Italian car turned into the main road. He thought he saw them wave back, but it was too far away to be sure.

His mother had never allowed him to have a dog, but she made no objection to P. T. being in the house. P. T. jumped up on his bed, and he slept all night with P.T.'s body curled against his chest.

THIRTEEN

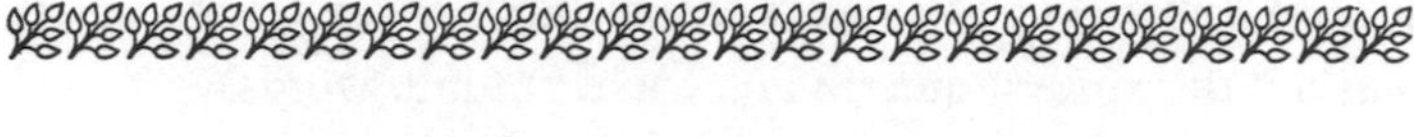

Building the Bridge

He woke up Saturday morning with a dull headache. It was still early, but he got up. He wanted to do the milking. His father had done it ever since Thursday night, but he wanted to go back to it, to somehow make things normal again. He shut P. T. in the shed, and the dog's whimpering reminded him of May Belle and made his headache worse. But he couldn't have P. T. yappping at Miss Bessie while he tried to milk.

No one was awake when he brought the milk in to put it away, so he poured a warm glass for himself and got a couple of pieces of light bread. He wanted his paints back, and he decided to go down and see if he could find them. He let P. T. out of the shed and gave the dog a half piece of bread.

It was a beautiful spring morning. Early wild flowers were dotting the deep green of the fields, and the sky was clean and blue. The creek had fallen well below the bank and seemed less terrifying than before. A large branch was washed up into the bank, and he hauled it up to the narrowest place and laid it bank to bank. He stepped on it, and it seemed firm, so he crossed on it, foot over foot, to the other side, grabbing the smaller branches which grew out from the main one toward the opposite bank to keep his balance. There was no sign of his paints.

He landed slightly upstream from Terabithia. If it was still Terabithia. If it could be entered across a branch instead of swung into. P. T. was left crying piteously on the other side. Then the dog took courage and paddled across the stream. The current carried him past Jess, but he made it safely to the bank and ran back, shaking great drops of cold water on Jess.

They went into the castle stronghold. It was dark and damp, but there was no evidence there to suggest that the queen had died. He felt the need to do something fitting. But Leslie was not here to tell him what it was. The anger which had possessed him yesterday flared up again. *Leslie. I'm just a dumb dodo, and you know it! What am I supposed to do?* The coldness inside of him had moved upward into his throat constricting it. He swallowed several times. It occurred to him that he probably had cancer of the throat. Wasn't that one of the seven deadly signs? *Difficulty in swallowing*. He began to sweat. He didn't want to die. Lord, he was just ten years old. He had hardly begun to live.

Leslie, were you scared? Did you know you were dying? Were you scared like me? A picture of Leslie being sucked into the cold water flashed across his brain.

"C'mon, Prince Terrien," he said quite loudly. "We must make a funeral wreath for the queen."

He sat in the clear space between the bank and the first line of trees and bent a pine bough into a circle, tying it with a piece of wet string from the castle. And because it looked cold and green, he picked spring beauties from the forest floor and wove them among the needles.

He put it down in front of him. A cardinal flew down to the bank, cocked its brilliant head, and seemed to stare at the wreath. P. T. let out a growl which sounded more like a purr. Jess put his hand on the dog to quiet him.

The bird hopped about a moment more, then flew leisurely away.

"It's a sign from the Spirits," Jess said quietly. "We made a worthy offering."

He walked slowly, as part of a great procession, though only the puppy could be seen, slowly forward carrying the queen's wreath to the sacred grove. He forced himself deep into the dark center of the grove and, kneeling, laid the wreath upon the thick carpet of golden needles.

"Father, into Thy hands I commend her spirit." He knew Leslie would have liked those words. They had the ring of the sacred grove in them.

The solemn procession wound its way through the sacred grove homeward to the castle. Like a single bird across a storm-cloud sky, a tiny peace winged its way through the chaos inside his body.

"Help! Jesse! Help me!" A scream shattered the quietness. Jess raced to the sound of May Belle's cry. She had gotten half-way across on the tree bridge and now stood there grabbing the upper branches, terrified to move either forward or back-ward.

"OK, May Belle." The words came out more steadily than he felt. "Just hold still. I'll get you." He was not sure the branch would hold the weight of them both. He looked down at the water. It was low enough for him to walk across, but still swift. Suppose it swept him off his feet. He decided for the branch. He inched out on it until he was close enough to touch her. He'd have to get her back to the home side of the creek. "OK," he said. "Now, back up."

"I can't!"

"I'm right here, May Belle. You think I'm gonna let you fall? Here." He put out his right hand. "Hold on to me and slide sideways on the thing."

She let go with her left hand for a moment and then grabbed the branch again.

"I'm scared, Jesse. I'm too scared."

" 'Course you're scared. Anybody'd be scared. You just gotta trust me, OK? I'm not gonna let you fall, May Belle. I promise you."

She nodded, her eyes still wide with fear, but she let go the branch and took his hand, straightening a little and swaying. He gripped her tightly.

"OK, now. It ain't far—just slide your right foot a little way, then bring your left foot up close."

"I forgot which is right."

"The front one," he said patiently. "The one closest to home."

She nodded again and obediently moved her right foot a few inches.

"Now just let go of the branch with your other hand and hold on to me tight."

She let go the branch and squeezed his hand.

"Good. You're doing great. Now slide a little ways more." She swayed but did not scream, just dug her little fingernails into the palm of his hand. "Great. Fine. You're all right." The same quiet, assuring voice of the paramedics on *Emergency*, but his heart was bongoing against his chest. "OK. OK. A little bit more, now."

When her right foot came at last to the part of the branch which rested on the bank, she fell forward, pulling him down.

"Watch it, May Belle!" He was off balance, but he fell, not into the stream, but with his chest across May Belle's legs, his

own legs waving in the empty air above the water. "Whew!" He was laughing with relief. "Whatcha trying to do, girl, kill me?"

She shook her head a solemn no, "I know I swore on the Bible not to follow you, but I woke up this morning and you was gone."

"I had to do some things."

She was scraping at the mud on her bare legs. "I just wanted to find you, so you wouldn't be so lonesome." She hung her head. "But I got too scared."

He pulled himself around until he was sitting beside her. They watched P. T. swimming across, the current carrying him too swiftly, but he not seeming to mind. He climbed out well below the crab apple and came running back to where they sat.

"Everybody gets scared sometimes, May Belle. You don't have to be ashamed." He saw a flash of Leslie's eyes as she was going in to the girls' room to see Janice Avery. "Everybody gets scared."

"P. T. ain't scared, and he even saw Leslie . . ."

"It ain't the same for dogs. It's like the smarter you are, the more things can scare you."

She looked at him in disbelief. "But you weren't scared."

"Lord, May Belle, I was shaking like Jello."

"You're just saying that."

He laughed. He couldn't help being glad she didn't believe him. He jumped up and pulled her to her feet. "Let's go eat." He let her beat him to the house.

When he walked into the basement classroom, he saw Mrs. Myers had already had Leslie's desk taken out of the front of the room. Of course, by Monday Jess knew; but still, but still, at the bus stop he looked up, half expecting to see her running up across the field, her lovely, even, rhythmic run. Maybe she was already at school—Bill had dropped her off, as he did some days when she was late for the bus—but then when Jess came into the room, her desk was no longer there. Why were they all in such a rush to be rid of her? He put his head down on his own desk, his whole body heavy and cold.

He could hear the sounds of the whispers but not the words. Not that he wanted to hear the words. He was suddenly ashamed that he'd thought he might be regarded with respect by the other kids. Trying to profit for himself from Leslie's death. *I wanted to be the best—the fastest runner in the school —and now I am*. Lord, he made himself sick. He didn't care what the others said or what they thought, just as long as they left him alone—just so long as he didn't have to talk to them or meet their stares. They had all hated Leslie. Except maybe Janice. Even after they'd given up trying to make Leslie miserable, they'd kept on despising her—as though there was one of them worth the nail on Leslie's little toe. And even he himself had entertained the traitorous thought that now he would be the fastest.

Mrs. Myers barked the command to stand for the allegiance. He didn't move. Whether he couldn't or wouldn't, he didn't really care. What could she do to him, after all?

"Jesse Aarons. Will you step out into the hall. Please."

He raised his leaden body and stumbled out of the room. He thought he heard Gary Fulcher giggle, but he couldn't be sure. He leaned against the wall and waited for Monster Mouth Myers to finish singing "O Say Can You See?" and join him. He could hear her giving the class some sort of assignment in arithmetic before she came out and quietly closed the door behind her.

OK. Shoot. I don't care.

She came over so close to him that he could smell her dime-store powder.

"Jesse." Her voice was softer than he had ever heard it, but he didn't answer. Let her yell. He was used to that.

"Jesse," she repeated. "I just want to give you my sincere sympathy." The words were like a Hallmark card, but the tone was new to him.

He looked up into her face, despite himself. Behind her turned-up glasses, Mrs. Myers' narrow eyes were full of tears. For a minute he thought he might cry himself. He and Mrs. Myers standing in the basement hallway, crying over Leslie Burke. It was so weird he almost laughed instead.

"When my husband died"—Jess could hardly imagine Mrs. Myers ever having had a husband—"people kept telling me not to cry, kept trying to make me forget." Mrs. Myers loving, mourning. How could you picture it? "But I didn't want to forget." She took her handkerchief from her sleeve and blew her nose. "Excuse me," she said. "This morning when I came in, someone had already taken out her desk." She stopped and blew her nose again. "It—it—we—I never had such a student. In all my years of teaching. I shall always be grateful—"

He wanted to comfort her. He wanted to unsay all the things he had said about her—even unsay the things Leslie had said. Lord, don't let her ever find out.

"So—I realize. If it's hard for me, how much harder it must be for you. Let's try to help each other, shall we?"

"Yes'm." He couldn't think of anything else to say. Maybe some day when he was grown, he would write her a letter and tell her that Leslie Burke had thought she was a great teacher or something. Leslie wouldn't mind. Sometimes like the Barbie doll you need to give people something that's for them, not just something that makes you feel good giving it. Because

Mrs. Myers had helped him already by understanding that he would never forget Leslie.

He thought about it all day, how before Leslie came, he had been a nothing—a stupid, weird little kid who drew funny pictures and chased around a cow field trying to act big—trying to hide a whole mob of foolish little fears running riot inside his gut.

It was Leslie who had taken him from the cow pasture into Terabithia and turned him into a king. He had thought that was it. Wasn't king the best you could be? Now it occurred to him that perhaps Terabithia was like a castle where you came to be knighted. After you stayed for a while and grew strong you had to move on. For hadn't Leslie, even in Terabithia, tried to push back the walls of his mind and make him see beyond to the shining world—huge and terrible and beautiful and very fragile? (Handle with care—everything—even the predators.)

Now it was time for him to move out. She wasn't there, so he must go for both of them. It was up to him to pay back to the world in beauty and caring what Leslie had loaned him in vision and strength.

As for the terrors ahead—for he did not fool himself that they were all behind him—well, you just have to stand up to your fear and not let it squeeze you white. Right, Leslie?

Right.

Bill and Judy came back from Pennsylvania on Wednesday with a U-Haul truck. No one ever stayed long in the old Perkins place. "We came to the country for her sake. Now that she's gone . . ." They gave Jesse all of Leslie's books and her paint set with three pads of real watercolor paper. "She would want you to have them," Bill said.

Jess and his dad helped them load the U-Haul, and noontime his mother brought down ham sandwiches and coffee, a little scared the Burkes wouldn't want to eat her food, but needing, Jess knew, to do something. At last the truck was filled, and the Aaronses and the Burkes stood around awkwardly, no one knowing how to say good-bye.

"Well," Bill said. "If there's anything we've left that you want, please help yourself."

"Could I have some of the lumber on the back porch?" Jess asked.

"Yes, of course. Anything you see." Bill hesitated, then continued. "I meant to give you P. T.," he said. "But"—he looked at Jess and his eyes were those of a pleading little boy —"but I can't seem to give him up."

"It's OK. Leslie would want you to keep him."

The next day after school, Jess went down and got the lumber he needed, carrying it a couple of boards at a time to the creek bank. He put the two longest pieces across at the narrow place upstream from the crab apple tree, and when he was sure they were as firm and even as he could make them, he began to nail on the crosspieces.

"Whatcha doing, Jess?" May Belle had followed him down again as he had guessed she might.

"It's a secret, May Belle."

"Tell me."

"When I finish, OK?"

"I swear on the Bible I won't tell nobody. Not Billy Jean, not Joyce Ann, not Momma—" She was jerking her head back and forth in solemn emphasis.

"Oh, I don't know about Joyce Ann. You might want to tell Joyce Ann sometime."

"Tell Joyce Ann something that's a secret between you and me?" The idea seemed to horrify her.

"Yeah, I was just thinking about it."

Her face sagged. "Joyce Ann ain't nothing but a baby."

"Well, she wouldn't likely be a queen first off. You'd have to train her and stuff."

"Queen? Who gets to be queen?"

"I'll explain it when I finish, OK?"

And when he finished, he put flowers in her hair and led her across the bridge—the great bridge into Terabithia—which might look to someone with no magic in him like a few planks across a nearly dry gully.

"*Shhh,*" he said. "Look."

"Where?"

"Can't you see 'um?" he whispered. "All the Terabithians standing on tiptoe to see you."

"*Me*?"

"*Shhh*, yes. There's a rumor going around that the beautiful girl arriving today might be the queen they've been waiting for."

The Great
GILLY HOPKINS

by the author

The Sign of the Chrysanthemum

Of Nightingales That Weep

The Master Puppeteer

Bridge to Terabithia

The Great Gilly Hopkins

Angels and Other Strangers

Jacob Have I Loved

The Great
GILLY HOPKINS

Katherine Paterson

HARPERCOLLINS*PUBLISHERS*

 Printed in the United States of America. For information address HarperCollins Children's Books, a division of HarperCollins Publishers, 10 East 53rd Street, New York, NY 10022.

Library of Congress Cataloging-in-Publication Data
Paterson, Katherine.
The great Gilly Hopkins.

Summary: An eleven-year-old foster child tries to cope with her longings and fears as she schemes against everyone who tries to be friendly.
[1. Foster care homes—Fiction] I. Title.
PZ7.P273Gr [Fic] 77-27075
ISBN 0-690-03837-2
ISBN 0-690-03838-0 (lib. bdg.)

"A Harper Trophy book"
ISBN 0-06-440201-0 (pbk.)

Published in hardcover by HarperCollins Publishers.
First Harper Trophy edition, 1987

For Mary
from her real
and adopted mother
with love

Contents

The Great GILLY HOPKINS

Welcome to Thompson Park

"GILLY," said Miss Ellis with a shake of her long blonde hair toward the passenger in the back seat. "I need to feel that you are willing to make some effort."

Galadriel Hopkins shifted her bubble gum to the front of her mouth and began to blow gently. She blew until she could barely see the shape of the social worker's head through the pink bubble.

"This will be your third home in less than three years." Miss Ellis swept her golden head left to right and then began to turn the wheel in a cautious maneuver to the left. "I would be the last person to say that it was all your fault. The Dixons' move to Florida, for example. Just one of those unfortunate things. And Mrs. Richmond having to go into the hospital"—it seemed to Gilly that there was a long, thoughtful pause before the caseworker went on—"for her nerves."

Pop!

Miss Ellis flinched and glanced in the rear-view mirror but continued to talk in her calm, professional voice while Gilly picked at the bits of gum stuck in her straggly bangs and on her cheeks and chin. "We should have been more alert to her condition before placing any foster child there. *I* should have been more alert." Cripes, thought Gilly. The woman was getting sincere. What a pain. "I'm not trying to *blame* you, Gilly. It's just that I need, we all need, your cooperation if any kind of arrangement is to work out." Another pause. "I can't imagine you *enjoy* all this moving around." The blue eyes in the mirror were checking out Gilly's response. "Now this new foster mother is very different from Mrs. Nevins." Gilly calmly pinched a blob of gum off the end of her nose. There was no use trying to get the gum out of her hair. She sat back and tried to chew the bit she had managed to salvage. It stuck to her teeth in a thin layer. She fished another ball of gum from her jeans pocket and scraped the lint off with her thumbnail before elaborately popping it into her mouth.

"Will you do me a favor, Gilly? Try to get off on the right foot?"

Gilly had a vision of herself sailing around the living room of the foster home on her right foot like an ice skater. With her uplifted left foot she was shoving the next foster mother square in the mouth. She smacked her new supply of gum in satisfaction.

"Do me another favor, will you? Get rid of that bubble gum before we get there?"

Gilly obligingly took the gum out of her mouth while Miss Ellis's eyes were still in the mirror. Then when the social worker turned her attention back to the traffic, Gilly carefully spread the gum under the handle of the left-hand door as a sticky surprise for the next person who might try to open it.

Two traffic lights farther on Miss Ellis handed back a towelette. "Here," she said, "see what you can do about that guck on your face before we get there."

Gilly swiped the little wet paper across her mouth and dropped it on the floor.

"Gilly—" Miss Ellis sighed and shifted her fancy on-the-floor gears. "Gilly—"

"My name," Gilly said between her teeth, "is Galadriel."

Miss Ellis appeared not to have heard. "Gilly, give Maime Trotter half a chance, OK? She's really a nice person."

That cans it, thought Gilly. At least nobody had accused Mr. or Mrs. Nevins, her most recent foster parents, of being "nice." Mrs. Richmond, the one with the bad nerves, had been "nice." The Newman family, who couldn't keep a five-year-old who wet her bed, had been "nice." Well, I'm eleven now, folks, and, in case you haven't heard, I don't wet my bed anymore. But I am not nice. I am brilliant. I am famous across this entire county. Nobody wants to tangle with the great Galadriel Hopkins. I am too clever and too hard to manage. Gruesome Gilly, they call me. She leaned back comfortably. Here I come, Maime baby, ready or not.

They had reached a neighborhood of huge trees and old houses. The social worker slowed and stopped beside a dirty white fence. The house it penned was old and brown with a porch that gave it a sort of potbelly.

Standing on the porch, before she rang the bell, Miss Ellis took out a comb. "Would you try to pull this through your hair?"

Gilly shook her head. "Can't."

"Oh, come on, Gilly—"

"No. Can't comb my hair. I'm going for the Guiness Record for uncombed hair."

"Gilly, for pete's sake . . ."

"Hey, there, I thought I heard y'all pull up." The door had opened, and a huge hippopotamus of a woman was filling the doorway. "Welcome to Thompson Park, Gilly, honey."

"Galadriel," muttered Gilly, not that she expected this bale of blubber to manage her real name. Jeez, they didn't have to put her in with a freak.

Half a small face, topped with muddy brown hair and masked with thick metal-rimmed glasses, jutted out from behind Mrs. Trotter's mammoth hip.

The woman looked down. "Well, 'scuse me, honey." She put her arm around the head as if to draw it forward, but the head resisted movement. "You want to meet your new sister, don't you? Gilly, this is William Ernest Teague."

The head immediately disappeared behind Mrs. Trotter's bulk. She didn't seem bothered. "Come in, come in. I don't mean to leave you standing on the porch like you was trying to sell me something. You belong here now." She backed up. Gilly could feel Miss Ellis's fingers on her backbone gently prodding her through the doorway and into the house.

Inside, it was dark and crammed with junk. Everything seemed to need dusting.

"William Ernest, honey, you want to show Gilly where her room is?"

William Ernest clung to the back of Mrs. Trotter's flowered housedress, shaking his head.

"Oh, well, we can see to that later." She led them down the hallway to a living room. "Just sit down and make yourself at home, now." She smiled all across her face at Gilly, like the "After" in a magazine diet ad—a "Before" body with an "After" smile.

The couch was brown and squat with a pile of cushions covered in graying lace at the far end. A matching brown chair with worn arms slumped at the opposite side of the room. Gray lace curtains hung at the single window between them, and beside the window was a black table supporting an old-time TV set with rabbit ears. The Nevinses had had color TV. On the right-hand wall between the door and the brown chair stood a black upright piano with a dusty brown bench. Gilly took one of the pillows off the couch and used it to wipe every trace of dust off the piano bench before sitting down on it.

From the brown chair Miss Ellis was staring at her with a very nonprofessional glare. Mrs. Trotter was lowering herself to the sofa and chuckling. "Well, we been needing somebody to rearrange the dust around here. Ain't we, William Ernest, honey?"

William Ernest climbed up behind the huge woman and lay behind her back like a bolster pillow, poking his head around from time to time to sneak another look at Gilly.

She waited until Mrs. Trotter and Miss Ellis were talking, then gave little W.E. the most fearful face in all her repertory of scary looks, sort of a cross between Count Dracula and Godzilla. The little muddy head disappeared faster than a toothpaste cap down a sink drain.

She giggled despite herself. Both of the women turned to look at her. She switched easily and immediately to her "Who, me?" look.

Miss Ellis stood up. "I need to be getting back to the office, Mrs. Trotter. You'll let me know"—She turned to Gilly with prickles in her big blue eyes—"you'll let me know if there're any problems?"

Gilly favored Miss Ellis with her best barracuda smile.

Meantime Mrs. Trotter was laboriously hefting herself to her feet. "Don't worry, Miz Ellis. Gilly and William Ernest and me is nearly friends already. My Melvin, God rest him, used to say that Trotter never met a stranger. And if he'd said kid, he woulda been right. I never met a kid I couldn't make friends with."

Gilly hadn't learned yet how to vomit at will, but if she had, she would have dearly loved to throw up on that one. So, lacking the truly perfect response, she lifted her legs and spun around to the piano, where she proceeded to bang out "Heart and Soul" with her left hand and "Chopsticks" with her right.

William Ernest scrambled off the couch after the two women, and Gilly was left alone with the dust, the out-of-tune piano, and the satisfaction that she had indeed started off on the right foot in her new foster home. She could stand anything, she thought—a gross guardian, a freaky kid, an ugly, dirty house—as long as she was in charge.

She was well on the way.

The Man Who Comes to Supper

THE room that Mrs. Trotter took Gilly to was about the size of the Nevinses' new station wagon. The narrow bed filled up most of the space, and even someone as skinny as Gilly had to kneel on the bed in order to pull out the drawers of the bureau opposite it. Mrs. Trotter didn't even try to come in, just stood in the doorway slightly swaying and smiling, her breath short from climbing the stairs.

"Why don't you just put your things away in the bureau and get yourself settled? Then when you feel like it, you can come on down and watch TV with William Ernest, or come talk to me while I'm fixing supper."

What an awful smile she had, Gilly thought. She didn't even have all her teeth. Gilly dropped her suitcase on the bed and sat down beside it, kicking the bureau drawers with her toes.

"You need anything, honey, just let Trotter know, OK?"

Gilly jerked her head in a nod. What she needed was to be left alone. From the bowels of the house she could hear the theme song from *Sesame Street.* Her first job would be to improve W.E.'s taste in TV. That was for sure.

"It's goin' to be OK, honey. I know it's been hard to switch around so much."

"I like moving." Gilly jerked one of the top drawers so hard it nearly came out onto her head. "It's boring to stay in one place."

"Yeah." The big woman started to turn and then hesitated. "Well—"

Gilly slid off the bed and put her left hand on the doorknob and stuck her right hand on her hip.

Mrs. Trotter glanced down at the hand on the knob. "Well, make yourself at home. You hear now?"

Gilly slammed the door after her. God! Listening to that woman was like licking melted ice cream off the carton. She tested the dust on the top of the bureau, and then, standing on the bed, wrote in huge cursive curlicues, "Ms. Galadriel Hopkins." She stared at the lovely letters she had made for a moment before slapping down her open palm in the middle of them and rubbing them all away.

The Nevinses' house had been square and white and dustless, just like every other square, white, dustless house in the treeless development where they had lived. She had been the only thing in the neighborhood out of place. Well, Hollywood Gardens was spotless once more. They'd got rid of her. No. She'd got rid of them—the whole stinking lot.

Unpacking even just the few things in her brown suitcase, always seemed a waste of time to Gilly. She never knew if she'd be in a place long enough to make it worth the bother. And yet it was something to fill the time. There were two little drawers at the top and four larger ones below. She put her underwear in one of the little ones, and her shirts and jeans in one of the big ones, and then picked up the photograph from the bottom of the suitcase.

Out of the pasteboard frame and through the plastic cover the brown eyes of the woman laughed up at her as they always did. The glossy black hair hung in gentle waves without a hair astray. She looked as though she was the star of some TV show, but she wasn't. See—right there in the corner she had written "For my beautiful Galadriel, I will always love you." She wrote that to me, Gilly told herself, as she did each time she looked at it, only to me. She turned the frame over. It was still there—the little piece of tape with the name on it. "Courtney Rutherford Hopkins."

Gilly smoothed her own straw-colored hair with one hand as she turned the picture over again. Even the teeth were gorgeous. Weren't girls supposed to look like their mothers? The word "mother" triggered something deep in her stomach. She knew the danger signal. Abruptly she shoved the picture under a T-shirt and banged the bureau drawer shut. This was not the time to start dissolving like hot Jell-O. She went downstairs.

"There you are, honey." Trotter turned away from the sink to greet her. "How about giving me a hand here with this salad?"

"No."

"Oh."

Score a point for Gilly.

"Well"—Trotter shifted her weight to her left foot, keeping her eyes on the carrots she was scraping—"William Ernest is in the living room watching *Sesame Street.*"

"My god, you must think I'm mental or something."

"Mental?" Trotter moved to the kitchen table and started chopping the carrots on a tiny round board.

"Dumb, stupid."

"Never crossed my mind."

"Then why the hell you think I'm going to watch some retard show like that?"

"Listen here, Gilly Hopkins. One thing we better get straight right now tonight. I won't have you making fun of that boy."

"I wasn't making fun of that boy." What was the woman talking about? She hadn't mentioned the boy.

"Just 'cause someone isn't quite as smart as you are, don't give you no right to look down on them."

"Who'm I looking down on?"

"You just said"—the fat woman's voice was rising, and her knife was crashing down on the carrots with vengeance—"you just said William Ernest was"—her voice dropped to a whisper—"retarded."

"I did not. I don't even know the stupid kid. I never saw him in my life before today."

Trotter's eyes were still flashing, but her hand and voice were under control. "He's had a rough time of it in this world, but he's with Trotter now, and as long as the Lord leaves him in this house, ain't anybody on earth gonna hurt him. *In any way.*"

"Good god. All I was trying to say—"

"One more thing. In this house we don't take the Lord's name in vain."

Gilly threw both her hands up in mock surrender. "All right, all right. Forget it." She started for the door.

"Supper's 'bout ready. How about going next door and getting Mr. Randolph? He eats here nights."

The word No was just about to pop out of Gilly's mouth, but one look at Trotter's eyes, and she decided to save her fights for something more important. "Which house?"

"The gray one on the right." She waved her knife vaguely uphill. "Just knock on the door. If you do it good and loud, he'll hear you. Better take your jacket. Cold out."

Gilly ignored the last. She ran out the door, through the picket gate, and onto the porch next door, stomping and jumping to keep warm. *Bam, bam, bam.* It was too cold for October. Mr. Randolph's house was smaller and more grubby-looking even than Trotter's. She repeated her knock.

Suddenly the door swung inward, revealing a tiny shrunken man. Strange whitish eyes stared out of a wrinkled, brown face.

Gilly took one look and ran back to Trotter's kitchen as fast as she could go.

"What's the matter? Where's Mr. Randolph?"

"I don't know. He's gone. He's not there."

"What d'you mean he's not there?" Trotter began wiping her hands on her apron and walking toward the door.

"He's gone. Some weird little colored man with white eyes came to the door."

"Gilly! That was Mr. Randolph. He can't see a thing. You've got to go back and bring him by the hand, so he won't fall."

Gilly backed away. "I never touched one of those people in my life."

"Well, then, it's about time, ain't it?" Trotter snapped. "Of course, if you can't manage, I can always send William Ernest."

"I can manage. Don't you worry about me."

"You probably got Mr. Randolph all confused and upset by now."

"Well, you shoulda warned me."

"Warned *you?*" Trotter banged a spoon on the table. "I shoulda warned poor Mr. Randolph. You want me to send William Ernest?"

"I said I could manage. Good god!" At this, Trotter's spoon went up in the air like a fly-swatter. "All right! I didn't say it. Hell, a person can't even talk around here."

"A smart person like you oughta be able to think of a few regular words to stick in amongst the cusses." The spoon went into the salad and stirred. "Well, hurry up, if you're going."

The little black man was still standing in the open doorway. "William Ernest?" he called gently as Gilly started up the steps.

"No," she said sharply. "Me."

"Oh." He smiled widely although his eyes did not seem to move. "You must be the new little girl." He stretched out his right hand. "Welcome to you, welcome."

Gilly carefully took the elbow instead of the hand. "Trotter said for me to get you for supper."

"Well, thank you, thank you." He reached behind, fumbling until he found the knob, and pulled the door shut. "Kind of chilly tonight, isn't it?"

"Yeah."

All she could think of was Miss Ellis. OK, so she hadn't been so great at the Nevinses', but she hadn't done anything to deserve this. A house run by a fat, fluff-brained religious fanatic with a mentally retarded seven-year-old—well, maybe he was and maybe he wasn't actually retarded, but chances were good the kid was running around with less than his full share of brains or why would Trotter make such a big deal of it? But she could've handled the two of them. It wasn't fair to throw in a blind black man who came to eat.

Or maybe Miss Ellis didn't know. Maybe Trotter kept this a secret.

The sidewalk was uneven. Mr. Randolph's toe hit a high corner, and he lurched forward.

"Watch it!" Without thinking, Gilly threw her arms around the thin shoulders and caught him before he fell.

"Thank you, thank you." Gilly dropped her arms. She thought for a horrible moment that he was going to try to grab her hand, but he didn't.

Boy, Miss Ellis, are you ever going to be sorry you did this to me.

"Now Mrs. Trotter did tell me your name, but I'm ashamed to say I don't seem to recall it." He tapped his head with its short, curly gray hair. "I can keep all the luxuries up here, but none of the necessities."

"Gilly," she muttered.

"I beg your pardon?"

"Gilly Hopkins."

"Oh, yes." He was shuffling painfully up Trotter's front steps. Jeez. Why didn't he get a white cane or something? "I am most pleased to make your acquaintance, Miss

Gilly. I feel mighty close to all Mrs. Trotter's children. Little William Ernest is like a grandson to me. So I feel sure . . ."

"Watch the door!"

"Yes, yes, I thank you."

"Is that you Mr. Randolph?" came Trotter's voice from inside.

"Yes, indeed, Mrs. Trotter, with the sweetest little escort you'd ever hope to see."

Trotter appeared in the hallway with her hands on her hips. "How you doing in this cold weather?"

"Not my best, I'm afraid. This sweet little girl had to keep me from falling right down on my face."

"Did she now?"

See there, Trotter? I managed.

"I guess this old house is going to be a bit more lively now, eh, Mrs. Trotter?"

"Wouldn't be surprised," answered Trotter in a flat voice that Gilly couldn't read the meaning of.

The meal proceeded without incident. Gilly was hungry but thought it better not to seem to enjoy her supper too much. William Ernest ate silently and steadily with only an occasional glance at Gilly. She could tell that the child was scared silly of her. It was about the only thing in the last two hours that had given her any real satisfaction. Power over the boy was sure to be power over Trotter in the long run.

"I declare, Mrs. Trotter," said Mr. Randolph, "every day I think to myself, tonight's supper couldn't be as delicious as last night's. But I tell you, this is the most delicious meal I have ever had the privilege of eating."

"Mr. Randolph, you could flatter the stripe off a polecat."

Mr. Randolph let out a giggling laugh. "It isn't flattery, I assure you, Mrs. Trotter. William Ernest and Miss Gilly will bear me out in this. I may be old, but I haven't lost my sense of taste, even if some folks maintain I've lost the other four."

They went on and on like that. Mr. Randolph flattering the fat woman, and the fat woman eating it up like hot-fudge sundae with all the nuts.

What I should do, thought Gilly, as she lay that night in the narrow bed with her arms folded under her head, What I should do is write my mother. Courtney Rutherford Hopkins would probably sue county welfare if she knew what kind of place they'd forced her daughter to come to.

Miss Ellis (whose eyebrows always twitched when Gilly asked questions about Courtney) had once told her that Courtney was from Virginia. Everybody knew, didn't they, that families like Courtney's did not eat with colored people? Courtney Rutherford Hopkins was sure to go into a rage, wasn't she, when she heard that news? Perhaps the self-righteous Trotter would be put into jail for contributing to the delinquency of a minor. Miss Ellis would, of course, be fired. *Yum!*

She'll come to get me then, for sure, thought Gilly. Her mother wouldn't stand for her beautiful Galadriel to be in a dump like this for one single minute, once she knew. But how was she to know? Miss Ellis would never admit it. What kind of lies was the social worker telling Courtney to keep her from coming to fetch Gilly?

As she dropped off to sleep, Gilly promised herself for the millionth time that she would find out where Courtney Rutherford Hopkins was, write to her, and tell her to come and take her beautiful Galadriel home.

More Unpleasant Surprises

IN the tiny mirror over the bureau Gilly noted with no little satisfaction that her hair was a wreck. Yesterday before the bubble gum got into it, it had looked as though it simply needed combing. Today it looked like a lot that had been partially bulldozed—an uprooted tree here, a half wall with a crumbling chimney there. It was magnificent. It would run Trotter wild. Gilly bounced down the stairs and into the kitchen.

She held her head very straight as she sat at the kitchen table and waited for the fireworks.

"I'll take you down to the school a little after nine, hear?" Trotter said.

Of course Gilly heard. She tilted her head a little in case Trotter couldn't *see*.

"If I take you down earlier," Trotter went on, "we'll just

have to sit and wait till they can take care of us. I'd as leave sit here at my own table with a cup of coffee, wouldn't you?" She put a bowl of steaming hot cereal down in front of Gilly.

Gilly nodded her head vigorously Yes.

William Ernest was staring at her, his glasses steamed up from the oatmeal. Gilly bared her teeth and shook her head violently No at him. The boy snuffled loudly and ducked his head.

"Need a tissue, William Ernest?" Trotter pulled one from her apron pocket and gently wiped his nose. "And here's a clean one for school, honey." Trotter leaned over and tucked a tissue into his pants pocket.

Gilly craned her neck over the table as though she were trying to see the contents of W.E.'s pocket. Her head was within a couple of feet of Trotter's eyes. The woman was sure to notice.

"William Ernest got promoted to the Orange reading group yesterday. Didn't you, William Ernest, honey?"

The little boy nodded his head but kept his eyes on his bowl.

"You're gonna have to do some reading out loud and show Gilly how great you're coming along with your reading these days."

W.E. looked up for one split second with terror in his eyes. Trotter missed the look, but not Gilly, who smiled widely and shook her half-bulldozed head emphatically.

"In Orange they use hardback books," Trotter was explaining. "It's a real big step to be Orange." She leaned over Gilly to put some toast on the table. "We really worked for this."

"So old W.E.'s getting a *head,* is he?"

Trotter gave her a puzzled look. "Yeah, he's doing just fine."

"Before you know it," Gilly heard herself saying loudly, "he'll be blowing his own nose and *combing his own hair.*"

"He already does," said Trotter quietly. "Leastways most of the time." She sat down with a loud sigh at the table. "Pass me a piece of toast, will you, Gilly?"

Gilly picked up the plate, raised it to the height of her hair, and passed it across to Trotter at that level.

"Thank you, honey."

At eight thirty Trotter got William Ernest off to school. Gilly had long since finished her breakfast, but she sat at the kitchen table, her head propped on her fists. From the doorway she could hear Old Mother Goose honking over her gosling. "OK, Big Orange, you show 'em down there today, hear?" Trotter said finally; and then the heavy door shut and she was heading back for the kitchen. As she got to the door, Gilly sat up straight and shook her head for all she was worth.

"You got a tic or something, honey?"

"No."

"I would've thought you was too young for the palsy," the huge woman murmured, sliding into her seat with the cup of coffee she'd promised herself earlier. "I see you got sneakers. That's good. You're supposed to have them for gym. Can you think of anything else you'll need for school?"

Gilly shook her head, but halfheartedly. She was beginning to feel like an oversharpened pencil.

"I think I'll go upstairs till it's time," she said.

"Oh, while you're up there, honey—"

"Yeah?" Gilly sprang to attention.

"Make the beds, will you? It does look messy to leave 'em unmade all day, and I'm not much on running up and down the stairs."

Gilly banged the door to her room for all she was worth. She spit every obscenity she'd ever heard through her teeth, but it wasn't enough. That ignorant hippopotamus! That walrus-faced imbecile! That—that—oh, the devil—Trotter wouldn't even let a drop fall from her precious William Ernest baby's nose, but she would let Gilly go to school—a new school where she didn't know anybody—looking like a scarecrow. Miss Ellis would surely hear about this. Gilly slammed her fist into her pillow. There had to be a law against foster mothers who showed such gross favoritism.

Well, she would show that lard can a thing or two. She yanked open the left top drawer, pulling out a broken comb, which she viciously jerked through the wilderness on her head, only to be defeated by a patch of bubble gum. She ran into the bathroom and rummaged through the medicine chest until she found a pair of nail scissors with which to chop out the offending hair. When despite her assault by comb and scissors a few strands refused to lie down meekly, she soaked them mercilessly into submission. She'd show the world. She'd show them who Galadriel Hopkins was—she was not to be trifled with.

"I see they call you Gilly," said Mr. Evans, the principal.

"I can't even pronounce the poor child's real name," said Trotter, chuckling in what she must believe was a friendly manner.

It didn't help Gilly's mood. She was still seething over the hair combing.

"Well, Gilly's a fine name," said Mr. Evans, which confirmed to Gilly that at school, too, she was fated to be surrounded by fools.

The principal was studying records that must have been sent over from Gilly's former school, Hollywood Gardens Elementary. He coughed several times. "Well," he said, "I think this young lady needs to be in a class that will challenge her."

"She's plenty smart, if that's what you mean."

Trotter, you dummy. How do you know how smart I am? You never laid eyes on me until yesterday.

"I'm going to put you into Miss Harris's class. We have some departmentalization in the sixth grade, but . . ."

"You got *what* in the sixth grade?"

Oh, Trotter, shut your fool mouth.

But the principal didn't seem to notice what a dope Trotter was. He explained patiently how some of the sixth-grade classes moved around for math and reading and science, but Miss Harris kept the same group all day.

What a blinking bore.

They went up three flights of ancient stairway to Miss Harris's room slowly, so that Trotter would not collapse. The corridors stank of oiled floors and cafeteria soup. Gilly had thought she hated all schools so much that they no longer could pain or disappoint her, but she felt heavier with each step—like a condemned prisoner walking an endless last mile.

They paused before the door marked "Harris–6." Mr. Evans knocked, and a tall tea-colored woman, crowned with a bush of black hair, opened the door. She smiled down on the three of them, because she was even taller than the principal.

Gilly shrank back, bumping into Trotter's huge breast, which made her jump forward again quickly. God, on top of everything else, the teacher was black.

No one seemed to take notice of her reaction, unless you counted a flash of brightness in Miss Harris's dark eyes.

Trotter patted Gilly's arm, murmured something that ended in "honey," and then she and the principal floated backward, closing Gilly into Harris–6. The teacher led her to an empty desk in the middle of the classroom, asked for Gilly's jacket, which she handed over to another girl to hang on the coatrack at the back of the room. She directed Gilly to sit down, and then went up and settled herself at the large teacher's desk to glance through the handful of papers Mr. Evans had given her.

In a moment she looked up, a warm smile lighting her face. "Galadriel Hopkins. What a beautiful name! From Tolkien, of course."

"No," muttered Gilly. "Hollywood Gardens."

Miss Harris laughed a sort of golden laugh. "No, I mean your name—Galadriel. It's the name of a great queen in a book by a man named Tolkien. But, of course, you know that."

Hell. No one had ever told her that her name came from a book. Should she pretend she knew all about it or play dumb?

"I'd like to call you Galadriel, if you don't mind. It's such a lovely name."

"No!" Everyone was looking at Gilly peculiarly. She must have yelled louder than she intended to. "I would prefer," she said tightly, "to be called Gilly."

"Yes"—Miss Harris's voice was more steel than gold now —"Yes. Gilly, it is then. Well"—she turned her smile on the rest of the class—"Where were we?"

The clamor of their answers clashed in Gilly's brain. She started to put her head down on the desk, but someone was shoving a book into her face.

It wasn't fair—nothing was fair. She had once seen a picture in an old book of a red fox on a high rock surrounded by snarling dogs. It was like that. She was smarter than all of them, but they were too many. They had her surrounded, and in their stupid ways, they were determined to wear her down.

Miss Harris was leaning over her. Gilly pulled away as far as she could.

"Did you do division with fractions at Hollywood Gardens?"

Gilly shook her head. Inside she seethed. It was bad enough having to come to this broken-down old school but to be behind—to seem dumber than the rest of the kids—to have to appear a fool in front of. . . . Almost half the class was black. And she would look dumb to *them.* A bunch of—

"Why don't you bring your chair up to my desk, and we'll work on it?"

Gilly snatched up her chair and beat Miss Harris to the front of the room. She'd show them!

At recesstime Monica Bradley, one of the other white girls in the class, was supposed to look after her on the playground. But Monica was more interested in leaning against the building and talking with her friends, which she did, keeping her back toward Gilly as she giggled and gossiped with two other sixth-grade girls, one of whom was black with millions of tiny braids all over her head. Like some African bushwoman. Not that Gilly cared. Why should she? They could giggle their stupid lives away, and she'd never let it bother her. She turned her back on them. That would show them.

Just then a ball jerked loose from the basketball game nearby and rushed toward her. She grabbed it. Balls were friends. She hugged it and ran over to the basket and threw it up, but she had been in too much of a hurry. It kissed the rim but refused to go in for her. Angrily she jumped and caught it before it bounced. She was dimly aware of a protest from the players, but they were boys and mostly shorter than she, so not worthy of notice. She shot again, this time with care. It arched and sank cleanly. She pushed someone out of the way and grabbed it just below the net.

"Hey! Who you think you are?"

One of the boys, a black as tall as she, tried to pull the ball from her hands. She spun around, knocking him to the concrete, and shot again, banking the ball off the backboard neatly into the net. She grabbed it once more.

Now all the boys were after her. She began to run across the playground laughing and clutching the ball to her chest. She could hear the boys screaming behind her, but she was too fast for them. She ran in and out of hopscotch games and right through a jump rope, all the way back to the basketball post where she shot again, missing wildly in her glee.

The boys did not watch for the rebound. They leaped upon her. She was on her back, scratching and kicking for all she was worth. They were yelping like hurt puppies.

"Hey! Hey! What's going on here?"

Miss Harris towered above them. The fighting evaporated under her glare. She marched all seven of them to the principal's office. Gilly noted with satisfaction a long red line down the tall boy's cheek. She'd actually drawn blood in the fracas. The boys looked a lot worse than she felt. Six to one—pretty good odds even for the great Gilly Hopkins.

Mr. Evans lectured the boys about fighting on the playground and then sent them back to their homerooms. He kept Gilly longer.

"Gilly." He said her name as though it were a whole sentence by itself. Then he just sat back in his chair, his fingertips pressed together, and looked at her.

She smoothed her hair and waited, staring him in the eye. People hated that—you staring them down as though they were the ones who had been bad. They didn't know how to deal with it. Sure enough. The principal looked away first.

"Would you like to sit down?"

She jerked her head No.

He coughed. "I would rather for us to be friends."

Gilly smirked.

"We're not going to have fighting on the playground." He looked directly at her. "Or anywhere else around here. I think you need to understand that, Gilly."

She tilted her head sassily and kept her eyes right on his.

"You're at a new school now. You have a chance to—uh —make a new start. If you want to."

So Hollywood Gardens had warned him, eh? Well, so what? The people here would have learned soon enough. Gilly would have made sure of that.

She smiled what she knew to be her most menacing smile.

"If there's anyway I can help you—if you just feel like talking to somebody. . . ."

Not one of those understanding adults. Deliver me! She smiled so hard it stretched the muscles around her eyes. "I'm OK," she said. "I don't need any help."

"If you don't want help, there's no way I can make you accept it. But, Gilly"—he leaned forward in his chair and spoke very slowly and softly—"you're not going to be permitted to hurt other people."

She snuffled loudly. Cute. Very cute.

He leaned back; she thought she heard him sigh. "Not if I have anything to do with it."

Gilly wiped her nose on the back of her hand. She saw the principal half reach for his box of tissues and then pull his hand back.

"You may go back to your class now." She turned to go. "I hope you'll give yourself—and us—a chance, Gilly."

She ignored the remark. Nice, she thought, climbing the dark stairs. Only a half day and already the principal was yo-yoing. Give her a week, boy. A week and she'd have the whole cussed place in an uproar. But this afternoon, she'd cool it a little. Let them worry. Then tomorrow or maybe even the next day, *Wham.* She felt her old powers returning. She was no longer tired.

"Sarsaparilla to Sorcery"

SHE met Agnes Stokes the next day at recess. Agnes was a shriveled-up-looking little sixth grader from another class. She had long red hair that fell rather greasily to her waist, and when she sidled up to Gilly on the playground, the first thing Gilly noticed was how dirty her fingernails were.

"I know who you are," the girl said. For a moment Gilly was reminded of the story of Rumpelstiltskin. Like that little creature, this girl had power over her. She knew who Gilly was, but Gilly didn't know who she was.

"Yeah?" said Gilly to let the evil little dwarf know that she wasn't interested.

"That was great about you beating up six boys yesterday."

"Yeah?" Gilly couldn't help but be a little interested.

"It's all over the school."

"So?"

"So." The girl leaned against the building beside her, as though assuming Gilly would be pleased with her company.

"So?"

The girl twitched her freckled nose. "I thought me and you should get together."

"How come?" Rumpelstiltskins were always after something.

"No reason." The smaller girl had on a jacket the sleeves of which were so long that they came down to her knuckles. She began to roll up first her left sleeve and then her right. She did it slowly and silently, as though it were part of some ceremony. It gave Gilly the creeps.

"What's your name?" Gilly blurted out the question, half expecting the girl to refuse to answer.

"Agnes Stokes"—she lowered her voice conspiratorily—"You can call me Ag."

Big deal. She was glad when the bell rang, and she could leave Agnes Stokes behind. But when she left school that afternoon, Agnes slipped out from the corner of the building and fell in step with her.

"Wanta come over?" she asked. "My grandma won't care."

"Can't." Gilly had no intention of going into Agnes Stokes's house until she found out what Agnes Stokes was up to. People like Agnes Stokes didn't try to make friends without a reason.

She walked faster, but Agnes kept up with funny, little skip steps. When they got all the way up the hill to Trotter's house, Agnes actually started up the walk after Gilly.

Gilly turned around fiercely. "You can't come in today!"

"How come?"

"Because," said Gilly. "I live with a terrible ogre that eats up little redheaded girls in one gulp."

Agnes stepped back, with a startled look on her face. "Oh," she said. Then she giggled nervously. "I get it. You're teasing."

"Arum golly goshee laboooooooo!" screamed Gilly, bearing down on the smaller girl like a child-eating giant.

Agnes backed away. "Wha—?"

Good. She had succeeded in unsettling Rumpelstiltskin. "Maybe tomorrow," said Gilly calmly and marched into the house without turning around.

"That you, William Ernest, honey?"

It made her want to puke the way Trotter carried on over that little weirdo.

Trotter came into the hall. "Oh, Gilly," she said. "You got home so quick today I thought it was William Ernest."

"Yeah." Gilly started past her up the stairs.

"Wait a minute, honey. You got some mail."

Mail! It could only be from—and it was. She snatched it out of Trotter's puffy fingers and raced up the stairs, slamming the door and falling upon the bed in one motion. It was a postcard showing sunset on the ocean. Slowly she turned it over.

My dearest Galadriel,

The agency wrote me that you had moved. I wish it were to here. I miss you.

All my love, Courtney

That was all. Gilly read it again. And then a third time. No. That was not all. Up on the address side, in the left-hand corner. The letters were squeezed together so you could hardly read them. An address. Her mother's address.

She could go there. She could hitchhike across the country to California. She would knock on the door, and her mother would open it. And Courtney would throw her arms around her and kiss her all over her face and never let her go. "I wish it were to here. I miss you." See, Courtney wanted her to come. "All my love."

Inside her head, Gilly packed the brown suitcase and crept down the stairs. It was the middle of the night. Out into the darkness. No. She shivered a little. She would pick a time when Trotter was fussing over W.E. or Mr. Randolph. She'd steal some food. Maybe a little money. People picked up hitchhikers all the time. She'd get to California in a few days. Probably less than a week. People were always picking up hitchhikers. And beating them up. And killing them. And pitching their dead bodies into the woods. All because she didn't have any money to buy a plane ticket or even a bus ticket.

Oh, why did it have to be so hard? Other kids could be with their mothers all the time. Dumb, stupid kids who didn't even like their mothers much. While she—

She put her head down and began to cry. She didn't mean to, but it was so unfair. She hadn't even seen her mother since she was three years old. Her beautiful mother who missed her so much and sent her all her love.

"You all right, honey?" Tap, tap, tap. "You all right?"

Gilly sat up straight. Couldn't anyone have any privacy around this dump? She stuffed the postcard under her pillow and then smoothed the covers that she'd refused to straighten before school. She stood up at the end of the bed like a soldier on inspection. But the door didn't open.

"Anything I can do for you, honey?"

Yeah. Fry yourself, lard face.

"Can I come in?"

"No!" shrieked Gilly, then snatched open the door. "Can't you leave me alone for one stupid minute?"

Trotter's eyelids flapped on her face like shutters on a vacant house. "You OK, honey?" she repeated.

"I will be soon as you get your fat self outta here!"

"OK." Trotter backed up slowly toward the stairs. "Call me, if you want anything." As an afterthought, she said, "It ain't a shameful thing to need help, you know."

"I don't need any help"—Gilly slammed the door, then yanked it open—"from anybody!" She slammed it shut once more.

"I miss you. All my love." I don't need help from anybody except from you. If I wrote you—if I asked, would you come and get me? You're the only one in the world I need. I'd be good for you. You'd see. I'd change into a whole new person. I'd turn from gruesome Gilly into gorgeous, gracious, good, glorious Galadriel. And grateful. Oh, Courtney—oh, Mother, I'd be so grateful.

"Lord, you are so good to us." Mr. Randolph was saying the supper blessing. "Yes, Lord, so very good. We have this wonderful food to eat and wonderful friends to enjoy it with. Now, bless us, Lord, and make us truly, truly grateful. Ah-men."

"Ay-men. My, Mr. Randolph, you do ask a proper blessing."

"Oh, Mrs. Trotter, when I sit before the spread of your table, I got so much to be thankful for."

Good lord, how was a person supposed to eat through this garbage?

"Well, Miss Gilly, how was school for you today?"

Gilly grunted. Trotter gave her a sharp look. "It was OK, I guess."

"My, you young people have such a wonderful opportunity today. Back when I was going to school—oh, thank you, Mrs. Trotter—what a delicious-smelling plate. My, my . . ."

To Gilly's relief, the blind man's attention was diverted from his tale of childhood schooldays to the organization of the food on his plate and the eating of it, which he did with a constant murmuring of delight, dropping little bits from his mouth to his chin or tie.

Disgusting. Gilly switched her attention to William Ernest, who, as usual, was staring at her bug-eyed. She smiled primly and mouthed, "How do you do, sweetums?"

Sweetums immediately choked on a carrot. He coughed until tears came.

"What's the matter, William Ernest, honey?"

"I think"—Gilly smiled her old lady principal smile—"the dear child is choking. It must be something he ate."

"Are you all right, baby?" asked Trotter.

W.E. nodded through his tears.

"Sure?"

"Maybe he needs a pat on the back," Mr. Randolph offered.

"Yeah!" said Gilly. "How about it, W.E., old man? Want me to swat you one?"

"*No!* Don't let her hit me."

"Nobody's gonna hit you, honey. Everybody just wants to help." Trotter looked hard at Gilly. "Right, Gilly?"

"Just want to help, little buddy." Gilly flashed her crooked-politician smile.

"I'm all right," the boy said in a small strangled voice. He slid his chair a couple of inches toward Trotter's end of the table, so that he was no longer directly across from Gilly.

"Say, W.E."—Gilly flashed her teeth at him—"how about you and me doing a little red-hot reading after supper? You know, squeeze the old orange reader?"

W.E. shook his head, his eyes pleading with Trotter to save him.

"My, oh, my, Mrs. Trotter. I can tell how old I am when I can't even understand the language of the young people about me," said Mr. Randolph.

Trotter was looking first at W.E. and then at Gilly. "Don't you fret yourself, Mr. Randolph." She leaned across the corner of the table and patted William Ernest gently, keeping her eyes on Gilly. "Don't you fret, now. Sometimes these kids'll tease the buttons off a teddy bear. Ain't nothing to do with age."

"Hell, I was just trying to help the kid," muttered Gilly.

"He don't always know that," Trotter said, but her eyes were saying "like heck you were." "I got a real good idea," she went on. "They tell me, Gilly, that you are some kind of a great reader yourself. I know Mr. Randolph would like to hear you read something."

The little wrinkled face brightened. "My, my! Would you do that, Miss Gilly? It would be such a pleasure to me."

Trotter, you rat. "I don't have anything to read," Gilly said.

"OK, that ain't a problem. Mr. Randolph's got enough books to start a public library, haven't you, Mr. Randolph?"

"Well, I do have a few," he chuckled. "Course you've got the Good Book right here."

"What good book?" demanded Gilly, interested in spite of herself. She did like a good book.

"I believe Mr. Randolph is referring to the Holy Bible."

"The *Bible?*" Gilly didn't know whether to laugh or cry. She had a vision of herself trapped forever in the dusty brown parlor reading the Bible to Trotter and Mr. Randolph. She would read on and on forever, while the two of them nodded piously at each other. She jumped up from her chair. "I'll get a book," she said. "I'll run over to Mr. Randolph's and choose something."

She was afraid they would try to stop her, force her to read the Bible, but they both seemed pleased and let her go.

Mr. Randolph's front door was unlocked. The house was pitch-black and mustier than Trotter's. Quickly, Gilly pushed a light switch. Nothing happened. Of course. Why should Mr. Randolph care if a bulb burned out? She stumbled from the hall to where she thought the living room should be, fumbling along the wall with her fingers until she found another switch. To her relief this one worked—only 40 watts worth, maybe—but still there was light.

Leaning against two walls of the crowded little room were huge antique bookcases that reached the ceiling. And stacked or lying upside down, even put in backward, were books—hundreds of them. They looked old and thick with dust. It was hard to think of funny little Mr. Randolph actually reading them. She wondered how long he had been blind. She wished she could push her mind past those blank white eyes into whatever of Mr. Randolph all these books must represent.

She went toward the larger shelf to the right of the door, but she felt strangely shy about actually touching the books. It was almost as though she were meddling in another person's brain. Wait. Maybe they were all for show. Maybe Mr. Randolph collected books, trying to act like some big-shot genius, even though he himself couldn't read a word. No one would ever catch on. They'd think he didn't read because he couldn't see. That was it, of course. She felt better. Now she was free to look at the books themselves.

Without thinking, she began to straighten out the shelves as she read the titles. She saw several volumes of an encyclopedia set: "Antarctica to Balfe," then "Jerez to Liberty." She looked around for other volumes. It bothered her to have everything in a muddle. High on the top shelf was "Sarsaparilla to Sorcery." She dragged a heavy stuffed chair backward to the shelf and climbed up on the very top of its back. On tiptoe, leaning against the rickety lower shelves to keep from toppling, she could barely reach the book. She pulled at it with the tip of her fingers, catching it as it fell. Something fluttered to the floor as she did so.

Money. She half fell, half jumped off the chair, and snatched it up. Two five-dollar bills had fallen out from behind "Sarsaparilla to Sorcery." She put the encyclopedia down and studied the old, wrinkled bills. Just when she was needing money so badly. Here they'd come floating down. Like magic. Ten dollars wouldn't get her very far, but there might be more where these came from. She climbed up again, stretching almost to the point of falling, but it was no good. Although she could just about reach the top shelf with her fingertips, she was very unsteady, and the lower shelves were much too wobbly to risk climbing.

Heavy footsteps thudded across the front porch. The front door opened. "You all right, Gilly, honey?"

Gilly nearly tripped over herself, leaping down and grabbing up "Sarsaparilla to Sorcery" from the chair seat, stretching her guts out to tip the book into its place on the shelf. And just in time. She got down on the chair seat, as Trotter appeared at the door.

"You was taking so long," she said. "Then Mr. Randolph remembered that maybe the bulbs was all burned out. He tends to forget since they really don't help him much."

"There's a light here," Gilly snapped. "If there hadn't been, I'd have come back. I'm not retarded."

"I believe you mentioned that before," said Trotter dryly. "Well, you find anything you wanted to read to Mr. Randolph?"

"It's a bunch of junk."

"One man's trash is another man's treasure," Trotter said in a maddeningly calm voice, wandering over to a lower shelf as she did so. She pulled out a squat leather-bound volume and blew the dust off the top. "He's got a yen for poetry, Mr. Randolph does." She handed the book up to Gilly, who was still perched on the chair. "This is one I used to try to read to him last year, but"—her voice sounded almost shy—"I ain't too hot a reader myself, as you can probably guess."

Gilly stepped down. She was still angry with Trotter for bursting in on her, but she was curious to know just what sort of poetry old man Randolph fancied. *The Oxford Book of English Verse.* She flipped it open, but it was too dark to see the words properly.

"Ready to come along?"

"Yeah, yeah," she replied impatiently. Holding her neck straight to keep from looking up at "Sarsaparilla," she followed Trotter's bulk back to her house.

"What did you bring?" Mr. Randolph's face looked like a child's before a wrapped-up present. He was sitting right at the edge of the big brown chair.

"The Oxford Book of English Verse," Gilly mumbled.

He cocked his head. "I beg your pardon?"

"The poems we was reading last year, Mr. Randolph." Trotter had raised her voice as she always did speaking to the old man.

"Oh, good, good," he said, sliding back into the chair until his short legs no longer touched the worn rug.

Gilly opened the book. She flipped through the junk at the beginning and came to the first poem. "Cuckoo Song," she read the title loudly. It was rather pleasant being able to do something well that none of the rest of them could. Then she glanced at the body of the poem.

Sumer is icumen in,
Lhude sing cuccu!
Groweth sed, and bloweth med,
And springth the wude nu—
Sing cuccu!

Cuckoo was right. "Wait a minute," she muttered, turning the page.

Bytuene Mershe ant Averil . . .

She looked quickly at the next.

Lenten ys come with love to toune, . . .

And the next—

Ichot a burde in boure bryht,
That fully semly is on syht, . . .

She slammed the book shut. They were obviously trying to play a trick on her. Make her seem stupid. See, there was Mr. Randolph giggling to himself. "It's not in English!" she yelled. "You're just trying to make a fool of me."

"No, no, Miss Gilly. Nobody's trying to make a fool of you. The real old English is at the front. Try over a way."

"You want the Wordsworth one, Mr. Randolph?" asked Trotter. "Or do you have that by heart?"

"Both," he said happily.

Trotter came over and leaned across Gilly, who was sitting on the piano bench. "I can find it," said Gilly, pulling the book out of her reach. "Just tell me the name of it."

"William Wordsworth," said Mr. Randolph. "There was a time when meadow, grove, and stream, . . ." He folded his small hands across his chest, his voice no longer pinched and polite, but soft and warm.

Gilly found the page and began to read:

"There was a time when meadow, grove, and stream,
The earth, and every common sight,
To me did seem
Apparell'd in celestial light,
The glory and the freshness of a dream."

She stopped a minute as though to listen to her own echo.

"It is not now . . . ," Mr. Randolph's velvet voice prompted her.

"It is not now as it hath been of yore:—
Turn wheresoe'er I may,
By night or day, . . ."

Leaning against the back of the chair, Mr. Randolph joined and with one voice they recited:

"The things which I have seen I now can see no more."

They continued to read that way. He would listen blissfully for a while and then join, turning her single voice into the sound of a choir.

She read:

"Our birth is but a sleep and a forgetting:
The Soul that rises with us, our life's Star,
Hath had elsewhere its setting,
And cometh from afar:
Not in entire forgetfulness,
And not in utter nakedness, . . ."

And then together

"But trailing clouds of glory do we come
From God, who is our home. . . ."

"Trailing clouds of glory do we come." The music of the words rolled up and burst across Gilly like waves upon a beach.

It was a long poem. Seven pages or so of small print. She couldn't understand really what it meant. But Mr. Randolph seemed to know each word, prompting her gently if she started to stumble on an unfamiliar one, and joining her, powerfully and musically, on his own favorite lines.

They chorused the final lines:

"Thanks to the human heart by which we live,
Thanks to its tenderness, its joys, and fears,
To me the meanest flower that blows can give
Thoughts that do often lie too deep for tears."

Mr. Randolph gave a long sigh. "Thank you, thank you," he said softly.

"She's a handsome reader, all right." Trotter was smiling proudly as though she might share the credit for Gilly's talent.

The smile irritated Gilly. She was a good reader because she had set her mind to be one. The minute that damn first-grade teacher had told Mrs. Dixon that she was afraid Gilly might be "slow," Gilly had determined to make the old parrot choke on her crackers. And she had. By Christmastime she was reading circles around the whole snotty class. Not that it made any difference. The teacher, Mrs. Gorman, had then explained very carefully to Mrs. Dixon that she had twenty-five other children to look out for and that there was no way to set up a private reading time for one individual. Gilly would just have to learn some patience and cooperation. That was all.

"Well, what do you think of Mr. Wordsworth, Miss Gilly?" asked Mr. Randolph, interrupting her angry thoughts.

"Stupid," she said to the memory of Mrs. Gorman rather than to him.

A look of pain crossed his face. "I suppose," he said in his pinched, polite voice, "in just one reading, one might. . . ."

"Like here"—Gilly now felt forced to justify an opinion which she didn't in the least hold—"like here at the end, 'the meanest flower that blows.' What in the hell—what's that supposed to mean? Whoever heard of a 'mean flower?' "

Mr. Randolph relaxed. "The word *mean* has more than one definition, Miss Gilly. Here the poet is talking about humility, lowliness, not"—he laughed softly—"not bad nature."

Gilly flushed. "I never saw a flower blow, either."

"Dandelions." They all turned to look at William Ernest, not only startled by the seldom-heard sound of his voice, but by the fact that all three had forgotten that he was even in the room. There he sat, cross-legged on the floor at the end of the couch, a near-sighted guru, blinking behind his glasses.

"You hear that?" Trotter's voice boomed with triumph. "Dandelions? Ain't that the smartest thing you ever heard? Ain't it?"

W.E. ducked his head behind the cover of the couch arm.

"That is probably exactly the flower that Mr. Wordsworth meant," Mr. Randolph said. "Surely it is the lowliest flower of all."

"Meanest flower, there is," agreed Trotter happily. "And they sure do blow, just like William Ernest says. They blow all over the place." She turned toward Gilly as though for agreement, but at the sight of Gilly's face, the woman's smile stuck.

"Can I go now?" Gilly's voice was sharp like the jagged edge of a tin-can top.

Trotter nodded. "Sure," she said quietly.

"I do appreciate more than you know—" but Gilly didn't wait to hear Mr. Randolph's appreciation. She ran up the stairs into her room. Behind the closed door, she pulled the two bills from her pocket, and lying on the bed, smoothed out the wrinkles. She would hide them beneath her underwear until she could figure out a better place, and tomorrow she would call the bus station and ask the price of a one-way ticket to San Francisco.

"I'm coming, Courtney," she whispered. "Trailing clouds of glory as I come."

It was only a matter of getting back into Mr. Randolph's house and getting the rest of the money. There was sure to be more.

William Ernest and Other Mean Flowers

AGNES Stokes was waiting outside when she started for school the next morning. Gilly's first impulse was to turn around and go back into the house until Agnes had left, but it was too late. Agnes was already waving and yelling to her. What a creep! Gilly walked past her quickly without speaking. She could hear Agnes's little scurrying steps behind her; then there was a dirty hand on her arm.

Disgusted, Gilly shook it off.

Agnes's hand was gone, but she hooked her chin over Gilly's upper arm, her face twisted up to look Gilly in the face. Her breath smelled. "What are we going to do today?" she asked.

We? Are you kidding?

"Want to fight the boys again? I'll help."

Gilly spun around and brought her nose down close to Agnes's stubby one. Ugh. "When are you gonna get it through that ant brain of yours that *I don't want help?*"

Agnes withdrew her nose and shook her greasy hair, but to Gilly's annoyance she clung like a louse nit, scurrying beside Gilly, two or three little steps to every one of Gilly's.

Though it was hard to ignore her the rest of the way to the school, Gilly managed by putting on her celebrity-in-a-parade face, staring glassy-eyed far into the crowd, blanking out everything within close range.

"I just live up the next block from you, you know."

Thrillsville.

"I'll stop by for you every day, OK?"

The little jerk couldn't even figure out that she was being ignored.

Just as they reached the schoolyard, Agnes waved a large unwrapped piece of gum before Gilly's nose. "Want some bubble gum?"

Oh, what the heck. The queen had used Rumpelstiltskin, hadn't she? Agnes might come in handy some day. The trick was in knowing how to dispose of people when you were through with them, and Gilly had had plenty of practice performing that trick.

She took the gum without speaking. Agnes flushed with pleasure. "See that kid over by the fence? The one with the big nose? Her mother run away with a sailor last May."

"So?"

Agnes put her hand up and whispered behind it. "My grandma says the whole family's nothing but trash."

"Yeah?" Gilly smacked her gum noisily. "What's your grandma say about your family?"

Agnes went as stiff as a dried sponge. "Who's been telling lies about my family?"

"Lucky guess."

"They're coming back. Both of them."

"Sure."

"Well, they are. Probably before Christmas."

"OK, OK, I believe you."

Agnes's eyes darted back and forth in their sockets, studying Gilly's expressionless face. "Are you making fun of me?" she asked finally.

"I wouldn't do that."

Agnes's uncertainty wavered. "I know a lot more stuff," she said. "You know—junk about people around here."

"I bet you do, sweetheart." Gilly carefully blew a medium-sized bubble which popped dangerously close to Agnes's stringy red hair.

Agnes let out a sharp little laugh. "Watch it!" she said nervously. The first bell rang. "See you at recess?"

Gilly shrugged and headed for Harris 6. "Maybe," she said.

Although a part of Gilly's head wanted to get on with her schemes of how to get Mr. Randolph's money, once she crossed the threshold of Harris 6, she forced herself to concentrate on her lessons. She had made up her mind that first day to pay attention in Miss Harris's class. She wasn't going to let a bunch of low-class idiots think they were smarter than she was. It was infuriating to find herself behind in almost every subject, but she knew that the fault lay in Hollywood Gardens Elementary and not in herself. She would work madly until she had not only caught up with but passed them all, and then she'd skid to a total halt. That kind of technique drove teachers wild. They took it personally when someone who could obviously run circles around the rest of the class completely refused to play the game. Yep. And in Miss Harris's case that was just how Gilly wanted it taken.

At lunchtime Agnes's class had gotten to the cafeteria first, so when Gilly left the line, Agnes was already seated and waved her over to her table. Gilly would have preferred to eat alone. Agnes wasn't the most appetizing luncheon companion, but since Gilly had decided Agnes might sometime come in handy, she might as well get used to her. She went over and sat down opposite Agnes, who smiled like a cartoon cat across the trays. "I get free lunch, too," she said.

Gilly glared at her. Nobody was supposed to know who got free lunch and who didn't. So much for privacy. The first thing she was going to teach Agnes Stokes was when to keep her big mouth shut.

"You know, don't you, Agnes, it makes me sick just looking at you?"

Agnes gave her kicked-dog expression. "Wha'cha mean?"

"Nothing personal. You just make me sick—that's all."

Agnes jerked the cafeteria bench closer to the table and started to roll up her dragging shirtsleeves.

"It's nothing personal," Gilly continued. "In fact, you probably can't help it. I don't blame you. I'm just not going to put up with it."

"Put up with what?"

Gilly leaned way across the table and right into Agnes's pink face. "Your big mouth!"

Agnes tilted backward to get her face out of Gilly's leering one. People were staring at them. They both straightened up, but Gilly kept the leer in place.

"I ain't got no big mouth," Agnes said quietly.

"Then keep it shut. We wouldn't want what's left of your brains to trickle out."

Agnes's mouth flew open and immediately slammed shut. She shrugged, gave an angry little sniff, and then began to eat her lunch.

Gilly paused to give a generous smile to the other people at the table while spreading her napkin delicately on her lap and picking up the milk carton with her pinky curled the way Mrs. Nevins used to do when she picked up her coffee cup.

After lunch she allowed Agnes to follow her around the playground like a stray puppy. Once Agnes ventured a tentative "Hey, Gil," but Gilly spun around with such a frightening look that any further words withered.

And when Gilly left school, Agnes fell in behind her without a word. They marched up the hill, Agnes tripping along double time to keep up with Gilly's exaggerated strides. When they got to Trotter's, Gilly went in. As she was closing the dirty white picket gate behind her, Agnes touched her arm and handed her a note. It said: "When can I talk?"

Gilly smiled benignly. "We'll see," she said. "We'll just see how it goes."

Agnes opened her mouth like a starved baby bird, but she didn't give a chirp. Good bird. Gilly patted the skinny, freckled arm and swept up the walk into the house, leaving the open-mouthed fledgling outside the gate.

"Zat you, William Ernest, honey?"

"Zat's me, Maime Trotter, baby," squeaked Gilly.

From the kitchen she could hear Trotter's laugh rumbling. "C'mon in here and get yourself a snack, Gilly, honey."

Gilly was tempted, but determined not to yield. She was too smart to be bought with food, no matter how hungry she felt. She stomped up the stairs past the open kitchen door from which came the definite smell of chocolate chip cookies. Double-damn you, Maime Trotter.

Later, behind her carefully closed door, Gilly took out the money from the bureau. Then she pulled out the whole drawer and dumped it upside down on the bed. She smoothed out the bills on the drawer bottom, and then took from her pocket the masking tape she'd taken care to steal from Miss Harris's desk and taped the bills to the bottom of the drawer.

Without warning, the door flew open. Gilly, to cover the money, fell chest down over the drawer.

A frog-eyed William Ernest stood on the threshold, trying to juggle a small tray which held a plate of cookies and a glass of milk.

"What in the devil?" screeched Gilly.

"Tr-tt-tt-tt-Trotter . . ." was all the child could manage in the way of an answer. He was rattling the tray so hard that the milk glass was threatening to jump the edge.

"Well, put 'em down, stupid."

W.E.'s eyes searched the room in desperation. Gilly was beginning to feel like a fool lying chest down on a bureau drawer. She raised herself enough to turn the drawer over. Then she sat up and turned to face him.

"Didn't Trotter ever tell you about knocking before you bust in?"

He nodded, eyes wide, tray rattling.

She sighed. What a weird little kid. "OK," she said, reaching out across the narrow space. "Give it here."

He shoved it at her and ran blamety-blam down the stairs. Gilly turned the drawer back over to make a table on the bed and put the milk and cookies on it. She shut the door and then sat down cross-legged on the bed and began to eat. Oh, thank you, thank you, Maime Trotter. What a delicious-smelling plate of cookies. My, my, and ahhhhh-men.

In the middle of the last cookie, an inspiration came to her. It wasn't Agnes Stokes whom she would use. Agnes couldn't be trusted between freckles. It was William Ernest. Of course. Trotter's honey baby engaged in a life of crime. She laughed out loud at the pleasure of it. Baby-Face Teague, the frog-eyed filcher. Wild-eyed William, the goose-brained godfather. The possibilities were unlimited and delectable. The midget of the Mafia. The Orange Reader Squeezer. No. The Orange Squirt.

She jumped up and put the room to order, danced down the stairs, balancing the tray high on one hand, and skipped into the kitchen.

Trotter looked up from the table where she was spooning cookie dough onto a baking sheet and gave her the eye. "Feeling good, now?"

Gilly gave her the 300-watt smile that she had designed especially for melting the hearts of foster parents. "Never better!" She spoke the words with just the right musical lilt. She put her dishes by the sink, started to wash them but thought better of it. Trotter might get suspicious if goodness was overdone.

She skated out into the hall and around the bottom of the

stairs right into the living room where W.E. sat on the floor staring at *Sesame Street.* She slid down beside him, and when his eyes checked her out sideways, she gave a quiet, sisterly kind of smile and pretended to be enthralled with Big Bird. She said nothing through *Sesame Street, Mr. Roger's Neighborhood,* and *The Electric Company* but occasionally hummed along with one of the songs in a friendly sort of way, never failing to smile at William when she caught him snatching a quick stare in her direction.

Her strategy seemed to be succeeding. At any rate when suppertime neared, she said to him, "Do you want to set the table or get Mr. Randolph?" and he answered with hardly a stutter, "Get Mr. Randolph."

So she set the kitchen table, humming under her breath the "Sunny Days" theme from *Sesame Street.* And after supper she folded an airplane for him from notebook paper, and at her suggestion he even followed her out on the front porch to fly it.

W.E. squinched his little nearsighted eyes together, wrinkled up his stubby nose, drew his arm way back, and pitched the airplane with all his might. "*Pow,*" he whispered. The plane swooped down off the porch, then suddenly caught an updraft and climbed higher than their heads, looped and glided smoothly to the grass.

He turned shining eyes on her. "See that?" he asked softly. "See that?"

"OK, OK." Gilly ran out and picked up the plane. It was the best one she'd ever made. She clambered up on the concrete post that held the porch railing in place and raised her arm. Then she thought better of it. "You do it, William Ernest, OK?"

She climbed down and gave him a boost up. He seemed

a little unsteady from the height of the post, glancing down, apparently afraid to move his feet.

"Look, I'm not going to let you fall, man." She put her hands loosely around his ankles. She could feel him relaxing under her fingers. He reared back and shot. *"Pow,"* he said a little louder than before, sending the white craft with its pale blue lines as high—well, almost as high—as the house, looping, climbing, gliding, resting at last in the azalea bush in Mr. Randolph's yard.

William Ernest scrambled off the post and down the steps. He was slowed by the fence, but not stopped. You could tell he'd never climbed a fence in his life, and it would have been faster by far to go through the gate and around, but he had chosen the most direct route to his precious plane.

He fell in Mr. Randolph's yard in such a way that one arm and leg seemed to arrive before the other pair, but he picked himself up at once and delicately plucked his prize from the bush. He turned around to grin shyly at Gilly and then, as though carrying the crown of England, came down Mr. Randolph's walk, the sidewalk, and into Trotter's gate.

About halfway up the walk, he said something.

"What you say?" Gilly asked.

"I say"—the veins on his neck stuck out with the effort of raising his voice to an audible level—"I say, It sure fly good."

He wasn't as dumb as he looked now, was he? thought Gilly smiling, without taking time to calculate which of her smiles to put on. "You throw good, too, William E."

"I do?"

"Sure. I was just admiring your style. I guess you've had lessons."

He cocked his head in puzzlement.

"No? You just taught yourself?"

He nodded his head solemnly.

"Gee, man, you're a natural. I've never seen such a natural."

He straightened his thin shoulders and marched up the stairs as though he were the President of the United States.

They were still flying the plane, or rather W.E. was flying it with Gilly looking on and making admiring remarks from time to time, when Trotter and Mr. Randolph came out on the porch.

"You gotta see this, Trotter. William Ernest can do this really good."

W.E. climbed unassisted to the top of the concrete post. He didn't need Gilly's hands or help now. "Watch," he said softly. "Watch here."

Mr. Randolph lifted his sightless face upward. "What is it, son?"

"Gilly made him a paper airplane, looks like," interpreted Trotter.

"Oh, I see, I see."

"Watch now."

"We're watching, William Ernest, honey."

W.E. leaned back and let fly—"*pow*"—for another swooping, soaring, slowly spiraling, skimming superflight.

Trotter sighed as the plane gracefully landed by the curb. William Ernest rushed to retrieve it.

"How was it?" Mr. Randolph asked.

"I 'clare, Mr. Randolph, sometimes it's a pity you gotta miss seeing things. I never thought paper airplanes was for anything but to drive teachers crazy before." She turned to Gilly. "That was really something," she said.

Gilly could feel herself blushing, but W.E. came up the steps and saved her. "It's 'cause I fly it so good," he said.

"Yeah," said Gilly, patting his shoulder. "You sure do." He looked up into her face, his squinty little eyes full of pure pleasure.

"Thank you," said Trotter softly.

For a moment Gilly looked at her, then quickly turned away as a person turns from bright sunlight. "Want me to walk Mr. Randolph home?" she asked.

"Thank you, Miss Gilly. I would appreciate that so much."

She took his elbow and guided him carefully down the stairs, taking care not to look back over her shoulder because the look on Trotter's face was the one Gilly had, in some deep part of her, longed to see all her life, but not from someone like Trotter. That was not part of the plan.

Harassing Miss Harris

By the third week in October, Gilly had caught up with her class and gone on ahead. She tried to tell herself that she had forced Miss Harris into a corner from which the woman could give her nothing but A's. Surely, it must kill old priss face to have to put rave notices—"Excellent" "Good, clear thinking" "Nice Work"—on the papers of someone who so obviously disliked her.

But Miss Harris was a cool customer. If she knew that Gilly despised her, she never let on. So at this point Gilly was not ready to pull her time-honored trick of stopping work just when the teacher had become convinced that she had a bloody genius on her hands. That had worked so beautifully at Hollywood Gardens—the whole staff had gone totally ape when suddenly one day she began turning in blank sheets of paper. It was the day after Gilly had overheard the principal telling her teacher that Gilly had made the highest score in the entire school's history on her national aptitude tests, but, of course, no one knew that she knew, so an army of school psychologists had been called in to try to figure her out. Since no one at school would take the blame for Gilly's sudden refusal to achieve, they decided to blame her foster parents, which made Mrs. Nevins so furious that she demanded that Miss Ellis remove Gilly at once instead of waiting out the year—the year Mrs. Nevins had reluctantly agreed to, after her first complaints about Gilly's sassy and underhanded ways.

But something warned Gilly that Miss Harris was not likely to crumble at the sight of a blank sheet of paper. She was more likely simply to ignore it. She was different from the other teachers Gilly had known. She did not appear to be dependent on her students. There was no evidence that they fed either her anxieties or her satisfactions. In Gilly's social-studies book there was a picture of a Muslim woman of Saudi Arabia, with her body totally covered except for her eyes. It reminded Gilly somehow of Miss Harris, who had wrapped herself up in invisible robes. Once or twice a flash in the eyes seemed to reveal something to Gilly of the person underneath the protective garments, but such flashes were so rare that Gilly hesitated to say even to herself what they might mean.

Some days it didn't matter to Gilly what Miss Harris was thinking or not thinking. It was rather comfortable to go to school with no one yelling or cajoling—to know that your work was judged on its merits and was not affected by the teacher's personal opinion of the person doing the work. It was a little like throwing a basketball. If you aimed right, you got it through the hoop; it was absolutely just and absolutely impersonal.

But other days, Miss Harris's indifference grated on Gilly. She was not used to being treated like everyone else. Ever since the first grade, she had forced her teachers to make a special case of her. She had been in charge of her own education. She had learned what and when it pleased her. Teachers had courted her and cursed her, but no one before had simply melted her into the mass.

As long as she had been behind the mass, she tolerated this failure to treat her in a special manner, but now, even the good-morning smile seemed to echo the math computer's "Hello, Gilly number 58706, today we will continue our study of fractions." *Crossing threshold of classroom causes auto-teacher to light up and say "Good morning." For three thousand dollars additional, get the personalized electric-eye model that calls each student by name.*

For several days she concentrated on the vision of a computer-activated Miss Harris. It seemed to fit. Brilliant, cold, totally, absolutely, and maddeningly fair, all her inner workings shinily encased and hidden from view. Not a Muslim but a flawless tamperproof machine.

The more Gilly thought about it, the madder she got. No one had a right to cut herself off from other people like that. Just once, before she left this dump, she'd like to pull a wire inside that machine. Just once she'd like to see Harris-6 scream in anger—fall apart—break down.

But Miss Harris wasn't like Trotter. You didn't have to be around Trotter five minutes before you knew the direct route to her insides—William Ernest Teague. Miss Harris wasn't hooked up to other people. It was like old *Mission*

Impossible reruns on TV: *Your mission, if you decide to accept it, is to get inside this computerized robot, discover how it operates, and neutralize its effectiveness.* The self-destructing tape never told the mission-impossible team how to complete their impossible mission, but the team always seemed to know. Gilly, on the other hand, hadn't a clue.

It was TV that gave her the clue. She hadn't been thinking about Miss Harris at all. She'd been thinking, actually, of how to get the rest of Mr. Randolph's money and hadn't been listening to the news broadcast. Then somehow it began sending a message into her brain. A high government official had told a joke on an airplane that had gotten him fired. Not just any joke, mind you. A dirty joke. But that wasn't what got him fired. The dirty joke had been somehow insulting to blacks. Apparently all the black people in the country and even some whites were jumping up and down with rage. Unfortunately the commentator didn't repeat the joke. She could have used it. But at least she knew now something that might be a key to Harris-6.

She borrowed some money from Trotter for "school supplies," and bought a pack of heavy white construction paper and magic markers. Behind the closed door of her bedroom she began to make a greeting card, fashioning it as closely as she could to the tall, thin, "comic" cards on the special whirlaround stand in the drugstore.

At first she tried to draw a picture on the front, wasting five or six precious sheets of paper in the attempt. Cursing her incompetence, she stole one of Trotter's magazines and cut from it a picture of a tall, beautiful black woman in an Afro. Her skin was a little darker than Miss Harris's, but it was close enough.

Above the picture of the woman she lettered these words carefully (She could print well, even if her drawing stank):

They're saying "Black is beautiful!"

Then below the picture:

But the best that I can figger
Is everyone who's saying so
Looks mighty like a

And inside in tiny letters:

person with a vested interest in
maintaining this point of view.

She had to admit it. It was about the funniest card she'd ever seen in her life. Gifted Gilly—a funny female of the first rank. If her bedroom had been large enough, she'd have rolled on the floor. As it was, she lay on the bed hugging herself and laughing until she was practically hysterical. Her only regret was that the card was to be anonymous. She would have enjoyed taking credit for this masterpiece.

She got to school very early the next morning and sneaked up the smelly stairs to Harris-6 before the janitor had even turned on the hall lights. For a moment she feared that the door might be locked, but it opened easily under her hand. She slipped the card into the math book that lay in the middle of Miss Harris's otherwise absolutely neat desk. She wanted to be sure that no one else would discover it and ruin everything.

All day long, but especially during math, Gilly kept stealing glances at Miss Harris. Surely at any minute, she would pick up the book. Surely she could see the end of the card sticking out and would be curious. But Miss Harris left the book exactly where it was. She borrowed a book from a student when she needed to refer to one. It was as though she sensed her own was booby-trapped.

By lunchtime Gilly's heart, which had started the day jumping with happy anticipation, was kicking angrily at her stomach. By midafternoon she was so mad that nothing had happened that she missed three spelling words, all of which she knew perfectly well. At the three o'clock bell, she slammed her chair upside down on her desk and headed for the door.

"Gilly."

Her heart skipped as she turned toward Miss Harris.

"Will you wait a minute, please?"

They both waited, staring quietly at each other until the room emptied. Then Miss Harris got up from her desk and closed the door. She took a chair from one of the front desks and put it down a little distance from her own. "Sit down for a minute, won't you?"

Gilly sat. The math book lay apparently undisturbed, the edge of the card peeping out at either end.

"You may find this hard to believe, Gilly, but you and I are very much alike."

Gilly snapped to attention despite herself.

"I don't mean in intelligence, although that is true, too. Both of us are smart, and we know it. But the thing that brings us closer than intelligence is anger. You and I are two of the angriest people I know." She said all this in a cool voice that cut each word in a thin slice from the next and then waited, as if to give Gilly a chance to challenge her. But Gilly was fascinated, like the guys in the movies watching the approach of a cobra. She wasn't about to make a false move.

"We do different things with our anger, of course. I was always taught to deny mine, which I did and still do. And that makes me envy you. Your anger is still up here on the surface where you can look it in the face, make friends with it if you want to."

She might have been talking Swahili for all Gilly could understand.

"But I didn't ask you to stay after school to tell you how intelligent you are or how much I envy you, but to thank you for your card."

It had to be sarcasm, but Harris-6 was smiling almost like a human being. When did the cobra strike?

"I took it to the teachers' room at noon and cursed creatively for twenty minutes. I haven't felt so good in years."

She'd gone mad like the computer in *2001*. Gilly got up and started backing toward the door. Miss Harris just smiled and made no effort to stop her. As soon as she got to the stairs, Gilly began to run and, cursing creatively, ran all the way home.

Dust and Desperation

ALL at once, leaving Thompson Park became urgent. Gilly knew in the marrow of her bones that if she stayed much longer, this place would mess her up. Between the craziness in the brown house and the craziness at school, she would become like W.E., soft and no good, and if there was anything her short life had taught her, it was that a person must be tough. Otherwise, you were had.

And Galadriel Hopkins was not ready to be had. But she must hurry. It didn't matter whether the people who hovered over her had fat laps or computer brains. For if a person could crack under heat or cold, a combination of the two seemed guaranteed to do in even the gutsy Galadriel.

By now she would have preferred to get Mr. Randolph's money on her own and leave both William Ernest and

Agnes Stokes out of it, but in her haste she acted stupidly and used them both.

The opportunity fell into her lap unexpectedly. Trotter had never asked her to baby-sit with William Ernest before, but suddenly two days after the card joke bombed, Trotter announced that she was taking Mr. Randolph to pick up a few things at the dime store and would Gilly watch William Ernest while they were gone.

It was too perfect. She should have realized that, but her anxiety to get the money and get going had fuzzed her common sense. With shaking hands, she leafed through the fat suburban phone book until she found the number for the Stokeses in Thompson Park who supposedly lived on Aspen Avenue. (Another of the world's lies. The senior Stokeses had long before left the Washington area, abandoning Agnes to a maternal grandmother, seventy-five-years-old, by the name of Gertrude Berkheimer. But Agnes's delinquent father was still listed in the directory just as though he had never left her.)

Agnes arrived immediately, nearly falling over herself with joy that Gilly had not only invited her over but was actually asking for her help in carrying out a secret and obviously illegal plot. She agreed, without objection, to being the lookout at Mr. Randolph's house, although Gilly suspected she would have preferred an inside role. Agnes was to do her whistle, which she claimed could be heard a mile away, should the taxi bearing Trotter and Mr. Randolph return while Gilly was still inside.

Prying W.E. away from the TV and explaining his part to him proved far more difficult.

"I don't understand," he said for what seemed to be

the thirtieth time, blinking stupidly behind his glasses.

Gilly started all over again from the beginning as patiently as she could.

"Mr. Randolph wants you and me to do him a favor. He's got something on the top shelf in his living room that he needs, and he can't see to get it down. I told him you and me weren't too busy this afternoon, so he says, 'Miss Gilly, could you and William Ernest, who is just like a grandson to me, do me a tremendous favor while I am busy at the store?' So of course I told him we'd be glad to help out. You being just like a grandson to him and all." She paused.

"What kind of favor?"

"Just get this stuff down off the shelf for him."

"Oh." Then, "What stuff?"

"William Ernest. I haven't got all day. Do you want to help or not?"

He guessed so. Well, it would have to do. They had already delayed far too long. She gave Agnes some last-minute instructions out of range of the boy's earshot. Agnes would have to be paid in cold cash to keep her big mouth you-know-what. Then she went and got W.E. by the hand, and using the key that Trotter kept, they let themselves into Mr. Randolph's house.

The house was dark and damp-feeling even in the daytime, but fortunately the boy was used to it and walked right in.

Gilly pointed out the top shelf of the bookcase. "He told me he had the stuff right behind that big red book."

W.E. looked up.

"See which one I'm talking about?"

He nodded, then shook his head. "I can't reach it."

"Of course not, stu—I can't reach it, either. That's why we both have to do it."

"Oh."

"Now look. I'm going to push this big blue chair over and stand on the arm. Then I want you to climb up the back of the chair and get on my shoulders . . ."

He drew back. "I want to wait for Trotter."

"We can't do that, William Ernest, honey. You know how hard it is on Trotter climbing up and down. It wouldn't be good for her." He was still hesitant. "Besides, I think it's kind of a surprise for Trotter. Mr. Randolph doesn't want her to know about it. Yet."

The boy came close to the chair and tiptoed up toward her. "I'm scared," he whispered.

"Sure you are. But just think, man, how proud everybody's going to be later. After the surprise can be told and everything. When they find out who it was that . . ."

He was already climbing up on the chair. It was an old, solid overstuffed one, so that when he stood on the arm and then on the back, it never moved. Gilly got up on the chair's fat arm and helped him onto her shoulders and held his legs. The little cuss was heavier than he looked.

"OK. First pull out that big red book I showed you."

He grabbed her hair with his left hand and stretched toward the shelf without straightening and pulled out the book. It fell to the floor with a crash.

"I dropped it."

"Don't worry about it! Just look back there behind where it was."

He leaned forward. Ouch—she was afraid he'd take her hair out like weeds from a wet garden.

"It's dark."

"Look, man! No, stick your hand up in there."

She had to shift her balance as he leaned forward to keep from crashing to the floor herself.

"*Pow,*" he said softly, bringing back a dusty fist. In it was a rubber-banded roll of bills.

Gilly reached up.

"Don't let go my legs!" He dropped the money and grabbed her hair with both hands.

"Is there any more?"

"*Wheeeeeeeeeet!*" Agnes's signal.

Gilly nearly fell off the chair as she snatched W.E. off her shoulders, then scrambled back on the top of the chairback, tilted "Sarsaparilla to Sorcery" back in place, jumped down, stuffed the roll of bills into her jeans, shoved the heavy chair forward, grabbed a startled William, and dragged him out the back door.

"I gotta give it to Mr. Randolph later, when Trotter isn't around," she explained to the blinking owl eyes. "Look I gotta go to the bathroom. You go help Trotter get Mr. Randolph into the house. Oh—and tell Agnes to go home. I'll see her tomorrow."

But Agnes was waiting for her in Trotter's hallway, lounging against the stairs. "Find what you was looking for?"

"No luck."

Agnes looked down at Gilly's jeans. "Then what's bulging your pocket?"

"OK. I found some, but I didn't find much."

"How much did you find?"

"Hell, Agnes, I don't know."

"I'll help you count."

"I swear, Agnes, I'll help you rearrange your nose if you don't get out of here. I promised I'd give you something for helping, and I will, but I can't now, and if you don't understand that, you're in worse shape than I thought."

Agnes stuck out her bottom lip. "If it wasn't for me, you'd be caught right now."

"I know, Agnes, and I won't forget that. But if you hang around now, we'll both be caught. So get out, and keep your mouth shut."

Without waiting for further sulks, Gilly pushed past Agnes and ran up the staircase. She shut her door and pulled the bureau in front of it. Then she took out the special drawer and began to tape the money to the bottom with a sinking heart. Thirty-four dollars. Thirty-four measly dollars. Forty-four, counting the ten she had already. It had seemed like more in William's fist and bulging in her jeans. She counted it again to make sure. No, there was no more. Five five-dollar bills and nine ones. It had seemed like more because of all the singles. She laid out a one to give to Agnes, then reluctantly swapped it for a five. Agnes would not be bought off cheaply, she knew. If only she had done it by herself. It cost too much to use people. Why had she thought she couldn't do it alone? She had been in too big a hurry. She should have taken more time, planned more carefully. Now she had gotten both Agnes and W.E. involved and all for a measly forty-four—no, thirty-nine—dollars. Then remembering the weight of W.E. on her neck and shoulders and the pain as he yanked her hair in terror, she started to count out another dollar, but that would leave her only thirty-eight. It would take a lot more to get even as far as the Mississippi River. She returned W.E.'s dollar to the stack.

She would have to search again, but she would go back by herself the next time. As soon as she figured out a plan.

Dust. The thought hit her after supper when they were all sitting in the living room watching the evening news. Suddenly she saw it, lying like a gray frost upon the TV set. Dust! She would go on a campaign, dusting first this house and then the other. She jumped to her feet.

"Trotter!"

Slowly Trotter shifted her attention from Walter Cronkite to Gilly. "Yeah, honey?"

"Mind if I dust in here?"

"Dust?" Trotter spoke the word as though it were the name of an exotic and slightly dangerous game. "I guess not." Her gaze slid back toward the screen. "Whyn't you wait till we're through watching TV, though?"

Gilly jiggled her foot through a Central American earthquake and the bribery trial of a congressman from who cared where.

She couldn't stand waiting. She ran into the kitchen. She now knew how she could get the money on her own and every minute seemed to matter. Under the sink were some old rags—and could you believe it?—a quarter bottle of furniture polish. She poured some on one of the rags which she had carefully dampened just as Mrs. Nevins always did and proceeded to clean the never-used dining room with its dark, heavy table and six chairs.

One side of the rag was black in two swipes, but Gilly turned it over and poured out more polish. The steady wiping and polishing with the "clean, dry cloth" fell into a rhythm that began to calm her inner frenzy. By the time she got to the picture over the buffet, she not only cleaned out the niches of the carved frame but she hunted up Windex and paper towels to wash the faces and so forths of the baby angels who were tripping around on clouds with only a ribbon or a stray wing to cover their private parts (as Mrs. Nevins used to call them).

Meantime in the living room, the volume of Trotter's voice told Gilly that Walter Cronkite had called it a day, but she no longer needed to rush. Gently she wiped off the last streak of Windex.

By supper the next night she had finished cleaning everything but the living-room chandelier. And how could one do that without a stepladder?

"Oh, forget it, Gilly, honey. The place looks beautiful. No one's going to notice the chandelier," said Trotter.

"I will," said Gilly. "I gotta have a tall stool or a stepladder or something. Then I could do the top kitchen cabinets, too."

"Mercy. Next thing I know you'll be wiping me right out with all the rest of the trash."

William Ernest looked up from his meat loaf in alarm.

Mr. Randolph was chuckling. "There is no danger of that, Mrs. Trotter."

"Well, you know what the Good Book says, Dust to dust . . ."

"No!" squeaked William Ernest. "You ain't dusty!"

"Oh, bless you, sweetheart. I was only talking crazy."

"Nobody will take away William Ernest's Mrs. Trotter; now, will they, Miss Gilly?" Mr. Randolph reached out and felt for the boy's head and patted it.

"Of course not," said Gilly sharply. "I just want something to stand on to finish my job."

"My, my," said Mr. Randolph, "You really have yourself

a prize helper here, Mrs. Trotter. Young people nowadays hardly . . ."

"If you want, Mr. Randolph . . ." She would have to be careful—talk slowly as though the idea were just occurring to her—"I could maybe do your house when I finish here. Course I'd have to have a stepladder, probably—"

"Didn't I say she was a prize, Mrs. Trotter?" Mr. Randolph was beaming. "I might even have a ladder in my basement . . ."

Gilly jumped up from the table, then caught herself—slow down, slow down. Her heart was pumping crazily. She made herself sit down.

"Maybe after supper I could take a look. I'd sure like to finish that chandelier tonight."

Trotter and Mr. Randolph nodded and chuckled happily. People were so dumb sometimes you almost felt bad to take advantage of them—but not too bad. Not when it was your only way to get where you had to go.

The stepladder was old and rickety, but it would beat trying to climb those bookshelves of Mr. Randolph's, which looked as though they might come right over on top of you if you pulled at them. She set the ladder up under Trotter's chandelier, and as she painstakingly wiped each piece of glass with her ammonia-water rag, she would have to grab the ladder from time to time, dizzy as she was with the smell of the ammonia and the thought that by tomorrow night at this time she'd be on her way to California.

Late that night she packed the brown bag and shoved it far under the bed. Tomorrow from the school pay phone, she'd call the bus station and find out how much the ticket cost. Then all she had to do was get the rest of the money.

Gilly was coming out of the phone booth the next day when Agnes appeared demanding her money. She pretended to be grumpy about the five dollars Gilly gave her, but there was a greedy gleam in her eyes. She was pleased, all right.

"Can we get more?" she asked.

Gilly shook her head. "That's all there was. I split it three ways."

"Looked like a lot in your pocket yesterday."

"Yeah, but the rest was all in ones."

"I don't see why you split equal with that weird kid. He wouldn't know the difference."

"He's not as dumb as he looks." Gilly looked Agnes straight in the eyes. "He acts stupid, maybe, but if he thought you and me were cheating on him . . ."

Agnes shrugged. "Well," she said, "next time, let's not use him."

"OK, sure, next time," Gilly agreed, knowing happily that there would be no next time with creepy Agnes the Stoke. Tonight she would be bound for her new life—her real life.

She got rid of Agnes at the front gate with some lie about Trotter forcing her to scrub all the dirty pots in the house. Agnes said she'd go on home. She wasn't too crazy about cleaning pots and pans.

The stepladder was in the hall. Gilly put her schoolbooks down on the table and went right to it. As she was leaning to pick it up—"Gilly, honey, want some snack?"

She straightened up quickly. It would be better to eat while she had the chance. She gave the ladder a pat and went into the kitchen.

Trotter was sitting at the table. She seemed to have

finished her daily Bible reading, for the Good Book, still open, was pushed to one side. Right before her was a piece of notebook paper, half filled with her square, laborious script. She had a nineteen-cent ball-point clutched tightly in her right hand. When Gilly came in, the huge woman smiled shyly at her over the top of her reading glasses.

"Writing one of my old children. I do miss 'em when they grow up and leave me, but the Good Lord knows I ain't much at writing." She looked down at her letter and sighed. "There's more of them cookies in the tin box next to the refrigerator."

Gilly poured herself a twelve-ounce glass of milk and took four of the cookies.

"Sit down, Gilly, honey. I ain't really busy."

Gilly sat down at the far side of the table.

"Things is going better for you now, ain't they, honey?

"OK."

"I been meaning to say to you how much I appreciate the way you've been making friends with William Ernest."

"Yeah, OK."

"Like Miz Ellis says, you're a special kind of person, Gilly. It makes me praise the Lord to see you so busy helping stead of hurting."

Shut up, Trotter.

"You got so much to give. Mercy, what most of us wouldn't give for half your brains."

Shut up, Trotter, shut up!

The silent commands were obeyed because just then William Ernest, honey, appeared, and Trotter roused her great hulk from the table to get him his snack.

Trotter, baby, if you had half my brains you'd know to let the boy do things for himself. If I were going to stay here,

I'd teach him how. You want to so hard, and you don't know how. Even the birds know to shove the babies out of the nest. If I were going to be here, I'd make a man of your little marshmallow. But I can't stay. I might go soft and stupid, too. Like I did at Dixons'. I let her fool me with all that rocking and love talk. I called her Mama and crawled up on her lap when I had to cry. My god! She said I was her own little baby, but when they moved to Florida, I was put out like the rest of the trash they left behind. I can't go soft —not as long as I'm nobody's real kid—not while I'm just something to play musical chairs with . . .

An elbow pierced her rib cage.

Gilly jerked awake. What the hell? W.E. was trying to attract her attention without getting Trotter's, mouthing some words through a full load of cookie crumbs.

Huh? She asked the question by raising her eyebrows.

He swallowed. Then "Surprise," he mouthed, pointing his head in Trotter's general direction.

She shook her head with exaggerated vigor. "Not yet!" she mouthed back. "Later."

A little grin escaped and danced around his face.

Gilly sighed. If she didn't watch herself, she'd start liking the little jerk. She excused herself. "I'm going to get on to my dusting over at Mr. Randolph's."

W.E. made as if to follow.

"Naw, William Ernest. You better watch *Sesame Street* today. I'm going to help you with your reading later on, and you have to be real sharp. Right, Trotter?"

"You better believe it."

She knocked several times at Mr. Randolph's door before he opened it, his tie and shirt awry and his face still clogged with sleep.

"I—uh—brought your stepladder back, Mr. Randolph."

"Oh? Oh, thank you, thank you. Just put it down out there on the porch."

"But—but—I thought since I was here and had the ladder and all, I might come on in and—uh—start to work."

"Oh, Miss Gilly. You don't have to worry. I was just talking the other night. What I can't see isn't likely to hurt me."

"I don't mind. I want to help."

"Every week or so my son over in Virginia comes and brings a lady to vacuum a little. It's really all I need."

"But I want to"—god—"What I mean is, I want to help Mrs. Trotter, and you know how she is, she really doesn't need my help. But I figured if I do something for you, it will be like doing something for her . . ."

"Bless you, you sweet little lady. How can I say No to that?"

It worked. He stepped aside for her to come in and shuffled along right behind her into the living room. Was he going to stay in there, his sightless eyes following the sound of her?

"Why don't you just go up and finish your nap, Mr. Randolph? I feel bad waking you up like this."

He chuckled and stretched out in the worn blue plush armchair, his feet up on the equally worn stool. He closed his eyes.

"Wouldn't you rest better up on your bed or something? I'm—I'm going to be working in here. Making a lot of noise."

"Mercy, Miss Gilly, I can rest in heaven. In the meantime, it is human company that I treasure. It won't bother you if I just sit here, will it? I promise not to make suggestions."

"Why don't I come back later? I don't want to bother you."

"Bother me? I'm delighted."

She kept her eyes on the little man as she carefully set up the stepladder at the far end of the bookcase wall. The blue plush chair was exactly where she'd shoved it two days earlier, catercornered three feet from the place she'd have to set up the ladder in order to reach "Sarsaparilla to Sorcery."

"Excuse me, Mr. Randolph." Her voice barely squeaked out. She cleared her throat. "Mr. Randolph!" Now she was yelling. "I'm going to have to move your chair."

He got up like an obedient child. Gilly shoved and pushed and tugged the heavy chair to a place opposite the red encyclopedia. She arranged the chair and then the stool, and then took Mr. Randolph's elbow and led him to them.

"Now your chair's just opposite from where it was before."

"I hope you haven't strained yourself, Miss Gilly."

"Right between the end of the couch and the corner of the desk. Couple of feet on either side, OK?"

"Fine, fine." He sat down and stretched out again.

Gilly went back to the stepladder, climbed the first step, and then backed down.

"I guess I'll begin with the windows over the desk."

He smiled his funny little blank-eyed smile. "You're the doctor, Miss Gilly."

She did the windows and the desk, then moved the ladder around Mr. Randolph to the smaller of the two giant bookcases. She went back and dusted the picture over the couch, which was of fancily dressed white people in another century having an elaborate picnic in a woods. She kept looking over her shoulder at Mr. Randolph, who lay motionless with his eyes closed. Since he'd been known to sleep on Trotter's couch with his eyes wide open, there was no way under heaven to tell if he were wide awake or dead asleep. But he wasn't snoring. That was worrisome.

But, hell. The man was blind and half deaf. Why should it matter in the least that he was sitting right there in the room while she robbed him of money he was too old to remember having? Still—the closer she got to "Sarsaparilla" the more her heart carried on like the entire percussion section of a marching band doing "The Stars and Stripes Forever."

At last she moved the stepladder directly in front of the place and took a step up, glancing sideways at Mr. Randolph. He didn't move. She eased up the ladder trying not to make any noise, but it creaked and swayed under her weight. From the next to the top step she could reach "Sarsaparilla to Sorcery" without stretching. She braced her left leg hard against the cold metal of the ladder, took out the now familiar volume, and laid it gently on the ladder top.

Nothing was visible except dust. She took out books on either side, dusting each one with a kind of fury. Still nothing.

Mr. Randolph was shifting in his chair across the room. She looked into his blank white eyes. Oh, god. Maybe he could really see. Maybe it was all a trick to fool people. She froze.

"You certainly are doing a beautiful job. So careful. My, my, I don't know when this room has been so thoroughly cleaned before."

"I—I—I'm sort of straightening up the book shelves."

"Fine, fine." He was bobbing his head. "Now if there were just some way you could straighten up this old brain of mine as well. . . ."

She was not going to panic. He couldn't see. Of course, he couldn't see. It was really better that he was in the room. Nobody would suspect her of stealing right from under his nose. She dusted the space and then moved "Sarsaparilla" down to the shelf that held the rest of the encyclopedia set. On the shelf from which it had come, she proceeded to remove, one by one, all the other books, wiping carefully behind each one to the dark-stained wood at the back of the case. With every book her hope rose and fell, rising a little less and falling a little more each time. At last she knew that her lie to Agnes had proved all too true. There was no more money.

Fear and anticipation curdled in her stomach. She wanted to throw up.

Mr. Randolph was chatting away happily. She couldn't seem to tune in the words, just the maddeningly cheerful tone of his high-pitched voice. She wanted to throw a book at the noise—kick over the stepladder—crash a chair through the window—at the very least scream out her frustration.

But, of course, she didn't. Wrapped in a silent, frozen rage, she folded the stepladder and carried it to the basement.

"You going now, Miss Gilly?" The voice followed her down and up the steps and out of the house. "Thank you, thank you. Come back for another little visit, won't you? Be sure to tell Mrs. Trotter what a lovely help you've been."

She made no attempt to answer him. It didn't matter

what he thought. He was of no use to her. Thirty-nine stinking dollars.

She went straight to her room, took the brown suitcase from under the bed, and unpacked it. Then she ripped out a sheet of paper through the rings of her notebook, lay down on the bed, and pressing on her math book, wrote:

1408 Aspen Ave.
Thompson Park, Md.

Dear Courtney Rutherford Hopkins,

I received your card. I am sorry to bother you with my problems, but as my real mother, I feel you have a right to know about your daughter's situation.

At the present time, it is very desperate, or I would not bother you. The foster mother is a religious fanatic. Besides that she can hardly read and write and has a very dirty house and weird friends.

She started to write "colored" but erased it, not sure how Courtney might react.

There is another kid here who is probably mentally retarded.

I am expected to do most of the work including taking care of him (the mentally retarded boy) which is very hard with all my schoolwork, too.

I have saved up $39 toward my ticket to California. Please send me the rest at your earliest convenience.

She wrote "Love" then changed it to:

Yours sincerely,
your daughter,
Galadriel Hopkins

P.S. I am very smart and can take care of myself, so I will not be a burden to you in any way.
P.S. Again. I have checked the cost of a bus ticket to San Francisco. It is exactly $136.60 one way. I will get a job and pay you back as soon as possible.

She listened at the top of the stairs until she heard Trotter go into the downstairs bathroom. Then she crept into the kitchen, stole an envelope and a stamp from the kitchen drawer, and ran to the corner to mail her letter before the rage could defrost and change her mind.

The One-Way Ticket

NOT everything in the letter to Courtney had been absolutely true, but surely the part about Trotter being a religious fanatic was. She read the Bible and prayed every day, always joining Mr. Randolph's grace over the food. Besides, anybody who started for church at nine in the morning on Sunday and didn't get home until after twelve thirty had to be peculiar.

Sunday mornings were torture to Gilly. The church was a strange little white frame building stuck up on a hill behind the police station, built when the city was a country town instead of part of the metropolitan Washington sprawl. The church didn't fit in the modern world anymore than the people who went there did.

The children's Sunday-school class, in which both Gilly and W.E. were lumped with the five other six- to twelve-year-olds in the church, was presided over by an ancient Miss Minnie Applegate, who reminded her seven charges every Sunday that she had been "saved" by Billy Sunday. Who in the hell was Billy Sunday? He sounded like a character from the comics. Billy Sunday meet Brenda Starr. Also, Miss Applegate neglected to say what Billy Sunday had saved her from. A burning building? The path of a speeding locomotive? Or indeed, having been so luckily preserved, what good had her pickling accomplished for either herself or the world?

Old Applegate would do things like lecture them on the Ten Commandments and then steadfastly refuse to explain what adultery was.

"But, Miss Applegate," an eight-year-old had sensibly asked, "if we don't know what adultery is, how can we know if we're doing it or not?"

Gilly, of course, knew all about adultery. In whispered conversations between Sunday school and church, she offered for sale not only the definition of the word but some juicy neighborhood examples (which had lately come to her attention, thanks to Agnes Stokes). In this way she gained seventy-eight cents in coins previously designated for the church collection plate.

The preacher was as young as the Sunday-school teacher was old. He, too, was high on getting saved and other matters of eternal preservation. But his grammar was worse than Trotter's, and, to Gilly's disgust, he'd stumble over words of more than one syllable whenever he read the Bible. Nobody but a religious fanatic would put up with such gross ignorance for over an hour every week of their lives—nobody but religious fanatics and the innocent victims they forced to go to church.

Unlike some of the women, Trotter didn't carry on over the preacher at the church door, which made Gilly bold enough to ask her once, "How can you stand him?" It was the wrong question. Trotter sucked in her breath and glowered down at her like Moses at the Israelites' golden calf. "Who am I," she thundered, "to pass judgment on the Lord's anointed?" Would anybody but a fanatic say a thing like that?

Mr. Randolph went to the black Baptist church. The same taxi that took Trotter and the children to the white Baptist church dropped him off on the way and picked him up on the way home. Gilly noted that the black Baptists dressed fancier and smiled more than the whites. But their services lasted even longer, and often W.E. would have to run in and get the old man out of his service while the taxi meter impatiently ticked away. It was usually past two by the time they got out of their Sunday clothes, cooked dinner, and finally sat down to their long, lazy meal.

The Sunday after the futile dusting, Mr. Randolph surprised everyone by refusing seconds.

"Oh, you must know, Mrs. Trotter, how it pains me to say No to this exquisite chicken, but my son is coming over about three."

At the word "son," something clanked inside Gilly's chest. Suppose the son noticed that something was funny in Mr. Randolph's living room? The chair on the opposite side, the books rearranged? Suppose he knew where the money should have been?

"Oh, you got time for a piece of pie, now, don't you, Mr. Randolph? It's cherry today."

"Cherry. My, my." Mr. Randolph held his bony thumb and index finger an inch apart. "About so much, all right?

I'm helpless before your cherry pies, Mrs. Trotter. Totally helpless."

He was chewing the pie blissfully when suddenly he stopped. "Oh, my. Have I got any spots on my clothes? My son gets so upset."

Trotter put her fork down and studied him. "You look good, Mr. Randolph. Only just a little something on your tie."

"Oh, mercy, mercy. The boy is always looking for some excuse to say I can't take care of myself so he can drag me over to his big house in Virginia." He dipped his napkin into his water glass and tried to dab his tie, completely missing the offending spots.

"Oh, shoot, Mr. Randolph. Let me get you one of Melvin's old ties to wear. I don't know why I still got so much of his stuff around anyhow." She sniffed as if to clear away a memory of the late Mr. Trotter. "Gilly, run up to my room and look in the back of the closet, will you? There's a dozen or more on a coat hanger." Before Gilly got out the door, she added, "Just pick a nice one, hear? Not one of the real loud ones." She turned, half apologetically to Mr. Randolph. "Sometimes in those last years, if Melvin was feeling low, he'd go out and buy some wild tie and wear it every day for a week." She shook her head. "I guess I should praise the Lord it wasn't some wild woman he was hanging round his neck."

Mr. Randolph giggled. "Why don't you bring me a wild one, Miss Gilly? I need to wake up that fifty-year-old senior citizen I've got for a son."

Trotter threw back her massive head and belly-laughed. "You're some kinda man, Mr. Randolph."

"Well, you're some kind of lady."

Gilly fled up the stairs. These scenes between Trotter and Mr. Randolph made her insides curl. It was weird to see old people carry on, old people who weren't even the same color.

But it was not that silly little flirtation that was bothering her. It was a vision of Mr. Randolph's prissy fifty-year-old son poking around his father's living room. So when she saw Trotter's purse with its no-good fastener lying wide open on the bed, inviting her, practically demanding her to look in, she did so. Good god. Trotter must have just cashed her check from county welfare. Gilly did a quick count—at least a hundred. Another hundred would get her all the way to California—all the way to Courtney Rutherford Hopkins, all the way home.

She stuffed the money in her pocket, went to the closet, and found the hanger full of Melvin's madness. She chose the gaudiest one there—four-inch-high ballet dancers in purple tutus, their pink legs pirouetting on a greenish four-in-hand. She tiptoed to her own room, slipped the fat wad of bills in her drawer under her T-shirts, and tiptoed back to Trotter's door, once there, she slammed her feet down and noisily descended the stairs.

"Oh, my sweet baby, what have you done?"

Gilly's blood went cold. How could Trotter know?

"That tie. It's the worst crime Melvin ever committed. Rest his precious soul."

"Oh, good, good." Mr. Randolph was standing up, rubbing his wrinkled hands together in excitement. "Tell me about it."

"You better not take this one, Mr. Randolph. It's got all these fat women jumping around."

"Really?" The little brown face beamed. "Are they decent?"

"Well, they ain't naked, but they might as well be. Little purple flimflams—"

"Tutus," prompted Gilly primly, gratefully recovering from her earlier shock.

"What?" asked Trotter.

"Tutus. They're wearing tutus."

Trotter roared. "Ain't that perfect? Too-toos. Too-too skimpy for words."

Mr. Randolph was already taking off his spotted black tie to make room for Melvin's dancing ladies.

"You sure now, Mr. Randolph? I don't want your son thinking I'm some kinda wicked influence on his good Baptist father."

Gilly began to wonder if poor Mr. Randolph was going to choke on his own giggles. "He doesn't ever need to know where the tie came from. I give you my solemn word"—this from a man hysterical with laughter. Jeez.

Trotter knotted the tie for him with the kind of assured expertise born of knotting one man's tie for more than a quarter of a century. She stepped back to appraise the effect.

"Well—what do you think, Gilly, honey? That do something for Mr. Randolph?"

"It's OK."

"OK? We gotta do better than that! How 'bout you William Ernest, honey? How do you like Mr. Randolph's new tie?"

"It's beautiful," the boy whispered reverently.

"See, well." Trotter was immediately sober. "William Ernest approves."

"Good, good," said Mr. Randolph, his dignity also once again intact. "Would you walk with me back to my house then, son?"

The boy slid out of his chair and took the old man's hand.

"See you tomorrow, hear?" Trotter said.

"Thank you. Yes. Thank you. And you, too, Miss Gilly. See you tomorrow."

"Yeah. OK," said Gilly, though by this time tomorrow she figured to be in Missouri at the very least.

She dried the dishes as Trotter washed them and put them to drain, her mind aboard the Greyhound bus skimming across something that looked like a three-dimensional version of the topographical map in her geography book.

Trotter beside her was chuckling again over Mr. Randolph's sporting Melvin's dancing ladies. "His son's this big lawyer"—lawyer!—"over in Virginia. I'd give a pretty penny to see his face when he gets a load of that tie. Mercy on us, wouldn't I ever?"

After they finished cleaning up in the kitchen, Trotter went into the living room and stretched out on the couch. Her one trip upstairs on Sundays was to change out of her good dress, so she'd be on the couch the rest of the day, napping or laboriously reading the Sunday paper. W.E., back from next door, turned on the TV and lay down on the rug to watch an old movie.

Now was the time. Gilly started for the stairs.

"You want to join us, honey? There's a football game on Channel 9, 'less W.E. cares about this movie."

W.E. got up, obediently ready to switch channels.

"No," Gilly said. "Not right now. I got things to do."

"Well, OK, honey."

If she was going to go, she would have to leave now. By tonight Trotter would go upstairs and find the money gone, and nothing was sure about what might happen with Mr. Randolph's lawyer son next door.

She packed quickly although her hands shook. The first thing was to gather all the money together and put it into her pocket. It made a lump as big as an orange. Too bad she'd thrown away that silly shoulder bag Mrs. Nevins had bought her last Christmas.

Her jacket—"First thing next week we're going to have to buy you a good, warm coat," Trotter had said. She had been waiting for the support check—her jacket was hanging by the front door, downstairs, past the open living-room door. Trotter was probably asleep, and, if Gilly was very quiet, perhaps W.E. wouldn't hear.

She crept down, keeping her suitcase under her right arm to conceal it as best she could with her body. Crossing the short, bright strip before the door, she glanced in. Neither head turned. She was safely to the front door. She took her jacket off the hook and poked it above the suitcase, so that she had a free hand for the knob.

"Where you going?" She jumped around at W.E.'s whisper. In the dark hallway his glasses flashed.

"Just out," she whispered back. Oh, god, make him shut up.

He did shut up and stood silently, looking first at her, then at the suitcase, then back at her.

"Don't go." His little face squeezed up at her like his tiny voice.

"I got to," she said through her teeth. Opening the door,

pulling it shut behind her, shifting the suitcase and jacket to either hand, and running, running, running, down the hill, the pulse in her forehead pounding as hard as her sneakered feet pounded the sidewalk.

Once around the corner, she slowed down. Someone might notice her if they saw her running. No bus came by. There were hardly any on Sundays. She settled herself at once to walk the mile or so to the bus station, stopping to put on her thin jacket against the November wind. The bus would be heated, she reminded herself, and in California the sun always shines.

It was dusk by the time she got to the bus station. She went straight to the ladies' room and combed her hair and tucked her shirt into her jeans. She tried to tell herself that she looked much older than eleven. She was tall, but totally bustless. Hell. She zipped up her jacket, stood up straight, and went out to the ticket counter.

The man didn't even look up.

"I want a ticket to California, please." As soon as the words were out, she heard her mistake.

"California where?" He glanced up now, looking at her through half-open lids.

"Uh—San Francisco. San Francisco, California."

"One-way or round trip."

Whatever happened to Lady Cool? "One—one way."

He punched some buttons and a ticket magically emerged. "One thirty-six sixty including tax."

She had it. She had enough. With trembling hands, she took the wad of bills from her pocket and began to count it out.

The man watched lazily. "Your mother know where you are, kid?"

Come on, Gilly. You can't fall apart now. She pulled herself straight and directed into his sleepy eyes the look she usually reserved for teachers and principals. "I'm going to see my mother. She lives in San Francisco."

"OK," he said, taking her money and recounting it before he handed her the ticket. "Bus leaves at eight thirty."

"Eight thirty?"

"Yeah. Want to check your bag?"

"It's only four-thirty now."

"That's right."

"That's four hours from now."

"Right again."

"But I want to leave as soon as I can."

"Look, kid, you came in here and asked me for a ticket. I gave you one on the next bus." He sighed. "OK," he said and consulted his book. "You can take the five o'clock into Washington and catch a six twenty-two out of there." He stuck out his hand. "I'll have to fix you another ticket."

She gave it back.

"It'll take me a while," he said. "I gotta check the routing." He nodded to the seats across the waiting room. "Just sit down over there. I'll call you."

She hesitated, then reluctantly obeyed. She didn't like the idea of leaving both the money and the ticket there, but she was afraid he'd ask more questions if she protested.

He was a long time at it. He was on the phone a while, talking in a muffled voice. Then he was poring through his books. Once he got up and went back into the baggage room and stayed away for several minutes.

It was almost four forty-five. If he didn't hurry, she might miss the five o'clock bus. She got up and got a drink from the water cooler. The water was warm, and somebody had dropped a piece of gum on the drain. She went back to the red plastic seat still thirsty.

The clock said four forty-eight when the clerk came back and sat down without even looking her way.

"My ticket?"

But just then a man and woman came in, and the clerk got busy with them. It wasn't fair. She'd been there waiting since four thirty. Gilly stood up and started for the counter. She didn't even see the policeman until she felt his hand on her arm.

Gilly snatched her arm back as she looked to see who had touched her.

"Where you headed, little girl?" He spoke quietly as though not to disturb anyone.

"To see my mother," said Gilly tightly. Oh, god, make him go away.

"All the way to San Francisco by yourself?" She knew then the clerk had called him. Damn!

"Yes."

"I see," he said with a quick look at the clerk, who was now staring at them with both eyes well open.

"I haven't done anything wrong."

"Nobody's charging you with anything." The policeman pulled his cap straight and said in a very careful, very patient voice, "Who you been staying with here in the area?"

She didn't have to answer him. It was none of his business.

"Look. Somebody's going to be worried about you."

Like hell.

He cleared his throat. "What about giving me your telephone number? So I can just check things out?"

She glared at him.

He coughed and cleared his throat again and looked up at the clerk. She might have gotten away in that instant—except for the money. Where could she go without the money? "I think," the policeman was saying, "I'd better take her in for a little talk."

The clerk nodded. He seemed to be enjoying himself. "Here's the money she brought in." He held up a manila envelope. The policeman took her gently by the arm and walked her to the counter. The clerk handed him the envelope.

"That's my money," Gilly protested.

"I'll just bet it is, kid," the clerk said with a fake smile.

If she had known what to do, she would have done it. She tried to make her brain tell her, but it lay frozen in her skull like a woolly mammoth deep in a glacier. All the way to the station she asked it, Shall I jump out of the car at the next light and run? Should I just forget about the damn money? But the woolly mammoth slept on, refusing to stir a limb in her behalf.

In a back room behind the police station's long counter two policemen tried to question her. The new one, a big blond, was asking the first one: "She ain't got no ID?"

"Well, I'm not going to search her, and Judy's gone out to get her supper."

"What about the suitcase?"

"Yeah, better check through there."

She wanted to yell at them to leave her stuff alone, but she couldn't break through the ice.

The blond policeman riffled carelessly through her clothes. He found Courtney's picture almost at once. "This your mother, kid?"

"Put that down," she whispered.

"Oh, now she's talking."

"She said to put her picture down, Mitchell."

"OK, OK. Just trying to do my job." He put the picture down and continued to poke through the suitcase. "Bingo," he said, picking up the postcard. He read it carefully before handing it to the other officer. "All here, Rhine. Name and current address. And big surprise! She does know somebody in San Francisco."

The one called Rhine read the postcard and then came and stooped down beside her chair.

"Is this your father's address here?" he asked, pointing at the address on the card.

She sat perfectly still, staring him down.

Rhine shook his head, stood up, and handed the card back to Mitchell. "Check out who lives at that address and give them a call, will you?"

Within a half hour, a red-faced Trotter, holding the hand of a white-faced William Ernest, puffed through the station-house door. Her eye immediately caught Gilly's, still seated in the room on the other side of the counter. She tried to smile, but Gilly jerked away from the gaze. The policewoman was back from her supper and on duty at the counter.

"Maime . . . Maime Trotter"—Trotter was puffing worse than if she'd run up her steps—"Got a . . . taxi . . . waiting . . . No money . . . to . . . pay . . . him."

"Just a minute, please." Judy, the policewoman, came in and spoke quietly to Rhine, and then Rhine got up and they both went out to the counter. The only part of the conversation Gilly could make out was Trotter's breathy replies:

"Foster child . . . Yes—somewhere . . . San Francisco, yes, maybe so . . . County Social Services . . . Uh—Miz Miriam Ellis . . . yes . . . yes . . . no . . . no . . . no . . . Can someone pay the taxicab? Still waiting out there. . . ." Officer Rhine gave Trotter the yellow envelope. She sighed and nodded, taking out some money which she handed to him. He handed it to Mitchell, who handed it to the policewoman, who frowned but went out anyway to pay the cab driver.

"No, no," Trotter was saying. "Of course not. She's just a baby . . ." Trotter was still shaking her head at Rhine as he brought her back around the counter, W.E. clutching at her shabby coat.

Trotter's breath had returned, but her voice shook as she spoke to Gilly from the doorway. "I come to take you home, Gilly, honey. Me and William Ernest come up to get you."

Rhine came all the way in and stooped down again beside her. "Mrs. Trotter is not going to press charges. She wants you to come back."

Press charges? Oh, the money. Did the stupid man think that Trotter would have her arrested? But how could she go back? Gilly the Great, who couldn't even run away? Botched the job. She stared at her fingers. The nails were grubby. She hated grubby fingernails.

"Gilly, honey . . ."

"Don't you want to go home?" Rhine was asking.

Want to go home? Don't I want to go home? Where in the hell do you think I was headed?

When she didn't answer him, Rhine stood up. "Maybe we should keep her tonight and call Social Services in the morning."

"You mean to lock the child up?"

"She'd be safe. It would just be overnight."

"You don't think for one minute I'm going to let you lock a child of mine up in jail?"

"Maybe it would be best," Rhine said quietly.

"Best? What do you mean? What are you trying to say?"

"She really doesn't seem to want to go with you, Mrs. Trotter. Now, I don't know . . ."

"O, my dear Lord, you don't—O, my dear Lord—"

It was the closest to cursing Gilly had ever heard Trotter come to. She looked up into the fat, stricken face.

"O, my dear Lord. What can I do?"

"Gilly! Gilly!" William Ernest streaked across the room and began to beat his fists on her knees. "Come home, Gilly. Please come home! Please, please!" The blood vessels stood out blue and strained on his white neck.

The ice in her frozen brain rumbled and cracked. She stood up and took his hand.

"Thank you, precious Jesus," Trotter said.

Rhine cleared his throat. "You don't have to go unless you want to. You know that, don't you?"

Gilly nodded. Trotter in the doorway lifted her arms, the brown purse dangling from one of them; the faulty clasp flew open as she did so. She dropped her arms, embarrassed, and forced the purse shut. "I need another taxi, officer."

"I'll get Mitchell to drive you," he said.

Pow

THERE was a fight between Trotter and Miss Ellis. Gilly heard the sounds of battle in the living room when she came in from school the next afternoon.

"Never, never, never!" Trotter was bellowing like an old cow deprived of its calf.

Gilly stopped still in the hallway, closing the door without a sound.

"Mrs. Trotter, nobody at the agency looks at it as any indication of failure on your part—"

"You think I care what the agency thinks?"

"You're one of our most capable foster parents. You've been with us for more than twenty years. This won't affect your record with us. You're too valuable—"

"I don't give a spit about no record. You ain't taking Gilly."

"We're trying to think of you—"

"No, you ain't. If you was thinking of me, you'd never come to me with such a fool notion."

"This is a troubled child, Maime. She needs special—"

"No! I ain't giving her up. Never!"

"If you won't think of yourself, think of William Ernest. He's come too far in the last year to let—I've seen myself how she upsets him."

"It was William Ernest got her to come home last night." Trotter's voice was square and stubborn.

"Because he saw how upset *you* were. That doesn't mean she can't damage him."

"William Ernest has lived with me for over two years. He's gonna make it. I know he is. Sometimes, Miz Ellis, you gotta walk on your heel and favor your toe even if it makes your heel a little sore."

"I don't understand what you're driving at."

"Somebody's got to favor Gilly for a little while. She's long overdue."

"That's exactly it, Mrs. Trotter. I'm quite aware of Gilly's needs. I've been her caseworker for nearly five years, and whether you believe it or not, I really care about her. But I don't think it's her needs we're talking about right now, is it?"

"What do you mean?"

"It's *your* needs." Said very quietly.

A silence and then, "Yes, Lord knows, I need her." A funny broken sound like a sob came from Trotter. "I like to die when I found her gone."

"You can't do that, Mrs. Trotter. You can't let them tear you to pieces."

"Don't try to tell a mother how to feel."

"You're a foster mother, Mrs. Trotter." Miss Ellis's voice was firm. "You can't afford to forget that."

Gilly's whole body was engulfed in a great aching. She opened and slammed the front door, pretending to have just come in. This time they heard her.

"That you Gilly, honey?"

She went to the doorway of the living room. Both women were on their feet, flushed as though they'd been running a race.

"Well, Gilly," Miss Ellis began, her voice glittering like a fake Christmas tree.

"Miz Ellis," Trotter broke in loudly, "was just saying how it's up to you." There was a flash of alarm from the social worker which Trotter pretended not to see. "You want to stay on here with William Ernest and me—that's fine. You want her to find you someplace else—that's fine, too. You got to be the one to decide." Her eyes shifted uneasily toward Miss Ellis.

"What about," Gilly asked, her mouth going dry as a stale soda cracker, "what about my real mother?"

Miss Ellis' eyebrows jumped. "I wrote her, Gilly, several months ago, when we decided to move you from the Nevinses. She never answered."

"She wrote me. She wants me to come out there."

Miss Ellis looked at Trotter. "Yes. I know about the postcard," the caseworker said.

Those damned cops reading people's mail and blabbing, passing it around, snickering over it probably.

"Gilly. If—if she had really wanted you with her—"

"She does want me. She said so!"

"Then why hasn't she come to get you?" A hard edge had come into Miss Ellis's voice, and her eyebrows were twitching madly. "It's been over eight years, Gilly. Even when she lived close by, she never came to see you."

"It's different now!"—wasn't it?—"She's gonna come! She really wants me!"—didn't she?

Trotter came over to her and laid her arm heavily on Gilly's shoulder. "If she knowed you—if she just knowed what a girl she has—she'd be here in a minute."

Oh, Trotter, don't be a fool. If she knew what I was like, she'd never come. It takes someone stupid like you—Gilly removed herself gently from under the weighty embrace and addressed herself to Miss Ellis, eye to eyebrow.

"Till she comes . . . till she comes for me, I guess I'll just stay here."

Trotter wiped her face with her big hand and snuffled. "Well, I'm sure we'll be seeing you sometime, Miz Ellis."

The social worker wasn't going to be swept out quite so easily. She set her feet apart as though fearing Trotter might try to remove her bodily and said, "Officer Rhine told me when he called that you had well over a hundred dollars with you last night."

"Yeah?"

It came out sassy, but Miss Ellis just squinted her eyes and went on: "It's hard to believe that it was all your money."

"So?"

"So I call taking other people's money *stealing,* Miss Hopkins."

"Yeah?"

Trotter patted Gilly's arm as if to shush her. "So do we, Miz Ellis. Surely you don't think this is the first time something like this has happened to me over the last twenty years?"

"No, I know it's not."

"Then how 'bout trusting me to handle it?"

Miss Ellis shook her head and smoothed her pants suit down over her rump before she put on her coat. "I'll be in close touch," she said.

Trotter nearly shoved her out the front door. "We're going to do just fine. Don't worry your pretty little head about us, hear?"

"I get paid to worry, Mrs. Trotter."

Trotter smiled impatiently and closed the door quickly. When she turned back toward Gilly, her face was like Mount Rushmore stone.

Gilly blinked in surprise at the sudden and absolute change.

"I don't take lightly to stealing, you know."

Gilly nodded. No use pretending sassiness.

"I figure that money ain't all mine, right?"

"No."

"Well, where'd you get it?"

"I found it," said Gilly softly.

Trotter came over and with two hands lifted Gilly's face to look into her own. "Where did you get it, Gilly?"

"I found it behind some books next door."

Trotter dropped her hands in disbelief. "You stole from Mr. Randolph?"

"It was just lying there behind the books. He probably didn't even—"

"Gilly, you stole it. Don't put no fancy name on it. It was his, and you took it, right?"

"I guess so."

"How much?"

"Uh, for—thir—"

"Don't fool with me. How much?"

"Forty-four dollars," Gilly said miserably.

"Well, you gotta take it back."

"I can't." Trotter stood there, hand on hip, staring at her until Gilly continued, "I gave five dollars to Agnes Stokes."

"You did, huh?"

Gilly nodded.

"Well"—a great sigh—"I'll lend you the five to pay Mr. Randolph back, and you can work it off."

Giving back Mr. Randolph's money was not as bad as it might have been. The old man apparently had no idea that there had been any money behind his books. Either he'd forgotten, or it had been put there by his wife, dead long before Trotter's Melvin. At any rate, when Gilly gave the forty-four dollars to him, Trotter looming behind her like a mighty army, he accepted her mumbled explanation without showing shock or undue curiosity, but with a strange little dignity.

"Thank you," he said, for once not doubling the phrase. He put the money in his pocket, rubbed his hands together briefly, and then put out his hand to be led to supper.

Gilly hesitated for a moment, waiting for the sermon that was bound to pour forth, if not from him, surely from Trotter. But neither spoke, so she took Mr. Randolph's hand, instead of his elbow as she usually did, as a kind of thank you.

Trotter had obviously never heard of either the minimum-wage or the child-labor laws. She posted the following sign in the kitchen:

Washing dishes and cleaning kitchen	*10¢*
Vacuuming downstairs	*10¢*
Cleaning both bathrooms including floors	*10¢*
Dusting	*10¢*
Helping William Ernest with schoolwork, one hour	*25¢*

Gilly began to spend a lot of time with W.E. She discovered several things. One was that the boy was not as dumb as he looked. If you held back and didn't press him, he could often figure out things for himself, but when you crowded him, he would choke right up, and if you laughed at him, he'd throw his hands up as if to protect his head from a blow. It finally occurred to Gilly that he really thought she would smack him every time he made a mistake.

Which was why, of course, Trotter tiptoed around the boy as though he would shatter at the least commotion, and why she was death on anyone she caught fooling around with him.

But it wasn't going to work. W.E. wasn't a fluted antique cup in Mrs. Nevins's china cupboard. He was a kid—a foster kid. And if he didn't toughen up, what would happen to him when there was no Trotter to look after him?

So Gilly asked him, "What do you do when somebody socks you?"

His squinty little eyes went wild behind the glasses.

"I'm not going to hit you. I was just wondering what you do."

He stuck his right index finger into his mouth and began to tug at the nail.

She took out the finger and studied his stubby-nailed

hand for a minute. "Nothing wrong with this, I can see. Ever think of smacking them back?"

He shook his head wide-eyed.

"You going to go through life letting people pick on you?"

He hung his head. The finger went back in.

"Look, William Ernest"—she bent over close to his ear and whispered hoarsely into it—"I'm going to teach you how to fight. No charge or anything. Then when some big punk comes up to you and tries to start something, you can just let them have it."

His finger dropped from his mouth as he stared at her, unbelieving.

"You hear how I fought six boys one day—all by myself?"

He nodded solemnly.

"Before I get through with you, you're going to do the same thing. *Pow! Pow! Pow! Pow! Pow! Pow!*" She landed six imaginary punches sending six imaginary bullies flying.

"Pow," he echoed softly, tentatively doubling up his fist and giving a feeble swing.

"First thing, when somebody yells at you, don't throw your hands up"—she imitated him—"and act like you think they're going to kill you."

"Pow?" He swung his little fist in a kind of question mark.

"Naw, not *first* thing. See, they may not be even meaning to hit you. First thing is, you take a deep breath—" She filled her diaphragm and waited while he tried to imitate her, his ribs poking through his shirt. "Then you yell like this: *Get the hell outa my way!*"

Before the sentence was out, Trotter was filling the doorway like the wrath of God Almighty.

"OK, OK," Gilly said. "Leave out the hell part. The main thing—"

"What are you kids doing? I thought I was paying you to help William Ernest with his reading?"

"Naw. This is on my own time. No charge."

Trotter looked anxiously at W.E. He was standing on tiptoe, fists clenched, eyes squeezed shut in his red face, sucking in a huge breath.

"Get the hell out my way!" He turned to Gilly, smiling. "Was that good, Gilly?"

"Better leave the hell part out in front of Trotter. But that was pretty good for a start. Really not bad."

"Gilly," said Trotter.

"Look, Trotter. He's got to learn to take care of himself, and I'm the best damn—the best teacher around."

Trotter just went on standing in the doorway as though she couldn't think what to do next, when the little guy marched over to her, put his fists up in front of her huge bosom, took in a breath, and said squeakily, "Get out my way."

Tears started in the woman's eyes. She threw her arms around W.E. and bear-hugged him.

"I was just practicing, Trotter. I didn't mean you."

"I know, William Ernest, honey," she said. "I know."

"He's got to learn to take care of himself in the world, Trotter."

The big woman wiped her face with her apron and sniffed. "Don't I know that, baby?" She patted the boy and straightened up. "How 'bout you finishing this lesson outside? I don't b'lieve it's something I want to listen to."

"C'mon, Gilly." William Ernest slid around Trotter and started for the back door. *"Pow! Pow!"* they could hear him exploding softly down the hall.

"I'm not going to teach him to pick on people," Gilly said, "just how to take care of himself. He can't come hiding behind your skirt every time someone looks at him cross-eyed."

"I s'pose not."

"Even real mothers can't watch out for kids the rest of their lives, and you're just his foster mother."

"So they keep telling me."

Gilly hadn't meant to be cruel, but she needed to make Trotter understand. "If he knows how to read and how to stick up for himself, he'll be OK."

"You got it all figured out, ain't you Gilly, honey?" She relaxed into a smile. "Well, I ain't stopping your boxing lessons. I just don't care to watch."

Boxing lessons? The woman was a throwback to another century. Gilly started to pass her at the door, but as she brushed by the big body, Trotter grabbed her and planted a wet kiss on her forehead. One hand went up automatically to wipe the spot, but a look at Trotter's face, and Gilly stopped her arm midway.

"Don't know what got into me," Trotter mumbled, trying to turn it into a joke. "I know you don't allow no kissing. Sometimes I just haul off and go crazy."

"At Sunday school Miss Applegate calls it demon possession."

"Does she now? Demon possession, is it?" She began to laugh so hard, Gilly could feel the boards vibrating under her feet. "Demon possession—Mercy, girl, I'd have to catch me a jet to keep one step ahead of you. Well—you better get going before the devil grabs me one more time."

She waved her hand to land a mock spank on Gilly's bottom, but by the time it swept the air, Gilly's bottom along with the rest of her was well down the hall.

The Visitor

THE week before Thanksgiving, Mr. Randolph came down with the flu. It wasn't a bad case as flu goes, but he was an old man, and any kind of sickness, as Trotter said, was harder on the old. So with many rest stops for Trotter to recapture her wind, she and Gilly brought the rollaway cot down from the attic and set it up in the dining room, turning the never-used room into a sickroom for Mr. Randolph.

There had been a great discussion as to whether big lawyer son should be notified. Mr. Randolph was sure that if his son knew he was sick, he would be snatched away to Virginia never to return again. Trotter recognized this appalling possibility, but maintained that there was some moral obligation to inform next of kin when one took to one's bed.

"Suppose he just shows up one day and finds you sick—then he won't trust you no more. He's sure to take you away then."

But Mr. Randolph thought it worth the risk, and they had compromised by having Mr. Randolph move in, so Trotter could keep a close eye on him.

"Now what happens if you die on me?"

"I promise not to die in your house. You have my solemn oath."

"Gilly, if he looks peaky, we carry him next door as fast as we can go. I ain't gonna be sued by no big Virginia lawyer."

Mr. Randolph raised up off the rollaway. "If I die on you, you can sue me, Mrs. Trotter. You can take me for every cent I have." He lay back, giggling and gasping.

"Humph, every cent. You won't even have no social security if you're dead. Better not die, that's all I got to say."

"I promise not to die, but with these two beautiful ladies nursing me, I may decide to remain ill for a long, long time."

"Well, that's a chance I got to take, beautiful as I am. But if you ain't well a week from today, you're gonna miss out on the turkey and stuffings."

So Mr. Randolph swore a solemn oath to be well by Thanksgiving. As it turned out, he was a little better, but by then both Trotter and William Ernest were down with the bug.

Trotter fought going to bed, but her fever was high, and she was too dizzy to stand up. Despite her protests, Gilly stayed home from school Tuesday and Wednesday to nurse the three of them, and Thanksgiving Day found her exhausted from going up and down the stairs and from bedside to bedside.

It occurred to her that if she could get sick, too, no one would blame her for collapsing, but, of course, she didn't catch anything, except irritability from not sleeping properly and worrying. She called Mr. Randolph's doctor, Trotter's doctor, and the pediatrician, but no one gave her any help. The patients were to stay in bed and take aspirin for the fever.

Gilly chopped an aspirin in half with the butcher knife for William Ernest. One piece flew out of sight under the stove and the other piece, which she got down the boy's throat with no little difficulty, came up again promptly, along with the bowl of soup she'd coaxed down earlier. She was afraid to try any more aspirin.

Trotter told her to wipe his face and arms and legs with a cold cloth, which seemed to help the fever a little, but the child was still miserable, and clean as she might, the smell of old vomit hung in the room.

The whole house was a mess, in fact. Even rooms like the living room and kitchen, which nobody but she went into, began to look as though they had been bombed. She was simply too whipped to pick up after herself.

By Thursday she couldn't have cared less about Thanksgiving. The turkey Trotter had bought was relentlessly defrosting on the refrigerator shelf, but there was nothing else to remind her as she sat at the kitchen table dressed in jeans and a shrunken T-shirt, chewing her late breakfast of bologna sandwich that the rest of the nation would soon be feasting and celebrating.

The doorbell rang. She jumped at the sound. Her first fear was that lawyer son had not believed Mr. Randolph's excuses for not coming to Virginia for Thanksgiving and had come to get him. Then, with annoyance, she realized that it was probably Agnes Stokes, sneaking around to find out why Gilly had skipped school for two days.

But when she opened the door, it was to a small, plump woman whose gray hair peaked out from under a close-fitting black felt hat. She wore black gloves and a black-and-tweed overcoat, which was a little too long to be fashionable, and carried a slightly worn black alligator bag over one arm. The woman, who was an inch or so shorter than she was, looked up into Gilly's face with a sort of peculiar expression, whether frightened or hungry, Gilly couldn't have said. At any rate, it made her shift uncomfortably and push at her bangs until she remembered two of Trotter's trusty sentences for emergency use and offered both of them.

"We're not buying anything today, thank you, and we're faithful members of the Baptist Church." She hurried to close the door.

"No, wait, please," the lady said. "Galadriel—Hopkins?"

Gilly yanked the door back open. "Who are you?" she blurted out, as awkwardly as William Ernest might have.

"I'm"—It was the woman's turn to look uncomfortable. "I'm—I suppose I'm your grandmother."

Somehow Gilly would have been less surprised if the woman had said fairy godmother.

"May I come in?"

Dumbly Gilly stepped back and let her.

The sound of snoring poured forth from the dining room. Gilly willed the woman not to look, not to stare at the funny little brown face poked up above the faded quilt, the mouth gaped and trembling with each noisy breath.

But, of course, the woman looked, jerked her head slightly at the sight, and then turned quickly back to Gilly.

"Gilly, honey, who is it?" Damn! Trotter must have heard the bell.

"OK, Trotter, I got it," Gilly yelled, as she tugged at her shrunken T-shirt (the last half-clean one) and tried to make it cover her navel. "Want to sit down?" she asked the visitor.

"Yes. Please."

Gilly led the way into the living room and backed up to the couch, sticking a hand out toward the brown chair.

Plunk. They both sat down in unison like string puppets, the lady right on the edge of the chair so that her short feet could touch the floor.

"So—" The woman was bobbing her little black hat. Did anyone in the world wear hats these days? "So—"

Gilly was trying to take it in. This—this little old lady in the old-fashioned hat and coat—was Courtney's mother? In all Gilly's fantasies, Courtney had never had a mother. She had always been—existing from before time—like a goddess in perpetual perfection.

"I'm right, aren't I? You are Galadriel?" Her voice was Southern but smooth, like silk to Trotter's burlap.

Gilly nodded.

"My daughter—" The woman fumbled in her purse and brought out a letter. "My daughter left home many—" She snapped the purse shut and raised her eyes to meet Gilly's puzzled ones. "—many years ago. I—my husband and I never . . . I'm sorry . . ."

Helplessly Gilly watched the little woman stumbling for words, trying to tell a painful story and not knowing how.

"My husband—" She tried to smile. "Your grandfather died—nearly twelve years ago."

Perhaps she should say something, thought Gilly. "Jeez, that's too bad."

"Yes. Yes, it was." The woman was pushing hard against the words to keep from crying. Gilly knew the trick. Oh, boy, how well she knew that one. "We—I tried to contact Courtney, your mother, at the time, of course. But—I was not able to. In fact—" The pitch of her voice went up. She stopped trying to talk and took a handkerchief from her purse, barely touching each nostril before putting it away.

Go ahead and blow, honey. It'll make you feel better. Trotter would have said it, but Gilly couldn't quite get it out.

"As a matter of fact—" The woman had recovered herself enough to continue. "As a matter of fact, this letter—this letter is the first direct word we've—I've had from my daughter in thirteen years."

"You're kidding," said Gilly. She felt sorry even though the woman's pain didn't seem to have anything to do with her.

"I didn't even know she'd had a ba— Wouldn't you think she'd want her own mother to know she'd had a baby?"

This was obviously the point where she, Gilly, was supposed to come into the story, but it still seemed far too remote, like something that had happened once to a friend of a friend. She tried to nod in a sympathetic manner.

"Gilly. I called you and called you." William Ernest stood clutching the doorway for support, his face still flushed with fever. He was dressed in his long grayish-white underwear. At the sight of a stranger, he stopped dead.

The woman looked at him once hard; then as she had done with Mr. Randolph, she looked quickly away.

"I'm sorry, W.E.," Gilly said. "I didn't hear you call me. What's the matter?" As soon as she asked, she knew. His long johns were wet all down the front. Gilly jumped up. " 'Scuse me, I'll be right back." She hustled the boy back to his room, as fast as you could hustle a boy who was still weak from fever and lack of food. It was hard to be patient with him on the stairs. "You shouldn't have come downstairs, William Ernest. You're sick."

"I wet," he said sadly. "I couldn't help it."

She sighed. "I know. When you're sick, you just can't help it." She got him the last clean underwear, which was short and wouldn't be as warm, and changed his sheets. She took a dry blanket off her own bed. He climbed in and turned his back to her at once, his strength exhausted.

"Gilly, honey," Trotter called drowsily as Gilly passed her door. "You got company down there?"

"Just playing the TV." Gilly smoothed her hair and tugged again at her shirt as she went down the stairs. She knew she looked a wreck. She must have shocked the poor old lady right out of her socks.

The woman gave a weak smile and nodded when Gilly came in. "You poor little thing," she said.

Gilly looked behind to see if W.E. had followed her down.

"Bless your heart." There was no one else around.

"Me?"

"Courtney didn't exaggerate. I'm just so glad you wrote her, my dear. How could they have put you in such a place?"

"Me?" What was the woman talking about? What place?

"I know I shouldn't have burst in upon you like this, but I felt I had to see for myself before I talked with your caseworker. Will you forgive me, my dear, for—"

There was a heavy thump, thump, thumping on the stairs. Both of them sat stark still and listened as it drew inexorably nearer.

"Ohhh!" The little lady gasped.

Swaying in the doorway was a huge barefoot apparition in striped men's pajamas, gray hair cascading over its shoulders, a wild look in its eyes.

"I forgot!" It was moaning as it swayed. "I forgot!" It grabbed frantically at the woodwork. "I forgot."

Gilly sprang to her feet. "What did you forget, dammit?"

"The turkey"—Trotter was almost sobbing now—"Fifteen dollars and thirty-eight cents, and I let it go to rot." She gave no sign that she noticed the visitor.

"Nothing's gone to rot. I would have smelled it, wouldn't I?"—Gilly couldn't help sneaking a sideways glance at the little woman, who looked almost as frightened as W.E. did when he spied a new word in his reading book—"Go back to bed, Trotter. I'll put it right in the oven."

The huge woman made an effort to obey, but nearly fell down just trying to turn around. "I better set a minute," she panted. "My head's light."

Gilly grabbed the back of the striped pajamas with both hands and half dragged, half supported the faltering frame toward the couch. But she knew—just as one knows when piling on one final block that the tower will fall—she knew they couldn't make it.

"Oh, mercy!" Trotter gave a little cry as she came crashing down, pinning Gilly to the rug beneath her. The woman lay there, flapping on her back like a giant overturned tortoise. "Well, I done it now." She gave a short hysterical giggle. "Squished you juicy."

"What? What is it?" The third night-clothed actor had made his entrance.

"You awright, ain't you, Gilly, honey?" asked Trotter, and without waiting for an answer, "S'awright, Mr. Randolph."

"But someone fell. I heard someone fall."

"Yeah, I fell awright." Trotter was rocking her huge trunk in a vain effort to get to her feet. "But it's OK, ain't it, Gilly, honey?"

"Just roll, Trotter," said a muffled voice. "Roll over and you'll be off me."

"What's that? What's that?" Mr. Randolph squeaked.

"It's poor little Gilly." Trotter grunted and with a supreme *ahhhhhhh* rolled off onto the floor.

"Miss Gilly?" he was asking anxiously.

"I'm OK, Mr. Randolph." Gilly got up, dusted herself off, then took him by the hand. "Let's get you back into bed."

By the time she returned from the dining room, Trotter had somehow hoisted herself into a sitting position on the couch, and dizzily clutching the cushions with both hands, had found herself face to face with a white-faced stranger.

"You said wasn't no one here," she accused Gilly.

The visitor, for her part, was teetering on the absolute brink of the brown chair in what Gilly took to be a state of total shock. But the small lady proved capable of speech. "I think I'd better go," she said, standing up. "I don't seem to have come at a very good time."

Gilly followed her to the door, eager to get her out of the looney bin the house had suddenly become.

"I'm glad to have met you," she said as politely as she could. She had no wish for the woman to think poorly of her. After all, she was—or, at least, she claimed to be—Courtney's mother.

The woman paused, resisting Gilly's efforts to hurry her out the door. She reached over abruptly and pecked Gilly on the cheek. "I'll get you out of here soon," she whispered fiercely. "I promise you, I will."

Fatigue had made Gilly stupid. She simply nodded and closed the door quickly behind the little form. It wasn't until she'd gotten Trotter back in bed and was putting the turkey in the oven that the woman's meaning came clear.

Oh, my god.

Well, it didn't matter what the woman thought. Miss Ellis could explain about today. No one could make her leave here, not when everyone needed her so. Besides—Trotter wouldn't let them take her. "Never," she had said. "Never, never, never."

Never and Other Canceled Promises

DREAD lay on Gilly's stomach like a dead fish on the beach. Even when you don't look at it, the stink pervades everything. She finally made herself admit the fact that it was her own letter that had driven Courtney to get in touch with her mother after a silence of thirteen years. What had it said? She couldn't even remember what the letter had said. And Courtney's letter had, in turn, brought the little lady up from Virginia to spy her out.

And now what? It was not at all the way she'd imagined the ending. In Gilly's story Courtney herself came sweeping in like a goddess queen, reclaiming the long-lost princess. There was no place in this dream for dumpy old-fashioned ladies with Southern speech, or barefoot fat women in striped pajamas, or blind old black men who recited poetry by heart and snored with their mouths open

—or crazy, heart-ripping little guys who went *"pow"* and still wet their stupid beds.

But she had done it. Like Bluebeard's wife, she'd opened the forbidden door and someday she would have to look inside.

By Saturday night, when the turkey was finally upon the kitchen table with the four of them gathered gratefully around it, there was still no word from either Miss Ellis or the Commonwealth of Virginia.

Trotter and W.E. looked deathly white, and Mr. Randolph was the shade of ashes, but they had thrown off the crankiness of their illness and were eating the cold dry meat with chirpy expressions of delight.

"I declare, Miss Gilly, you are the only person I know who can rival Mrs. Trotter's culinary skill." A statement Gilly knew for a bald-faced if kindly intended lie.

"The potatoes are lumpy," she responded, doing some tardy mashing with the tines of her fork.

"Mine ain't lumpy," W.E. whispered loyally.

"They're just fine, Gilly, honey. I think you gave yourself the only lump in the pot. Mine's smooth as ice cream. I don't know how long it's been"—Trotter paused, head tilted as though reaching far back into her memory—"I don't think food's tasted this good to me since . . . since before Melvin took sick the last time." She beamed, having delivered the ultimate compliment.

Gilly blushed despite herself. They were all liars, but how could you mind?

"Gilly, honey"—Trotter stopped a forkful in midair—"who was that woman come here the other day? What she want?"

Now it was Gilly's turn to lie. "Well, I think she was about to ask us to join her church, but before I could tell her about being faithful Baptists, all of you came roaring in looking like three-day-old death. Scared her straight out the door."

"Me, too?" asked W.E.

"You were the worst one, William Ernest. She saw you standing there, all tall and white and skinny, calling my name, '*Gi——lyeeeeeee. Gi——lyeeeeeee.*' She nearly swallowed her dentures."

"Really?"

"Would I lie?"

"*Pow,*" he said.

"Well, she sure got up and hightailed it when I come in and bulldozed poor Gilly clean through the carpet." Trotter snickered. "I reckon she thought she was fixing to be next."

"What you do?" asked W. E.

"I fell smack down on Gilly and couldn't get back up for the life of me."

Mr. Randolph was giggling. "I was awakened by a terrible crash. I came as fast as I could. . . ."

"Then all you could hear was this little squeak, "Roll off me, Trotter. Roll off me!' " Trotter repeated herself getting nearer to hysterics with each repetition. "Roll off me!' "

"Did you roll off her?"

"Mercy, boy, it weren't that easy. I huffed and I puffed . . ."

"And you blew the house down!" William Ernest pounded the table, and they all laughed until the tears came, taking turns to cry out, "Roll off me!" and "Not by the hair of my chinny-chin-chin!"

"Roll off me!" was not what Gilly remembered saying,

but it didn't matter. It was so good to have them all well, laughing, and eating together. Besides, in their merriment, the little gray-haired lady had slipped from their thoughts.

But Monday came, and the long holiday weekend was over. Gilly, armed with an absence excuse that looked more like a commendation for bravery in battle, and William Ernest, cheerful but pale, went back to school. Mr. Randolph moved home again, and Trotter, taking time to rest every few minutes, began to straighten up the house. And, as Gilly learned later, by the time Miss Ellis reached her desk at twelve after nine, there was already a note upon it directing her to call a Mrs. Rutherford Hopkins in Loudoun County, Virginia.

Gilly had waited after school at William Ernest's classroom door. She didn't want him taking on any fights while he was still wobbly from the flu, and she knew, with her reputation, that no one would sneeze in his direction, if he were walking with her.

Agnes Stokes danced along beside them, trying to entice Gilly to join her in a trip to the deli, but Gilly was too intent on getting W.E. home.

"Or we could go to my house and call people on the phone and breathe weird."

"Come off it, Agnes. That is so dumb."

"No, it really scares 'em. I've had 'em screaming all over the place at me."

"It is dumb, Agnes. Dumb, dumb, dumb."

"You always say that when you don't think it up yourself."

"Right. I don't think up dumb things."

"C'mon, Gilly. Let's do *something.* You ain't done nothing with me for a long time."

"My family's been sick."

Agnes sneered. "What family? Everybody knows . . ."

"My brother." At this William Ernest raised his head up proudly. "My mother. And my—uncle."

"Gilly Hopkins. *That* is the dumbest idea . . ."

Gilly spun around and jammed her nose down onto Agnes's face, her mouth going sideways and narrow exactly like Humphrey Bogart's on TV. "You want to discuss this further—sweetheart?"

Agnes backed up. "It's too dumb to talk about even," she said, still backing. "Really dumb."

William Ernest slid close to Gilly so they couldn't help touching as they walked. "Bet I could beat her up," he whispered.

"Yeah," Gilly said. "But don't bother. Hell, it wouldn't be fair. You against that poor little puny thing."

Trotter was at the door, opening it before they reached the porch. Gilly went cold. You could tell something was badly wrong by the way the woman's smile twisted and her body sagged.

Sure enough. Miss Ellis was sitting on the brown chair. This time the two women had not been fighting, just waiting for her. Gilly's heart gave a little spurt and flopped over like a dud rocket. She sat down quickly on the couch and hugged herself to keep from shaking.

Suddenly Miss Ellis began to speak, her voice bright and fake like a laxative commercial: "Well, I've got some rather astounding news for you, Gilly." Gilly hugged herself tighter. The announcement of "news" had never meant anything in her life except a new move. "Your mother . . ."

"My mother's coming?" She was sorry immediately for

the outburst. Miss Ellis' eyebrows launched into the twitchy dance they always seemed to at the mention of the words, "my mother."

"No." Twitch, twitch. "Your mother is still in California. But your grandmother . . ."

What have I to do with her?

". . . your mother's mother called the office this morning, and then drove up all the way from Virginia to see me."

Gilly stole a look at Trotter, who was sitting bolt upright at the far end of the couch, rubbing W.E.'s back, her hand up under his jacket and her eyes like those of a bear on a totem pole.

"She and your mother"—twitch—"want you to go with her."

"With who?"

"With your grandmother. *Permanently.*" The social worker seemed to be dangling that last word before Gilly's nose, as if expecting her to jump up on her hind legs and dance for it.

Gilly leaned back. What did they take her for? "I don't want to live with her." she said.

"Gilly, you've been saying ever since you were old enough to talk . . ."

"I never said I wanted to live with *her!* I said I wanted to live with my *mother.* She's not my mother. I don't even know her!"

"You don't know your mother, either."

"I do, too! I remember her! Don't tell me what I remember and what I don't!"

Miss Ellis suddenly looked tired. "God help the children of the flower children," she said.

"I remember her."

"Yes." The pretty face grew sharp with tension, as the social worker leaned forward. "Your mother wants you to go to your grandmother's. I talked to her long distance."

"Didn't she tell you she wanted me to come to California like she wrote me?"

"No, she said she wanted you to go to your grandmother's house."

"They can't make me go there."

Gently, "Yes, Gilly, they can."

She felt as though the walls were squeezing in on her; she looked around wildly for some way to escape. She fixed on Trotter.

"Trotter won't let them take me, will you Trotter?"

Trotter flinched but kept on looking wooden-faced at Miss Ellis and rubbing W.E.'s back.

"Trotter! Look at me! You said you'd never let me go. I heard you." She was yelling at the totem pole now. "Never! Never! Never! That's what you said!" She was on her feet stamping and screaming. The two women watched her, but numbly as though she were behind glass and there was no way that they could reach in to her.

It was William Ernest who broke through. He slid from under Trotter's big hand and ran to Gilly, snatched the band of her jacket, and pulled on it until she stopped screaming and stood still. She looked down into his little near-sighted eyes, full of tears behind the thick lenses.

"Don't cry, Gilly."

"I'm not crying"—she jerked her jacket out of his hands—"I'm yelling!" He froze, his hands up as though the jacket were still between his fingers.

"Oh, hell, kid." She grabbed his two fists. "It's gonna be

OK." She sighed and sat down. He sat down next to her, so close that she could feel the warmth of him from her arm through her thigh. It gave her the strength to look up again defiantly.

Miss Ellis was looking at the two of them like a bird watcher onto a rare species. But the big woman—Gilly could see the pain breaking up the totem-pole stare—Trotter shuddered to her feet like an old circus elephant.

"You tell the child what's got to be done. C'mon William Ernest, honey." She stuck out her big hand. "We ain't helping here." When he hesitated, she reached down and gently pulled him to his feet. They closed the door behind them, leaving Gilly cold and alone.

"You seem to have changed your mind about a lot of things."

"So?"

"So you goofed it, right?"—Gilly didn't answer. What did it matter?—"I'd really like to know what you wrote that fool letter for."

"You wouldn't understand."

"You bet I wouldn't. I don't understand why a smart girl like you goes around booby-trapping herself. You could have stayed here indefinitely, you know. They're both crazy about you." Miss Ellis shook her long blonde hair back off her shoulders. "Well, it's done now. Your grandmother will come to pick you up at my office tomorrow. I'll come about nine to get you."

"Tomorrow?"

"Gilly, believe me, it's better. Waiting around is no good in these situations."

"But I got school"—not even a good-bye for cool, beautiful Miss Harris or silly little Agnes?

"They'll send your records on." Miss Ellis stood up and began to button her coat. "I must admit that last month when you ran away, I thought, Uh-oh, here we go again, but I was wrong, Gilly. You've done well here. I'm very pleased."

"Then let me stay." Galadriel Hopkins had rarely come so close to begging.

"I can't," Miss Ellis said simply. "It's out of my hands."

The Going

FOR dinner that night Trotter fried chicken so crisp it would crackle when you bit it, and she beat the potatoes into creamy peaks with the electric mixer. She had made Mr. Randolph his favorite green beans with ham bits and for Gilly and W.E. there was a fruit salad with baby marshmallows. The sweet-sour smell of cherry pie filled the kitchen where the four of them sat around the table without appetite for food or speech.

Only William Ernest cried, big, silent tears catching in the corners of the frame of his glasses and then spilling down his cheeks. Mr. Randolph, smaller and thinner than ever, sat forward on his chair, with a shy, half smile on his face, which meant he was just about to say something but he never quite got it out. Trotter was breathing as hard as if she had just climbed the stairs. She kept rearranging the serving dishes as though just about to offer seconds, but since the four plates were still piled high, the gesture was useless.

Gilly watched her and tried to decide how much Miss Ellis had told her. Did she know the Thanksgiving visitor was Gilly's grandmother? Did Trotter know—she hoped not—about the crazy letter? She still couldn't remember what she had said in the letter. Had she said W.E. was retarded? Her mind blanked in self-defense. Oh, god, don't let Trotter know. I never meant to hurt them. I just wanted —what had she wanted? A home—but Trotter had tried to give her that. Permanence—Trotter had wanted to give her that as well. No, what she wanted was something Trotter had no power over. To stop being a "foster child," the quotation marks dragging the phrase down, almost drowning it. To be real without any quotation marks. To belong and to possess. To be herself, to be the swan, to be the ugly duckling no longer—Cap O'Rushes, her disguise thrown off—Cinderella with both slippers on her feet—Snow White beyond the dwarfs—Galadriel Hopkins, come into her own.

But there was to be no coming, only a going.

"If you all don't start eating this supper, I'm gonna"—Trotter stopped, fishing around for a proper threat. She took a deep breath—"Jump up and down on the table, squawking like a two-hundred-pound lovesick chicken!"

"Really?" William Ernest took off his glasses and wiped them on his pants to prepare for a better view.

Mr. Randolph's fixed smile crumbled into a nervous titter. Gilly swallowed to clear her clogged-up throat and took a large noisy bite of her drumstick.

"Now, that's more like it." Trotter patted her shiny face with the tail of her apron. "This was supposed to be a party, not some kinda funeral." She turned to Mr. Randolph and half shouted. "Gilly's folks are from Loudoun County, Mr. Randolph."

"Oh, that's lovely, lovely country, Miss Gilly. Real Virginia horse country."

"You got horses, Gilly?

"I don't know, W.E." She found it hard to imagine the little pudgy lady on horseback, but who could tell?

"Can I see 'em?"

"Sure. If I got 'em, you can see 'em."

She caught a flicked warning from Trotter over the boy's head, but Gilly ignored it. "It's not as if I'm going to Hong Kong. Hell. You can just hop on a bus and come to see me —any time."

Trotter was shaking her head. She put her hand over on W.E.'s shoulder. "When folks leave, William Ernest, honey, they gotta have a chance to settle in and get used to things. Sometimes it's best not to go visiting, right away."

If you mean "never" Trotter, say so. Is that it? Will I never see the three of you again? Are you going to stand by and let them rip me out and fold me up and fly me away? Leave me a string, Trotter, a thread, at least. Dammit. She'd tie her own.

"I'll write you, W.E. The mailman will bring you a letter with your name on it. Just for you."

"Me?" he said.

"Nobody else." She looked belligerently at Trotter, but Trotter was so busy making the meat platter and the salad bowl switch places that the expression was wasted.

After supper Gilly did her homework, knowing it was useless, that Miss Harris would never see the neat figures, row on row, that proved that Gilly Hopkins had met and mastered the metric system. When she finished, she thought briefly of calling Agnes, but what should she say? "Good-bye" when she'd never really said "hello"? Poor Agnes, what would become of her? Would she stomp herself angrily through the floor, or would someone's kiss turn her magically into a princess? Alas, Agnes, the world is woefully short on frog smoochers.

No, she wouldn't call, but maybe, someday, she'd write.

William Ernest walked Mr. Randolph home and returned carrying *The Oxford Book of English Verse* for Gilly—a farewell present from Mr. Randolph.

"Gilly, honey, do you know what kind of present that is?"

Gilly could guess.

"Like he tore a piece off hisself and gave it to you."

Gilly ran a finger over the wrinkled brown leather, which could almost have been a piece of Mr. Randolph, but the observation seemed too raw, so she kept it to herself.

She waited for Trotter to puff up the stairs to take W.E. to bed before she began to look for the poem:

Our birth is but a sleep and a forgetting:
The Soul that rises with us, our life's Star,
Hath had elsewhere its setting
And cometh from afar:
Not in entire forgetfulness,
And not in utter nakedness,
But trailing clouds of glory do we come
From God, who is our home.

She didn't understand it any more than she had the first time. If birth was a sleep and a forgetting, what was death? But she didn't really care. It was the sounds she loved—the sounds that turned and fell in kaleidoscopic wonder.

"And not in utter nakedness," Who would have thought those five words could fall into such a pattern of light? And her favorite "But trailing clouds of glory do we come." Was it all the *l*'s that did it or the mental picture that streaked cometlike across the unfocused lens of her mind?

"From God, who is our home." Again the lens was unfocused. Was that God with the huge lap smelling of baby powder? Or was that home?

She awoke in the night, trying to remember the dream that had awakened her. It was a sad one, or why did her heart feel like a lump of poorly mashed potatoes? It was something about Courtney. Courtney coming to get her, and then, having seen her, turning away sorrowing: "Never, never, never." But the voice was Trotter's.

She began to cry softly into her pillow, not knowing why or for whom. Maybe for all the craziness she had tried so hard to manage and was never quite able to.

And then Trotter was beside her, making the bedsprings screech at the burden of her body. She leaned over, her hair, loose from its daytime knot, falling across Gilly's own hair.

"You OK, baby?"

Gilly turned to face her, this mountain smelling of Johnson's baby powder and perspiration. In the dark, she could hardly make out the lines on Trotter's face.

"Yeah," she sniffed. "OK."

Trotter took the hem of the striped pajama top and

gently wiped Gilly's eyes and nose. "I ain't supposed to let on how I feel. I ain't got no blood claim on you, and the Lord in Heaven knows I want you to have a good life with your own people. But"—her huge bass voice broke up into little squeaky pieces—"but it's killing me to see you go." The whole mammoth body began to shake with giant sobs.

Gilly sat up and put her arms as far as they could go around Trotter. "I'm not going to go," she cried. "They can't make me!"

Trotter quieted at once. "No, baby. You got to go. Lord forgive me for making it harder for you."

"I'll come back and see you all the time."

Trotter stuck her big warm hand underneath Gilly's pajama top and began to rub her back, the way Gilly had often seen her rub W.E.'s. "No, Gilly, baby. It don't work that way. Like I tried to tell you at supper. Once the tugboat takes you out to the ocean liner, you got to get all the way on board. Can't straddle both decks."

"I could," said Gilly.

The big hand paused in its healing journey around and up and down her back, then began again as Trotter said softly, "Don't make it harder for us, baby."

Perhaps Gilly should have protested further, but instead she gave herself over to the rhythmic stroking under whose comfort she wished she could curl up her whole body like a tiny sightless kitten and forget about the rest of the whole stinking world.

She could almost forget, lying there in the silence, letting the soothing warmth of the big hand erase all the aching. At last, overcome with drowsiness, she slid down into the bed.

Trotter pulled the covers up around Gilly's chin and patted them and her.

"You make me proud, hear?"

"OK," she murmured and was asleep.

Jackson, Virginia

THE ride in Mrs. Hopkins's ten-year-old Buick station wagon to Jackson, Virginia, took just over an hour. To Gilly it seemed like a hundred years. Every other time she'd moved, she'd been able to think of the destination as a brief stop along the way, but this one was the end of the road. Always before she had known she could stand anything, because someday soon Courtney would come and take her home. But now she had to face the fact that Courtney had not come. She had sent someone else in her place. Perhaps Courtney would never come. Perhaps Courtney did not want to come.

The heaviness dragged her down. What was she doing here in this old car with this strange woman who surely didn't want her, who had only taken her out of some stupid idea of duty, when she could be home with Trotter and

William Ernest and Mr. Randolph who really wanted her? Who—could she dare the word, even to herself?—who loved her.

And she loved them. Oh, hell. She'd spent all her life—at least all of it since the Dixons went to Florida and left her behind—making sure she didn't care about anyone but Courtney. She had known that it never pays to attach yourself to something that is likely to blow away. But in Thompson Park, she'd lost her head. She loved those stupid people.

"Would you like to turn on the radio?"

"No, that's all right."

"I'm not familiar with the latest music, but I don't really mind, as long as it's not too loud."

Can't you just leave me alone?

There were several miles of silence before the woman tried again: "Miss Ellis seems like a nice person."

Gilly shrugged. "She's OK, I guess."

"She—uh—seems to think I got a rather wrong impression of that foster home she'd put you in."

Something dark and hot began to bubble up inside of Gilly. "They were all sick last week," she said.

"I see."

How in the hell could you see?

"Miss Ellis tried to tell me that you had really liked it there—despite everything. From your letter—"

That damn letter. "I lie a lot," Gilly said tightly.

"Oh." A quick side glance and then back to the windshield. The woman was so short she was almost peering through the top of the steering wheel. Gilly saw her small hands tighten on the wheel as she said, "I'd hoped you'd be glad to come with me. I'm sorry."

If you're sorry, turn this old crate around and take me back. But, of course, the woman didn't.

The house was on the edge of the village. It was a little larger, a little older, and considerably cleaner than Trotter's. No horses for W.E. Oh, well, she hadn't really expected any.

"I thought you might like to have Courtney's room. What do you think?"

"Anything is all right." But when she got to the door of Courtney's room, she hung back. Everything was pink with a four-poster canopied bed complete with stuffed animals and dolls. She couldn't make herself go in.

"It's all right, my dear. It's a big house. You may choose."

The room which she found most to her liking had a bunk bed with brown corduroy spreads and models of airplanes hanging on delicate wires from the ceiling. In a metal-wire wastebasket was a basketball and a football and a baseball mitt still cradling a stained and scruffed-up ball. The grandmother explained quietly without her having to ask that it was the room of Chadwell, Courtney's older brother, a pilot who had one day crashed into the steaming jungles of Vietnam. Nonetheless, his room seemed less haunted than his sister's.

"Would you like me to help you unpack?"

Inside her head, she was screaming, "I don't need any help!" but for Trotter's sake, she said only, "No, I can do it."

They ate lunch in the dining room with real monogrammed silver off silver-rimmed china set on lace mats.

The woman caught Gilly eying the layout. "I hope you

don't mind my celebrating a little." She seemed to be apologizing. "I usually eat in the kitchen since I've been alone."

The word "alone" twanged in Gilly's head. She knew what it meant to be alone. But only since Thompson Park did she understand a little what it meant to have people and then lose them. She looked at the person who was smiling shyly at her, who had lost husband, son, daughter. That was alone.

As lunch progressed, the woman began almost to chatter, as though she were overcoming her shyness, or forcing herself to. "I feel very silly saying to you, Tell me all about yourself, but I wish you would. I want to get to know you."

That's not how you get to know people. Don't you know? You can't talk it out, you got to live into their lives, bad and good. You'll know me soon enough. What I want you to know.

"Miss Ellis says you're very bright."

"I guess so."

"Do you want to see about school right away? Or would you rather settle in here first?"

"I don't know. It doesn't matter."

"I'm afraid you'll get bored just sitting around with me all day. I want you to make friends your own age. I'm sure there are some nice girls your age somewhere around."

I have never in my life been friends with a "nice girl."

"What kinds of things do you enjoy doing?"

Please shut up. I can't stand your trying so hard. "I don't know. Anything."

"If you like to read, I still have Chadwell and Courtney's books. There may even be a bicycle in the shed. Do you suppose it's any good after all these years? Would you like a bicycle? I'm sure we could find the money for a bicycle if you'd like one."

Stop hovering over me. I'll smother.

They did the dishes. Gilly wiped silently while her grandmother nervously put-putted on and on. It didn't seem necessary to answer her questions. She went right on whether or not Gilly bothered to reply. What had happened to the quiet little lady in the car? It was as though someone had turned on a long-unused faucet. The problem was how in the world to get it shut off again. Gilly had to try. She yawned elaborately and stretched.

"Are you tired, dear?"

Gilly nodded. "I guess I haven't caught up on my sleep. I had to be up a lot last week with everyone sick and all."

"Oh, my dear. How thoughtless of me! Here I go on and on . . ."

"No. It's all right. I think I'll just go up and lie down, though, if you don't mind."

"What a good idea. I often lie down a little in the afternoon myself."

In the quiet of Chadwell's room, Gilly lay back and gazed out the window at the blue expanse of sky. If she lifted up on her elbow she could see the rolling fields beyond the margin of the tiny town, and beyond the hills, the mountains dark and strong. She felt herself loosening. Had Chadwell been homesick for this sight as he dropped his bombs into the jungle? Why would anyone leave such peace for war? Maybe he had to go. Maybe they didn't give him any choice. But Courtney had had a choice. Why had she left? You don't just leave your mother because she talks too much. Why should she leave and not look back a single time—until now?

She must care about me, at least a little. She wrote her mother to come and get me because she was worried about me. Doesn't that prove she cares? Gilly got up and took Courtney's picture out from underneath her T-shirts. How silly. She was in Courtney's house now. Courtney didn't have to hide in a drawer any longer. She propped the picture up against the bureau lamp. Maybe her grandmother would let her buy a frame for it. She sat down on the bed and looked back at Courtney on the bureau. Beautiful, smiling Courtney of the perfect teeth and lovely hair.

But something was wrong. The face didn't fit in this room any more than it had fit in all the others. Oh, Courtney, why did you go away and leave her? Why did you go away and leave me? She jumped up and slid the picture face-down under the T-shirts again.

She'll Be Riding Six White Horses (When She Comes)

P.O. Box 33
Jackson, Va.
December 5

Dear William Ernest,

Ha! I bet you thought I'd forget. But don't worry. I wouldn't forget you. I have just been so busy looking after the horses I have hardly had a minute to myself. I practically fall into bed I'm so worn out from all the work. Have you ever shoveled horse manure?

Just kidding. Actually, it is a lot of fun. We are getting six of the horses ready to race at the Charles Town track soon, so I have to help them train. I am sure one of them, named Clouds of Glory, is going to win. The prize is about a half a million dollars, so we will be even richer when he does. Not that we need the money, being millionaires and all.

How is school? I bet you zonked Miss McNair with all those new words you learned last month. You should keep in practice by reading out loud to Mr. Randolph.

Tell Trotter we have three maids and a cook, but the cook isn't half as good as she is, even though she uses lots of fancy ingredients. (Ha! Bet you knock Miss McNair over when you read her that word.)

Write soon.

Gilly

P.S. My grandmother told me to call her "Nonnie." Aren't rich people weird?

Thompson Park Elementary School
Thompson Park, Maryland
December 7

Dear Gilly,

If anyone had told me how much I would miss having you in my class, I'd never have believed it. I hope, however, that you are enjoying your new school and that the people there are enjoying you as well. You might like to know that when I send your records to Virginia, I do not plan to include any samples of your poetry.

You will be receiving soon some paperbacks that I'd been meaning to lend you, but now that you've left us, I want you to keep them as a souvenir of our days together in Harris 6.

I certainly won't forget you even if you never write, but it would be good to hear how you're getting along.

Best wishes,
Barbara Harris

December 10

Dear Gilly,

How are you? I am fine. I liked your letter. I liked your horses. Write me soon.

Love,
William Ernest Teague

P.S. Did you win the race?

P.O. Box 33
Jackson, Virginia
December 15

Dear Miss Harris,

The books by J. R. R. Tolkien came the day after your letter. Now I know who Galadriel was. Do you think Frodo should keep trying to take back the magic ring? I think it would be better if he kept it and took charge of things himself. Do you know what I mean? Anyhow, thank you for the books. They are really exciting.

They help a lot because this school is terrible. Nobody knows anything, including the teachers. I wish I was back in Harris 6.

Your former student,
Gilly Hopkins

P.S. It's OK if you want to call me Galadriel.

December 16

Dear William Ernest,

Of course we won the race. Now we are training for the Kentucky Derby. I guess I will have to miss a lot of school to go to that, but it won't matter. They have already told me that I will probably skip to the ninth grade, because I am so far ahead of all the sixth graders in this dumb school. When you are old enough, I will take you to a horse race. How about that?

Tell Trotter and Mr. Randolph hello for me. Are you reading to Mr. Randolph like I told you to?

Take care.

Gilly

P.S. Why don't you ask Santa to bring you some karate lessons?

December 17

Dear William Ernest, Trotter, and Mr. Randolph,

I just wrote William Ernest yesterday, but now I got some real news. I just heard that my mother is coming on December 23. I know I lie a lot, so you won't believe this, but it is really the truth this time. She is really coming. I hope you all have a Merry Christmas and a Happy New Year.

Galadriel (Gilly) Hopkins

Her mother was really coming. At least Nonnie, who had talked to her on the telephone while Gilly was at school, believed she was. She was due at Dulles Airport at 11 A.M. on December twenty-third. A whole week to wait. Gilly thought she might die waiting. She dulled the agony somewhat by plunging into housecleaning for Nonnie.

Nonnie was all right. She could still chatter Gilly straight into a pounding headache, but she meant well. And then, whenever Gilly would lose patience with her, she'd remember the first day Nonnie had taken her into Jackson Elementary School.

They had marched into the principal's office, and Nonnie had said: "Margaret, this is my granddaughter, Galadriel Hopkins."

The principal had raised her eyebrows. She had obviously known Nonnie for years, and this was the first mention she'd ever had of a granddaughter. "Your granddaughter?" she said giving Gilly's new blouse and jumper the once over. "Hopkins, did you say?"

You had to hand it to old Nonnie. She didn't blink an eye. "Yes, I said Hopkins. She's Courtney's child."

"I see," said the principal, and you could practically see the wheels spinning in that prissy head of hers. "I see. Hopkins. Now how do you spell her Christian name?" Had she exaggerated Christian ever so slightly? If so, Nonnie took no notice.

Nonnie spelled out Galadriel as patiently as Gilly might have spelled out a hard word for W.E. "Her school records will be sent directly to you. She's been in school in Maryland."

"Maryland?" The same tone of voice used earlier for Hopkins.

It was a scene that was to repeat itself with variations many times in those first couple of weeks. "Hopkins?" they always asked. "Galadriel? How do you spell that?" "Maryland, did you say?"

Gilly had had plenty of practice staring down sneers, but it was hard to imagine that someone like Nonnie had. But Nonnie looked straight down her short nose at every sneer and they stopped, at least the face-to-face ones did. Nonnie was gutsier than she looked.

But everything would be all right for them both now. Courtney was coming.

"It's silly to be nervous, isn't it?" Nonnie said. "She's my own daughter. It's just that it's been so long. And she was hardly speaking to her father and me in those days. What will we say to each other?"

Oh, Nonnie. If I knew what mothers and daughters said to each other, wouldn't I tell you? How should I know?

"She'll think I've gotten terribly old. My hair was quite dark when she left."

"Yeah?" She tried to put Courtney's hair on Nonnie's head. It didn't work.

"Would you think it was very silly of me to get a rinse?"

"A rinse?"

"Just to cover a little of the gray?"

Nonnie a Clairol girl? "Why not?"

"Let's do it!" So while Nonnie was rinsed and curled, Gilly was cut and blown.

"You look lovely, my dear."

Nonnie looked totally unnatural, but then Gilly had never seen her with black hair before. Maybe she'd look great to Courtney. "You look nice, too," she lied.

Money, though not as scarce as at Trotter's, was hardly in the supply hinted at in the letters to W.E. Nevertheless, Nonnie seemed determined to prepare royally for Courtney's return. They bought a Christmas tree that would touch the high ceiling of the living room and had to hire a neighbor's boy to carry it from the back of the old station wagon into the house and help them set it up.

Every ornament they hung had a family history, and Gilly half listened as Nonnie recounted each tale. She was too excited to concentrate fully, but she did grasp that the lopsided pasteboard star was one that Chadwell had made in the third grade. Most of the glued-on glitter had long departed. There was a yarn snowman that Courtney had made when a Brownie, it was gray now, and beginning to ravel. And there were yards of tattered paper chains. "You sure you want to put these chains on?" Gilly asked Nonnie.

"Oh, we have to have the chains. We always had the chains."

So Gilly glued the chains together as best she could and hung them. The whole effect was appalling—a pile of junk. But then she put on three boxes of tinsel, one strand at a time, so that the entire tree was under a silver veil. In a dark room with only the Christmas tree lighted, it wasn't bad. Not a department-store display, but not bad.

Nonnie slipped her glasses on and off her nose, trying to take in the sight, and finally let them hang on the ribbon around her neck while she clapped her hands like a little girl. "I can't remember ever before having such a lovely tree," she said.

Neither, after she thought about it, could Gilly.

December 20

Dear Gilly,

So your Mom is coming to see you? You must be real excited. Mr. Randolph, William Ernest, and me wishes you lots of luck.

By the way, William Ernest come home yesterday with a bloody nose. You know me, I like to die, but he was prouder than a punch-drunk pickle. Mr. Evans call me up to complain about my kid fighting at school but took to laughing too hard to finish. What do you think about that?

Sincerely, your friend,
Maime M. Trotter

Pow! That's what she thought of that.

Homecoming

THE plane was late. It seemed to Gilly that everything in this world that you can't stand to wait one extra minute for is always late. Her stomach was pretzeled with eagerness and anxiety. She stood sweating in the chill of the huge waiting room, the perspiration pouring down the sleeves of her new blouse. She'd probably ruin it and stink besides.

Then, suddenly, when she'd almost stopped straining her eyes with looking at it, the door opened, and people began to come off the motor lounge into the airport. All kinds of people, all sizes, all colors, all of them rushing. Many looking about for family or friends, finding them with little cries of joy and hugs. Tired fussy babies, children dragging on their mothers. Businessmen, heads down, swinging neat thin leather briefcases. Grandparents laden with shopping bags of Christmas presents. But no Courtney.

The pretzel turned to stone. It was all a lie. She would never come. The door blurred. Gilly wanted to leave. She didn't want to cry in the stupid airport, but just at that moment she heard Nonnie say in a quavering voice, "Courtney."

"Hello, Nonnie."

But this person wasn't Courtney. It couldn't be Courtney! Courtney was tall and willowy and gorgeous. The woman who stood before them was no taller than Nonnie and just as plump, although she wore a long cape, so it was hard to make out her real shape. Her hair was long, but it was dull and stringy—a dark version of Agnes Stokes's, which had always needed washing. A flower child gone to seed. Gilly immediately pushed aside the disloyal thought.

Nonnie had sort of put her hand on the younger woman's arm in a timid embrace, but there was a huge embroidered shoulder bag between the two of them. "This is Galadriel, Courtney."

For a second, the smile, the one engraved on Gilly's soul, flashed out. The teeth were perfect. She was face to face with Courtney Rutherford Hopkins. She could no longer doubt it. "Hi." The word almost didn't come out. She wondered what she was supposed to do. Should she try to kiss Courtney or something?

At this point Courtney hugged her, pressing the huge bag into Gilly's chest and stomach and saying across her shoulder to Nonnie, "She's as tall as I am," sounding a little as though Gilly weren't there.

"She's a lovely girl," said Nonnie.

"Well, of course, she is," Courtney stepped back and

smiled her gorgeous heart-shattering smile. "She's mine, isn't she?"

Nonnie smiled back, rather more weakly than her daughter had. "Maybe we should get your luggage."

"I've got it," said Courtney, slapping her shoulder bag. "It's all right here."

Nonnie looked a little as though she'd been smacked in the face. "But—" she began and stopped.

"How many clothes can you wear in two days?"

Two days? Then Courtney had come to get her after all.

"I told you on the phone that I'd come for Christmas and see for myself how the kid was doing. . . ."

"But when I sent you the money, . . ."

Courtney's face was hard and set with lines between the brows. "Look. I came, didn't I? Don't start pushing me before I'm hardly off the plane. My god, I've been gone thirteen years, and you still think you can tell me what to do." She slung the bag behind her back. "Let's get out of here."

Nonnie shot Gilly a look of pain. "Courtney—"

She hadn't come because she wanted to. She'd come because Nonnie had paid her to. And she wasn't going to stay. And she wasn't going to take Gilly back with her. "I will always love you." It was a lie. Gilly had thrown away her whole life for a stinking lie.

"I gotta go to the bathroom," Gilly said to Nonnie. She prayed they wouldn't follow her there, because the first thing she was going to do was vomit, and the second was run away.

She tried to vomit, but nothing happened. She was still shaking from the effort when she dropped her coins in the pay telephone beside the restroom and dialed. It rang four times.

"Hello."

"Trotter, it's me, Gilly." God, don't let me break down like a baby.

"Gilly, honey. Where are you?"

"Nowhere. It doesn't matter. I'm coming home."

She could hear Trotter's heavy breathing at the other end of the line. "What's the matter, baby? Your mom didn't show?"

"No, she came."

"Oh, my poor baby."

Gilly was crying now. She couldn't help herself. "Trotter, it's all wrong. Nothing turned out the way it's supposed to."

"How you mean supposed to? Life ain't supposed to be nothing, 'cept maybe tough."

"But I always thought that when my mother came. . . ."

"My sweet baby, ain't no one ever told you yet? I reckon I thought you had that all figured out."

"What?"

"That all that stuff about happy endings is lies. The only ending in this world is death. Now that might or might not be happy, but either way, you ain't ready to die, are you?"

"Trotter, I'm not talking about dying. I'm talking about coming home."

But Trotter seemed to ignore her. "Sometimes in this world things come easy, and you tend to lean back and say, 'Well, finally, happy ending. This is the way things is supposed to be.' Like life owed you good things."

"Trotter—"

"And there is lots of good things, baby. Like you coming to be with us here this fall. That was a mighty good thing for me and William Ernest. But you just fool yourself if you expect good things all the time. They ain't what's regular —don't nobody owe 'em to you."

"If life is so bad, how come you're so happy?"

"Did I say bad? I said it was tough. Nothing to make you happy like doing good on a tough job, now is there?"

"Trotter, stop preaching at me. I want to come home."

"You're home, baby. Your grandma is home."

"I want to be with you and William Ernest and Mr. Randolph."

"And leave her all alone? Could you do that?"

"Dammit, Trotter. Don't try to make a stinking Christian out of me."

"I wouldn't try to make nothing out of you." There was a quiet at the other end of the line. "Me and William Ernest and Mr. Randolph kinda like you the way you are."

"Go to hell, Trotter," Gilly said softly.

A sigh. "Well, I don't know about that. I had planned on settling permanently somewheres else."

"Trotter"—She couldn't push the word hard enough to keep the squeak out—"I love you."

"I know, baby. I love you, too."

She put the phone gently on the hook and went back into the bathroom. There she blew her nose on toilet tissue and washed her face.

By the time she got back to an impatient Courtney and a stricken Nonnie, she had herself well under control.

"Sorry to make you wait," Gilly said. "I'm ready to go home now." No clouds of glory, perhaps, but Trotter would be proud.

About the Author

Katherine Paterson is the author of JACOB HAVE I LOVED *and* BRIDGE TO TERABITHIA, *both Newbery Medal winners. She has twice been awarded the National Book Award for Children's Literature, and several of her novels have been chosen as Notable Children's Books by the American Library Association.*

Katherine Paterson was born in China and spent part of her childhood there. After her education in both China and the United States, she lived for four years in Japan. There she studied at the Japanese Language School in Kobe and taught in a rural area of Shikoku Island.

Her four children and their friends have provided her with some of the subject matter for her sharply observant stories of family life. She and her family live in Barre, Vermont.

JACOB HAVE I LOVED

ALSO BY KATHERINE PATERSON

Angels & Other Strangers

The Great Gilly Hopkins

Bridge to Terabithia

The Master Puppeteer

Of Nightingales That Weep

The Sign of the Chrysanthemum

Katherine Paterson

JACOB HAVE I LOVED

HARPERCOLLINS*PUBLISHERS*

For information address HarperCollins Children's Books, a division
of HarperCollins Publishers, 10 East 53rd Street, New York, NY 10022.
Designed by Al Cetta

Library of Congress Cataloging-in-Publication Data
Paterson, Katherine.
Jacob Have I Loved.
Summary: Feeling deprived all her life of schooling, friends, mother, and
even her name by her twin sister, Louise finally begins to find her identity.
[1. Twins—Fiction. 2. Brothers and sisters—Fiction.
3. Chesapeake Bay region—Fiction] I. Title.
PZ7.P273Jac 1980 [Fic] 80-668
ISBN 0-690-04078-4.—ISBN 0-690-04079-2 (lib. bdg.)
(A Harper Trophy book) ISBN 0-06-440368-8 (pbk.)

Published in hardcover by HarperCollins Publishers.
First Harper Trophy edition, 1990.

For

Gene Inyart Namovicz

I wish it were EMMA, *but, then,*

you already have two or three

copies of that.

With thanks and love.

ACKNOWLEDGMENTS

The impetus for this book came from reading William W. Warner's *Beautiful Swimmers: Watermen, Crabs and the Chesapeake Bay*, Little, Brown and Company, 1976, which justly deserved the Pulitzer Prize it won the following year. Since then, there have been many people and books that have helped me learn more about life on the Chesapeake Bay. I should like especially to mention the Smith Island watermen I met at the Folk Life Festival at the Smithsonian: Mr. Harold G. Wheatley of Tangier Island, Virginia, and Dr. Varley Lang of Tunis Mills, Maryland. Dr. Lang, who is a writer and scholar as well as a Maryland waterman, was kind enough to read this manuscript. Any errors that remain are, of course, my fault and not his. His book about Maryland watermen entitled *Follow the Water*, John F. Blair, 1961, was also a great help to me.

Rass Island

As soon as the snow melts, I will go to Rass and fetch my mother. At Crisfield I'll board the ferry, climbing down into the cabin where the women always ride, but after forty minutes of sitting on the hard cabin bench, I'll stand up to peer out of the high forward windows, straining for the first sight of my island.

The ferry will be almost there before I can see Rass, lying low as a terrapin back on the faded olive water of the Chesapeake. Suddenly, though, the steeple of the Methodist Church will leap from the Bay, dragging up a cluster of white board houses. And then, almost at once, we will be in the harbor, tying up beside Captain Billy's unpainted two-story ferry house, which leans wearily against a long, low shed used for the captain's crab shipping business. Next door, but standing primly aloof in a coat of fierce green paint, is Kellam's General Store with the post office inside, and behind them, on a narrow spine of fast land, the houses and white picket fences of the village. There are only a few spindly trees. It is the excess of snowball bushes that lends a semblance of green to every yard.

The dock onto which I'll step is part of a maze of docks. My eye could travel down the planking of any one of them and find at the end a shack erected by a waterman for storage and crab packing. If I arrive in late spring, the crab houses will be surrounded by slat floats that hold and protect peeler crabs in the water of the Bay until they have shed. Then the newly soft crabs will be packed in eelgrass and the boxes taken to Captain Billy's for shipping to the mainland.

More important than the crab houses, however, are the boats, tied along the docks. Though each has a personality as distinctive as the waterman who owns it, they look deceptively alike—a small cabin toward the bow, washboards wide enough for a man to stand on running from the point of the bow to the stern. In the belly of the hull, fore and aft of the engine are a dozen or so barrels waiting for the next day's catch, a spare crab pot or two, looking like a box made of chicken wire, and a few empty bait baskets. Near the winch that pulls the line of pots up from the floor of the Chesapeake is a large washtub. Into it each crab pot will be emptied and from it the legal-sized crabs—hard, peeler, and soft—will be culled from their smaller kin as well as from the blowfish, sea nettles, seaweed, shells, and garbage, all such unwelcome harvest as the Bay seems ever generous to offer up. On the stern, each boat bears its name. They are nearly all women's names, usually the name of the waterman's mother or grandmother, depending on how long the boat has been in the family.

The village, in which we Bradshaws lived for more than two hundred years, covers barely a third of our island's length. The rest is salt water marsh. As a child I secretly welcomed the first warm day of spring by yanking off my shoes and standing waist deep in the cordgrass to feel the cool mud squish up between my toes. I chose the spot with care, for cordgrass alone is rough enough to rip the skin, and ours often concealed a bit of curling tin or shards of glass or crockery or jagged shells not yet worn smooth by the tides. In my nostrils, the faint hay smell of the grass mingled with that of the brackish water of the Bay, while the spring wind chilled the tips of my ears and raised goosebumps along my arms. Then I would shade my eyes from the sun and search far across the water hoping to see my father's boat coming home.

I love Rass Island, although for much of my life, I did not think I did, and it is a pure sorrow to me that, once my mother leaves, there will be no one left there with the name of Bradshaw. But there were only the two of us, my sister, Caroline, and me, and neither of us could stay.

1

During the summer of 1941, every weekday morning at the top of the tide, McCall Purnell and I would board my skiff and go progging for crab. Call and I were right smart crabbers, and we could always come home with a little money as well as plenty of crab for supper. Call was a year older than I and would never have gone crabbing with a girl except that his father was dead, so he had no man to take him on board a regular crab boat. He was, as well, a boy who had matured slowly, and being fat and nearsighted, he was dismissed by most of the island boys.

Call and I made quite a pair. At thirteen I was tall and large boned, with delusions of beauty and romance. He, at fourteen, was pudgy, bespectacled, and totally unsentimental.

"Call," I would say, watching dawn break crimson over the Chesapeake Bay, "I hope I have a sky like this the day I get married."

"Who would marry you?" Call would ask, not meanly, just facing facts.

"Oh," I said one day, "I haven't met him yet."

"Then you ain't likely to. This is a right small island."

"It won't be an islander."

"Mr. Rice has him a girl friend in Baltimore."

I sighed. All the girls on Rass Island were half in love with Mr. Rice, one of our two high school teachers. He was the only relatively unattached man most of us had ever known. But Mr. Rice had let it get around that his heart was given to a lady from Baltimore.

"Do you suppose," I asked, as I poled the skiff, the focus of my romantic musings shifting from my own wedding day to Mr. Rice's, "do you suppose her parents oppose the marriage?"

"Why should they care?" Call, standing on the port washboard, had sighted the head of what seemed to be a large sea terrapin and was fixing on it a fierce concentration.

I shifted the pole to starboard. We could get a pretty little price for a terrapin of that size. The terrapin sensed the change in our direction and dove straight through the eelgrass into the bottom mud, but Call had the net waiting, so that when the old bull hit his hiding place, he was yanked to the surface and deposited into a waiting pail. Call grunted with satisfaction. We might make as much as fifty cents on that one catch, ten times the price of a soft blue crab.

"Maybe she's got some mysterious illness and doesn't want to be a burden to him."

"Who?"

"Mr. Rice's finance." I had picked up the word, but not the pronunciation from my reading. It was not in the spoken vocabulary of most islanders.

"His *what*?"

"The woman he's engaged to marry, stupid."

"How come you think she's sick?"

"Something is delaying the consumption of their union."

Call jerked his head around to give me one of his looks, but the washboards of a skiff are a precarious perch at best, so he didn't stare long enough to waste time or risk a dunking. He left me to what he presumed to be my looniness and gave his attention to the eelgrass. We were a good team on the water. I could pole a skiff quickly and quietly, and nearsighted as he was he could spy a crab by just a tip of the claw through grass and muck. He rarely missed one, and he knew I wouldn't jerk or swerve at the wrong moment. I'm sure that's why he stuck with me. I stuck with him not only because we could work well together, but because our teamwork was so automatic that I was free to indulge my romantic fantasies at the same time. That this part of my nature was wasted on Call didn't matter. He didn't have any friends but me, so he wasn't likely to repeat what I said to someone who might snicker. Call himself never laughed.

I thought of it as a defect in his character that I must try to correct, so I told him jokes. "Do you know why radio announcers have tiny hands?"

"Huh?"

"Wee paws for station identification," I would whoop.

"Yeah?"

"Don't you get it, Call? Wee paws. *Wee Paws.*" I let go the pole to shake my right hand at him. "You know, little hands—paws."

"You ain't never seen one."

"One what?"

"One radio announcer."

"No."

"Then how do you know how big their hands are?"

"I don't. It's a joke, Call."

"I don't see how it can be a joke if you don't even know if they have big hands or little hands. Suppose they really have big hands. Then you ain't even telling the truth. Then what happens to your joke?"

"It's just a joke, Call. It doesn't matter whether it's true or not."

"It matters to me. Why should a person think a lie's funny?"

"Never mind, Call. It doesn't matter."

But he went on, mumbling like a little old preacher about the importance of truth and how you couldn't trust radio announcers anymore.

You'd think I'd give up, but I didn't.

"Call, did you hear about the lawyer, the dentist, and the p-sychiatrist who died and went to heaven?"

"Was it a airplane crash?"

"No, Call. It's a joke."

"Oh, a joke."

"Yeah. You see, this lawyer and this dentist and this p-sychiatrist all die. And first the lawyer gets there. And Peter says—"

"Peter who?"

"Peter in the Bible. The Apostle Peter."

"He's dead."

"I know he's dead—"

"But you just said—"

"Just shut up and listen to the joke, Call. This lawyer comes to Peter, and he wants to get into heaven."

"A minute ago you said he was already in heaven."

"Well, he wasn't. He was just at the pearly gates, okay? Anyhow, he says he wants to get into heaven, and Peter says he's sorry but he's looked at the book and the lawyer was wicked and evil and cheated people. So he's got to go to hell."

"Does your mother know you use words like that?"

"Call, even the preacher talks about hell. Anyhow, this lawyer has to give up and go to hell. Then this dentist comes up and he wants to get into heaven, and Peter looks at his book and sees that this guy pulled people's teeth out just to get their money even when their teeth were perfectly good and he knew it."

"He did *what?*"

"Call, it doesn't matter."

"It don't matter that a dentist pulls out perfectly good teeth just to make money? That's awful. He ought to go to jail."

"Well, he went to hell for it."

"Pulling out perfectly good teeth—" he mumbled, pinching his own with the fingers of his left hand.

"Then the p-sychiatrist—"

"The what?"

I was an avid reader of *Time* magazine, which, besides the day-old Baltimore *Sun,* was our porthole on the world in those days, so although psychiatry was not yet a popular pastime, I was quite aware of the word, if not the fact that the p was silent. *Time* was probably the source of the joke I was laboring to recount.

"A p-sychiatrist is a doctor that works with people who are crazy."

"Why would you try to do anything with people who're crazy?"

"To get them well. To make their minds better. Good heavens." We paused to net a huge male crab, a true number one Jimmy, swimming doubled over a she-crab. He was taking her to the thick eelgrass, where she would shed for the last time and become a grown-up lady crab—a sook. When she was soft, there would be a proper crab wedding, of course, with the groom staying around to watch out for his bride until her shell was hard once more, and she could protect herself and her load of eggs on her own.

"Sorry, Mr. Jimmy," I said, "no wedding bells for you."

Now this old Jimmy didn't much like being deprived of his sweetheart, but Call pinched him from behind and threw each of them in a separate bucket. She was a rank peeler—that is, it wouldn't be more than a couple of hours before she shed. Our bucket for rank peelers was almost full. It was a good day on the water.

"Well, like I was saying, this p-sychiatrist comes up to Peter, and Peter looks him up in the book of judgment and finds out he's been mean to his wife and kids and tells him to go to hell."

"What?"

I ignored him. Otherwise I'd never get the story finished. "So the p-sychiatrist starts to leave, and then Peter says all of a sudden: 'Hey! Did you say you were a p-sychiatrist?' And the guy says, 'Yes, I did.'" I was talking so fast now, I was almost out of breath. "And Peter says, 'I think we can use you around here after all. You see, we got this problem. God thinks he's Franklin D. Roosevelt.'"

"God *what*?"

"You know when people are crazy they think they're somebody important—like Napoleon or something."

"But, Wheeze, God *is* important."

"It's a joke, Call."

"How can it be a joke? There ain't neither funny about it." He had broken into a waterman's emphatic negative.

"Call, it's funny because Franklin D. Roosevelt has got too big for his britches. Like he's better than God or something."

"But that's not what you said. You said—"

"I know what I said. But you gotta understand politics."

"Well, what kinda joke is that? Fiddle." Call's cuss words were taught to him by his sainted grandmother and tended to be as quaint as the clothes she made for him.

When the sun was high and our stomachs empty, Call stepped off the washboards into the boat. I shipped the pole and moved up with him to the forward thwart, where we put the oars into the locks and rowed the boat out of the eelgrass into deeper water and around to the harbor.

Captain Billy's son Otis ran the crab shipping part of his father's business, while his father and two brothers ran the ferry. We sold our soft crabs, peelers, and the terrapin to Otis, then split the money and the hard crabs. Call ran home to dinner, and I rowed back around the island as far as the South Gut, where I traded oars for the pole and poled the rest of the way home. The South Gut was a little ditch of water, one of many that crisscrossed Rass, and a natural garbage dump. The summer before, Call and I had cleaned it out (it had been clogged with rusting cans and crab pots, even old mattress springs) so I could pole the skiff through it all the way to my own backyard. Rass might be short on trees, but there was a loblolly pine sapling and a fig tree that my mother had planted on our side of the gut, as well as an orphan cedar on the other. I hitched my skiff to the pine and started at a trot for the back porch, a bucket of hard crabs in one hand and a fistful of money in the other.

My grandmother caught me before I got to the door. "Louise Bradshaw! Don't you go coming in the house dirty like that. Oh, my blessed, what a mess! Susan," she called back in to my mother, "she's full ruined every scrap of clothes she owns."

Rather than argue, I put my crab bucket and money on the edge of the porch and stepped out of my overalls. Underneath I had on my oldest cotton dress.

"Hang them overhalls on the back line, now."

I obeyed, pinning the straps securely to the clothesline. Immediately, the breeze took them straight out, as though Peter Pan had donned them to fly across our yard toward never-never land across the Bay.

I was humming with goodwill, "Come, Thou Fount of every blessing, tune my heart to sing Thy grace . . ." My grandmother was not going to get me today. I'd had a right smart haul.

Caroline was shelling peas at the kitchen table. I smiled at my sister benevolently.

"Mercy, Wheeze, you stink like a crab shanty."

I gritted my teeth, but the smile was still framing

them. "Two dollars," I said to my mother at the stove, "two dollars and forty-five cents."

She beamed at me and reached over the propane stove for the pickle crock, where we kept the money. "My," she said, "that was a good morning. By the time you wash up, we'll be ready to eat."

I liked the way she did that. She never suggested that I was dirty or that I stank. Just—"By the time you wash up—" She was a real lady, my mother.

While we were eating, she asked me to go to Kellam's afterward to get some cream and butter. I knew what that meant. It meant that I had made enough money that she could splurge and make she-crab soup for supper. She wasn't an islander, but she could make the best she-crab soup on Rass. My grandmother always complained that no good Methodist would ever put spirits into food. But my mother was undaunted. Our soup always had a spoonful or two of her carefully hoarded sherry ladled into it. My grandmother complained, but she never left any in the bowl.

I was sitting there, basking in the day, thinking how pleased my father would be to come home from crabbing and smell his favorite soup, bathing my sister and grandmother in kindly feelings that neither deserved, when Caroline said, "I haven't got anything to do but practice this summer, so I've decided to write a book about my life. Once you're known," she explained carefully as though some of us were dim-witted, "once you're famous, information like that is very valuable. If I don't get it down now, I may forget." She said all this in that voice of hers that made me feel slightly nauseated, the one she used when she came home from spending all Saturday going to the mainland for her music lessons, where she'd been told for the billionth time how gifted she was.

I excused myself from the table. The last thing I needed to hear that day was the story of my sister's life, in which I, her twin, was allowed a very minor role.

2

If my father had not gone to France in 1918 and collected a hip full of German shrapnel, Caroline and I would never have been born. As it was, he did go to war, and when he returned, his childhood sweetheart had married someone else. He worked on other men's boats as strenuously as his slowly healing body would let him, eking out a meager living for himself and his widowed mother. It was almost ten years before he was strong enough to buy a boat of his own and go after crabs and oysters like a true Rass waterman.

One fall, before he had regained his full strength, a young woman came to teach in the island school (three classrooms plus a gymnasium of sorts), and, somehow, though I was never able to understand it fully, the elegant little schoolmistress fell in love with my large, red-faced, game-legged father, and they were married.

What my father needed more than a wife was sons. On Rass, sons represented wealth and security. What my mother bore him was girls, twin girls. I was the elder by a few minutes. I always treasured the thought of those minutes. They represented the only time in my life when I was the center of everyone's attention. From the moment Caroline was born, she snatched it all for herself.

When my mother and grandmother told the story of our births, it was mostly of how Caroline had refused to breathe. How the midwife smacked and prayed and cajoled the tiny chest to move. How the cry of joy went up at the first weak wail—"no louder than a kitten's mew."

"But where was I?" I once asked. "When everyone was working over Caroline, where was I?"

A cloud passed across my mother's eyes, and I knew that she could not remember. "In the basket," she said. "Grandma bathed you and dressed you and put you in the basket."

"Did you, Grandma?"

"How should I know?" she snapped. "It was a long time ago."

I felt cold all over, as though I was the newborn infant a second time, cast aside and forgotten.

Ten days after our birth, despite the winter wind

and a threat of being iced in, my mother took Caroline on the ferry to the hospital in Crisfield. My father had no money for doctors and hospitals, but my mother was determined. Caroline was so tiny, so fragile, she must be given every chance of life. My mother's father was alive in those days. He may have paid the bill. I've never known. What I do know is that my mother went eight or ten times each day to the hospital to nurse Caroline, believing that the milk of a loving mother would supply a healing power that even doctors could not.

But what of me? "Who took care of me while you were gone?" The story always left the other twin, the stronger twin, washed and dressed and lying in a basket. Clean and cold and motherless.

Again the vague look and smile. "Your father was here and your grandmother."

"Was I a good baby, Grandma?"

"No worse than most, I reckon."

"What did I do, Grandma? Tell me about when I was a baby."

"How can I remember? It's been a long time."

My mother, seeing my distress, said, "You were a good baby, Louise. You never gave us a minute's worry." She meant it to comfort me, but it only distressed me further. Shouldn't I have been at least a minute's worry? Wasn't it all the months of worry that had made Caroline's life so dear to them all?

When Caroline and I were two months old, my mother brought her back to the island. By then I had grown fat on tinned milk formula. Caroline continued at my mother's breast for another twelve months. There is a rare snapshot of the two of us sitting on the front stoop the summer we were a year and a half old. Caroline is tiny and exquisite, her blonde curls framing a face that is glowing with laughter, her arms outstretched to whoever is taking the picture. I am hunched there like a fat dark shadow, my eyes cut sideways toward Caroline, thumb in mouth, the pudgy hand covering most of my face.

The next winter we both had whooping cough. My mother thinks that I was sick enough to have a croup tent set up. But everyone remembers that Captain Billy got the ferry out at 2:00 A.M. to rush Caroline and my mother to the hospital.

We went that way through all the old childhood diseases except for chicken pox. We both had a heavy case of that, but only I still sport the scars. That mark on the bridge of my nose is a chicken pox scar. It was more noticeable when I was thirteen than it is now. Once my father referred to me teasingly as "Old Scarface" and looked perfectly bewildered when I burst into tears.

I suppose my father was used to treating me with a certain roughness, not quite as he would have treated a son, but certainly differently from the way he treated Caroline. My father, like nearly every man on our island, was a waterman. This meant that six days a week, long before dawn he was in his boat. From November to March, he was tonging for oysters, and from late April into the fall, he was crabbing. There are few jobs in this world more physically demanding than the work of those men who choose to follow the water. For one slightly lame man alone on a boat, the work was more than doubled. He needed a son and I would have given anything to be that son, but on Rass in those days, men's work and women's work were sharply divided, and a waterman's boat was not the place for a girl.

When I was six my father taught me how to pole a skiff so I could net crabs in the eelgrass near the shore. That was my consolation for not being allowed to go aboard the *Portia Sue* as his hand. As pleased as I was to have my own little skiff, it didn't make up for his refusal to take me on his boat. I kept praying to turn into a boy, I loved my father's boat with such a passion. He had named it after my mother's favorite character from Shakespeare to please her, but he had insisted on the Sue. My mother's name is Susan. In all likelihood he was the only waterman on the Chesapeake Bay whose boat was named for a woman lawyer out of Shakespeare.

My father was not educated in the sense that my

mother was. He had dropped out of the island school at twelve to follow the water. I think he would have taken easily to books, but he came home at night too tired to read. I can remember my mother sometimes reading aloud to him. He would sit in his chair, his head back, his eyes closed, but he wasn't asleep. As a child, I always suspected he was imagining. Perhaps he was.

Although our house was one of the smaller of the forty or so houses on the island, for several years we owned the only piano. It came to us on the ferry after my mainland grandfather died. I think Caroline and I were about four when it arrived. She says she remembers meeting it at the dock and following while six men helped my father roll it on a dolly to our house, for there were no trucks or cars on the island.

Caroline also says that she began at once to pick out tunes by ear and make up songs for herself. It may be true. I can hardly recall a time when Caroline was not playing the piano well enough to accompany herself while she sang.

My mother not being an islander and the islanders not being acquainted with pianos, no one realized at the beginning the effect of damp salt air on the instrument. Within a few weeks it was lugubriously out of tune. My inventive mother solved this problem by going to the mainland and finding a Crisfield piano tuner who could also give lessons. He came by ferry once a month and taught a half-dozen island youngsters, including Caroline and me, on our piano. During the Depression he was glad to get the extra work. For food, a night's lodging, and the use of our piano, he tuned it and gave Caroline and me free lessons. The rest, children of the island's slightly more affluent, paid fifty cents a lesson. During the month each paid twenty cents a week to practice on our piano. In those days, an extra eighty cents a week was a princely sum.

I was no better or worse than most. We all seemed to get as far as "Country Gardens" and stay there. Caroline, on the other hand, was playing Chopin by the time she was nine. Sometimes people would stand outside the house just to listen while she practiced. Whenever I am tempted to dismiss the poor or uneducated for their vulgar tastes, I see the face of old Auntie Braxton, as she stands stock still in front of our picket fence, lips parted to reveal her almost toothless gums, eyes shining, drinking in a polonaise as though it were heavenly nourishment.

By the time we were ten, it became apparent, though, that Caroline's true gift was her voice. She had always been able to sing clearly and in tune, but the older she grew, the lovelier the tune became. The mainland county schoolboard, which managed the island school more by neglect than anything else, suddenly, and without explanation, sent the school a piano the year Caroline and I were in the fifth grade, and the next year, by what could only have been the happiest of coincidences, the new teacher appointed as half of the high school staff was a young man who not only knew how to play a piano but had the talent and strength of will to organize a chorus. Caroline was, of course, his inspiration and focal point. There was little to entertain the island youth, so we sang. And because we sang every day and Mr. Rice was a gifted teacher, we sang surprisingly well for children who had known little music in their lives.

We went to a contest on the mainland the spring we were thirteen and might have won except that when the judges realized our chief soloist was not yet in high school, we were disqualified. Mr. Rice was furious, but we children figured that the mainland schools were too embarrassed to be beaten out by islanders and so made up a rule to save their faces.

Sometime before that Mr. Rice had persuaded my parents that Caroline should have voice lessons. At first they refused, not because of the time and effort it would take to get Caroline to the mainland every Saturday, but because there was no money. But Mr. Rice was determined. He took Caroline to the college in Salisbury and had her sing for the head of the music department. Not only did the man agree to take Caroline on as a private pupil, he waived the fee. Even then the two round-trip tickets on the ferry plus the taxi fare to Salisbury put an unbelievable strain on the weekly budget, but Caroline is the kind of person other people sacrifice for as a matter of course.

I was proud of my sister, but that year, something began to rankle beneath the pride. Life begins to turn upside down at thirteen. I know that now. But at the time I thought the blame for my unhappiness must be fixed—on Caroline, on my grandmother, on my mother, even on myself. Soon I was able to blame the war.

3

Even I who read *Time* magazine from cover to cover every week was unprepared for Pearl Harbor. The machinations of European powers and the funny mustached German dictator were as remote to our island in the fall of 1941 as *Silas Marner,* which sapped our energies through eighth-grade English.

There were hints, but at the time I didn't make sense of them: Mr. Rice's great concern for "peace on earth" as we began at Thanksgiving to prepare for our Christmas concert; overhearing a partial conversation between my parents in which my father pronounced himself "useless," to which my mother replied, "Thank the Lord."

It was not a phrase my mother often used, but it was a true island expression. Rass had lived in the fear and mercy of the Lord since the early nineteenth century, when Joshua Thomas, "The Parson of the Islands," won every man, woman, and child of us to Methodism. Old Joshua's stamp remained upon us—Sunday school and Sunday service morning and evening, and on Wednesday night prayer meeting where the more fervent would stand to witness to the Lord's mercies of the preceding week and all the sick and straying would be held up in prayer before the Throne of Grace.

We kept the Sabbath. That meant no work, no radio, no fun on Sunday. But for some reason my parents were out on the Sunday afternoon that was December 7, my grandmother was snoring loudly from her bed, and Caroline was reading the deadly dull Sunday school paper—our only permitted reading on the Sabbath other than the Bible itself. So I, bored almost to madness, had wandered into the living room and turned on the radio, very low so that no one could hear, and pressed my ear against the speaker.

"The Japanese in a predawn surprise attack have destroyed the American fleet at Pearl Harbor. I repeat. The White House has confirmed that the Japanese . . ."

I knew by the chill that went through my body that it meant war. All my magazine reading and overheard remarks fell at once into a grotesque but understandable pattern. I rushed up to our room where Caroline, still innocent and golden, lay stomach down on her bed reading.

"Caroline!"

She didn't even look up. "Caroline!" I ripped the paper from under her hands. "The Japanese have invaded America!"

"Oh, Wheeze, for pity sake." And hardly looking up, she grabbed for her paper. I was used to her ignoring me, but this time I would not allow it. I snatched her arm and dragged her off her bed and down the stairs to the radio. I turned the volume up full. The fact that the Japanese had attacked Hawaii rather than invaded the continental United States was a distinction that neither of us bothered to quibble over. She, like me, was totally caught by the tone of fear that even the smooth baritone of the announcer's voice could not conceal. Caroline's eyes went wide, and, as we listened, she did something she had never done before. She took my hand. We stood there, squeezing each other's hand to the point of pain.

That is how our parents found us. There was no remonstrance for having broken the Fourth Commandment. The crime of the Japanese erased all lesser sinning. The four of us huddled together before the radio set. It was one of those pointed ones that remind you of a brown wood church, with long oval windows over a cloth-covered speaker.

At six, Grandma woke, hungry and petulant. No one had give any thought to food. How could one think of supper when the world had just gone up in flames? Finally, my mother went to the kitchen and made plates of cold meat and leftover potato salad, which she brought to the three of us hunched about the set. She even brought coffee for us all. Grandma insisted on being served properly at the table. Caroline and I had never drunk coffee in our lives, and the fact that our mother served us coffee that night made us both realize that our secure, ordinary world was forever in the past.

Just as I was about to take my first solemn sip, the announcer said, "We pause, now, for station identification." I nearly choked. The world had indeed gone mad.

Within a few days we learned that Mr. Rice had volunteered for the army and would be leaving for the war soon after Christmas. In chorus one morning the irony of celebrating the birth of the Prince of Peace suddenly seemed too much. I raised my hand.

"Yes, Louise?"

"Mr. Rice," I said, standing and dramatically darkening my voice to what I imagined to be the proper tone for mourning, "Mr. Rice, I have a proposal to make." There were a few snickers at my choice of words, but I ignored them. "I feel, sir, that under the circumstances, we should cancel Christmas."

Mr. Rice's right eyebrow shot up. "Do you want to explain that, Louise?"

"How," I asked, my glance sweeping about to catch the amused looks of the others, "how dare we celebrate while around the world thousands are suffering and dying?" Caroline was staring down at her desk, her cheeks red.

Mr. Rice cleared his throat. "Thousands were suffering and dying when Christ was born, Louise." He was clearly discomfited by my behavior. I was sorry now that I had begun but was in too deeply to retreat.

"Yes," I agreed grandly. "But the world has not seen, neither has it heard, such a tragic turn of events as we face in this our time."

Tiny little one-syllable explosions went off about the room like a string of Chinese firecrackers. Mr. Rice looked stern.

My face was burning. I'm not sure whether I was more embarrassed by the sound of my own voice or the snorts of my schoolmates. I sat down, my whole body aflame. The snorts broke into open laughter. Mr. Rice tapped his baton on his music stand to restore order. I thought he might try to explain what I had meant, would try in some way to mediate for me, but he said only, "Now then, let's try it once more from the beginning—"

"God rest ye merry, gentlemen, let nothing you dismay," sang everyone except me. I was afraid if I opened my mouth, I might let go the enormous sob that was lurking there, right at the top of my throat.

It was nearly dark when school got out that afternoon. I rushed out before anyone could catch up with me and walked, not home, but across the length of the marsh on the one high path to the very southern tip of the island. The mud had a frozen brown crust and the cordgrass was weighed down by ice. The wind cut mercilessly across the barren end of Rass, but the hot shame and indignation inside me made me forget the wind as I walked. I was right. I knew I was right, so why had they all laughed? And why had Mr. Rice let them? He hadn't even tried to explain what I meant to the others. It was only when I came to the end of the path and sat down upon a giant stump of driftwood and stared at the sickly winter moon waveringly reflected on the black water that I realized how cold I was and began to cry.

I should not forget that it was Caroline who came and found me there. Sitting on the stump, my back to the swamp and the village, I was crying aloud, so that I did not even hear the crunch of her galoshes.

"Wheeze."

I jerked around, angry to be found out.

"It's past time for your supper," she said.

"I'm not hungry."

"Oh, Wheeze," she said. "It's too cold to stay out here."

"I'm not coming back. I'm running away."

"Well, you can't run away tonight," she said. "There's no ferry until tomorrow morning. You might as well come in and have supper and get warm."

That was Caroline. I would hope for tears and pleadings. She offered facts. But they were facts I couldn't argue with. It would be next to impossible to run away in a skiff at any time of year. I sighed, wiped my face on the back of my hand, and rose to follow her. Even though I could have walked the path blindfolded, I felt foolishly grateful for the homely bobbing comfort of her flashlight.

The watermen of Rass had their own time system. Four-thirty was suppertime winter and summer. So when Caroline and I walked in, our parents and grandmother were already eating. I expected a reprimand from my father or a tongue-lashing from my grandmother, but to my relief they simply nodded as we came in. Mother got up to bring us some hot food from the stove, which she put before us when we had washed and sat down. Caroline must have told them what had happened at school. I was torn between gratitude that they should sympathize and anger that they should know.

The school concert was Saturday night. Sunday was the only day the men did not get up before dawn, and therefore Saturday night was the only night anyone of the island would consider spending in a frivolous manner. I didn't want to go, but it would have been harder to stay away and imagine what people were saying about me than to go and face them.

The boys had helped Mr. Rice rig up footlights, really a row of naked bulbs behind reflectors cut from tin cans, but they gave the tiny stage at the end of the gymnasium a magical distance from the audience. As I stood there on the stage floor in front of the risers, I could barely make out the familiar features of my parents in the center of the second row of chairs. I felt as if those of us on the stage were floating in another layer of the world, removed from those below. When I squinted my eyes, the people all blurred like a film that has jumped the sprockets and is racing untended through the machine. I think I sang most of the program with my eyes squinted. It was a very comforting feeling thus to remove myself from the world I imagined was laughing at me.

Betty Jean Boyd sang the solo for "O Holy Night," and I hardly flinched when she went flat on the first "shining." Betty Jean was considered to have a lovely voice. In any other generation on Rass she would have been worshiped for it, flat as it was, but in my day on Rass, everyone had heard Caroline sing. No one should have had to bear that comparison. Poor Betty Jean. I was puzzled that Mr. Rice should give her this solo. Caroline had sung it last year. Everyone would remember. But this year Mr. Rice had chosen a different solo for Caroline, a very simple one. I had been angry the first time he had sung it over for us. Caroline's voice, after all, was our school treasure. Why had he given the showy song to Betty Jean and a strange thin melody to Caroline?

Now Mr. Rice left the piano and stood before us, his arms tense, his long fingers slightly curved. His dark eyes traveled back and forth, willing every eye to meet his. There were a few polite coughs from the shadowy darkness behind him. It was time. In just a few seconds it would begin. I didn't dare to shift my gaze from Mr. Rice's face to Caroline's head, two rows behind and to the right of me in the back row, but my stomach knotted for her.

Mr. Rice's hands went down, and from the center of the back row Caroline's voice came suddenly like a single beam of light across the darkness.

I wonder as I wander out under the sky
Why Jesus the Savior did come for to die
For poor on'ry people like you and like I
I wonder as I wander—out under the sky.

It was a lonely, lonely sound, but so clear, so beautiful that I tightened my arms against my sides to keep from shaking, perhaps shattering. Then we were all singing, better than we had all night, better than we ever had, suddenly judged, damned, and purged in Caroline's light.

She sang once more by herself, repeating the words of the first verse so quietly that I knew surely I would shatter when she went up effortlessly, sweetly, and, oh, so softly, to the high G, holding it just a few seconds longer than humanly possible and then returning to the last few notes and to silence.

A sharp report of applause suddenly rattled the room like gunfire. I jumped, first startled by the sound and then angered. I looked from the dark noisy blur to Mr. Rice, but he was already turning to take a bow. He motioned Caroline to step down and come forward, which she did. And when she turned to go back to her place, I was disgusted to see her dimpled and smiling. She was pleased with herself. It was the same expression she wore when she had thoroughly trounced me in checkers.

When we left the gymnasium, the stars were so bright, they pulled me up into the sky like powerful magnets. I walked, my head back, my own nearly flat chest pressed up against the bosom of heaven, dizzied by the winking brilliance of the night. "I wonder as I wander..."

Perhaps I would have drowned in wonder if Caroline, walking ahead with my parents, had not turned and called my name sharply. "Wheeze, you better watch out walking that way," she said. "You're likely to break your neck." She had now moved beyond my parents in the narrow street and was walking backward, the better, I suppose, to observe me.

"Better watch out yourself," I snapped, annoyed and embarrassed to be so yanked away from the stars. I realized suddenly how cold the wind had become. She laughed merrily and, still walking backward, doubled her speed. She was not likely to run into anything. She never stumbled or bumped into things. That, she seemed to be saying, was what I did—often enough for both of us.

Grandma was prone to arthritis and did not go out on a winter's night, even to prayer meeting. So once home, we had to tell her all about the concert. Caroline did most of the talking, singing a snatch of this or that to remind Grandma of a carol she claimed never to have heard before.

"Did you sing the Holy Night one again?"

"No, Grandma, remember, I told you Betty Jean Boyd was doing that this year."

"Why was that? She can't half sing like you can."

"Caroline sang a different one this year, Mother." My mother was making cocoa for us and calling in a word here and there from the kitchen. "Betty Jean sounded very sweet."

Caroline gave me a look and snorted out loud. I knew she was expecting me to contradict Momma, but I wasn't going to. If Caroline wanted to be snobbish about Betty Jean, she could do it on her own.

Caroline had begun to imitate Betty Jean's singing of "O Holy Night." It was almost perfect, just a fraction flatter and shakier than Betty Jean's voice had been, the o's and ah's parodies of Betty Jean's pretentious ones. She ended the performance with a mournful shriek more than a little off pitch and looked around, grinning for her family's approval.

All the way through I had expected my parents to stop her, invoking, if nothing else, the nearness of the neighbors. But no one had. And now, she had finished and was waiting for our applause. It came in the form of a smile working at the firm corners of my father's mouth. Caroline laughed happily. It was all she desired.

Surely Momma would protest. Instead she handed Grandma a cup to drink in her chair. "Here's your cocoa, Mother," she said. Caroline and I went to the table for ours, Caroline still smiling. I had a burning desire to hit her in the mouth, but I controlled myself.

That night I lay in bed with an emptiness chewing away inside of me. I said my prayers, trying to push it away with ritual, but it kept oozing back round the worn edges of the words. I had deliberately given up "Now I lay me down to sleep" two years before as being too babyish a prayer and had been using since then the Lord's Prayer attached to a number of formula "God blesses." But that night "Now I lay me" came back unbidden in the darkness.

Now I lay me down to sleep,
I pray the Lord my soul to keep.
If I should die before I wake,
I pray the Lord my soul to take.

"If I should die . . ." It didn't push back the emptiness. It snatched and tore at it, making the hole larger and darker. "If I should die . . ." I tried to shake the words away with "Yea, though I walk through the valley of the shadow of death, I shall fear no evil, for behold, thou art with me . . ."

There was something about the thought of God being with me that made me feel more alone than ever. It was like being with Caroline.

She was so sure, so present, so easy, so light and gold, while I was all gray and shadow. I was not ugly or monstrous. That might have been better. Monsters always command attention, if only for their freakishness. My parents would have wrung their hands and tried to make it up to me, as parents will with a handicapped or especially ugly child. Even Call, his nose too large for his small face, had a certain satisfactory ugliness. And his mother and grandmother did their share of worrying about him. But I had never caused my parents "a minute's worry." Didn't they know that worry proves you care? Didn't they realize that I needed their worry to assure myself that I was worth something?

I worried about them. I feared for my father's safety every time there was a storm on the Bay, and for my mother's whenever she took the ferry to the mainland. I read magazine articles in the school library on health and gave them mental physical examinations and tested the health of their marriage. "Can this marriage succeed?" Probably not. They had nothing in common as far as I could tell from the questionnaires I read. I even worried about Caroline, though why should I bother when everyone else spent their lives fretting over her?

I longed for the day when they would have to notice me, give me all the attention and concern that was my due. In my wildest daydreams there was a scene taken from the dreams of Joseph. Joseph dreamed that one day all his brothers and his parents as well would bow down to him. I tried to imagine Caroline bowing down to me. At first, of course, she laughingly refused, but then a giant hand descended from the sky and shoved her to her knees. Her face grew dark. "Oh, Wheeze," she began to apologize. "Call me no longer Wheeze, but Sara Louise," I said grandly, smiling in the darkness, casting off the nickname she had diminished me with since we were two.

4

"I hate the water."

I didn't even bother to look up from my book. Grandma had two stock phrases. The first was "I love the Lord," and the second, "I hate the water." I had grown fully immune to both by the time I was eight.

"What time's the ferry due?"

"The same time as always, Grandma." I wished only to be left to my book, which was a deliciously scary one about some children who had been captured by a bunch of pirates in the West Indies. It was my mother's. All the books were hers except the extra Bibles.

"Don't be sassy."

I sighed and put down my book and said with

greatly exaggerated patience, "The ferry is due about four, Grandma."

"Doubt but there's a northwest wind," she said mournfully. "Likely to be headed into the wind all the way in." She rocked her chair slowly back and forth with her eyes closed. Or almost closed. I usually had the feeling she was watching through slits. "Where's Truitt?"

"Daddy's working on the boat, Grandma."

She opened her eyes wide and sat up straight. "Not tonging?"

"Tonging's done, Grandma. It's April." It was spring vacation, and here I was sitting all day with a cranky old woman.

She settled back. I thought she might tell me not to be sassy once more for good measure, but instead she said, "That ferry of Billy's is too old. One of these days it's going to sink right there in the middle of the Bay, and no one will find neither plank of it never again."

I knew Grandma's fears were idle, but they stirred up a little fuzz ball of fear in my stomach. "Grandma," I said, as much to myself as to her, "it's got to be okay. Government's always checking it out. Ferryboat's got to be safe or it won't get a license. Government controls it."

She sniffed loudly. "Franklin D. Roosevelt thinks

he can control the whole Chesapeake Bay? Ain't no government can control that water."

God thinks he's Franklin D. Roosevelt.

"What are you grinning about? Ain't nothing to grin about."

I pulled in my cheeks in an attempt to appear solemn. "You want some coffee, Grandma?" If I made her some coffee, it would distract her, and maybe she'd let me get back to my book in peace.

I slipped my book under the sofa cushion because it had a picture of a great sailing vessel on the front. I didn't want Grandma upset because I was reading a book about the water. The women of my island were not supposed to love the water. Water was the wild, untamed kingdom of our men. And though water was the element in which our tiny island lived and moved and had its being, the women resisted its power over their lives as a wife might pretend to ignore the existence of her husband's mistress. For the men of the island, except for the preacher and the occasional male teacher, the Bay was an all-consuming passion. It ruled their waking hours, sapped their bodily strength, and from time to tragic time claimed their mortal flesh.

I suppose I knew that there was no future for me on Rass. How could I face a lifetime of passive waiting? Waiting for the boats to come in of an afternoon, waiting in a crab house for the crabs to shed, waiting at home for children to be born, waiting for them to grow up, waiting, at last, for the Lord to take me home.

I gave Grandma her coffee and stood by while she noisily sucked in air and coffee. "Not enough sugar."

I whipped the sugar bowl out from behind my back. She was clearly annoyed that I'd been able to anticipate her complaint. I could see on her face that she was trying to decide how to shift to something that I wouldn't be prepared for. "Hmm," she said finally in a squeaky little tone and spooned two heaping measures of sugar into her cup. She didn't thank me, but I hadn't expected thanks. I was so delighted to have outsmarted her that I forgot myself and began whistling "Praise the Lord and Pass the Ammunition" as I returned the sugar bowl to the kitchen.

"Whistling women and crowing hens never come to no good end."

"Oh, I don't know, Grandma, we might be terrific in a circus freak show."

She was clearly shocked but couldn't seem to put her finger on my specific sin. "Thou shalt not—thou shalt not—"

"Whistle?"

"Sass!" She almost screamed. I had clearly gotten

the best of her, so I sobered to an elaborate caricature of humility. "Can I get you anything else, Grandma?"

She humphed and hemmed and slurped her coffee without answering, but as soon as I'd gotten my book again and was settled down on the couch and reading, she said, "It's onto four o'clock."

I pretended not to hear.

"Ain't you going down for the ferry?"

"I hadn't thought to."

"It wouldn't hurt you to think a little. Your mother's likely to have heavy groceries."

"Caroline's with her, Grandma."

"You know full well that little child ain't got the strength to carry heavy groceries."

I could have said several things but all of them were rude, so I kept my mouth shut.

"Why do you look at me like that?" she asked.

"Like what?"

"With bullets in your eyes. Like you want to shoot me dead. All I want you to do is help your poor mother."

It was useless to argue. I took the book upstairs and hid it in my underwear drawer. Grandma was less likely to poke around in there. She considered modern female undergarments indecent and if not precisely "of the devil," certainly in that vicinity. I got a jacket, as the wind would be chilly, and went downstairs. When I reached the front door, the rocking stopped.

"Where you think you're going?"

Fury began to swoosh up inside me. I kept my voice as flat as I could and said, "Down to meet the ferry, Grandma. Remember? You said I should go and help Momma bring back the groceries."

She looked strangely blank. "Well, hurry," she said at last, beginning to rock again. "I don't favor waiting here by myself."

A small crowd of islanders had come by foot or bicycle and were already waiting the arrival of the ferry. They greeted me as I approached, pulling the red metal wagon that we used for hauling.

"Your Momma coming in?"

"Yes, Miss Letty. She had to take Caroline to the doctor."

Sympathetic looks all round. "That child has always been so delicate."

It was useless to withhold information; besides, for once, I didn't care. "She had an earache, and Nurse thought she ought to go have Dr. Walton check it."

Heads shook knowingly. "You can't be too careful 'bout the earache."

"Surely cannot. Remember, Lettice, when little Buddy Rankin come down with that bad ear? Martha thought nothing of it, and the next thing she knowed he got this raging fever. A pure miracle of the Lord the child didn't go deaf, they said."

Little Buddy Rankin was a seasoned waterman with two children of his own. I wondered idly what fixed memory they would have of me in twenty or thirty years.

Captain Billy's son Otis emerged from the unpainted crab shipping shed. That meant the boat was coming in. He walked to the end of the pier ready to catch the line. Those of us waiting moved out of the lee of the building to watch the ferry chug in. It was small and, even before it was close enough to reveal its peeling paint, seemed to sag in the water. Grandma was right. It was an old boat, a tired boat. My father's boat was far from new. It had belonged to another waterman before he bought it, but it was still lively and robust, like a man who's spent his life on the water. Captain Billy's ferry, though much larger, drooped like an old waiting woman. I buttoned my jacket against the wind and concentrated on Captain Billy's sons Edgar and Richard who had jumped ashore and were helping Otis tie up the ferry with graceful, practiced steps.

My father had walked up. He smiled at me and touched my arm in greeting. For a happy moment, I thought he'd spied me from his boat and had come on purpose to say hello. And then I saw his gaze turn toward the hatch of the under deck passenger cabin.

It was Momma he had come to meet and Caroline, of course. Hers was the first head out of the opening, wrapped against the wind in a sky blue scarf. Just enough of her hair had escaped to make her look fresh and full like a girl in a cigarette ad.

"Hey, Daddy!" she called out as she came. "Daddy's here, Momma," she said back over her shoulder toward the cabin. Our mother's head appeared. She was having more trouble on the ladder than Caroline, for, in addition to a large purse, she was trying to negotiate a huge shopping bag.

Caroline, meantime, had skipped quickly around the narrow deck and jumped lightly to the dock. She kissed our father on his cheek, a gesture that never failed to embarrass me. Caroline was the only person I knew who kissed in public. It was simply not done on our island. At least she wouldn't try to kiss me. I was sure of that. She nodded, grinning. "Wheeze," she said. I nodded back without the smile. Daddy met Momma halfway round the deck and took the shopping bag. No unnecessary touching, but they were smiling and talking when they got off the boat.

"Oh, Louise. Thank you for bringing the wagon. They're still more groceries in the hold."

I smiled, proud of my thoughtfulness, conveniently forgetting it was Grandma who had sent me down to the dock.

Two other island women emerged from the cabin

door, and then, to my surprise, a man. Men usually rode up top on the bridge with Captain Billy. But this was an old man, one whom I had never seen before. He had the strong stocky build of a waterman. His hair, under a seaman's cap, was white and thick and hung almost halfway down his neck. He had a full mustache and beard, both white, and was wearing a heavy winter overcoat, despite the fact that it was April. And he was carrying what I imagined one might call a "valise." It must have been heavy because he put it down on the dock as he waited quietly with the rest of us for Captain Billy's sons to hand up the luggage and groceries from the hold.

Momma pointed out her two boxes, which my father and I loaded precariously onto the wagon. They were too large to fit into the bed of the wagon, so we perched them slantwise, tilting down into the middle. I knew I would have to go slowly, for if I hit a bump, there were likely to be groceries all over the narrow street.

All the time I was watching the stranger out of the corner of my eye. Two more ancient bags and a small trunk were brought up and put beside him. By now everyone was staring. No one would have so much baggage unless he planned to stay for quite some time.

"Somebody meeting you?" Richard asked, not unkindly.

The old man shook his head, staring down at the luggage piled around him. He looked a little like a lost child.

"Got a place to stay?" the young man asked.

"Yes." He lifted his overcoat collar up as though to protect himself from the cold island wind and jerked his hat down almost to his bushy eyebrows.

By now the crowd upon the dock was positively leaning in his direction. The island held few secrets or surprises beyond the weather. But here was a perfectly strange man. Where had he come from, and where was he planning to stay?

I felt my mother's elbow. "Come along," she said quietly, nodding a good-bye at my father. "Grandma will be worrying."

I had seldom felt so exasperated—to have to go home in the middle of this unfolding drama. But both Caroline and I obeyed, leaving the little scene on the dock behind, making our slow progress up the narrow oyster-shell street between the picket fences that enclosed each house. The street was only wide enough for four people to walk abreast. The crushed oyster shells underfoot rattled the wagon so that I could feel the vibrations in my teeth.

There was such a scarcity of high land on Rass that for generations we had buried our dead in our front yards. So to walk down the main street was to walk between the graves of our ancestors. As a child I thought nothing of it, but when I became an adolescent, I began to read the verses on the tombstones with a certain pleasant melancholy.

Mother, are you gone forever
To a land so bright and fair?
While your children weep unstopping
Can you hear us? Do you care?

Most of them were more bravely Methodist in flavor.

God will keep you little angel
Till we greet you by and by,
For a moment is our sorrow
Joy forever in the sky.

My favorite was for a young man who had died more than a hundred years before, but to whom I had attached more than one of my romantic fantasies.

Oh, how bravely did you leave us
Sailing for a foreign shore
How our hearts did break within us
At the thought of Nevermore.

He had been only nineteen. I fancied that I would have married him, had he lived.

I needed to concentrate on the groceries. Momma still had the large shopping bag. Caroline could hardly bear to go as slowly as the two of us had to, so she tended to skip on ahead and then come back to share some of the details of her trip to the mainland. It was one of these times when she was walking toward us that she suddenly lowered her voice.

"There he is. There's that man from the ferry."

I looked back over my shoulder, being careful to keep my free hand on the grocery boxes.

"Don't be rude," Momma said.

Caroline leaned toward me. "Edgar is pulling all his stuff in a cart."

"Hush," Momma warned. "Turn around."

Caroline was slow to obey. "Who is he, Momma?"

"Shh. I don't know."

Despite his age the man was walking remarkably fast. We couldn't hurry because of the wagon, so he soon overtook us and walked purposefully down the street ahead as though he knew exactly where he was going. There was no longer any sense of a lost child in his manner. The Roberts' house was the last one on the street, but he walked right past it, to where the oyster-shell street gave way to the dirt path across the southern marsh.

"Where's he think he's going?" Caroline asked.

The only thing farther along the path besides the marsh itself was one long-abandoned house.

"I wonder—" Momma began, but we were turning in at our own gate, and she didn't finish the sentence.

5

The stranger from the ferry offered no explanation for his presence on the island. Gradually, the people of Rass built one from ancient memory lavishly cemented with rumor. The man had gone to the Wallace place, which had been deserted for twenty years since the death of old Captain Wallace six months after his wife. He had found it without asking anyone the way and had moved in and begun to put it into repair as though he belonged there.

"He's Hiram Wallace," Grandma had announced—everyone over fifty had come to the same conclusion. "The old ones thought he was dead. But here he is. Too late to bring them neither comfort."

Bit by bit, straining my short patience to its utmost limit, the story of Hiram Wallace emerged. Call's grandmother told him that when she was a child, there had been a young waterman by that name, the only child of Captain Charles Wesley Wallace. It was back in the days when nearly every boat on the Bay was under sail, before hard blue crabs brought in much money. Captain Wallace and his son tonged for oysters in the winter, and in the summer they netted fish, chiefly menhaden and rockfish. That they had made a tidy profit was evidenced by the size of their house, which stood apart from the rest of the village. As my grandmother remembered it, their land had been large enough in those days for real grass to grow in a pasture, enough to support one of the few cows in the island's history.

What was left of the land was now all marsh, but the house, though neglected, had survived. We children had always regarded it as haunted. There were tales that Captain Wallace's ghost appeared to chase off intruders. It took me years to figure out that the purpose of the ghost story was to keep young courting couples from wandering down the path to the old Wallace place and taking advantage of the privacy.

One day I had talked Call into exploring the house with me, but just as we stepped onto the porch, a huge orange-colored tomcat came shrieking out a broken window at us. It was the only time in our lives that Call outran me. We sat gasping for breath on my front stoop. One part of my mind was saying that it had only been one of Auntie Braxton's cats.

She was said to keep sixteen, and anyone who had ever been as close as her front door would have sworn by the smell that there were at least that many and more. The other part of my mind was reluctant to let it go as simply as that.

"Have you ever heard," I asked, "have you ever heard that ghosts will take an animal form when they are angry?" Now that my breath was back I let my voice glide out in a dreamy way.

Call jerked around to look me in the face. "No!" he said.

"I was reading this book," I began to improvise (of course, I'd never seen any such book). "In this book, this scientist investigated places where ghosts were supposed to be. He started out saying that there was no such thing as ghosts, but being a scientist he had to admit finally that he couldn't explain certain things any other way."

"What things?"

"Oh—" I thought fast while drawing out the syllable. "Oh—certain furry beasts that took on the personality of a dead person."

Call was clearly shaken. "What do you mean?"

"Well, for instance, suppose old Captain Wallace when he was alive didn't want any visitors."

"He didn't." Call said darkly. "My grandma told me. After Hiram left, they lived all by themselves. Never spoke to nobody hardly."

"See?"

"See what?"

"We were fixing to visit him without an invitation," I whispered. "He was yelling at us and chasing us away."

Call's eyes were the size of clam shells. "You're making that up," he said. But I could tell that he believed every word of it.

"Only one way to be sure," I said.

"How you mean?"

I leaned close and whispered again. "Go back and see what happens."

He jumped to his feet. "Suppertime!" He started out the yard.

I had done my work too well. I was never able to persuade Call to return to that old empty house with me, and somehow, I was never quite able to go there alone.

Now that the strange old man was there, the house was no longer empty, and the whole island was trying to unravel the mystery. All the old people agreed that Hiram Wallace was in his youth the hope of every island maiden's heart, but that he had left Rass with his father's money and blessing to go to college. It was an unusual enough occurrence that even someone from our island who had gone to college fifty years ago was remembered for it. People also recalled, though this point was discussed at considerable length, that he had returned home without a degree, and that he had, in some undefinable way, changed. He had never been too sociable before he left, but he was positively silent when he returned. This only made the hearts of the young girls beat the harder, and no one had suspected that anything was wrong with him until the day of the storm.

The Bay is famous for its sudden summer storms. Before they can read their school primers, watermen learn how to read the sky and to head for the safety of a cove at the first glimmer of trouble. But the Bay is wide, and sometimes safety is too far away. In the old days, the watermen would lower their sails and use them as tents to protect themselves from the rain.

This is the story that the old people told: Captain Wallace and his son, Hiram, had let down their sails and were waiting out the storm. The lightning was so bright and near that it seemed to flash through the heavy canvas of the sail, the roaring and cracking enough to wake the dead sleeping in the depths of the water. Now, a man who is not afraid at a time like this is a man without enough sense to follow the water. But to fear is one thing. To let fear grab you by the tail and swing you around is another. This, Call's grandmother said, was what Hiram Wallace had done: terrified that the lightning would strike the tall mast of his father's skipjack, he had rushed out from under his sail cover, taken an ax, and chopped the mast to the level of the deck. After the storm passed, they were sighted drifting mastless on the Bay and were towed home by an obliging neighbor. When it became apparent that the mast had been chopped down, rather than felled by lightning, Hiram Wallace became the butt of all the watermen's jokes. Not long after, he left the island for good. . . .

Unless, of course, the strong old man rebuilding the Wallace house was the handsome young coward who had left nearly fifty years before. He never said he was, but then again, he never said he wasn't. Some of the islanders thought a delegation should be sent to ask the old man straight out who he was, for if he were not Hiram Wallace, what right did he have taking over the Wallace property? The delegation was never sent. April was nearly over. The one slow month of the watermen's year was coming to an end. There was a flurry of overhauling and painting and mending to be done. Crabs were moving and the men had to be ready to go after them.

"I bet he isn't Hiram Wallace," I said to Call one day in early May.

"Why not?"

"Why would a man come to Rass in the middle of a war?"

"Because he's old and has nowhere else to go."

"Oh, Call. Think. Why would a person come to the Bay right now of all times?"

"Because he's old—"

"The Bay is full of warships from Norfolk."

"So? What does that have to do with Hiram Wallace?"

"Nothing. That's just it, dummy. Who would want to know about warships?"

"The navy."

"Call. Don't you get it?"

"There's nothing to get."

"Warships, Call. What better place to spy on warships than from a lonely house right by the water?"

"You read too much."

"I suppose if someone was to catch a spy they'd take him to the White House and pin medals on him."

"I never heard of kids catching spies."

"That's just it. If two kids were to catch a spy—"

"Wheeze. It's Hiram Wallace. My grandma knows."

"She *thinks* he's Hiram Wallace. That's what he wants everyone to think. So they won't suspect him."

"Suspect him of what?"

I sighed. It was obvious that he had a long way to go before he was much of a counterspy, while I was putting myself to sleep at night performing incredible feats of daring on behalf of my embattled country. The amount of medals Franklin D. Roosevelt had either hung around my neck or pinned to my front would have supplied the army with enough metal for a tank. There was a final touch with which I closed the award ceremony.

"Here, Mr. President," I would say, handing back the medal, "use this for our boys at the front."

"But, Sara Louise Bradshaw—" Franklin D. Roosevelt for all his faults never failed to call me by my full name. "But, Sara Louise Bradshaw, this medal is yours. You have earned it with your great cunning and bravery. Keep it and hand it down to your children's children."

I would smile, a slightly ironic little smile. "Do you think, Mr. President, with the life I lead, that I will live long enough to have children?" That question never failed to reduce Franklin D. Roosevelt to silence touched with awe.

In my dreams I always went in alone, but in real life it seemed selfish. Besides, I was used to doing things with Call.

"Okay, Call. First we got to work out a plan."

"A plan for what?"

"To catch this kraut in the very act of spying."

"You're not going to catch him spying."

"Why not?"

"Because he's not a spy."

What can you do with a man who has no faith? "All right. Who is he then? Just answer me that."

"Hiram Wallace."

"Good heavens."

"You're cussing again. My grandma—"

"I am not cussing. Cussing is like 'God' and 'hell' and 'damn.'"

"See!"

"Call. How about pretending? Just for fun, pretend the guy is a spy, and we've got to get the proof."

He looked uncertain. "Like one of your jokes?"

"Yes. No." Sometimes Call could be perfectly sensible and at other times you could have gotten more sense out of a six-year-old. "It's like a game, Call." I didn't wait for him to answer. "Come on." I started running for the path through the salt meadow marsh with Call puffing behind me.

If Call's family was as poor as my grandmother said they were, I could never figure out how Call got so fat. As a matter of fact, both his mother and grandmother were fat. I thought that if you were poor you were skinny. But the evidence seemed to contradict this. And Call had other problems with running besides his weight. Like all of us, his shoes came from the Sears, Roebuck catalog. To order shoes from a catalog, you stood on a piece of brown wrapping paper, and your mother drew a pencil line around both your feet. These outlines were sent to the mail-order house, and they sent you shoes to fit the brown wrapping-paper feet. But the brown paper outlines didn't tell the mail-order house how fat your feet were on the top. For that reason, poor Call never had a pair of shoes that would lace properly. The tops of his feet were so fat that once he got his shoes laced up, there was nothing left to make a proper bow. So when he ran, his shoes often came unlaced and flapped up and down on his heels.

It was low tide, so I left the path and began making my way through the marsh. My plan was to give the old Wallace house a wide berth and come up on it from the south side. The old man would never expect people from that direction.

"Wait!" Call cried out. "I lost my shoe."

I went back to where Call was standing on one leg like an overweight egret. "My shoe got stuck," he said.

I pulled his shoe out of the mud for him and tried to clean it off on the cordgrass.

"My grandma will beat me," he said. It was hard for me to imagine Call's tubby little grandmother taking a switch to a large fifteen-year-old boy, but I held my peace. I had a greater problem than that. What would Franklin D. Roosevelt say about a spy who lost his shoe in the salt marsh and worried aloud that his grandma would beat him? I sighed and handed Call the shoe. He put it on and limped back to the path.

"Sit down," I commanded.

"On the ground?"

"Yes, on the ground." What did he expect, an easy chair? Then I cleaned his shoes and mine as best I could with my handkerchief. My mother had trouble persuading me to carry one because I was a lady, but I now realized that a handkerchief was an invaluable tool for a counterspy—to erase fingerprints, and so forth. "Now," I said, "I'm going to fix your shoestrings." I unlaced his strings and started again, skipping the second and fourth holes. This way I could make the lace long enough to provide a decent bow.

"There," I said, tying them for him as though he were a little child.

"You left out four holes."

"Call. I did it on purpose. So they wouldn't come loose all the time."

"They look dumb."

"Not as dumb as you'd look in your sockfeet."

He pretended to ignore this and stared at his shoelaces, as though trying to decide whether to retie them or to leave them be.

"Why don't you think of it as a secret signal?"

"A *what*?"

"Counterspies have to have ways of identifying themselves to other counterspies. Like secret code words. Or wearing a special kind of flower. Or—tying their shoes a certain way."

"You can't make me believe that spies tie their shoestrings funny."

"Just ask Franklin D. Roosevelt when we meet him."

"That's one of your jokes."

"Oh, come on. You can tie them again later, after the mission."

He had his mouth set to argue, but I didn't wait for a retort. Good heavens. The war would be over and he'd still be sitting there fussing about his shoestrings. "Follow me and keep low."

The cordgrass was about two feet high. There was no way, short of crawling through the mud on our bellies, that we could approach the Wallace house unseen. But there is a way of feeling invisible that makes one almost believe it's true. At any rate, I felt invisible, creeping bent over toward that great gray clapboard house. My heart was beating as fast and noisily as the motor of the *Portia Sue*.

There was no sound of life from the house. Earlier I had heard sawing and pounding. Now everything was quiet except the gentle lapping of the water on the nearby shore and the occasional cry of a water bird.

I signaled for Call to follow me to the southwest corner of the house, and then, keeping close to the side, we slipped silently to the first window facing south. Carefully, I raised my head until my eyes could peer over the sill into the room. It was evidently the room that the old man had chosen for his workshop. Weather-beaten chairs, their cane bottoms sagging and broken, were arranged to serve as sawhorses. The floor was covered with wood curls and sawdust. The sounds I had heard from across the marsh came from here, but the old man was no longer in the room. I gestured Call to stay down, that there was nothing to see, but of course he stuck his head up and peered in, just as I had done.

"No one there," he said in what he mistook for a whisper.

"Shhhhh!" I waved my hand in a violent "get down," but he was in no hurry. He gazed into the room as though it were full of great art rather than pine boards and wood curls.

I gave up trying to signal him and crept ahead to the next window. Slowly, very slowly, bracing my hand against the side of the house for support, I raised my head to the level of the window—straight into a great staring glass eye. I must have screamed. At least I did something to make Call begin to run as fast as he could around the house and in the direction of the path. I didn't run—not because I wasn't terrified, not because I wouldn't have liked to run, but because my feet had lost all power of movement.

The glass eye raised itself slowly from my face and a human voice said, "There you are. I didn't mean to scare you."

I tossed my head, trying vainly to imitate the

counterspy of my imagination, hoping that a clever, careless remark would float effortlessly from my lips, but my mouth was dry as sawdust and no remark, careless or otherwise, was about to emerge.

"Would you like to come in?"

I turned frantically to find Call and located him a hundred feet away on the path toward the village. He had stopped running. I felt a surge of gratitude for him. He hadn't deserted, not really.

"Your friend, too," the old man said, putting his periscope down on a table and smiling warmly through his white beard.

I licked my mouth, but my tongue was almost as dry as my lips. Franklin D. Roosevelt was hanging the Congressional Medal of Honor around my neck, saying, "Without regard for her personal safety, she entered the very stronghold of the foe."

"Ca-all." My voice cracked wide open on the word. "Ca-all."

He started back in a sort of zombielike walk. I could feel the presence of the man in the window above me. Call came up and stood right behind me, his breath coming from his open mouth in noisy pants. We were both fixed on the form above us.

"Won't you come in and have a cup of tea, or something?" the man said invitingly. "I haven't had any visitors since I got here except for an old tom-cat."

I could feel Call stiffen like a dead fish.

"He acted like the place belonged to him. I had a time convincing him otherwise."

Call butted me in the back with his stomach. I butted him back with my behind. Good heavens. Here we were on the very trail of a spy and Call was going to get upset by a ghost—a made-up ghost, one I had made up. Annoyance drove out panic.

"Thank you," I said. My voice was a little too loud and there was a distinct quaver in it, so I tried again. "Thanks. We'd like tea, wouldn't we?"

"My grandma don't allow me to drink tea."

"The boy will have milk," I said grandly and flounced around to the front door. Call followed at my heels. By the time we got around the house, the man was there, holding the door open for us. *Without regard for her personal safety . . .*

There was very little to sit on inside the house. The man pulled a rough plank bench around for Call and me, and after he'd put a kettle on a two-burner propane stove and puttered about his kitchen a bit, he came in and sat down on a homemade stool.

"Now. You are—"

I was still in the process of deciding whether or not counterspies gave their actual names in a situation like this when Call spoke up. "I'm Call and she's Wheeze."

The man began unaccountably to laugh. "Wheeze and Call," he said gleefully. "It sounds like a vaudeville act."

How rude—to sit there laughing at our names.

"It would be better if it was Wheeze and Cough. Still, Wheeze and Call is pretty good."

I sat up very straight on the bench. To my utter amazement, not to say disgust, I realized that Call was giggling. I gave him a look.

"It's a joke, Wheeze."

"How can it be a joke?" I asked. I almost said *"It's not funny,"* but I stopped myself in time. Fortunately, the kettle whistled, and the man got up to make the tea. I gave Call a glare that should have stopped the tide, but he kept on laughing. I'd never heard him laugh in my life and here he was shrieking like a gull over garbage about something that was just plain insulting.

The man handed me a mug of very black tea. "I've only got tinned milk," he said to Call while returning to the kitchen.

"That's okay," Call said, wiping the tears off his face with the back of his wrist. "Wheeze and Cough," he repeated to me. "Don't you get it?"

"Of course I get it." I was trying to figure out how I was going to get down the black stuff I had been handed. "I just don't think it's funny."

The man came back from the kitchen carrying a mug. "Not funny, eh? Oh, well, I'm out of practice." He handed the mug to Call. "It's half tinned milk and half water."

Call tasted it. "Good," he said.

I waited for him to offer me something to put in my tea, but he didn't. He just got himself a mug of the black brew and sat down.

"My real name is Sara Louise Bradshaw," I said, forgetting that minutes ago I had decided against revealing my true name.

"That's a very nice name," he said politely.

"My real name is McCall Purnell, but everybody calls me Call."

"I see," he said slyly. "If I want you, I just call Call."

"Call Call!" cried Call, as though it was the most original idea as well as the funniest thing he had ever heard. "Call Call! Did you get that, Wheeze? It's a joke."

Good heavens. "I don't suppose," I said, loading my voice with significance, "I don't suppose that you would tell us your name."

The man feigned surprise. "I thought everyone on this island knew my name."

Both Call and I leaned forward, waiting for him to say more, but he didn't. I was puzzling it out, whether to press him further or to play it casually, when Call blurted out, "You don't seem like neither spy."

The old man raised an eyebrow at me. I'm sure I turned the color of steamed crab. How do counterspies keep from blushing? He stared at me unmercifully for a minute. I was shrinking into the bench. "Why," he asked accusingly, "why aren't you drinking your tea?"

"Tin—tin—tin," I stammered.

"Rin tin tin," shrieked Call.

The man laughed, too, but at least he got up and brought the tin of milk over to me. My hands were shaking with rage or frustration or exasperation, who knew which, but I managed to fill the mug to the brim with the thick yellowish milk. He waited in front of me until I had sampled the brew. I took a scalding sip. It was too hot to know how it tasted, but I shook my head to indicate that it was fine. Halfway into the mug, I realized I should have asked for sugar, but then it seemed too late.

That was the way most of our early visits to the Captain's house went. We decided, Call and I, simply to call him "the Captain." On Rass any waterman who owned his own boat was called Captain So and So after he had passed fifty. I wouldn't call him Captain Wallace, because he'd never actually claimed the name. I kept going to see him in the fading hope that he'd turn out to be a real spy and I could have a medal after all. Call kept going because the Captain told great jokes, "not like yours, Wheeze, really good ones."

At any rate, it was Call the Captain liked, not me. If I'd been a more generous person, I'd have been happy that Call had found a man to be close to. He didn't remember his own father, and if any boy needed a father it was Call. But I was not a generous person. I couldn't afford to be. Call was my only friend. If I gave him up to the Captain, I'd have no one.

6

It is hard, even now, to describe my relationship to Caroline in those days. We slept in the same room, ate at the same table, sat for nine months out of each year in the same classroom, but none of these had made us close. How could they, when being conceived at the same time in the same womb had done nothing to bind us together? And yet, if we were not close, why did only Caroline have the power, with a single glance, to slice my flesh clear through to the bone?

I would come in from a day of progging for crab, sweating and filthy. Caroline would remark mildly that my fingernails were dirty. How could they be anything else but dirty? But instead of simply acknowledging the fact, I would fly into a wounded rage. How dare she call me dirty? How dare she try to make me feel inferior to her own pure, clear beauty? It wasn't my fingernails she was concerned with, that I was sure of. She was using my fingernails to indict my soul. Wasn't she content to be golden perfection without cutting away at me? Was she to allow me no virtue—no shard of pride or decency?

By now I was screaming. Wasn't it I who brought in the extra money that paid for her trips to Salisbury? She ought to be on her knees thanking me for all I did for her. How dare she criticize? How dare she?

Her eyes would widen. Even as I yelled, I could feel a tiny rivulet of satisfaction invading the flood of my anger. She knew I was right, and it unsettled her. But the lovely eyes would quickly narrow, the lips set. Without a word, she would turn and leave me before I was through, shutting off my torrent, so that my feelings, thus dammed, raged on in my chest. She would not fight with me. Perhaps that was the thing that made me hate her most.

Hate. That was the forbidden word. I hated my sister. I, who belonged to a religion which taught that simply to be angry with another made one liable to the judgment of God and that to hate was the equivalent of murder.

I often dreamed that Caroline was dead. Sometimes I would get word of her death—the ferry had sunk with her and my mother aboard, or more often the taxi had crashed and her lovely body had been consumed in the flames. Always there were two feelings in the dream—a wild exultation that now I was free of her and . . . terrible guilt. I once dreamed that I had killed her with my own hands. I had taken the heavy oak pole with which I guided my skiff. She had come to the shore, begging for a ride. In reply I had raised the pole and beat, beat, beat. In the dream her mouth made the shape of screaming, but no sound came out. The only sound of the dream was my own laughter. I woke up laughing, a strange shuddering kind of laugh that turned at once into sobs.

"What's the matter, Wheeze?" I had awakened her.

"I had a bad dream," I said. "I dreamed you were dead."

She was too sleepy to be troubled. "It was only a dream," she said, turning her face once more to the wall and snuggling deep under her covers.

But it was I who killed you! I wanted to scream it out, whether to confess or frighten, I don't know. *I beat you with my pole. I'm a murderer. Like Cain.* But she was breathing quietly, no longer bothered by my dream or by me.

Sometimes I would rage at God, at his monstrous almighty injustice. But my raging always turned to remorse. My wickedness was unforgivable, yet I begged the Lord to have mercy on me, a sinner. Hadn't God forgiven David who had not only committed murder, but adultery as well? And then I would remember that David was one of God's pets. God always found a way to let his pets get by with murder. How about Moses? How about Paul, holding the coats while Stephen was stoned?

I would search the Scriptures, but not for enlightenment or instruction. I was looking for some tiny shred of evidence that I was not to be eternally damned for hating my sister. Repent and be saved! But as fast as I would repent, resolving never again to hate, some demon would slip into my soul, tug at the corner, and whisper, "See the look on your mother's face as she listens to Caroline practice? Has she ever looked at you that way?" And I would know she hadn't.

Only on the water was there peace. When school let out in the middle of May, I began getting up long before dawn to go crabbing. Call went along, somewhat grudgingly, because I was unwilling to explain my great zeal for work. I had formulated a plan for escape. I was going to double my crab catch and keep half the money for myself, turning over to my mother the usual amount. My half I would save until I had enough to send myself to boarding school in Crisfield. On Smith Island to the south of us there was no high school, not even the pretense of one that we had on Rass. The state, therefore, sent any Smith Islanders who continued school after the elementary level to a boarding school in Crisfield. The prices were not out of sight. Too high, it was true, for an island family without state aid to contemplate, but low enough for me to dream and work toward. It seemed to me that if I could get off the island, I would be free from hate and guilt and damnation, even, perhaps, from God himself.

I was too clever to pin all my hopes on crabs. Crabs are fickle creatures. They always know when you need them too much and pick precisely that season to make themselves scarce. I must give the impression, therefore, despite my early risings, that I didn't much care how lucky we were. When we were on the water, poling through the eelgrass, I took pains to say at just about dawn, "This is the nicest time of day, isn't it, Call? Who cares if the crabs are here or not? Let's just relax and enjoy ourselves."

Call would give me a look that indicated that I had lost my mind, but he was smart enough not to think it out loud. I can't swear that I fooled the crabs, but our catches were good that summer. Still, I wasn't going to count too heavily on crabs. I began casting about for other ways to make money.

I found what seemed a sure thing in the back of a Captain Marvel comic book in Kellam's store. I even squandered a dime of my hard-earned cash to buy the book, which I hid with my other treasures in the underwear drawer.

WANTED: Song Lyrics
Cash for your poems!

Cash. That was a word to make the creative juices flow. The fact that most of the poetry I'd ever read came off tombstones didn't stop me. I listened to the radio, didn't I?

There'll be bluebirds over
The white cliffs of Dover
Tomorrow, just you wait and see.
There'll be love and laughter
And peace ever after
Tomorrow, when the world is free.

Any idiot could figure it out. Two rhyming lines, stuffed with romance, a third that neither rhymes nor makes sense right away, two more romantic ones, then the third that also rhymes with the earlier unrhymed one and sort of makes sense.

When the gulls fly over the Bay
They cry that you're far away.
But we didn't part.
Though you're far across the sea,
You're not far away to me,
You're in my heart.

It had all the elements—romance, sadness, an allusion to the war, and faithful love. I fancied myself the perfect lyricist—romantic, yet knowledgeable.

I tried it out on Call in the boat one day.

"What's that supposed to mean?"

"The girl's boyfriend is away at war."

"Then why are the gulls crying? Why should they care?"

"They don't really care. In poems you can't say plain out what you mean."

"Why not?"

"Then it's not poetry anymore."

"You mean a poem's supposed to lie?"

"It's not lying."

"Go on. Ain't neither gull on this Bay up there boohooing 'cause some sailor's gone to war. If that ain't a plain out lie, I don't know what is."

"It's a different way of talking. Makes it prettier."

"It ain't pretty to lie, Wheeze."

"Forget about the gulls. How about the rest of it?"

"The rest of what?"

"The rest of my poem, Call. How does it sound?"

"I forget."

I gritted my teeth to keep from yelling at him and then with super patience read it through again.

"I thought you's going to forget about the gulls."

"No, *you* forget them. How does the rest sound?"

"It don't make neither sense."

"What do you mean?"

"Either the guy's away or he ain't. You got to make up your mind."

"Call. It's a poem. In real life he is far away, but she thinks about him all the time, so she feels like he's real close."

"I call it dumb."

"Just wait until you fall in love."

He looked at me as though I'd proposed some indecent act.

I sighed. "Did you hear the one about the Australian who wanted to buy a new boomerang but he couldn't get rid of his old one?"

"No. What about him?"

"Get it? A boomerang. He wanted to buy a new boomerang, but he kept getting the old one back every time he threw it away."

"Why should he even want a new one? The old one's still perfectly good, isn't it?"

"Call. Just forget it."

He shook his head, the picture of patient disbelief,

and I forgot I was pretending not to care about crabs and devoted my full attention to the pesky varmints. I like to recall that we netted two full baskets of rank peelers that day.

No one had told me to turn over all the money I made crabbing. I just always had. When I started, I guess, it hadn't occurred to me that it was mine to keep. We always lived so close to the edge of being poor. It made me feel proud to be able to present the family with a little something extra to hold onto. While my parents never carried on much over it, I was always thanked. When my grandmother would criticize me, I could remember, even if the laws of respect kept me silent, that I was a contributing member of the household in which she and Caroline were little more than parasites. It was a private comfort.

But no one ever said I had to turn over *every* penny I made to the stoneware pickle crock in which the household money was kept.

Why then did I feel so guilty? Wasn't it my right to keep some of my hard-won earnings? But what if Otis should say something to my father about all the crabs he was buying from us? What if Call's mother should brag to my mother about how much money Call was bringing home these days? I divided my share exactly down the middle. If there was a penny in doubt, the penny went into the crock. I was contributing almost as much as I had during the previous summer, but I wasn't taking the money proudly to Momma for her to count out and put into the crock. I was slipping it in myself and then saying later, "Oh, by the way, I left a little in the crock." And my mother would thank me quietly, just as she always had. I never said I was putting everything in. I never lied. But then no one ever asked.

If only there were some other way to make money. Call's total lack of enthusiasm for my poem had had a dampening effect. I knew perfectly well that he was as qualified to judge poetry as he was to judge jokes, which was not at all, but still, he was the only human being I could risk reading it aloud to. If only he could have said something like, "I don't know anything about poetry, but it sounds fine to me." That would have been gracious, almost honest, and would have given me a real boost when I needed it.

As it was, I waited a week or so, then pulled myself together enough to copy the poem out on clean notebook paper and mail it to Lyrics Unlimited. Even before it could have been delivered to the P.O. Box in New York, I began haunting the docks when the ferry (which also served as the mail boat) came in. I didn't have the nerve to ask Captain Billy directly if there was any mail for me, but I hoped that if I just happened to be standing there, he'd see me and let me know. I didn't know that he never opened the sack before he took it to Mrs. Kellam, who served as postmistress. But I did know that Mrs. Kellam was a noisy gossip. I dreaded the thought of her asking my grandmother about a mysterious letter arriving from New York addressed to me.

It was about that time that our day-old Baltimore *Sun* carried huge headlines about the eight German saboteurs. They had been landed by submarine on Long Island and Florida and almost immediately caught. I knew, of course I knew, that the Captain was not a spy, but as I read, it felt as though I were swallowing an icicle. Suppose he had been. Suppose Call and I had caught him and become heroes? It seemed such a near miss that suddenly it was important to me to find out more about the old man. If he was not a spy, if he was indeed Hiram Wallace, why had he come back after all these years to an island where he was hardly remembered except with contempt?

7

Call and I had been so busy crabbing since school let out that we'd hardly been to visit the Captain together. Call, I knew, usually went to see him on Sunday afternoons, but my parents liked me to stay closer by on Sundays. I didn't mind. The long sleepy afternoon was perfect for writing lyrics. By now I had nearly a shoe box full, just waiting for Lyrics Unlimited to write and demand all that I could deliver.

So Call was surprised when, on a Tuesday, I proposed that we wind up the crabbing an hour early and pay a visit to the Captain.

"I thought you didn't like him," Call said.

"Of course I like him. Why shouldn't I like him?"

"Because he tells good jokes."

"That's a stupid reason not to like somebody."

"Yeah. That's what I thought."

"What d'you mean?"

"Nothing."

I decided to ignore the implied insult. "You can learn a lot from someone who comes from the outside. Take Mr. Rice. I guess Mr. Rice taught me more than all my other teachers put together." All two of them.

"About what?"

I blushed. "About everything—music, life. He was a great man." I talked and thought about Mr. Rice as though he were dead and gone forever. That's how far away his Texas army post seemed.

Call was quiet, watching my face. I knew he was fixing to say something but didn't quite know how to say it. "What's the matter?" I asked him. As soon as I asked, I knew. He didn't want me to visit the Captain with him. He wanted the Captain all to himself. Besides, he was suspicious of me. I decided to tackle the matter directly.

"Why don't you want me to visit the Captain?"

"I never said I didn't want you to visit the Captain."

"Well, what are we waiting for? Let's go."

He shrugged his shoulders unhappily. "Free country," he muttered. It didn't make any sense, but I knew what he meant—that if there had been a way to stop me, he would have.

The Captain was tending crab lines on his broken-down dock. I poled the boat in close before he heard us and looked up.

"Well, if it isn't Wheeze and Cough," he said, smiling widely and touching the bill of his cap.

"Wheeze and Cough, get it?" Call yelled back to me from the bow. He shook his head, smiling all over his face. "Wheeze and Cough, that's really good."

I tried to smile, but my face had too much basic integrity for me even to pretend I had heard something funny.

Call and the Captain gave each other a "don't mind her" look, and Call threw the Captain the bowline and he tied us up. I don't mind admitting I wasn't too keen to step out on that ramshackle dock, but after Call had jumped onto it, and it had only shuddered a bit, I climbed carefully out and walked off to the shore as quickly as I dared.

"I'm going to fix it." The Captain hadn't missed my anxiety. "Just so many things to do around here." He nodded at Call. "I tried to get your friend here to give me a hand, but—"

Call blushed. "You can't hammer on a Sunday," he said defensively.

Hiram Wallace would have known that. Nobody on the island worked on the Sabbath. It was as bad as drinking whiskey and close to cursing and adultery. I racked my brain for the next question—the one that would prove to Call beyond doubt that the Captain was no more Hiram Wallace than I was. "Don't you recall the Seventh Commandment?" I asked slyly.

He lifted his cap and scratched his hair underneath. "Seventh Commandment?"

I had him. That is, I almost had him. I hadn't reckoned on Call. Call who snorted and almost yelled, "Seventh? Seventh? Seventh don't have neither to do with hammering on Sunday. Seventh's the one," he stopped, suddenly embarrassed and lowered his voice, "on adultery."

"Adultery?" The Captain started laughing out loud. "Well, I'm too old to worry about that one. Now there was a time—" He grinned mischievously. I suspect Call wanted him to go on as much as I did, but the old man stopped right there. Like offering candy to a child and then yanking back your hand with some excuse about saving his teeth, I thought.

"Today is Tuesday," Call said as we started for the house.

"Tuesday! Then—then—" the Captain seemed terribly excited. "Then tomorrow is Wednesday, and after that comes Thursday! Friday! Saturday! Sunday! And Monday!!"

I thought Call would die laughing on the spot, but he managed to control himself enough to gasp, "Get it, Wheeze? Get it?"

If I couldn't smile at "Wheeze and Cough," how was I to force a laugh at a recitation of the days of the week?

"Don't mind her, Captain. She don't catch on too good."

"Too well." At least I could demonstrate proper grammar. "Too well."

"Too well. Too well," repeated the Captain chirpily, lifting his hand to his ear. "Hark? Do I hear the mating call of a feathered friend of the marshland?"

Call, naturally, collapsed. All I could think of was if we'd netted a spy like this, Franklin D. Roosevelt would have thrown him back. Good heavens.

Eventually, Call recovered from his hysterics enough to explain to the Captain that since it was Tuesday and not yet suppertime, he and I would be glad to lend a hand fixing up the old dock or house or whatever else the Captain might want doing around the place. In fact, Call added, we could come at about this time *every* afternoon, except Sunday of course, and help out.

"I'd want to pay you something," the Captain said. My ears stretched practically to the top of my head, and I opened my mouth to utter a humble thanks.

"Oh, *no,*" said Call. "We couldn't think of taking money from a neighbor."

Who couldn't? But for once in his life Call talked

faster than I could think, and the two of them snatched away my time and energy and sold me into slavery before I had breath to hint that I wouldn't be insulted by a small tip every now and then.

That was how we came to spend two hours every afternoon slaving for the Captain. I noticed grimly that he didn't mind at all ordering us around, even though we were supposed to be doing him a favor. We didn't have our tea break after the first week because tin was becoming scarce and the Captain was short on canned milk. And, as he explained, since he could no longer offer Call milk, it would have been mean for the two of us to stop for tea. I would have been glad to stop for any excuse, even that awful tea. When you're fourteen and your body is changing as mine was that summer, you just plain get tired, but I couldn't admit it. Both Call and the Captain seemed to regard me as mentally deficient, since I couldn't appreciate their marvelous humor. I couldn't let them make fun of me physically as well.

Nothing went right for me that summer, unless you count the fact that when my periods began, almost a year after Caroline's of course, they began on a Sunday morning *before* I left the house for church instead of after, but the stain went clear through my pants and slip to my only good dress. Momma let me pretend to be sick. What else could she do? I couldn't wash and dry my dress in time for Sunday school.

My grandmother kept saying things like "What's the matter with her? She don't look sick to me. Just don't want to worship the Lord." And "If she was mine, I'd give her a good smack on the rear. That'd perk her up fast enough."

I was terrified that Momma would betray me and tell Grandma the real reason I was staying home. But she didn't. Even Caroline tried to shush Grandma up. I don't know what Grandma told her old friends, but for weeks after that they'd all ask sweetly about my health, both physical and spiritual.

My spiritual health was about on a par with a person who's been dead three days, but I wasn't about to admit it and get prayed for out loud on Wednesday night by that bunch of old sooks.

8

I used to try to decide which was the worst month of the year. In the winter I would choose February. I had it figured out that the reason God made February short a few days was because he knew that by the time people came to the end of it they would die if they had to stand one more blasted day. December and January are cold and wet, but, somehow, that's their right. February is just plain malicious. It knows your defenses are down. Christmas is over and spring seems years away. So February sneaks in a couple of beautiful days early on, and just when you're stretching out like a cat waking up, bang! February hits you right in the stomach. And not with a lightning strike like a September hurricane, but punch after punch after punch. February is a mean bully. Nothing could be worse—except August.

There were days that August when I felt as though God had lowered a giant glass lid over the whole steaming Bay. All year we had lived in the wind, now we were cut off without a breath of air. On the water the haze was so thick it was like trying to inhale wet cotton. I began to pray for a real blow. I wanted relief that badly.

In February the weather sometimes gave us a vacation, in August, never. We just got up earlier every morning until finally we met ourselves going to bed. Call and I didn't get up quite as early as my father, who may have never gone to bed between tending to his floats and going out to crab, but we were up well before dawn, trying to sneak a fair catch of crabs from the eelgrass before the sun drove us off the water.

I had a faint hope that the Captain, not being an islander, would take the heat as an excuse to slow down a bit. But Call fixed that.

"We're coming in from crabbing early these hot mornings," he blabbed. "We could come on over here and get lots more done of a day."

"I can't come before dinner," I said. "Momma expects me home to eat."

"Well, fiddle, Wheeze," Call said. "You all eat by eleven. Don't take more'n ten minutes to eat."

"We don't stuff like scavengers at our house," I

said. "I couldn't possibly get here that fast. Besides, I got chores."

"We'll be here by noon," he told the Captain cheerily. I could have choked him. That meant at least four and a half hours of gut-ripping work in the heat for nothing. Nothing.

The Captain, of course, was delighted. His one concession to the temperature was that we work indoors and not on the dock in the sun. He began planning out loud all the projects the three of us could complete by the time school opened. I managed, with a lie about my mother needing me, to get away by four-fifteen. I wanted to get to the post office before supper. It would have been better perhaps if I had not, for there it was, my letter from Lyrics Unlimited. I ran with it to the tip of the island, to my driftwood stump, and sat down to open it, my hands shaking so they made a poor job of it.

Dear Miss Bandshaw:

CONGRATULATIONS!!! YOU ARE A WINNER! LYRICS UNLIMITED is delighted to inform you that your song, while not a money prize winner, is a WINNER in our latest contest. Given an appropriate musical setting, YOUR LYRICS could become a POPULAR SONG played on the radio waves all over America and even to our boys overseas. We urge you to let us set your words to music and give them this OUTSTANDING OPPORTUNITY. You might well be the lyricist of an all-time hit. You might well hear your song on the HIT PARADE. Your lyrics deserve this chance. All you need to do is send a check or money order (no stamps, please) for $25 and leave the rest to us.

We will

Set YOUR WORDS to music

Print the sheet music

Make copies available to

THE PEOPLE in the world

of POPULAR MUSIC

And WHO KNOWS?! The next song to top the HIT PARADE may be YOURS!!!!

Don't lose this chance! Time is limited! Send in your $25 today and put yourself on the ROAD TO FAME AND FORTUNE.

Sincerely,
your friends at
LYRICS UNLIMITED

Even I, wanting so much to believe, could tell it was mimeographed. The only thing typed in was my name, and that had been misspelled. I was a fool, but

I'm proud to say, not that big a fool. Heartsick, I ripped the letter down to its last exclamation point and flung it like confetti out into the water.

August and February are both alike in one way. They're both dream killers.

The next day the orange tomcat reappeared. It was the same cat, I'm sure, that had scared Call and me that time four years before when we had decided to investigate the house, and the same cat that the Captain had finally driven out after the first week or so he had lived there. The cat marched in through the open front door as though he were the long-absent landlord popping in to check out the tenants.

The Captain was furious. "I thought I got rid of that fool thing months ago." He got his broom and took after the huge tom, who calmly jumped onto the kitchen table. When the Captain took a swing at him there, he leaped daintily to the floor, taking a cup down with his tail.

"Damn it to hell!"

I had the capacity to imagine such language, but neither Call nor I had ever really heard it spoken. I think we were as fascinated as we were shocked.

"Captain," said Call, when he recovered himself slightly, "do you know what you said?"

The Captain was still stalking the cat and answered impatiently, "Of course I know what I said. I said—"

"Captain. That's against the commandments."

He took another futile swing before he answered. "Call, I know those blasted commandments as well as you do, and there is not one word in them about how to speak to tomcats. Now stop trying to play preacher and help me catch that damn cat and let's get him out of here."

Call was too shocked now to do anything but obey. He ran out after the cat. I started laughing. For some reason, the Captain had at last said something I thought was funny. I wasn't just giggling either. I was belly laughing. He looked at me and grinned. "Nice to hear you laugh, Miss Wheeze," he said.

"You're right!" I screeched through my laughter. "There's not—I bet there's not one word in the whole blasted Bible on how to speak to cats."

He began to laugh, too. Just sat down on the kitchen stool, the broom across his knees, and laughed. Why was it so funny? Was it because it was so wonderful to discover something on this island that was free—something unproscribed by God, Moses, or the Methodist conference? We could talk to cats any way we pleased.

Call reappeared carrying the struggling tom. He looked first at the Captain and then at me, apparently baffled. He had never seen us laughing together, of course. Maybe he didn't know whether to be pleased or jealous.

"Who—who—" puffed out the Captain. "Who is going to take that damned animal back to Trudy Braxton?"

"Trudy Braxton!" I think both Call and I yelled it. We had never heard anyone call Auntie Braxton by her Christian name. Even my grandmother, who must have been nearly the old woman's age, called her "Auntie."

After the first shock, my feeling was one of pleasure. It really was. I no longer wanted the Captain to be a Nazi spy or an interloper. I wanted him to be Hiram Wallace, an islander who had escaped. That was far more wonderful than being a saboteur to be caught or an imposter to be exposed.

"I'll take the cat back," I said. "If the stink don't get me first."

For some reason my irreverent description of Auntie Braxton's house triggered Call. "Did you hear what she said?" he asked the Captain. "'If the stink don't get me first.'" Then he and the Captain were laughing their heads off.

I grabbed the cat from Call just as it wriggled free. "Come along," I said, "before I call you a stinking name or two." I wasn't quite bold enough to use the forbidden curse word aloud, but I thought of it several times quite happily as I made my way up the path and to Auntie Braxton's house.

I hadn't exaggerated the smell. The windows of

the house were open and the overwhelming ammonia essence of cat stood like an invisible wall between me and the front yard. The tom was scratching and struggling to get out of my grasp, leaving stinging red lines all over my bare arms. If I hadn't been afraid that he would turn and run straight back to the Captain's, I would have dropped him on the front walk and run back myself. I had, however, a duty to perform, so I marched bravely up the walk to Auntie Braxton's door.

"Auntie Braxton!" I yelled her name over unhappy cat sounds coming from the other side of the door. If I let go the tom to knock or open the door, I might lose him, so I just stood there on the dilapidated porch and hollered. "Auntie Braxton. I got your cat."

From within a cat howled in reply, but no human voice accompanied it. I called again. Still no answer from the old lady. It occurred to me that I might be able to push the cat through the torn window screen. I went over to the window. The hole was large enough if I stuffed the creature in a bit. As I stooped to do so, I saw something dark lying on the front room floor. There were cats perched on top of it and cats walking across it, so for a minute I simply stared at it, not recognizing it for what it was—a human form. When I did, I panicked. Throwing the cat down, I half tripped over it in my hurry to be gone. I raced back to the Captain's house where I nearly fell over the door stoop, panting out my terror.

"Auntie Braxton!" I said. "Lying dead on the floor with cats crawling all over her."

"Slow down," said the Captain. I tried to catch my breath and repeat myself, but after two words he was already past me and walking, almost running up the path toward the old woman's house. Call and I followed. We were both terrified, but we ran to catch up to him and stayed at his heels. No matter what terrible thing was going on, we wanted to be with him and each other.

The Captain pushed open the door. People never locked their houses on Rass. Most doors didn't even have locks. The three of us went in. No one was bothering about the smell anymore. The Captain knelt down beside the old woman, scattering cats in every direction.

Call and I hung back a little, wide-eyed and breathing fast.

"She's alive," he said. "Call, you go down to the dock. As soon as the ferry docks, Captain Billy's going to have to take her to the hospital."

Relief washed over me like a gentle surf. It wasn't that I'd never seen a dead body. On an island, you can't get away from death. But I'd never found one.

Never been the first person accidentally to stumble in on death. It seemed more terrible somehow to be the first one.

"Don't just stand there, Sara Louise. Go find some men to help me carry her down to the dock."

I jumped and ran to obey. It was not until later that I realized that he had called me by my full name, Sara Louise. No one bothered, not even my mother, to call me Sara Louise, but he had done it without thinking. Strange how much that meant to me.

I got my father and two other men from their crab houses, and we raced back to Auntie Braxton's. The Captain had found a cot mattress, and he and my father gently rolled the old woman over and lifted her to the mattress. The Captain covered her with a cotton blanket. I was glad, for her thin legs seemed indecent somehow poking out from her faded housedress. Then the four men began to lift the awkward makeshift stretcher. As they did so, the old lady moaned, like someone disturbed by a bad dream.

"It's all right, Trudy, it's me, Hiram," the Captain said. "I'll take care of you." My father and the other two men gave one another funny looks, but no one said anything. They had to get her to the hospital.

9

"Trudy" was what did it. Simply by using Auntie Braxton's first name, the Captain confirmed himself as the true Hiram Wallace. He still didn't go to meet the ferry in the afternoon like most folks, or hang around Kellam's after supper matching water stories, or go to church. But despite these aberrations he seemed to be accepted as an islander, simply because he had called Auntie Braxton "Trudy," a name nobody had used for her since she was a young woman.

Call's life and mine took a strange turn at that time. The Captain decided that while Auntie Braxton was in the hospital, the three of us should tackle her house. I tried weakly to argue that it was like trespassing to clean up someone's house without her permission, and trespassing was something Methodists were forever bent on getting forgiveness for, so it was likely to be a fairly serious sin. The Captain just snorted impolitely at that. If we didn't do it, he said, the Ladies' Society of the Methodist church was likely to take it on as a good deed. Although Auntie Braxton went regularly to church, she had, for years, been considered strange, and once her cat population had passed four or five, she had been on very strained terms with the other women of Rass.

"Would Trudy rather have them poking about her property than us?"

"She'd rather have nobody, I bet."

He sadly admitted that I was right, but since the alternative to our doing the cleaning was having it become a missionary endeavor, I had to agree that we were certainly the lesser of two evils.

The problem, of course, was the cats. Until something could be done about them, there was no hope of getting the house in any kind of order.

"How in the world did she feed them?" I asked. It had always seemed to me that Auntie Braxton was below even Call's family on the poverty scale.

"The wonder is she didn't feed them better," the Captain said. "These poor things look half-starved."

"Cat food costs a lot of money," I said, trying to remember if Auntie Braxton had ever been known to buy fish from a local waterman to feed to her cats.

Anyone else would have used scraps, but anyone else would have had more people than cats in the house.

"I would have thought Trudy had more money than most people on the island," the Captain said.

Even Call was flabbergasted. "What makes you think a thing like that?" he asked. We both remembered that Auntie Braxton got a basket from the Ladies' Society at Thanksgiving and Christmas. Not even Call's family rated a basket.

"I was here when her father died," the Captain said, as though the two of us should have known such a simple fact as that. "Old Captain Braxton had plenty, but he never let on. He let his wife and child scrimp by on next to nothing. Trudy found the money after they both died. And it scared her something silly to suddenly find all this cash, so she come running to my mother. My mother treated her like she was her own daughter. Poor Momma," he shook his head, "she never gave up hoping I'd marry Trudy. Well, anyway, Momma told her to put it in a bank, but I doubt that Trudy did. What did she know about mainland banks? What's left of it after all these years is probably hidden right here in this house, if the damn cats haven't chewed it up."

"Maybe it ran out," I said. "It's been a long time."

"Maybe. It was a lot of money." He suddenly looked at us both, changing his tone abruptly.

"Look," he said, "don't say anything about any money. If she'd have wanted anyone else to know about it, she would have told them. I'm not even supposed to know. Just my mother."

Call and I nodded solemnly. Real intrigue was far more delicious than the pretend kind. The fact that there might be money hidden convinced me beyond a doubt that the Ladies' Society must not take over the housecleaning.

But the distasteful problem of the cats remained. The Captain made both me and Call sit down in his clean, refurbished living room. He served me tea and Call some of his precious tinned milk, and then, very gently, he tried to explain to us what he believed had to be done.

"The only way to resolve the problem of the cats," he said, "is to dispose of them humanely."

Either I was a little slow or the language was too elegant, because I was nodding my head in respectful agreement when, suddenly, it hit me what he meant.

"You mean shoot them?"

"No. I think that would be hard to do. Besides it would make a mess and bring the neighbors running. I think the best method—"

"Kill them? You mean kill them all?"

"They're almost starving now, Sara Louise. They'll die slowly with no one to care for them."

"I'll take care of them," I said fiercely. "I'll feed them until Auntie Braxton gets back." Even as I heard myself say it, the words hacked at my stomach. All my crab money, my boarding school money—to feed a pack of yowling, stinking cats. I hated cats.

"Sara Louise," the Captain said kindly, "even if you had the money to feed them, we can't leave them in the house. They're a health hazard."

"A person's got the right to choose their own hazards."

"Maybe so. But not when it's getting to be a problem for the whole community."

"Thou shalt not kill!" I said stubbornly, remembering at the same time that only the day before I had been rejoicing that not one word of the blasted Bible applied to cats. He was gracious enough not to remind me.

"What are you fixing to do with 'em, Captain?" Call asked, his voice cracking in the middle of his question.

The Captain sighed, polishing his mug with the back of his thumb. Without lifting his eyes, he said softly, "Take them couple miles out and leave them."

"Drown them?" I was getting hysterical. "Just take them out and throw them in?"

"I don't like the idea, either," he said.

"We could take them to the mainland," I said. "They have places there like orphanages for animals. I read about it in the *Sun.*"

"The SPCA," he said. "Yes, in Baltimore—or Washington. But even there, they'd just have to put these creatures to sleep."

"Put them to sleep?"

"Kill them as gently as possible," he explained. "Even there they can't take care of everyone's unwanted cats on and on."

I tried not to believe him. How could anything that called itself the "Society for the Prevention of Cruelty to Animals" engage in wholesale murder? But even if I was right, Baltimore and Washington were too far away to do Auntie Braxton's cats any good.

"I'll borrow a boat," he said. "One that will get us out fast. You two round up the cats." He started out the door and up the path. In a moment he was back. "There's three gunnysacks on the back porch," he said. "You'll need something to put the cats in." Then he was gone again.

Call got off the bench. "C'mon," he said. "We can't catch neither cat sitting here on our bottoms all day."

I shuddered and got up reluctantly. It would be better not to think, I told myself. If you could hold your nose to avoid a stink, or close your eyes to cut out a sight, why not shut off your brain to avoid a thought? Thus, the catching of the cats became a sport with no consequences. We took turns, one holding the bag while the other dodged about the furniture and up the stairs in pursuit. They were amazingly lively despite their half-starved appearance, and once seized and thrown into the sack, they went after one another with ungodly shrieks. Five were in the first bag—they proved to be the hardest to get—and the bag was tied tightly with cord I found in the kitchen drawer.

By the second bag, I had become more wily. In addition to the cord, I had found some cans of tuna and sardines in the kitchen. I divided a can of sardines between the two remaining gunnysacks and then smeared the oil on my hands. I risked being eaten alive, but it worked. I lured those fool cats right to me and into those infernal sacks. We got them all, all that is but the orange tom, which was nowhere in the house. Neither Call nor I had the heart to track him down. Besides, sixteen snarling cats were more than enough.

I sneaked down to our house and got the wagon. Very gingerly we loaded the live sacks onto it. We were already scratched and bitten enough. Those claws could reach through the burlap as though it weren't there. Once one of the sacks writhed and wiggled its way off the wagon and into the street, but we got it back on and down the path to the Captain's dock. He sat there waiting for us in a skiff with an outboard. He was wearing a black tie and his old blue seaman's suit. I had the feeling he was dressed for a funeral.

Without a word, Call and I put the sacks into the bottom of the boat and climbed in after them. The cats must have exhausted themselves fighting, for the sacks lay almost quiet at our feet. The Captain yanked the starter cord two or three times and the motor finally coughed and then hummed. Slowly he turned the bow and headed for open water.

It was midafternoon and the heat closed in on us unmercifully. I was aware of the smells of cat and the awful spoiled sardine smell of my own hands. I jerked them off my lap.

Just then, a piteous little cry rose from the sack nearest my feet. It sounded more like a baby than a cat, which is why, I suppose, it suddenly tore the blinders from my mind. "Stop!" I screamed, standing up in the boat.

The Captain cut the motor abruptly, telling me to sit down. But as soon as the motor died, I jumped over the washboard and swam with all my might for shore. I could dimly hear the Captain and Call yelling after me, but I never stopped swimming or running until I was home.

"Wheeze. What happened?" Caroline jumped up

from the piano at the sight of me, hair streaming, clothes dripping all over the floor. I stomped past her and my mother, who had come to the kitchen door, up the stairs to our bedroom and slammed the door. I didn't want to see anyone, but of all people in the world, Caroline was the last one I wanted to talk to. I still smelled of sardines, for goodness' sake.

She opened the door a crack and slid through, leaning on it to shut it gently behind her. There was no way, now, to get down to the kitchen and wash.

"Can't you see I'm dressing?" I turned my back to the door.

"Want me to get you a towel?"

"Don't bother."

She slid out the door and came back carrying a towel. "You're a mess," she said pleasantly.

"Oh, shut up."

"What happened to you?"

"None of your business."

She got that hurt look in her great blue eyes that always made me want to smack her. She didn't say anything, just put the towel down on her bed and climbed up and sat down cross-legged beside it, dropping her shoes neatly to the floor.

"You and Call didn't go swimming, did you?"

No one was supposed to know that Call and I sometimes went swimming together.

I tried to run my fingers through my wet knotted

hair. She slipped off her bed and came over carrying the towel. "Want me to rub your hair?"

My first impulse was to shake her off, but she was trying to be kind. Even I could tell that. And I was feeling so awful that the kindness broke down all my usual defenses. I began to cry.

She got my bathrobe for me, and then she dried my hair with those powerful fingers of hers as gently as she might coax a nocturne from our old piano. So although she never seemed to urge me to talk, I began to do so, until, finally, I was pouring out my anguish, not for the cats, but for myself as murderer. It didn't matter that I had not actually thrown them into the Bay. I had cleverly lured them to their death. That was enough.

"Poor Wheeze," she said quietly. "Poor old cats."

At last I stopped crying, dressed, and combed my hair.

"Where are you going?" she asked. It was none of her business, but she had been too nice for me to say so.

"Auntie Braxton's," I said. "We have to get it cleaned up before the Ladies' Society makes it a missionary project."

"Can I come?"

"Why would you want to come? It's a filthy stinking mess."

She shrugged, blushing a little. "I don't know," she said. "Nothing better to do."

We borrowed a bucket and mop and a bottle of disinfectant as well as a pile of rags from my mother, whose face was set in a question she did not ask. As we entered Auntie Braxton's house, I watched Caroline closely. I suppose I wanted to see some sign of weakness. "Smells terrible," she said cheerfully.

"Yeah," I said, a bit disappointed that she hadn't at least gagged.

We had hardly filled the bucket with water when Call and the Captain appeared at the front door. They just stood there, hanging back a little, like a pair of naughty kids.

"Well," I said. "Back so soon."

The Captain shook his head sadly. "We couldn't do it."

Call looked as though he were about to cry. "They sounded just like little babies," he said.

I'm sure I should have felt joy and relief. Actually, what I felt was annoyance. I had spent a lot of guilt and grief over the death of those dratted cats. They had no right to be alive. "Well," I said, the dried salt was making my skin itch and adding to my irritation, "what are you going to do with them, then? We can't keep them here. You said so yourself."

Wearily, the Captain sat down in Auntie Braxton's

easy chair right on top of the pile of rags I'd left there. He scrunched around under himself and fished them out. "I don't know," he was saying. "I just don't know."

"We can give them away." It was Caroline, taking over the problem just as though someone had asked her to.

"What do you mean, 'we'?" I was furious at her.

"I—you," she said. "What I mean is, just give the cats to as many people as will take them—"

"Nobody is going to take these cats," I said. "They're wild as bobcats and half-starved to boot. Nobody in their right mind would take a cat like that."

The Captain sighed his agreement. Call nodded his Methodist preacher nod. "They're wild as bobcats," he repeated. Not that any of us had ever seen a bobcat.

"So?" Caroline was undaunted. "We tame them."

"Tame them?" I snorted. "Why don't you just teach a crab to play the piano?"

"Not permanently," she said. "Just long enough to get them new homes."

"How, Caroline?" Call was definitely interested.

She grinned. "Paregoric," she said.

Call went to his house to fetch the family bottle, and I went to our house and got ours. Meantime, Caroline had prepared an assortment of sixteen saucers, cups, and bowls, rationing out the cans of tuna fish to each container. She laced each liberally with paregoric. We set them all around the kitchen floor and then brought in the gunnysacks and untied them.

Lured by the smell of food, the cats came staggering out of the bag. At first there was a bit of snarling and shoving, but since there were plenty of dishes for all, each cat eventually found a place for itself and set itself to cleaning away every trace of the drugged feast set before it.

In the end, it was as much Caroline's charm as the paregoric that worked. She took one cat to each house along the street, leaving Call and me to mind the sacks, slightly out of sight. Nobody on Rass would dare slam a door in Caroline's face. And no matter how determined the housewife might be against taking in a cat, Caroline's melodiously sweet voice would remind her that it was no small thing to save a life—a life precious to God if not to man—and then she would hold out a cat who was so doped up with paregoric that it was practically smiling. Some of them even managed a cuddly, kittenish mew. "See," Caroline would say, "he likes you already."

When the last cat was placed, we went back to Auntie Braxton's. The Captain had put chairs on top of tables and was beginning to mop the floor with hot water and disinfectant. Call told him the whole story of Caroline's feat, house by house, cat by cat. They laughed and imitated the befuddled women at the door. Caroline threw in imitations of the happy, drunken cats while the Captain and Call hooted with delight, and I felt as I always did when someone told the story of my birth.

10

The blow that I had been praying for struck the next week. While not as severe as the storm of '33, which became a legend before its waters receded, the storm of '42 is the one I will never forget.

During the war, weather was classified information, but on Rass we didn't need a city man on a radio to warn us of bad weather. My father, like any true waterman, could smell the storm coming up, even before the ominous rust-colored sunset. He had made his boat fast and boarded up the windows of our house. There was not much he could do about the peelers in our floats, except hope the storm would leave him a few of the floats and spare his crab shanty for one more season.

It is a mysterious thing how cheerful people become in the face of disaster. My father whistled as he boarded up the windows, and my mother from time to time would call to him happily out the back door. She obviously was enjoying the unusual pleasure of having him home on a weekday morning. Tomorrow they might be ruined or dead, today they had each other. And then there are things you can do to prepare for a hurricane. It is not like a thunderstorm on the water or sudden illness before which you are helpless.

Just before noon Call came by and asked if Caroline or I was going down to the Captain's.

"Sure," said Caroline cheerfully. "Soon as we finish carrying the canning upstairs." High water had more than once washed through our downstairs, and my mother didn't want to take a chance on having the fruits and vegetables she had bought on the mainland and put up for the winter dashed to the floor or swept away. "You coming, Wheeze?"

Who did she think she was, inviting me to go see the Captain? As if she owned both him and Call. Call, who had always belonged to me because nobody else besides his mother and grandmother would have him, and the Captain, who finally through all our troubles and misunderstandings had become mine as well. Now, because of one afternoon of giving away a batch of drugged cats, she thought she could snatch them both for herself. I muttered something angry but unintelligible.

"What's the matter, Wheeze?" she asked. "Don't you think we ought to help the Captain get ready for the storm?"

There she was, trying to make me look bad in front of Call. Her voice had its usual sweet tone, and her face was all concern. I wanted to smack it. "Go on down," I said to Call. "We'll get there when we can."

Later the four of us boarded up the Captain's windows. Call, Caroline, and the Captain were calling back and forth cheerfully while we worked. The Captain didn't want to move anything to the second floor, and he laughed away my fear that the water might rise higher than his front stoop. We carried our hammers and nails and boards up to Auntie Braxton's and started on her windows. Before long my father joined us, and with his help, the work was quickly done.

"Want to spend the night at our place, Hiram?" my father asked.

The Captain smiled quickly as though thanking my father for calling him by name. "No," he said. "But I thank you. Any port in a storm, they say, but I take home port if I got a choice."

"It's going to blow mean tonight."

"I wouldn't be surprised." But the Captain gathered his tools, waved, and headed for home.

I was a sound sleeper in those days and it was my father, not the wind that woke me up.

"Louise."

"What? What?" I sat up in bed.

"Shh," he said. "No need to wake your sister."

"What is it?"

"The wind's come up right smart. I'm going to go down and take off my motor and sink the boat."

I knew that to be an extreme measure. "Want me to help?"

"No, there'll be plenty of men down there."

"Okay," I said and turned over to sleep again. He shook me gently. "I think you better go down and get the Captain. Bring him up here in case it gets worse."

I was fully awake now. My father was worried. I jumped up and pulled on my work overalls over my nightgown. The house was shuddering like Captain Billy's ferry.

"Is it raining yet?" I asked my father at the front door. The wind was so loud that it was hard to tell.

"Soon," he said, handing me the largest flashlight. "Better wear your slicker. Now you take care and be quick."

I nodded. "You, too, Daddy."

The blow came up faster than even my father had

guessed. Every now and then I would grab the paling of one of the picket fences lining the street to steady myself against the wind. It was blowing from the northwest, so making my way southeast toward the Captain's house, I had the feeling that at any moment the wind might lift me off my feet and deposit me in the Bay. When I reached the last house, where the narrow street turned into a path across the marsh, I went down on my hands and knees, shoved my slicker up out of the way, and crawled. The wind seemed too powerful now to tempt with my upright body.

If our house had been shaking, protected as it was in the middle of the village, imagine the Captain's, hanging there alone so near the water. The beam of my flashlight caught for a frightening moment the waters of the Bay, which the wind had whipped into a fury. *And everyone that heareth these sayings of mine and doeth them not, shall be likened unto a foolish man, which built his house upon the sand: And the rain descended and the floods came, and the winds blew, and beat upon that house. . . .*

I began to cry out the Captain's name. How he heard me over the roar of the wind, I don't know, but he was out on the porch before I reached the house.

"Sara Louise? Where are you?"

I stood up, bracing my body as best I could against

the wind. "Hurry!" I yelled. "You got to come to our house."

He came quickly, put his body in front of mine, and pulled my arms about his waist. He took my flashlight so I could grasp my hands together in front of him. "Hold tight!"

Even with his stocky waterman's body to break the wind, our journey back up the path was a treacherous one. The rain was coming down now like machine-gun fire, and the water from the marsh began to swirl up around our feet. The Captain cried out something to me, but his voice was lost in the moaning of the wind. Like all the rest of me, my hands were wet. Once they slipped apart. The Captain caught my left arm and held on tightly. Even when we got to the first picket fence, he held on. The pain in my arm became the only real thing, a sharp point of comfort in the midst of a nightmare. In the narrow street the dark houses of the village gave us some shelter from the wind, but the water of the Bay was already washing across the crushed oyster shells.

My father was not home when the Captain and I got there. The electricity was out. My mother, white-faced in the light from the kerosene lamp, was at the stove getting coffee. Grandma was rocking back and forth in her chair, her eyes squinched shut. "Oh, Lord," she was praying out loud. "Why don't you come down and still the wind and waves? Oh, Jesus, you told the storm on Galilee, 'Peace, be still,' and it obeyed your word. Ohhh, Lord, come down now and quiet this evil wind."

As if in defiance, the moan of the wind shifted into a shriek. We were all so startled that it took us several seconds to realize that my father had come in the front door and was now pushing the old food safe against it. The door was leeward, but we all knew that later the wind would shift. We had to be ready.

"Best douse the lamp, Susan," my father said. "And the stove. Things get banging around down here and we'll have a first-class fire."

Momma handed him a cup of coffee before she obeyed.

"Now," he said. "Best be getting upstairs." He had to shout to be heard but the words were as calm as someone telling the time. "Come along, Momma," he called to Grandma. "Can't have you floating away on your rocker." He waved his flashlight toward the staircase.

Grandma had stopped her litany. Or else the wind had swallowed it. She went to the steps and began to climb slowly. My father nudged me to follow. "Oh, my blessed," Grandma was saying as she climbed. "Oh, my blessed. I do hate the water."

Caroline slept on. Caroline would probably have

slept through the Last Trumpet. I started toward her bed to wake her up. Daddy called me from the hallway. "No," he said. "Let her sleep."

I came back to where he was. "She'll miss the whole hurricane."

"Yeah. Probably will," he said. "Better get off those wet things, now. Then you should try to get some sleep yourself."

"I couldn't sleep through this. I wouldn't want to."

Even through the shriek of the wind, I could hear his chuckle. "Nope," he said. "Probably wouldn't."

When I had changed out of my wet things and cleaned myself off as best I could, I went into my parents' room. Daddy had gone down and fetched Grandma's chair so she could rock and moan as was her custom. Somehow, the Captain had changed from his wet clothes into my father's bathrobe, which barely met at his middle. Daddy and Momma were perched on the side of their bed, and the Captain sat on the edge of the only other chair. They had lit a candle in the room, which flickered because of the wind coming through the chinks of the house. Momma patted the bed beside her. I went and sat down. I wanted to snuggle up on her lap like a toddler, but I was fourteen, so I sat as close to her body as I dared.

We gave up trying to talk. It was too hard to fight the wind screaming like a giant wounded dove. We could no longer hear the sounds of Grandma's prayers or the rain or the water.

Suddenly there was silence. "What happened?" Though as soon as I asked, I knew. It was the eye. We were in the quiet eye of the storm. Daddy got up, took the flashlight, and went to the stairs. The Captain rose, pulled the bathrobe together, and followed him. I started to get up, too, but Momma put her arm across my lap.

"You can't tell how long it will last," she said. "Just let the men go."

I wanted to object, but I was tired. It wouldn't have mattered. The men were back almost before they started.

"Well, Sue, there's two foot of Bay water sloshing about down there." Daddy sat down beside her. "I'm feared it'll make a mess of your nice parlor."

She patted his knee. "As long as we're all safe," she said.

"Ohhhh, Lord," Grandma cried out. "Why must the righteous suffer?"

"We're all safe, Momma," my father said. "We're all safe. Nobody's suffering."

She began to cry then, bawling out like a frightened child. My parents looked at each other in consternation. I was angry. What right had she, a grown woman, who had lived through many storms, to carry on like that?

Then the Captain got up and went to kneel beside her chair. "It's all right, Louise," he said, as though he were indeed talking to a child. "A storm's a fearsome thing." When he said that I remembered the tale I'd heard about him cutting down his father's mast. Was it possible that a man so calm had once been so terrified? "Would you like me to read to you?" he asked. "While it's still quiet?"

She didn't answer. But he got up and, taking the Bible from the bedside table, pulled his chair in close to the candle. As he was flipping through for the place, Grandma looked up. "T'ain't fitting a heathen should read the Word of God," she said.

"Hush, Momma!" I had never heard my father speak so sharply to her before. But she did hush, and the Captain began to read.

"God is our refuge and strength, a very present help in trouble." He read well, better than the preacher, almost as well as Mr. Rice. "Therefore we will not fear, though the earth be removed, and though the mountains be carried into the midst of the sea; Though the waters thereof roar and be troubled, though the mountains shake with the swelling thereof . . ."

Into my mind came a wonderful and terrible picture of great forested mountains, shaken by a giant hand that scooped them up, finally, and flung them into the boiling sea. I had never seen a mountain, except in a geography text. I was fourteen, and I had never even seen a real mountain. I was going to, though. I was not going to end up like my Grandma, fearful and shriveled.

They told me later that I finally slept through the worst part of the hurricane. When the eye passed, the wind came up from the south even more fiercely than before. "Grabbed this old house by the scruff of the neck and shook the bejeebers out of it," my father said. "But I couldn't wake you for nothing. Snoring away like an old dog."

"I didn't snore!" I was horrified at the thought of the Captain watching me while I snored.

"Snored so loud, you plumb drowned the wind." He was teasing me. At least I hoped my father was teasing.

It was not one of those hurricanes like the one that was to hit the Atlantic Coast in '44, not one of those hurricanes that go down in the books. No island lives were lost in the storm of '42. No human lives, at any rate. The storm did accomplish without conscience what we had been too fainthearted to do. It reduced the island's cat population by at least two-thirds.

11

It was the bluest, clearest day of the summer. Every breath of air was delicious with just enough of a clean, salt edge to wake up all your senses. If the Captain and I had just stood on the porch with our eyes closed, it would have been a perfect day. For while our noses and lungs feasted on nature's goodness, our eyes were assaulted by evidence of her savagery.

The water had left our living room, but it was still in the yard, level with the porch. Riding the muddy surface were sections of picket fence, giant tree limbs, crab pots, remnants of floats and crab houses, boats, and . . . "What's that?" I had grabbed the Captain's arm.

"A coffin," he said matter of factly. "These storms

will dig them up sometimes. Just replant them is all." His mind was clearly not on the dead. "Look here," he said. "There's no safe walking to my place this morning. We'd best go back in and give your mother a hand."

The thought of our sodden, muck-filled downstairs dragged at me like a lead weight on a crab pot. "Don't you want to see what happened to your house?" I asked. This was a day for adventure, not drudgery.

"Plenty of time to see later when the water's down," he said, turning to go back inside.

"My boat!" That was it. We could pole the skiff down to his house, maneuvering around the debris as we would ice floes. He cocked his head. I'm sure he doubted that my stubby little skiff could have survived the storm.

At first we couldn't tell. The gut had disappeared under the foot of water flooding the yard, bringing with it the same floating dump heap we had seen swirling about the front yard. The day before, my father had tied the boat, not just to the pine to which I usually secured her bowline; he had run lines from her stern to the fig tree on one side and the cedar on the other. The three trees were still there, looking a bit like little boys after their summer haircuts, but still there. From the porch I could, at last, make out the three now taut lines, and then I caught sight of her washboards just above the water line.

"She's here!" I was half off the porch when the Captain grabbed me.

"You want lockjaw or typhoid or a combination?" He indicated my bare legs and feet.

I was too happy to be offended. "Okay," I said. "Just a minute." He waited until I fetched my father's old boots. He had worn his good ones when he left earlier to see about his own boat and the crab shanty.

We bailed out the skiff until it was bobbing merrily on the surface. The Captain loosed the lines on the house side of the still invisible gut, and then I climbed into the boat, pulled myself along the rope to the cedar tree, and loosed that knot as well. The Captain fetched the pole from the kitchen, and after he had handed it in to me in the stern, he climbed in and sat down facing me, his arms tightly folded across his chest.

He let me maneuver the skiff through the wreckage of the flood without even peeking over his shoulder to see what I might be about to hit. I poled us along what I thought might be the line of the gut. The water was too murky and trash-filled to tell. Usually my pole was only a foot or so in the water, but then suddenly it would go down three feet and I knew I had found the gut again.

The Captain looked so somber, I could almost imagine I was an Egyptian slave taking Pharaoh on a tour of the flooded Nile Delta. In fifth-grade history we had spent a lot of time worrying about the flooded river deltas of the ancient world. I would be one of those wise slaves who could read and write and dare to advise their masters. Now, for example, I would be reassuring the Pharaoh that the flood was a gift from the gods, that once it receded, the rich black earth of the delta would bring forth abundant grain. Our storehouses would be full to overflowing even as they had been when the great Joseph had been the Pharaoh's minister.

My reverie was punctured by a raucous cackling and complaining from a tiny house floating past us. "Hey!" I said. "That looks like the Lewises' chicken coop." The live occupants of the coop were squawking their unhappiness to the world as they traveled along.

The storm had been capricious. Some roofs were gone, while the next door house was not only intact but the fence and shed as well. In some yards people were already trying to collect things and clean up the debris lodged against their fences. I called out to them and waved.

They waved back and shouted greetings like, "Hey there, Wheeze. Y'all make out all right?"

And I'd answer, "Yessir. Least the house is all

right." Seldom had I felt such warmth from my island neighbors. I nodded and waved and smiled. I loved everyone that morning.

I was well past and around the last house on the village street when I realized that I had lost my bearings. I should be over the marsh now. The sun was starboard, so I should have been heading straight for the Captain's house.

I made a funny squeak in my throat that startled the Captain. "What is it?" He jerked around to see what I was staring at.

I was staring at nothing. Nothing. Not a tree, not a board. Nothing was left at the spot where the Captain's house had stood the night before.

It took us both a few minutes to take it in. I circled the spot in the boat, or tried to. My pole was going down too deep for me to dare venture out too far. There was nothing to tell us if we were over the south marsh or the place where the Wallace house had stood. It was all Bay now.

At first I could do nothing but stare at the muddy water. Finally, I stole a look at the Captain. His eyes looked glazed, and he was pulling at the hair of his beard with the fingers of his left hand. He realized that I was watching him and cleared his throat.

"We used to have cows," he said. "Did you know that?"

"I heard it. Yes."

"Though the earth be removed," he was mumbling. "Though the mountains be carried into the midst of the sea."

I wanted to say how sorry I felt, but it seemed childish. I hadn't even lost my boat pole. He had lost everything.

He crossed his arms once more even more tightly across his chest. Squinting his eyes, he said in a rough voice, "Well. That's that."

As I turned the boat, I tried to read his meaning. At last I said, "Where do you want to go?"

His laugh came out something like a snort. I shipped the pole and sat down on the thwart opposite him. "I'm really sorry," I said.

He shook his head as though to shake off my concern, his eyes glittering. His hands dropped to his lap. He was wearing clothes borrowed from my father, an old blue workshirt and denim pants that were a little too tight for him. He seemed to be watching his right thumb rub the knuckles of his left hand. For all his white beard, he looked like a little boy trying not to cry. I was terrified that I might actually see tears in his eyes and so to avoid that sight more than anything else, I slipped off the thwart, crossed the narrow space between us on my knees, and put my arms around him. The rough shirt scraped my chin, and I was aware of the pressure of his knees against my stomach.

Then, suddenly, something happened. I can't explain it. I had not put my arms around another person since I was tiny. It may have been the unaccustomed closeness, I don't know. I had only meant to comfort him, but as I smelled his sweat and felt the spring of his beard against my cheek, an alarm began to clang inside my body. I went hot all over, and I could hear my heart banging to be let out of my chest. "Let go, stupid," part of me was saying, while another voice I hardly recognized was urging me to hold him tighter.

I pulled back abruptly and, putting the thwart between us, grabbed up the hard, solid pole, stood and jammed it down into the water. I didn't dare speak, much less look at him. What must he think of me? I knew that anything that made a person feel the way I felt at that moment had to be a deadly sin. But I was less concerned at the moment with God's judgment than the Captain's. Suppose he laughed? Suppose he told someone? Call or, God forbid, Caroline?

I dared a glance at his hands. The fingers of his right hand were nervously tapping his knee. I had never noticed how long his fingers were. His nails were large, rounded at the bottom and blunt and neat at the tips. He had the cleanest fingernails of any man I'd ever seen—it was the male hand in the ad reaching to put the diamond on the Pond'scaressed female hand. Why had I never noticed before how beautiful his hands were? I wanted to hold one in both of my hands and kiss the fingertips. Oh, my blessed, I was going crazy. Just looking at his hands was doing the same wild things to the secret places of my body that holding him had done.

I poled faster and tried to keep my eyes and mind totally on getting the boat back to the house. I kept banging into debris. I was sure he could tell how agitated I was. I kept waiting for him to say something. Anything.

"Well," he said. My heart went straight through my ribs at the sound. "Well." A short explosive sigh. "That's that."

That's what? something inside my head was crying. I rammed the boat into the back porch, leaped out, and secured the line on a post. Then, without looking back, I raced into the house up into the sanctuary of my bedroom.

"What's the matter, Wheeze?" No sanctuary. No hiding place. Caroline was there to question me as I dived onto my bed and buried my head under the pillow. "For goodness' sake, Wheeze? What on earth is going on?"

When I refused to answer, she finished dressing and went downstairs. I could hear voices, muffled as they were by the pillow. I waited for laughter. Slowly, as I calmed, I knew that the Captain would never tell my mother or my grandmother what had happened in the boat. Call and Caroline, perhaps, but not the others.

But even if he never told a soul, how was I to face him again? Just thinking of his smell, his feel, his hands, made my body go hot all over. "He's older than your grandmother," I kept saying to myself. "When your grandmother was a child, he was nearly a man already." My grandmother was sixty-three. She seemed like a hundred, but she was sixty-three. I knew because my father had been born when she was sixteen. The Captain had to be seventy or more. I was fourteen, for mercy's sake. Fourteen from seventy was fifty-six. *Fifty-six*. But then my mind would go to the curve of his perfect thumbnail, and my body would flame up like pine pitch.

I heard my father come in the front door. I jumped off the bed and tried to compose myself before our small streaky mirror. I could not pretend I had not heard him, and no one would understand any excuse for my not coming down to hear his report. I would have to be stretched out dead to remain upstairs. I ran a comb through my wild hair and banged down the steps. Everyone turned at the racket. I just caught the Captain's face. He was smiling. I'm sure I flushed all over, but no one, after that first glance, was taking notice of me. They wanted to find out what was happening at the harbor.

"The boat's all right." That was the first and only really vital thing we needed to know.

"Thank the Lord," Momma said quietly, but with a force that surprised me.

"There's plenty," Daddy went on, "that aren't so lucky. A lot of the boats not sunk are all tore up. It'll be a hard year for many." Our crab house was gone and the floats as well, but we had our boat. "The dock's tore up right smart, but folks got their homes."

"Not the Captain." Caroline said it so quickly and loudly that no one else had a chance. It didn't seem right to me that the Captain should be robbed of the chance to tell his own tragedy. He had nothing else to call his own. He should have at least had his story. But Caroline was like that, snatching other people's rights without even thinking.

"Oh, my blessed," said my father. "And here I was thinking how lucky we were. Is it clean gone?"

The Captain nodded, tightening his arms across his chest as he had earlier. "Even the fast land where she stood," he said. We were all quiet. My grandmother ceased her eternal rocking for a time. At last he said, "That whole marsh was a meadow back when I was a boy. We used to keep cows." It bothered me intensely that he should be repeating the information about the cows. I couldn't understand why it meant so much to him.

"Well," my father said. "Well." He went over to the table and sat down heavily on a chair. "You best stay with us for a while."

The Captain opened his mouth to protest, but Grandma beat him to it. "Ain't neither room for another body in this house," she said. She was right, but I wanted to kill her for saying it. Just the look on the Captain's face ripped my heart right out of my chest.

"The girls can double up for a few days, Mother," my father said. "And you can have the other bed up there."

She opened her mouth wide, but he shushed her with a look. "Louise'll help you carry up a few things now."

"I couldn't think of putting you to trouble," the Captain said. The tone was a meek, broken one I'd never heard before.

"It's no trouble," I said loudly before my grandmother could interfere again. I rushed into her room and cleared her drawers in a few swoops and carried her things upstairs on a run. Half of me was bursting with joy at the thought of having him so close, the other half was in mortal terror. I seemed to have no control over myself, I who had always prided myself on keeping the deepest parts of me hidden from view. I dumped my own things into a bag and pushed it under Caroline's bed, and then as neatly as I could, folded Grandma's things and put them in my drawers. I was shaking all over. Grandma had come thumping up the stairs. She was in a rage.

"I can't think what your daddy's up to," she said, still panting from her rush up the stairs. "Letting that heathen into our house. Into my bed. Oh, my blessed. Into my very bed."

"Stop it!" I didn't say it loudly, but I said it into her face. It may have scared her. She sniffed and backed up. She climbed up on my bed. Naturally, she assumed that I would be the one to give up a bed. "I'm resting," she said. "If anybody cares."

I slammed the drawer shut and went back downstairs. How dare she hurt his feelings? He had lost everything he had in this world. I saw his beautiful hands lovingly sanding the back of one of his old chairs. He had worked so hard on that house. We all had. He and Call and I. Not Caroline. It didn't belong to her, just to the three of us. But when I got to the living room, there was Caroline, giving him a cup of coffee, practically falling all over him while she did so. Then she got herself a cup and sat down beside him, her beautiful eyes mooning with pity.

"Would you like some coffee, Louise?"

"No," I said sharply. "Somebody's got to remember this is no picnic." There was no place to run to, no tip of the marsh where I could sit alone on a stump of driftwood and watch the water. I wanted to cry and scream and throw things. Instead, under almost perfect control, I got a broom and began savagely to attack the sand that was stuck like cement in the corner of the living room.

12

For the three days that the Captain lived with us, I avoided looking him in the eye. I was, instead, obsessed with his hands. They were always moving because he was intent on paying his way by helping to clean the house. By the time the water had left the yard and street, most of our downstairs, though smelling more like a crab shanty than a proper house, was at least cleaned out. We carried the stuffed chair and the couch to the front porch to let them air as best we could. Grandma's high bed had escaped the water but still smelled damp, so we put the mattress on the porch roof to sun.

The Captain treated me as though nothing had happened between us. At least I think he did. My brain was so feverish, it couldn't have judged what was natural and what was not. He called me "Sara Louise," but he had done that for some time, hadn't he? Why then did his voice speaking my name seem so heartbreakingly sweet? Tears would start in my eyes at the sound.

The second afternoon after the water was gone, he left the house for several hours. I wanted to go with him, but I couldn't trust myself. What insane thing might I do, finding myself suddenly alone with him? But after he was gone I began to worry. Would he do something foolish now that he had lost everything? I had one horrible vision of him walking straight out into the Bay until he was swallowed up. Oh, if only I could tell him that he had me—that I would never desert him. But I couldn't. I knew I couldn't.

I forgot my work and began to watch for him. Caroline and I were supposed to be putting fresh paper on the lower kitchen cabinet shelves, so that the canned goods could be brought down once more from upstairs and put away.

"Wheeze, what on earth are you doing? You've been to the front door five times in the last five minutes."

"Oh, leave me alone."

"I know what she's doing." Grandma was rocking as usual in the living room. "She's peeking around for that heathen Captain of hers."

Caroline burst into a giggle and then tried to cover

it up with fake coughing. Once we were both in the kitchen and out of sight, she rolled her eyes at me and twirled her finger at her temple to indicate that she thought our grandmother was nuts.

"Yep. Yep." The voice continued from the other room. "Can't keep her eyes off that wicked man. I see it. 'Deed I do."

Caroline began to giggle in earnest then. I didn't know which one I wanted to kill more.

"I told Susan no good would come of letting that man into the house. Like letting the devil himself march in. Don't take much to bedevil a foolish girl, but still—"

My throat choked up like a swamp pond listening to her drone on and on.

"But still, they that lets the devil in cannot count themselves blameless."

I was holding a jar of string beans in my hand, and I swear, if my mother had not happened down the stairs at that moment, I might have hurled that quart at the old woman's nodding head. I don't know what my mother heard, if anything, but I suppose she sensed the hatred, the air was so thick with it. At any rate, she gently pried my grandmother from the rocker and helped her upstairs for her afternoon nap.

When she came back to the kitchen, Caroline was practically dancing across the linoleum, simply bursting to tattle. "You know what Grandma said?"

I turned on her like a red-bellied water snake. "Shut your mouth, you fool!"

Caroline blanched, then recovered. "Whosoever shall say, 'Thou fool,' shall be in danger of hell fire," she quoted piously.

"Oh, my blessed," said Momma. She didn't often resort to such a typical island expression. "Is the world so short on trouble that you two crave to make more?"

I opened my mouth but shut it again hard. *Momma,* I wanted to cry out, *tell me I'm not in danger of hell fire.* My childhood nightmares of damnation were rising fast, but there was no place for me to run. How could I share with my mother the wildness of my body or the desperation of my mind?

As I finished putting away the canned goods in frozen silence, my own hands caught my eye. The nails were broken and none too clean, the cuticles ragged. There was a crack of red at the edge of my index finger where a hangnail had been chewed away.

"She's lovely, she's engaged, she uses Pond's" the advertisement read, showing two exquisitely white hands with perfectly formed and manicured nails, long nails, and a diamond ring sparkling on the gracefully curved left hand. A man with strong clean hands would never look at me in love. No man would. At the moment, it seemed worse than being forsaken by God.

The five of us were already at the supper table when the Captain got back. He knocked formally at the door. I jumped and ran to the screen to open it, even though my mother had not indicated that I must. He was standing there, his blue eyes sagging with tiredness, but with a warm smile parting his lips above the beard. In his arms he was carrying the huge orange tomcat.

"Look what found me," he said, as I opened the door.

Caroline came running. "You found the old orange cat!" she cried, just as though she had had some relation to the creature. She reached out for it. I was almost glad because I figured the tom would go wild at her touch. But it didn't. The storm must have broken its spirit, for it lay purring close to Caroline's chest. "You sweet old thing," she murmured, rubbing her nose in its fur. If Caroline had been relegated to the devil, she probably would have tamed him as well. She gave the cat some of our supper fish in a bowl and set it on the kitchen floor. The cat plunged its head blissfully into the bowl.

The Captain followed Caroline to the kitchen and rinsed his hands by pouring a scant dipper of our precious fresh water over them. Then he took out a large white handkerchief and wiped them carefully before he came back into the living room to sit down at the table. I concentrated on keeping my eyes off his hands, knowing now that they were more dangerous for me than his face, but sometimes I couldn't help myself.

"Well," he said, as though someone had asked him, "I hitched a ride to Crisfield today."

Everyone looked up and mumbled, though it was evident that he was going to tell us what he had been up to whether or not we prodded.

"I went to see Trudy in the hospital," he said. "She has that perfectly good house standing there empty. It occurred to me she might not mind my staying there until I can work out something more permanent." He carefully unfolded his large cloth napkin and lay it across his lap, then looked up as though awaiting our judgment.

My grandmother was the first to speak. "I knowed it," she muttered darkly without a hint of what it was she knew.

"Hiram," my father said, "no need for you to rush away. We're proud to have you with us."

The Captain flicked a glance at Grandma, who had her mouth open, but before she got her words past her teeth, he said, "You're mighty gracious. All of you. But I could be cleaning out her place while I live there. Make it fit for her to come home to. It would be a help to both of us."

He left right after supper. He had nothing to move, so he simply walked out with the orange tom at his heels.

"Wait," called Caroline. "Wheeze and I will walk you over." She grabbed her light blue scarf and tied it loosely about her hair. She always looked like a girl in an advertisement when she wore that scarf. "Come on," she said, as I hung back.

So I went with them, my legs so heavy that I could hardly lift them. It's better, I tried to tell myself. As long as he is here I will be in danger. Even if I do not give myself away, Grandma will see to it. But, oh, my blessed, did I hate to see him go.

School opened, and I suppose that helped. With Mr. Rice gone, there was only one teacher for the whole high school. Our high school, which had about twenty students at full strength, was down now to fifteen since two had graduated the previous spring and three had gone off to war. Six of us, including Call and Caroline and me, were freshmen, five were sophomores, three juniors, and a lone senior girl, Myrna Dolman, who wore thick glasses and doggedly maintained the ambition she had harbored since first grade to become a primary schoolteacher. Our teacher, Miss Hazel Marks, used to hold Myrna up to the rest of us as an example. Apparently, the ideal pupil in Miss Hazel's eyes was one who wrote neatly and never smiled.

I wasn't smiling much that fall, but my handwriting didn't improve a whit thereby. Without Mr. Rice, all the fun of school was gone. Although he had not been our teacher when we were in the eighth grade, we had been allowed every day to join the high school for music since the chorus could not do without Caroline. Even having to acknowledge that debt could not diminish my delight in our hour of music. Now, however, there was nothing to look forward to.

On the other hand, there was a certain safety in the unrelenting boredom of each day. I heard once that there are people who commit crimes with the sole purpose of being caught and put in jail. I rather understand that mentality. There are times when prison must seem a haven.

The ninth grade was seated in the worst possible place in the classroom, at the front, and to the right, away from the window. I spent hours gazing into the disapproving face of George Washington as painted by Gilbert Stuart. This experience left me with the conclusion that our first president, besides having frizzy hair, a large red hooked nose, and apple cheeks, had a prissy, even old-ladyish mouth and a double chin. All of these would have rendered him harmless, except that he also had staring blue eyes, eyes that could read everything that was going on underneath my forehead.

"Really, Sara Louise," he seemed to say everytime he caught my eye.

My mental project that fall was a study of all the hands of the classroom. It was my current theory that hands were the most revealing part of the human body—far more significant than eyes. For example, if all you were shown of Caroline's body were her hands, you would know at once that she was an artistic person. Her fingers were as long and gracefully shaped as those on the disembodied hands in the Ponds ad. Her nails were filed in a perfect arc, just beyond the tip of her finger. If the nails are too long, you can't take the person seriously, too short, she has problems. Hers were exactly the right length to show that she was naturally gifted and had a strength of will to do something about it.

In contrast I observed that Call's hands were wide with short fingers, the nails bitten well below the quick. They were red and rough to show he worked hard, but not muscled enough to give them any dignity. Reluctantly, I concluded that they were the hands of a good-hearted but second-rate person. After all, Call had always been my best friend, but, I said to myself, one must face facts however unpleasant.

Then there were my hands. But I've already spoken of them. I decided one day in the middle of an algebraic equation to change my luckless life by changing my hands. Using some of my precious crab money, I went to Kellam's and bought a bottle of Jergen's lotion, emery boards, orange sticks, cuticle remover, even a bottle of fingernail polish, which though colorless seemed a daring purchase.

Every morning as soon as there was enough light to see by without turning on the lamp, I'd work on my hands. It was a ritual as serious as the morning prayers of a missionary, and one which I took pains to finish well before Caroline could be expected to wake up. I carefully stashed my equipment at the very back of my bottom drawer in the bureau we shared.

Despite all my cunning, I came in one afternoon to find her generously slathering her hands with my Jergen's.

"Where did you get that?"

"From your drawer," she said innocently. "I didn't think you'd mind."

"Well, I do mind," I said. "You have no right to go poking around my drawers, stealing my stuff."

"Oh, Wheeze," she said, placidly helping herself to more lotion. "Don't be selfish."

"Okay," I screamed, "take it! Take it! Take everything I own!" I picked up the bottle and hurled it at the wall above her bed. It smashed there and fell, leaving a mixture of shattered glass and lotion to ooze down the wall after it.

"Wheeze," she said quietly, looking first at the wall and then at me, "have you gone crazy?"

I fled the house and was headed for the south marsh before I remembered it was no longer there. I stood shaking at the spot where the head of the old marsh path had begun, and through my tears, I thought I could just make out across the water a tiny tump of fast land, my old refuge now cut off from the rest of the island, orphaned and alone.

13

Caroline kept the Jergen's lotion incident to herself, so no one else suspected that I was going crazy. I kept the knowledge locked within myself, taking it out from time to time to admire in secret. I was quite sure I was crazy, and it was amazing that as soon as I admitted it, I became quite calm. There was nothing I could do about it. I seemed relatively harmless. After all, I hadn't thrown the lotion bottle at anyone, just the wall. There was no need to warn or disturb my parents. I could probably live out my life on the island in my own quiet, crazy way, much as Auntie Braxton always had. No one paid much attention to her, and if it hadn't been for the cats she would have probably lived and died in our midst, mostly forgotten by the rest of us. Caroline was sure to leave the island, so the house would be mine after my grandmother and my parents died. (With only a slight chill I contemplated the death of my parents.) I could crab like a man if I chose. Crazy people who are judged to be harmless are allowed an enormous amount of freedom ordinary people are denied. Thus as long as I left everyone alone, I could do as I pleased. Thinking about myself as a crazy, independent old woman made me feel almost happy.

So since no one knew about me, the crisis demanding the family's attention centered around Auntie Braxton. She was going to be released from the hospital, which meant that the Captain would soon be homeless again.

To my father it was perfectly simple. We were the Captain's friends, we would take him in. But my grandmother was adamant. "I'll not have that heathen in my house, much less in my bed. That's what he craves. To get in my bed with me in it."

"Mother Bradshaw!" Momma was genuinely shocked. My father glanced nervously at Caroline and me. She was on the verge of laughing. I was numb with rage.

"Oh, you just think when a woman gets old no man is going to look at her that way again."

"Mother," my father said. His intenseness made her pause. "The girls—" He nodded at us.

"Oh, she's the one stirred him up," Grandma said.

"She thinks he craves her, but I know. I know who he's really after. 'Deed I do."

My father turned to Caroline and me and spoke quietly. "Go to your room," he said. "She's old. You got to make allowances."

We knew we had to obey, and for once I was eager to. Caroline hung back, but I grabbed her arm and started for the staircase. I couldn't help what my parents heard, but I didn't want Caroline to hear. It was she who knew that I, not Grandma, was the crazy one.

As soon as our door was shut Caroline burst out laughing. "Can you imagine?" She shook her head. "What do you suppose is going on in that head of hers?"

"She's old," I said fiercely. "She's not responsible."

"She's not that old. She's younger than the Captain and he's not the least bit crazy." She didn't even look up to see how I was reacting. "Well," she continued in a chatty tone of voice. "At least we know he can't stay here. I can't imagine what she'd do if we invited him in again." She pulled her legs up and sat cross-legged on her bed facing toward mine. I was lying on my stomach with my head on my hands. I turned my face toward the pillow, trying not to betray myself any more than I had already. "I don't see why he can't just keep on living at Auntie Braxton's," she said.

"Because they're not married," I said. If I weren't more careful my voice alone would give me away. I cleared my throat and said as steadily as I could, "People who are not married do not live together."

She laughed. "It's not as if they'd want to do anything. My gosh, they're both too old to bother with that."

I was so hot all over at the suggestion of the Captain doing something that I could hardly breathe.

"Well?" Obviously she wanted some comment from me.

"It doesn't matter," I muttered. "It's how it looks. People don't think it looks right for people who aren't married to live together in the same house."

"Well, if people are going to be that way, they should just get married."

"What?" I swung my legs over the side of the bed and sat bolt upright.

"Sure," she said calmly, as though she were explaining a math problem. "What difference would it make? They should just get married and shut everybody up."

"Suppose he doesn't want to marry a crazy old woman?"

"He doesn't have to do anything, silly. They'd just—"

"Will you shut up about *doing* things? You have

got the filthiest mind. All you can think about is *doing* things."

"Wheeze. I was talking about *not* doing anything. It would be a marriage of convenience."

"That's not the same." I'd read more than she had and knew about these things.

"Well, a marriage in name only." She grinned at me. "Like that better?"

"No. It's terrible. It's peculiar. And don't you even suggest it. It will make him think we're peculiar, too."

"It will not. He knows us better than that."

"If you mention it to him, I'll kill you."

She shrugged me off. "You will not. Honestly, Wheeze, what's got into you?"

"Nothing. It's just that he might want to marry someone else. How would it be if we made him marry Auntie Braxton and then later on, too late, he finds he's really in love with someone else?"

"What on earth have you been reading, Wheeze? In the first place, if you don't count Grandma who's really nuts, and Widow Johnson who still worships the image of her sainted captain, and Call's grandma, who's too fat, there is no one else. In the second place, we can't *make* him do anything. He's a grown man."

"Well, I think it's filthy even to suggest it."

She stood up, choosing to ignore my comment. At

the door she listened for what might be going on downstairs and then, apparently satisfied that all was quiet, turned to me. "Come on," she said. "If you want to."

I jumped off my bed. "Where do you think you're going?"

"I'm going to get Call."

"Why?" I knew why.

"The three of us are going to see the Captain."

"Please stop it, Caroline. It's none of your business. You hardly even know him." I was trying to force my voice to remain calm with the result that all the unreleased shrieks were clogging my throat.

"I do know him, Wheeze. And I care about what happens to him."

"Why? Why do you always try to take over everybody else's life?" I thought I might strangle on the words.

She gave me her look which indicated that once again I had lost all sense of proportion. "Oh, Wheeze" was all she said.

It was up to Call to stop her. He would, I was sure—he and his tight little sense of propriety. But once she'd explained to him what a marriage "in name only" consisted of, he blushed and said, "Why not?"

Why not? I followed them to Auntie Braxton's house like a beaten hunting pup. Why not? Because,

I yearned to say, people aren't animals. Because it is none of our business. Because, oh, my blessed, I love him and cannot bear the thought of losing him to a crazy old woman, even in name only.

The Captain was making tea and cooking potatoes for his supper when we arrived. He was uncommonly cheerful for a man who was about to be cast out on his ear for the second time straight. He offered to share his supper, but there was hardly enough for one person, so we all politely refused, insisting that he go ahead—at least, Caroline and Call were insisting. I was sitting tight-lipped on the other side of the room, but when Caroline and Call started to sit down at the kitchen table with him I dragged myself across the living room and dumped myself into the empty chair. As little as I wanted to be a part of the coming scene, I didn't want to be left out of it either.

Caroline waited until he had generously salted and peppered his potatoes, then she laid her elbows on the table and propelled herself a bit closer to it and thus to him. "We heard that Auntie Braxton is going to be back in a couple of days," she said.

"That's right," he said, taking a large bite of potato.

"We've been worried about where you're going to live."

He raised his hand to stop her talking and held it

there until he had chewed and swallowed the bite. "I know what you're going to say, and I thank you, but I just can't."

See? See? I was smiling inside and out.

Caroline was not. "How do you know what I'm going to say?"

"You're going to ask me back to your house—and I'm grateful, but you know I can't come in on you again."

Caroline laughed. "Oh, I've got a much better idea than that."

All my smiles had dried up.

"Have you now, Miss Caroline?" He was spearing another piece of potato with his fork.

"I sure do." She leaned toward him with the kind of smile you see a woman give a man when she's got something more than politeness on her mind. "I'm proposing that you marry Miss Trudy Braxton."

"Marry?" he asked, putting down his fork and staring wide-eyed into her face. "You're suggesting that Trudy and I get married?"

"Don't worry," Call began earnestly, "you wouldn't have to—" at which point my bare heel slammed down on his bare toes. He stopped talking to give me a look of hurt surprise.

Caroline ignored us both. "Think of it this way," she said in her most sophisticated tone of voice. "She needs someone to take care of her and her house, and you need a house to live in. It would be a marriage of convenience." I noticed she didn't say "in name only." At least she had a whiff of delicacy.

"I be damned," he said under his breath, looking from one face to another. I pretended to study a torn cuticle to miss his scrutiny. "You kids do beat the limit. Who would have ever thought?"

"Once you get used to the idea, it'll make a lot of sense to you," Caroline said. "It's not," she added quickly, "that you couldn't find someplace else. Plenty of folks would take you in. But no one else *needs* you. Not like Auntie Braxton." She turned to me, then to Call for support.

By now I was biting away at the offending cuticle, but out of the corner of my eye I could see Call nodding his head vigorously, pumping up for a big affirmative statement. "It'll make sense," he repeated Caroline's theme. "It'll make plenty of sense, once you get used to it."

"It will, will it?" The Captain was shaking his head and grinning. "You sound like my poor old mother." Eventually he picked up his fork and, using one side of it, thoughtfully scraped the pepper off one of the potatoes. "People," he said at last, no shadow of a grin remaining, "people would say I did it for the money."

"What money?" Caroline asked.

"Nobody but you ever heard tell of no money,"

Call said. "Me and Wheeze are the only ones you told. And now Caroline."

"I wouldn't take a cent of her money, you know."

"Of course you wouldn't," Caroline said. What did she know?

"There probably isn't any," I said huffily. "We cleaned good and we never saw any."

He smiled appreciatively at me as though I had helped him. "Well," he said grinning. "It's a crazy idea." Something about the way he said it made me feel cold all over.

"You're going to think about it," Caroline said, rather than asked.

He shrugged. "Sure," he said. "No harm thinking crazy."

The next day he caught the ferry to Crisfield. He never even told us he was going. We had to get the word from Captain Billy. And he didn't come home that night or the next. We knew because we met the ferry each evening.

On the third day there he was, waving to us from the deck. My heart jumped to see him, and my body felt all over again how it was to be crushed against the rough material of his clothes, his heart beating straight through my backbone. Call and Caroline were waving back and calling out to him, but I was standing there shivering, my arms crossed, my hands hooked up under my arms and pressed against my breasts.

The boat was tied up, and now he was calling us by name. He wanted Caroline and me to see to something in the hold and Call to come aboard and give him a hand.

Caroline, as usual, moved faster than I. "Come, look here!" she yelled. When I got to where Captain Billy's sons were handing up the freight, I saw the chair. It was huge and dark brown with a wicker seat and back and large metal wheels rimmed in hard black rubber. It took both Edgar and Richard to lift it up onto the pier. Caroline was grinning all over. "I bet he's done it," she said.

Whatever was in my look made her correct herself. "I mean," she said with an impatient sigh, "I just mean, I bet he's gone and married her."

I had no place to run to, and even if I had, it was too late. They were already emerging from the cabin. Very slowly up the ladder, first Call's head, his neck bent. Then at last the three of them, the Captain and Call carrying Auntie Braxton on a hand sling between them, she with an arm about each's shoulder. When the three of them turned around at the top of the ladder, I could see that she was wearing on her shoulder a huge chrysanthemum corsage.

"He did marry her." Caroline said it softly, but it was exploding like shrapnel inside my stomach. She ran for the wheelchair and pushed it to the end of the gangplank as proud as though she were rolling out the red carpet for royalty. Call and the Captain carefully lowered the old woman into the chair.

As he straightened up, the Captain saw me hanging back and called to me. "Sara Louise," he said. "Come on over. I want you to shake hands with Miz Wallace here."

The old woman looked up at him when he said that, as worshipful as a repentant sinner testifying in church. When I came close, she put out her hand. Shaking her hand was like holding a bunch of twigs, but her eyes were clear and steady. I think she said, "How are you, Sara Louise?" The words were hard to decipher.

"Welcome home, Miss Trudy," I muttered. I couldn't for the life of me call her by his name.

14

I suppose if alcohol had been available to me that November, I would have become a drunk. As it was, the only thing I could lose my miserable self in was books. We didn't have many. I know that now. I have been to libraries on the mainland, and I know that between my home and the school there was very little. But I had all of Shakespeare and Walter Scott and Dickens and Fenimore Cooper. Every night I pulled the black air raid curtains to and read on and on, huddled close to our bedroom lamp. Can you imagine the effect of *The Last of the Mohicans* on a girl like me? It was not the selfless Cora, but Uncas and Uncas alone whom I adored. Uncas, standing ready to die before the Delaware, when an enemy warrior tears off his hunting shirt revealing the bright blue tortoise tattooed on Uncas's breast.

Oh, to have a bright blue tortoise—something that proclaimed my uniqueness to the world. But I was not the last of the Mohicans or the only of anything. I was Caroline Bradshaw's twin sister.

I cannot explain why, seeing how the storm had affected our family's finances, I never told anyone that I had almost fifty dollars hidden away. Among the first things that had to be given up were Caroline's mainland voice and piano lessons. Even on generous scholarships, the transportation was too much for our slender resources. I suppose it is to Caroline's credit that she seldom sulked about this deprivation. She continued to practice regularly with the hope that spring would mark the end of a successful oyster season and give us the margin we needed to continue her trips to Salisbury. I might say to my own credit, as I needed every bit of credit available in those days, that I did not rejoice over Caroline's misfortune. I never hated the music. In fact, I took pride in it. But though it occurred to me to offer the money I had saved to help her continue her lessons, I was never quite able to admit that I had put it away. Besides, it was not that much money—and it was mine. I had earned it.

I went once to see the Captain after he got married. He invited the three of us—Caroline, Call, and me—to dinner. I suppose he meant it for a celebration. At any rate, he pulled out a small bottle of wine and offered us some. Call and I were shocked and refused. Caroline took some with a great deal of giggling about what would happen if anyone found out he had smuggled spirits onto our very dry little island. I was annoyed. The absence of alcohol on Rass (we never counted Momma's sherry bottle as real alcohol) was a matter of religious, not civil, law. We didn't even have a policeman, and there certainly was nothing resembling jail. If people had known about the Captain's wine, they would have simply condemned him as a heathen and prayed over him on Wednesday night. They'd been doing that ever since he arrived.

"I used to buy this kind of wine in Paris," the Captain explained. "It's been hard to get since the war." I assumed, of course, that he meant the war of the moment. Thinking back, I guess he must have meant World War I. I had a hard time keeping in mind how old he was.

With Auntie Braxton, there was no question. She sat at the head of the table in her wooden and wicker wheelchair, smiling a lopsided, almost simple smile. Her hair was white and so thin you could see the pink of her skull shining through. I suppose the strange angle of her smile was the result of the stroke, which is what had caused her to fall and break her hip. She tried to hold her glass in the tiny claw of her hand, but the Captain was there to hold it steady at her mouth. She took a sip, a bit of which dribbled down her chin. She seemed not to mind, keeping her clear, childlike eyes devoted to his face.

He patted her chin with a napkin. "My dear," he was saying. "Did I ever tell you about the time I had to drive a car across the city of Paris?"

For those of us who had lived all our lives on Rass, an automobile was almost more exotic than Paris. It irritated me that the Captain had never thought to tell, or chosen to tell Call and me about this adventure. For it was an adventure, the way the Captain told it.

Settling back in his own chair, he explained that he had driven a car only once before in his life, and that on a country road in America, when his companion, a French seaman, suggested that they buy a car someone was hawking on the dock at Le Havre and take it into Paris. The Frenchman felt that it would be a wonderful way to pick up some girls, and the Captain, his pockets full of francs and with a week's shore leave in which to spend them, saw the car as a means to independence and excitement. He did not know until after the purchase was made that his companion had never driven a car before.

"'But no matter,'" the Captain imitated the

Frenchman. "'Is easy.'" With difficulty, the Captain persuaded his friend to let him drive and then began their hair-raising trip from Le Havre to Paris, culminating in a cross-city ride at the busiest time of the afternoon.

"And then I came to a huge intersection—carts and automobiles and trucks coming at me from what seemed to be eight directions. If I stayed still I would be plowed under but to go forward was suicide."

"What did you do?" Call asked.

"Well—I shifted into first gear, grabbed the wheel as tight as I could with one hand, squeezed the horn with the other, jammed down on the accelerator with both feet, shut my eyes, and zoomed across."

"What?" cried Call. "Didn't you kill yourself?"

A peculiar noise, more like a chicken cackle than anything else, came from the end of the table. We all turned. Auntie Braxton was laughing. The others all began to laugh then, even Call, who knew the joke was at his expense. Everyone began to laugh but me.

"Don't you get it, Wheeze?" Call asked. "If he'd of killed himself—"

"Of course I get it, stupid. I just don't happen to think it's funny."

Caroline turned to Auntie Braxton and said, "Don't mind her." She flashed a beautiful smile at Call. "Wheeze doesn't think anything's funny."

"I do, too. You liar! All you do is lie, lie, lie."

She gave me her most pained expression. "Wheeze," she said.

"Don't call me Wheeze! I'm a person, not a disease symptom." It would have sounded more impressive if my voice hadn't cracked in the middle of the word *disease*.

Caroline laughed. She acted as though she thought I had meant to be funny. When she laughed, Call laughed. They looked at each other and hooted with pleasure as though something enormously witty had been said. I propped my forehead on my elbowed hand and steeled myself for the cackle from Auntie Braxton and the laugh, which reminded me of an exuberant tuba, that would come from the Captain. They didn't come. Instead, I felt a scratchy arm about my shoulder and a face close to my ear.

"Sara Louise," he was saying gently. "What's wrong, my dear?"

God have mercy. Didn't he know that I could stand anything except his kindness? I pushed back my chair, nearly knocking him down as I did so, and fled from that terrible house.

I never saw Auntie Braxton again, until she was laid out for her funeral. Caroline reported to me regularly how happy both the old woman and the Captain were. She and Call visited them almost every day. The Captain always asked Caroline to sing for them because "Trudy loves music so." He seemed to know a lot about this old woman that most people who had lived all their lives on the island didn't.

"She can talk, you know," Caroline said to me. "Sometimes you can't understand, but he always seems to. And whenever I sing she listens, really listens. Not with half her mind somewhere else. The Captain's right. She loves it. I never saw anyone who loved music so much, not even Momma." When she would say things like this, I'd just bury myself more deeply in my book and pretend I hadn't heard.

On the anniversary of Pearl Harbor, Auntie Braxton suffered a massive stroke and was rushed to the hospital by ferry in the middle of the night. She was dead by Christmas.

There was a funeral service for her in the church. It seemed ironic. Neither she nor the Captain had been to church for as long as anyone could remember, but the preacher in those days was young and earnest and gave her what was warmly regarded as a "right purty service." The Captain wanted our family to sit with him in the front pew, so we did, even Grandma who, I'm glad to say, behaved herself. The Captain sat between Caroline and me. While the congregation recited the Twenty-third Psalm—"Yea, though I walk through the valley of the shadow of death, I shall fear no evil; for thou art with me . . ." Caroline reached over and took his hand as though he were a small child in need of guidance and protection. He reached up with his free hand and wiped his eyes. And, sitting closer to him than I had in months, I realized with a sudden coldness how very old he was and felt the tears start in my own eyes.

Afterward my mother asked the Captain to come home and have supper with us, but when he refused, no one pressed him to change his mind. Caroline and Call and I walked him to the door of what was now his house. No one said a word along the way, and when he nodded to us at the door, we just nodded back and headed home. As it turned out, it was a good thing he had not come home with us. Grandma went on one of her worst rampages to date.

"He killed her, you know."

We all gaped in astonishment. Even from Grandma this was strong stuff.

"He wanted her house. I knew soon as he moved in there this was bound to happen."

"Mother," my father said quietly. "Don't, Mother."

"I reckon you want to know how he did it."

"Mother—"

"Poisoned her. That's how." She gazed about the table in triumph. "Rat poison." She took a large bite of food and chewed it noisily. The rest of us had stopped eating entirely.

"Louise knows," she said in a sneaky little voice. She smiled at me. "But you wouldn't tell, would you? And I know why." She broke into a child's singsong jeer. "Nah nah nah nah *nah nah.*"

"Shut up!" It was Caroline who yelled what I could not.

"Caroline!" both our parents said.

Caroline's face was red with rage, but she pinched her lips together.

Grandma continued unperturbed. "Ever see how she looks at him?"

"Mother."

"She thinks I'm only a foolish old woman. But I know. 'Deed I do." She stared at me full in the eyes. I was too afraid to look away. "Maybe you helped. Did you, Louise? Did you help him?" Her eyes were glittering.

"Girls," my father was almost whispering. "Go to your room."

This time both of us obeyed immediately. Even behind the safety of our door we could not speak. There were no more jokes or excuses to be made for the silly, grumpy old woman we'd known from birth. The shock was so enormous that I found my own puny fear of exposure melting into a much larger darker terror that seemed to have no boundaries.

"Who knows?" the voice from *The Shadow* asks. "Who knows what evil lurks in the hearts of men?" Now we knew.

Much later, when we were getting ready for bed,

Caroline said, "I've got to get away from here before she runs me nuts."

You? I thought but did not say. You? What harm can she possibly do? You do not need to be delivered from evil. Can't you see? It's me. Me—I who am so close to being swallowed up in all that eternal darkness. But I didn't say it. I wasn't angry at her—just deadly tired.

In the light of the next day, I tried to tell myself that I had only imagined the great evil of the scene the night before. Hadn't I once tried to convince Call that the Captain was a Nazi—a U-boat delivered spy? Why, then, was I so upset over Grandma's accusation? I saw again in my mind those glittering eyes and knew it was not the same. Grandma, however, seemed to have forgotten everything. She was quite her grumpy, silly self again, and we were relieved to pretend that we, too, had forgotten.

In February, Call dropped out of school. His mother and grandmother were destitute, and my father offered to take him aboard the *Portia Sue* as an oyster culler. My father would tong, bringing up oysters with his long fir-wood tongs, which looked like scissors with a metal rake at the end of each shaft. He would open the rakes and drop his catch onto the wooden culling board. There Call, his hands in heavy rubber gloves, would cull, using a culling hammer. With the hammer head he knocked off the excess shell, and with the blade at the other end he struck off the small oysters. The debris was shoved into the Bay and the good oysters forward until they could be sold to a buy boat, which would take them to market. From Monday well before dawn to Saturday night, they would be gone, sleeping all week on cramped bunks in the *Portia Sue*'s tiny cabin, for the best oyster beds were up the Eastern Shore rivers, too far away for daily commuting when gas was so strictly rationed.

Of course I was jealous of Call, but I was surprised to realize how very much I missed him. All my life my father had followed the water, so it had never seemed strange to have him gone, but Call had always been around, either with me or close by. Now we only saw him at church.

Caroline made a fuss over him every Sunday. "My, Call, we sure do miss you." How could she know? Besides, it didn't seem quite ladylike to say something like that, straight out.

Each week, he seemed to grow taller and thinner, and his hands were turning more and more into the rough brown bark of a waterman's. Even his manner seemed to change. The solemnity that had always lent him, as a small child, a rather comic air, now seemed a sort of youthful dignity. You could sense his pride that he had come at last into a man's estate, the sole support of the women upon whom he had until now depended. I knew we had been growing apart since summer, but I had been able to blame that on Caroline. Now it was more painful, for the very things that made him stronger and more attractive were taking him deep into the world of men—a place I could never hope to enter.

Later that winter I began going again to see the Captain. I always went with Caroline. It wouldn't have been proper for either of us to go alone. He taught us how to play poker, which I had to be persuaded to do, but once I began it made me feel deliciously wicked. He probably owned the only deck of regular playing cards on Rass. Those were the days when good Methodists only indulged in Rook or Old Maid. We played poker for toothpicks, as though they were gold pieces. At least I did. Nothing gave me greater satisfaction than totally cleaning out my sister. It must have shown, because I can remember her saying on more than one occasion in a very annoyed tone of voice, "For goodness' sakes, Wheeze, it's only a game" as I would lick my chops and scrape all her tumbled stacks of toothpicks across the table with my arm.

One day after a particularly satisfying win, the Captain turned from me to Caroline and said, "I miss your singing now that Trudy's gone. Those were some happy times."

Caroline smiled. "I liked them too," she said.

"You're not letting down on your practicing now, are you?"

"Oh," she said. "I don't know. I guess it's all right."

"You're doing fine." I was impatient to get on to another game.

She shook her head. "I really miss my lessons," she said. "I hadn't realized how much they meant."

"Well, it's a pity," I said the way a grown-up speaks to a child to shut her up. "Times are hard."

"Yes," the Captain said. "I suppose lessons take a lot of money."

"It's not just the money," I said quickly, trying to ignore the vision of my own little hoard of bills and change. "It's the gas and all. Once you get to Crisfield, it's worth your life to get a taxi. Now if the county would just send us to boarding school like they do the Smith Island kids—"

"Oh, Wheeze, that wouldn't help. What kind of a music program could they have at that school? We beat them all to pieces in the contest last year."

"Well, we should be able to request a special school on account of special circumstances."

"They'd never pay for us to go to any school, much less a really good school," she said sadly.

"Well, they ought to." I wanted to dump the blame on the county and deal the cards. "Don't you think they should, Captain?"

"Yes, somebody should."

"But they won't," I said. "Anything dumber than a blowfish, it's a county board of education."

They laughed, and to my relief the subject was closed. It was too bad about Caroline's lessons, but she'd had a couple of good years at Salisbury. Besides, it wasn't my fault. I hadn't started the war or caused the storm.

The Captain did not come to our house. He was invited perfunctorily every Sunday, but he seemed to know that he oughtn't to come and always managed an excuse. So I was startled one afternoon a week or so later to see him hurrying up the path to our porch, his face flushed with what looked like excitement and not just the effects of his rushing. I opened the door before he had stepped up onto the porch.

"Sara Louise," he said, waving a letter in his hand as he came. "Such wonderful news!" He paused at the door. "Your father's not here, I guess." I shook my head. It was only Wednesday. "Well, please get your mother. I can't wait." He was beaming all over.

Grandma was rocking in her chair, reading or pretending to read her large leather-bound Bible. He nodded at her. "Miss Louise," he said. She didn't look up. Mother and Caroline were coming in from the kitchen.

"Why, Captain Wallace," said my mother, wiping

her hands on her apron. "Sit down. Louise, Caroline, will you fix some tea for the Captain?"

"No, no," he said. "Sit down, all of you. I've got the most wonderful news. I can't wait."

We all sat down.

He put the letter on his lap and pressed out a crease with his fingertip. "There are so few opportunities for young people on this island," he began. "I'm sure, Miss Susan, a woman of your background and education must suffer to see her children deprived."

What was he leading up to? I could feel a faint stir of excitement in my breast.

"You know how much I think of you, how indebted both Trudy and I are—were—to all of you. And now—" He could hardly contain himself. He smiled at me. "I have Sara Louise to thank for the idea. You see, Trudy left a little legacy. I didn't know what to do with it, because I swore to myself I would never touch her money. There isn't a great deal, but there is enough for a good boarding school." He was beaming all over. "I've investigated. There will be enough for Caroline to go to Baltimore and continue her music. Nothing would make Trudy happier than that, I know."

I sat there as stunned as though he had thrown a rock in my face. Caroline!

Caroline jumped up and ran over and threw her arms around his neck.

"Caroline, wait," my mother was saying. Surely she would point out that she had two daughters. "Captain, this is very generous, but I can't—I'd have to talk with my husband. I couldn't—"

"We must convince him, Miss Susan. Sara Louise, tell her how you were saying to me just the other day that someone should understand that special circumstances demand special solutions—that Caroline ought to be sent to a really good school where she could continue her music. Isn't that right, Sara Louise?"

I made a funny sound in my throat that must have resembled a "yes." The Captain took it for approval. My grandmother twisted in her chair to look at me. I looked away as fast as I could. She was smiling.

"Isn't that right, Sara Louise?" she asked in a voice intended to mimic the Captain's. "Isn't that right?"

I jumped toward the kitchen with the excuse of making tea. I could hear the Captain talking on to Mother and Caroline about the academy he knew in Baltimore with the wonderful music program. The words roared in my ears like a storm wind. I put the kettle on and laid out cups and spoons. Everything seemed so heavy I could hardly pick them up. I struggled to pry the lid from the can of tea leaves, aware that my grandmother had come in and was standing close behind me. I stiffened at the sound of her hoarse whisper.

"Romans nine thirteen," she said. "'As it is written, Jacob have I loved, but Esau have I hated.'"

15

I served the tea with a smile sunk in concrete pilings.

"Thank you, Louise," my mother said.

The Captain nodded at me as he took his cup off the tray. Caroline, distracted with happiness, seemed not to see me at all. I took the cup that I had prepared for her back to the kitchen, brushing past my grandmother, who was grinning at me in the doorway. After I had put down the tray, I had to squeeze past her once more to get to the protection of my room. "Jacob have I loved—" she began, but I hurried by and up the steps as quickly as I could.

I closed the door behind me. Then, without thinking, I took off my dress and hung it up and put on my nightgown. I crawled under the covers and closed my eyes. It was half-past three in the afternoon.

I suppose I meant never to get up again, but of course I did. At suppertime my mother came in to ask if I were ill, and being too slow-witted to invent an ailment, I got up and went down to the meal. No one said much at the table. Caroline was positively glowing, my mother quiet and thoughtful, my grandmother grinning and stealing little peeks at my face.

At bedtime Caroline finally remembered that she had a sister. "Please don't mind too much, Wheeze. It means so much to me."

I just shook my head, not trusting myself to reply. Why should it matter if I minded? How would that change anything? The Captain, who I'd always believed was different, had, like everyone else, chosen her over me. Since the day we were born, twins like Jacob and Esau, the younger had ruled the older. Did anyone ever say Esau and Jacob?

"Jacob have I loved . . ." Suddenly my stomach flipped. Who was speaking? I couldn't remember the passage. Was it Isaac, the father of the twins? No, even the Bible said that Isaac had favored Esau. Rebecca, the mother, perhaps. It was her conniving that helped Jacob steal the blessing from his brother. Rebecca—I had hated her from childhood, but somehow I knew that these were not her words.

I got up, pulled the blackout curtains, and turned on the table lamp between our beds.

"Wheeze?" Caroline propped herself up on one elbow and blinked at me.

"Just have to see something." I took my Bible from our little crate bookcase, and bringing it over to the light, looked up the passage Grandma had cited. Romans, the ninth chapter and the thirteenth verse. The speaker was God.

I was shaking all over as I closed the book and got back under the covers. There was, then, no use struggling or even trying. It was God himself who hated me. And without cause. "Therefore," verse eighteen had gone on to rub it in, "hath he mercy on whom he will have mercy, and whom he will he hardeneth." God had chosen to hate me. And if my heart was hard, that was his doing as well.

My mother did not hate me. The next two days part of me watched her watching me. She wanted to speak to me, I could tell, but my heart was already beginning to harden and I avoided her.

Then Friday after supper while Caroline was practicing, she followed me up to the room.

"I need to talk with you, Louise."

I grunted rudely. She flinched but didn't correct me. "I've been giving this business a lot of thought," she said.

"What business?" I was determined to be cruel.

"The offer—the idea of Caroline going to school in Baltimore."

I watched her coldly, my right hand at my mouth.

"It—it—well, it is a wonderful chance for her, you know. A chance we, your father and I, could never hope—Louise?"

"Yes?" I bit down savagely on a hangnail and ripped it so deeply that the blood started.

"Don't do that to your finger, please."

I grabbed my hand from my mouth. What did she want from me? My permission? My blessing?

"I-I was trying to think—we could never afford this school in Baltimore, but maybe Crisfield. We could borrow something on next year's earnings—"

"Why should Caroline go to Crisfield when she has a chance—"

"No, not Caroline, you. I thought we might send you—"

She did hate me. There. See. She was trying to get rid of me. "Crisfield!" I cried contemptuously. "Crisfield! I'd rather be chopped for crab bait!"

"Oh," she said. I had plainly confused her. "I really thought you might like—"

"Well, you were wrong!"

"Louise—"

"Momma, would you just get out and leave me alone!" If she refused, I would take it for a sign, not only that she cared about me but that God did. If she stayed in that room— She stood up, hesitating.

"Why don't you just go?"

"All right, Louise, if that's what you want." She closed the door quietly behind her.

My father came home as usual on Saturday. He and my mother spent most of Sunday afternoon at the Captain's. I don't know how the matter was settled in a way that satisfied my father's proud independence, but by the time they returned it was settled. Within two weeks we were on the dock to see Caroline off to Baltimore. She kissed us all, including the Captain and Call, who turned the color of steamed crab at her touch. She was back for summer vacation a few days before Call left for the navy, at which time she provided the island with another great show of kissing and carrying on. You couldn't doubt that she'd go far in grand opera judging by that performance.

After Call left, I gave up progging and took over the responsibility of my father's crab floats. I poled my skiff from float to float, fishing out the soft crabs and taking them to the crab house to pack them in boxes filled with eelgrass for shipping. I knew almost as much about blue crabs as a seasoned waterman. One look at a crab's swimming leg and I could tell almost to the hour when the critter was going to shed. The next to the last section is nearly transparent and if the crab is due to moult in less than a couple of weeks, the faint line of the new shell can be seen growing there beneath the present one. It's called a "white sign." Gradually, the shadow darkens. When a waterman catches a "pink sign," he knows the moulting will take place in about a week, so he gently breaks the crab's big claws to keep it from killing all its neighbors and brings it home to finish peeling in his floats. A "red sign" will begin to shed in a matter of hours and a "buster" has already begun.

Shedding its shell is a long and painful business for a big Jimmy, but for a she-crab, turning into a sook, it seemed somehow worse. I'd watch them there in the float, knowing once they shed that last time and turned into grown-up lady crabs there was nothing left for them. They hadn't even had a Jimmy make love to them. Poor sooks. They'd never take a trip down the Bay to lay their eggs before they died. The fact that there wasn't much future for the Jimmies once they were packed in eelgrass didn't bother me so much. Males, I thought, always have a chance to live no matter how short their lives, but females, ordinary, ungifted ones, just get soft and die.

At about seven I would head home for breakfast

and then back to the crab house and floats until our four-thirty supper. After supper sometimes one of my parents would go back with me, but more often I went alone. I didn't really mind. It made me feel less helpless to be a girl of fifteen doing what many regarded as a man's job. When school started in the fall, I, like every boy on Rass over twelve, was simply too busy to think of enrolling. My parents objected, but I assured them that when the crab season was over, I would go and catch up with the class. Secretly, I wasn't sure that I could stand school with neither Caroline nor Call there with me, but, of course, I didn't mention this to my parents.

We had another severe storm that September. It took no lives, in the literal sense, but since it took another six to eight feet of fast land off the southern end of the island, four families whose houses were in jeopardy moved to the mainland. They were followed within the month by two other families who had never quite recovered from the storm of '42. There was plenty of war work on the mainland for both men and women at what seemed to us to be unbelievable wages. So as the water nibbled away at our land, the war nibbled away at our souls. We were lucky, though. In the Bay we could still work without fear. Fishermen of the Atlantic coast were being stalked by submarines. Some were killed, though we like the rest of the country were kept ignorant of those bodies that washed ashore just a few miles to the east of us.

Our first war deaths did not come until the fall of 1943, but then there were three at once when three island boys who had signed aboard the same ship were lost off a tiny island in the South Pacific that none of us had ever heard of before.

I did not pray anymore. I had even stopped going to church. At first I thought my parents would put up a fight when one Sunday morning I just didn't come back from the crab house in time for church. My grandmother lit into me at suppertime, but to my surprise my father quietly took my part. I was old enough, he said, to decide for myself. When she launched into prophecies of eternal damnation, he told her that God was my judge, not they. He meant it as a kindness, for how could he know that God had judged me before I was born and had cast me out before I took my first breath? I did not miss church, but sometimes I wished I might pray. I wanted, oddly enough, to pray for Call. I was so afraid he might die in some alien ocean thousands of miles from home.

If I was being prayed for mightily at Wednesday night prayer meetings, I was not told of it. I suppose people were a little afraid of me. I must have been a strange sight, always dressed in man's work clothes, my hands as rough and weathered as the sides of the crab house where I worked.

It was the last week in November when the first northwest blow of winter sent the egg-laden sooks rushing toward Virginia and the Jimmies deep under the Chesapeake mud. My father took a few days off to shoot duck, and then put the culling board back on the *Portia Sue* and headed out for oysters. One week in school that fall had been enough for me and one week alone on the oyster beds was enough for him. We hardly discussed it. I just got up at two Monday morning, dressed as warmly as I could with a change of clothes in a gunnysack. We ate breakfast together, my mother serving us. No one said anything about my not being a man—maybe they'd forgotten.

I suppose if I were to try to stick a pin through that most elusive spot "the happiest days of my life," that strange winter on the *Portia Sue* with my father would have to be indicated. I was not happy in any way that would make sense to most people, but I was, for the first time in my life, deeply content with what life was giving me. Part of it was the discoveries—who would have believed that my father sang while tonging? My quiet, unassuming father, whose voice could hardly be heard in church, stood there in his oilskins, his rubber-gloved hands on his tongs, and sang to the oysters. It was a wonderful sound, deep and pure. He knew the Methodist hymnbook by heart. "The crabs now, they don't crave music, but oysters," he explained shyly, "there's nothing they favor more than a purty tune." And he would serenade the oysters of Chesapeake Bay with the hymns the brothers Wesley had written to bring sinners to repentance and praise. Part of my deep contentment was due, I'm sure, to being with my father, but part, too, was that I was no longer fighting. My sister was gone, my grandmother a fleeting Sunday apparition, and God, if not dead, far removed from my concern.

It was work that did this for me. I had never had work before that sucked from me every breath, every thought, every trace of energy.

"I wish," said my father one night as we were eating our meager supper in the cabin, "I wish you could do a little studying of a night. You know, keep up your schooling."

We both glanced automatically at the kerosene lamp, which was more smell than light. "I'd be too tired," I said.

"I reckon."

It had been one of our longer conversations. Yet once again I was a member of a good team. We were averaging ten bushels of oysters a day. If it kept up, we'd have a record year. We did not compare ourselves to the skipjacks, the large sailboats with five or six crew members, that raked dredges across the bottom to harvest a heavy load of muck and trash and bottom spat along with oysters each time the mechanical winch cranked up a dredge. We tongers stood perched on the washboards of our tiny boats, and, just as our fathers and grandfathers had before us, used our fir-wood tongs, three or four times taller than our own bodies, to reach down gently to the oyster bed, feel the bottom until we came to a patch of market-sized oysters, and then closing the rakes over the catch, bringing it up to the culling board. Of course, we could not help but bring up some spat, as every oyster clings to its bed until the culling hammer forces a separation, but compared to the dredge, we left the precious bottom virtually undisturbed to provide a bed for the oysters that would be harvested by our children's children.

At first, I was only a culler, but if we found a rich bed, I'd tong as well, and then when the culling board was loaded, I'd bring in my last tong full hand over hand, dump it on the board, and cull until I'd caught up with my father.

Oysters are not the mysterious creatures that blue crabs are. You can learn about them more quickly. In a few hours, I could measure a three-inch shell with my eyes. Below three inches they have to go back. A live oyster, a good one, when it hits the culling board has a tightly closed shell. You throw away the open ones. They're dead already. I was a good oyster in those days. Not even the presence at Christmastime of a radiant, grown-up Caroline could get under my shell.

The water began to freeze in late February. I could see my culling like a trail behind us on the quickly forming ice patches. "Them slabs will grow together blessed quick," my father said. And without further discussion, he turned the boat. We stopped only long enough to sell our scanty harvest to a buy boat along the way and then headed straight for Rass. The temperature was dropping fast. By morning we were frozen in tight.

There followed two weeks of impossible weather. My father made no attempt to take the *Portia Sue* out. The first day or so I was content simply to sleep away some of the accumulated exhaustion of the winter. But the day soon came when my mother, handing me a ten o'clock cup of coffee, was suggesting mildly that I might want to take in a few days of school since the bad weather was likely to hold out for some time.

Her kindly intended words lay on me like a wet sail. I tried to appear calm, but I was caught and suffocated by the idea of returning to school. Didn't she realize that I was by now a hundred years older than anyone there, including Miss Hazel? I put my coffee down, sloshing it over the saucer onto the table. Coffee was rationed then and to waste it, inexcusable. I jumped up mumbling an apology to get a rag, but she was quicker and began sponging the brown liquid off the oilcloth before I could move, so I sat down again and let her do it.

"I worry about you, Louise," she said, mopping carefully and not looking at me. "Your father and I are grateful, indeed. I hardly know what we'd have done without you. But—" She trailed off, reluctant, I suppose, to predict what might become of me if I went on in my present manner of life. I didn't know whether to seem touched or annoyed. I was certainly irritated. If they were willing to accept the fruits of my life, they should at least spare me the burden of their guilt.

"I don't want to go back to school," I said evenly.

"But—"

"You can teach me here. You're a teacher."

"But you're so lonely."

"I'd be lonelier there. I've never belonged at that school." I was becoming, much to my own displeasure, a bit heated as I spoke. "I hate them and they hate me." There. I had overstated my case. They had never cared enough about me one way or the other to hate me. I might have from time to time served as the butt of their laughter, but I had never achieved enough status to earn their hatred.

She straightened up, sighing, and went over to the

sink to wash the coffee from her cloth. "I suppose I could," she said finally. "Teach you, I mean, if Miss Hazel would lend me the books. Captain Wallace might be willing to do the math."

"Can't you do that?" Although I was no longer in love with the Captain, I did not wish to be thrown in such close company with him again—just the two of us. There was a residue of pain there.

"No," she said. "If you want to be taught at home, I'd have to ask someone else to do the math. There is no one else with the—with the time." She was always very careful not to seem to sneer at the rest of the islanders for their lack of education.

I'm not sure how my mother persuaded Miss Hazel to go along with the arrangement. The woman was very jealous of her position as the one high school teacher on Rass. Perhaps my mother argued that my irregular attendance would be disruptive, I don't know, but she came home with the books, and we began our kitchen-table school.

As for my lessons with the Captain, my mother, sensitive to the least hint of inappropriate behavior, always went with me. She would sit and knit while we had our very proper lesson, no more poker or jokes, and afterward, she and the Captain would chat across my head. He was always eager for news of Caroline, who was prospering in Baltimore as the Prophet Jeremiah claimed only the wicked do. Her letters were few and hurried but filled with details of her conquests. In turn, the Captain would share news from Call, from whom he heard nearly as often as we heard from Caroline. Between letters there was a lot of "Did I remember to tell you . . . ?" or "Did I read the part about . . . ?" Censorship kept Call from revealing very much about where he was or what was going on, but in what he didn't say there was enough to make my flesh crawl. The Captain, having been through naval battles before, seemed to regard the whole thing with more interest than fear.

There were only a few more days of oystering left that winter of '44. During the end of March and most of April, my father caught and salted alewives for crab bait, overhauled the motor on the *Portia Sue,* and converted it once more for crabbing. After he had caught and salted his crab bait, he did a little fishing to pass the days and even some house repairs. I crammed in as much schooling at home as possible, because once the crabs were moving, I'd be back on duty at the floats and in the crab house.

My mother heard the report of D day on our ancient radio and walked up to the crab house to tell me. She seemed more excited than I, to whom it signified only more war and killing. Besides, it was not the European war that concerned me.

16

Roosevelt was elected to a fourth term in the fall of 1944 without the help of Rass, which went solidly Republican as usual. And yet, when he died the following April, we shared the shock of the nation. As I heard the news, I remembered instantly the day the war had begun, Caroline and I standing hand in hand before the radio. The chill that went through me was the same coldness of that winter day in 1941 when Caroline and I had begun to grow up.

Some days after Roosevelt's death, I received the only letter I had ever gotten from Call. I was surprised to see how my hands trembled opening it, so much that I was obliged to turn my back on my mother and grandmother in the living room and go to the kitchen. It was very brief.

Dear Wheeze,

What do you think St. Peter said to Franklin D. Roosevelt? Get it?

Call

I got it, but as was usually the case with Call's jokes, I didn't find it the least bit funny.

On April 30, the day that Hitler committed suicide, I was permitted to take the exams for graduation. I passed, much to my satisfaction, with the highest grades recorded from Rass. Not that Miss Hazel told my mother this. It was the mainland school supervisor who had graded the exams who took time to write me a note of congratulations.

When the war in Europe ended eight days later, it was overshadowed by the news from Baltimore that Caroline had been accepted by the Juilliard School of Music in New York on a full scholarship.

I looked upon this announcement with enormous relief as the end of any sacrifice I would ever be asked to make for Caroline. My parents hoped it meant that she could take a rest and come home for the summer, but she wrote at the last minute to say that she had been offered a chance to go to summer school at Peabody—an opportunity her voice teacher felt she must not pass up. I'm sure my parents were disappointed, but I was not. The war was coming quickly to a close. Soon, I felt sure, Call would be back.

Exactly what Call's return would mean to me, I could not say. I had not despised my life of the past two years, but I began to realize that it had been a time of hibernation, for I felt stirrings I had almost forgotten. Perhaps when Call came home—perhaps—well, at the very least when he came I could turn over my tasks to him. My father would be overjoyed to have a man to help him. And I—what was it I wanted? I could leave the island, if I wished. I could see the mountains. I could even take a job in Washington or Baltimore if I wanted to. If I chose to leave—there was something cold about the idea, but I shook it away.

I began to cream my hands each night, sloshing lotion all over them and sleeping in a pair of mother's worn white cotton gloves—perhaps the pair she was married in. Is that possible? It was stupid, I decided, to resign myself to being another Auntie Braxton. I was young and able, as my exams had proved. Without God, or a man, I could still conquer a small corner of the world—if I wanted to. My hands stubbornly refused to be softened. But I was determined not to give up on them this time.

Something was happening inside of Grandma, too. Suddenly that summer she decided that my mother was the woman who had stolen her husband. One afternoon I came in for supper from the crab house to find Momma trying to bake bread. I say trying, because it was a sweltering August day, which was hard enough to fight on the island, but as Momma worked, her face shining with sweat, her hair plastered against her head, Grandma was reading aloud to her, in a voice that could be heard from the street, the section in Proverbs chapter six entitled, "The mischiefs of whoredom."

"'Can a man take fire in his bosom, and his clothes not be burned?'" my grandmother was crying out as I came into the back door. We were used to Grandma reading the Bible to us, but the selections were not usually quite so purple. I didn't even understand what it was all about until Grandma, seeing that I had come in, said, "Tell that viperish adulteress to listen to God's Word!" And proceeded to read on into chapter seven, which details the seduction of a young man by a "strange woman."

I looked down at my poor mother, struggling to pull several loaves of bread out of the oven. It was all I could do to keep from bursting out laughing. Susan Bradshaw as a scarlet woman? It's a joke, get it? I began banging pots and pans, more to cover my giggles than to help with supper.

I looked up to see my father in the front doorway. He seemed to be waiting there, taking in the scene, before he determined what his part should be.

Grandma had not seen him. She stumbled on through the passage. " 'He goeth after her straightway, as an ox to the slaughter . . .' "

Without even removing his boots, my father walked straight across the living room to the kitchen and, pretending not to care who watched, kissed my mother on her neck where a tendril of hair had pulled loose from her bun. I blushed despite myself, but he didn't seem to notice me. He whispered something into her ear. She gave a wry grin.

" 'Till a dart strike through his liver . . .' "

"Liver?" My father mouthed the word in mock horror. Then he turned to Grandma, all teasing dropped. "Mother. I think your supper is on the table."

She seemed a little startled by his voice, but she came to the table determined to finish the terrible passage, yet not willing to miss her supper to do so. " 'Her house is the way to hell—' " My father took the Bible gently from her hands and put it on a bookshelf above her head.

She twisted away from him like a startled child, but he took her arm and led her to the table and held her chair for her. The gesture seemed to satisfy her. She directed a triumphant look at my mother and then set herself with great energy to her food.

My father smiled across the table at my mother. She pushed her wet hair off her face and smiled back.

I turned away from the sight. Don't look at each other like that. Grandma might see you. But was it only the fear of Grandma's foolish jealousies that made me want to weep?

It was, ironically, the news of Hiroshima that made our lives easier. My grandmother, catching somehow the ultimate terror that the bomb promised, turned from adultery to Armageddon. We were all admonished to fight the whore of Babylon, who was somehow identified in Grandma's mind with the pope of the Roman Catholic Church, and repeatedly warned to prepare to meet our God. A rapid scurrying through her well-worn Bible and she had located several passages to shake over our heads—telling us of the sun turning to darkness and the moon to blood. How could she know that the Day of the Lord's Anger was an almost welcome relief from her accusations of lust and adultery? There never had been any Catholics on Rass, and the end of all things was, after all, almost unimaginable, and therefore had far less power to shake one's core.

We did not take a holiday when peace was declared. There were still crabs moving in the Bay and peeling in the floats. But we ate our supper with a special delight. Toward the end of the meal, my father, turning to me as though peace had brought with it some great change to our meager fortunes, said, "Well, Louise, what will you do now?"

"Do?" Was he trying to get rid of me?

"Yes," he said. "You're a young woman now. I can't keep you on as a hand much longer."

"I don't mind," I said. "I like the water."

"I mind," he said quietly. "But I'm grateful to have had you with me."

"When Call comes back," my mother said as my heart fluttered at the words, "when Call comes back he could lend a hand and you could take a trip. Wouldn't you like that?"

A trip. I'd never been farther than Salisbury.

"You might go to New York and see Caroline." She was getting excited for me.

"Maybe," I said. I wouldn't hurt her by saying that I had no desire to see either New York or my sister. There was that old dream of mountains. Maybe I would go far enough to see a mountain.

At the tail end of the crab season Call came home. I was still at the crab house, but bored with lack of crabs to watch and pack, when suddenly the light from the doorway was blocked. The body of a large man in uniform was filling the door. There was a bass laugh that sounded vaguely familiar and a voice. "Crabby as ever, I see," it said. And then, "Get it?"

"Call!" I jumped, nearly tripping over a stack of packing boxes. He was holding out both his arms, inviting an embrace, but I was suddenly shy. "Oh, my blessed, Call. You done growed up," I said to cover my confusion.

"That's what the navy promised," he said.

I was aware of his clean, masculine smell and at the same time of the smell of salt water and crab, which was my only perfume. I wiped my hands on my pants. "Let's get out of here," I said.

He glanced around. "Can you leave?"

"Mercy, yes," I said. "I don't get more'n a boxful every couple hours."

We walked the board planking to where the skiff was tied. He handed me down into the bow as if I were a lady. Then he jumped into the stern and took up the pole. He stood there in his petty officer's uniform, tall and almost shockingly broad-shouldered and thin-hipped, his cap pushed slightly back, the sun lighting on the patch of reddish hair that showed. His eyes were bright blue and smiling down at me, and his nose had mysteriously shrunk to fit his face. I realized that I was staring at him and that he was enjoying it. I looked away, embarrassed.

He laughed. "You haven't changed, you know." If he'd meant it as a compliment he couldn't have failed more. He himself had changed so marvelously over the past two years, surely something should have happened to me. I crossed my arms over my chest and held my hands tightly under the protection of my upper arms. They scratched like dry sand.

"Aren't you going to ask me about myself?" I had the feeling he was trying to tease me about something. I didn't like it.

"Well," I said, trying not to sound irritated. "Tell me where you been and what you saw."

"I think I seen every island in the world," he said.

"And you come home to the purtiest one of all," I answered.

"Yeah," he said, but his focus blurred for a moment. "The water's about to get her, Wheeze."

"Only a bit, to the south," I said defensively.

"Wheeze, open your eyes," he said. "In two years I've been gone, she's lost at least an acre. Another good storm—"

It wasn't right. He should have been more loyal. You don't come home after two years and suddenly inform your mother that she's dying. I don't know what he saw in my face, but what I actually said was, "I guess you been to see the Captain already."

"No. That's why I came to get you. So we could go see him together like we used to." He shifted the pole to port side. "I guess he's gotten a lot older, huh?"

"What would you expect?"

"Crabby as ever, huh?" he repeated, trying to

make it sound like a joke, to tease me out of my mood.

"He's nearly eighty," I said, and added, "I leave the skiff at the slip now. It's handier than the gut."

He nodded and steered toward the main dock.

"Miss Trudy's death took a lot out of him, didn't it?"

He was beginning to annoy me as much as he had when he was a chubby boy. "I wouldn't say that."

He squinted down at me. "Well, it did, you know. Caroline and I both remarked on it. He was never the same after that."

"Caroline," I said, so anxious to change the subject I was even willing to speak of my sister's good fortune, "Caroline is at a music school in New York City."

"Juilliard," he said. "Yes, I know."

We were at the slip now. I wanted to ask how he knew, but I was afraid to. So I jumped out and tied up the skiff, next to where my father would tie the *Portia Sue*. He shipped the pole and climbed out after me.

We walked without talking down the narrow street. When we got to our gate, I stopped. "I'd like to change my clothes before I go calling."

"Sure," he said.

I carried a pitcher of water to the washstand upstairs to bathe as best I could from the basin. Below I could hear Call's new deep voice rumbling in reply to my mother's soft alto. Every now and then a staccato interjection from my grandmother. I strained to make out the words but couldn't through the door. When I put on my Sunday dress, which I hadn't worn for almost two years, it strained across my breasts and shoulders. I could hardly bring myself to look in the mirror, first at my brown face and then at my sun-scorched hair. I dampened it with water and tried to coax it into a few waves about my forehead. I slopped hand lotion all over my hands and then on my face and legs, even my arms and elbows. It had a cheap fragrance, which I tried to fool myself would cover the essence of crab.

I nearly stumbled on the stairs. All three of them looked up. My mother smiled and would have spoken—her mouth was pursed with some encouraging comment—but I glared her into silence.

Call stood up. "Now," he said. "That is an improvement." It was not the encouragement needed at that moment.

My grandmother half rose from the rocker, "Where you going with that man, Louise? Huh? Where you going?" I grabbed Call's elbow and shoved him toward the door.

He was laughing silently as the voice followed us

out onto the porch. He shook his head at me, as though we were sharing a joke. "I see she hasn't changed, either," he said at the gate.

"She's worse. The things she calls Momma . . ."

"Well," he said, "you mustn't take it to heart," dismissing the years of aggravation with a flick of his hand.

The Captain greeted me with courtesy, but he was overjoyed to see Call. He embraced him almost as though Call were a woman. Men on Rass did not hug each other, but Call returned the embrace without any sign of embarrassment. I could see tears glittering in the old man's eyes when at last he pulled away.

"Well," he said. "My. Well."

"It's good to be back," Call said, covering the old man's discomposure.

"I've saved a tin of milk," the Captain said. "Saved against this day." He started for the kitchen. "Let me just put on the kettle."

"Do you want some help?" I asked, half-rising.

"Oh, no, no. You sit right there and entertain our conquering hero." Call laughed. "You heard about Caroline?" the Captain called.

"Yessir, and she's everlastingly grateful to you."

"It was Trudy's money. Nothing would have made Trudy happier than to know she helped Caroline go on with her music." There was a pause. Then he stuck his head in the doorway. "You been keeping up with each other lately?"

"I saw her," Call said. "I stopped in New York on the way home."

My body understood long before my mind did. First it chilled, then it began to burn, with my heart thumping overtime in alarm.

They were exchanging inanities about the size and terrors of New York, but my body knew that the conversation was about something far more threatening. The Captain brought in the black tea and the tin of milk, which he had neatly poked open with an ice pick—two holes on one side, one on the other.

"I'm guessing you can take the tea now," he said, handing a chipped cup and saucer, first to me, and then to Call. "Not just the milk."

"That's right," Call said grinning. "They made me a man."

"So." The Captain seated himself carefully, and compensating for the tremor in his hands, slowly lifted his own cup to his mouth and took a long sip. "So. What's Miss Caroline got to say for herself these days?"

Call's face flamed in pleasure. It was the question he had been bursting to answer. "She—she said, 'Yes.'"

I knew, of course, what he meant. There was no

need to press him to explain. But something compelled me to hear my own doom spelled out. "'Yes' to what?" I asked.

"Let's just say," he was eyeing the Captain slyly. "Let's just say she answered her Call."

The Captain gave a great tuba laugh, sloshing his tea out onto his lap. He patted away at it with his free hand, still laughing.

"Get it?" Call turned to me. "She answered—"

"I guess it took you most of the train trip from New York to work that one out." Call stopped smiling. I suppose it was the bitterness in my tone. "She's only seventeen," I said, trying to justify myself.

"Eighteen in January." As though I needed to be told. "My mother was married at fifteen."

"So was my grandmother," I said nastily. "Great advertisement for early marriage, wouldn't you say?"

"Sara Louise." The Captain was almost whispering.

I stood up so quickly that the room seemed to spin. I grabbed the arm of the chair, rattling the tea cup all around the saucer. I staggered to the kitchen and put it down, then came back into the room. I knew I was making a scene, but I didn't know how to escape. How unjust to throw everything at me at once.

"Well," I said, "I guess you won't be culling for Daddy this winter."

"No," he said. "I've got a part-time job lined up in New York as soon as I'm discharged. With that and my GI Bill, I can go to school there."

"What about Caroline's school? Have you thought of her? What she'll have to give up to marry you?"

"Oh, my blessed," he said. "It's not like that. I'd never let her give up her chance to sing. She'll go ahead with all her plans. I wouldn't ever hold her back. Surely you know that, Wheeze." He was asking me humbly to understand. "I can help her. I can—"

"Give her a safe harbor," the Captain offered quietly.

"Caroline?" I snorted.

"She's alone in that world, Wheeze. She needs me."

You? I was thinking. You, Call? I said nothing, but he heard me anyhow.

"I guess," he was saying softly, "I guess it's hard for you to think someone like Caroline might favor me." He gave a short laugh. "You never did think I was much to brag about, now did you?"

Oh, God. If I had believed in God I could have cursed him and died. As it was, I extricated myself as quickly as I could from them and made my way, not home, but back to the crab house where I proceeded to ruin my only decent dress fishing the floats.

17

Call was not discharged as soon as he had hoped, so it was the next year, the day before Christmas 1946, that he and Caroline were married. My parents went up for the ceremony in the Juilliard chapel, which, I gathered, was stark in word and dress, but rich in Bach and Mozart, thanks to Caroline's school friends.

I stayed home with Grandma. It was my choice. My parents spoke of getting a neighbor to stay with her, and each offered to remain and let me go instead. But I felt they were greatly relieved by my insistence. The way Grandma was or could be, we dreaded the thought of asking someone outside the family to endure even a few days alone with her. Besides, as they said later, it was the first trip of any length that the two of them had ever taken together. They left, with apologies to me, on the twenty-second. Perhaps my soul, now as calloused as my hands, could have borne such a wedding. I don't know. I was glad not to be put to the test.

Grandma was like a child whose parents have gone off and left her without making plain where they have gone or when they could be expected to return. "Where's Truitt?"

"He's gone to New York for Caroline's wedding, Grandma."

She looked blank, as though she were not quite sure who Caroline was but felt she shouldn't ask. She rocked quietly for a few minutes, picking a thread on her knitted shawl. "Where's Susan?"

"She went with Daddy to New York."

"New York?"

"For Caroline's wedding."

"I know," she snapped. "Why did they leave me?"

"Because you hate to ride the ferry, Grandma, especially in the wintertime."

"I hate the water." She dully observed the worn-out ritual. Suddenly she stopped rocking and cocked her head at me. "Why are you here?"

"You hate to be alone, Grandma."

"Humph." She sniffed and pulled the shawl tight about her shoulders. "I don't need to be watched like one of your old peelers."

The image of Grandma as an old sook caught in my mind. *Get it?* I wanted to say to somebody.

"What you cutting on?"

"Oh, just whittling." It was in fact a branch of almost straight driftwood, which I had decided would make a good cane for Grandma. I had spread out part of the Sunday *Sun* and was trimming the wood down before sanding it.

"I ain't seen that old heathen about," she said. "I guess he's dead like everybody else."

"No. Captain Wallace is just fine."

"He don't ever come around here." She sighed. "Too snobby to pay attention to the likes of me, I reckon."

I stopped whittling. "I thought you didn't like him, Grandma."

"No, I don't favor him. He thinks he's the cat's pajamas. Too good for the daughter of a man who don't even own his own boat."

"What are you talking about, Grandma?"

"He never paid me no mind. Old heathen."

I felt as though I had stumbled off a narrow path right into a marsh. "Grandma, do you mean *now*?"

"You was always a ignorant child. I wouldn't have him on a silver plate *now*. I mean *then*."

"Grandma," I was still trying to feel my way, "you were a lot younger than the Captain."

She flashed her eyes at me. "I would've growed,"

she said like a stubborn child. "He run off and left before I had a chance." Then she put her head down on her gnarled hands and began to cry. "I turned out purty," she said between sobs. "By the time I was thirteen I was the purtiest little thing on the island, but he was already gone. I waited for two more years before I married William, but he never come back 'til now." She wiped her eyes on her shawl and leaned her head back watching a spot on the ceiling. "He was too old for me then, and now it 'pears he's too young. After scatter-headed children like you and Caroline. Oh, my blessed, what a cruel man."

What was I to do? For all the pain she had caused me, to see her like that, still haunted by a childish passion, made me want to put my arm around her and comfort her. But she had turned on me so often, I was afraid to touch her. I tried with words.

"I think he'd be glad to be your friend," I said. "He's all alone now." At least she seemed to be listening to me. "Call and Caroline and I used to go to see him. But—they are gone now, and it isn't proper for me to go down alone."

She raised her head. For a moment I was sure she was about to hurl one of her biblical curses at me, but she didn't. She just eased back and murmured something like "not proper."

So I took another bold step. "We could ask him for Christmas dinner," I said. "There'll be just the two of us. Wouldn't it seem more like Christmas to have company?"

"Would he be good?"

I wasn't sure what she meant by "good," but I said I was sure he would be.

"Can't have no yelling," she explained. "You can't have a body yelling at you when you're trying to eat."

"No," I said. "You can't have that." And added, "I'll tell him you said so."

She smiled slyly. "Yes," she said. "If he wants to come calling here, he better be good."

I wonder if I shall ever feel as old again as I did that Christmas. My grandmother with her charm, gaudy and perishable as dime-store jewelry—whoever had a more exasperating child to contend with? The Captain responded with the dignity of a young teen who is being pestered by a child whose parents he is determined to impress. While I was the aged parent, weary of the tiresome antics of the one and the studied patience of the other.

But I shouldn't complain. Our dinner went remarkably well. I had a chicken—a great treat for us in those days—stuffed with oysters, boiled potatoes, corn pudding, some of Momma's canned beans, rolls, and a hot peach cobbler.

Grandma picked the oysters out of the stuffing and pushed them to the side of her plate. "You know

I don't favor oysters," she said pouting at me.

"Oh, Miss Louise," said the Captain. "Try them with a bit of the white meat. They're delicious."

"It's all right," I said quickly. "Just leave them. Doesn't matter."

"I don't want them on my plate."

I jumped up and took her plate to the kitchen, scraped off the offending oysters, and brought it back, smiling as broadly as I could manage.

"How's that now?" I asked, sitting down.

"I don't favor corn pudding neither," she said. I hesitated, not sure if I should take the pudding off her plate or not. "But I'll eat it." She flashed a proud smile at the Captain. "A lot of times I eat things I don't really favor," she told him.

"Good," he said. "Good for you." He was beginning to relax a bit and enjoy his own dinner.

"Old Trudy died," she said after a while. Neither the Captain nor I replied to this. "Everybody dies," she said sadly.

"Yes, they do," he answered.

"I fear the water will get my coffin," she said. "I hate the water."

"You got some good years to go yet, Miss Louise."

She grinned at him saucily. "Longer than you anyway. I guess you wish now you was young as me, eh, Hiram Wallace?"

He put down his fork and patted his napkin to his beard. "Well—"

"One time I was too young and too poor for you to pay me any mind."

"I was a foolish young man, but that's a long time ago, now, Miss Louise."

"You had no cause to leave, you know. There was ones who would have had you, coward or no."

"Grandma? How about some more chicken?"

She was not to be distracted. "There's others who's not favored lightning, you know."

"Lightning?"

"'Course, chopping down your daddy's mast—" She tittered.

"That's just an old story, Grandma. The Captain never—"

"But I did," he said. "Took me twenty minutes to chop it down and fifty years to set it back." He smiled at me, taking another roll from the tray I was offering. "It's so good to be old," he said. "Youth is a mortal wound."

"What's he talking about, Wheeze? I don't know what he's saying."

He put down his roll and reached over and took her gnarled hand, stroking the back of it with his thumb. "I'm trying to tell the child something only you and I can understand. How good it is to be old."

I watched her face go from being startled by his

gesture to being pleased that he had somehow joined her side against me. Then she seemed to remember. She drew back her hand. "We'll die," she said.

"Yes," he said. "But we'll be ready. The young ones never are."

She would not leave us that day, even for her nap, but rocking in her chair after dinner, she fell asleep, her mouth slightly open, her head rolled awkwardly against her right shoulder.

I came in from washing the dishes to find the two of them in silence, she asleep and he watching her. "I thank you," I said. He looked up at me. "This would have been a lonesome day without you."

"I thank you," he said. And then, "It's hard for you, isn't it?"

I sat down on the couch near his chair. There was no need to pretend, I knew. "I had hoped when Call came home—"

He shook his head. "Sara Louise. You were never meant to be a woman on this island. A man, perhaps. Never a woman."

"I don't even know if I wanted to marry him," I said. "But I wanted something." I looked down at my hands. "I know I have no place here. But there's no escape."

"Pish."

"What?" I couldn't believe I'd heard him correctly.

"Pish. Rubbish. You can do anything you want to. I've known that from the first day I met you—at the other end of my periscope."

"But—"

"What is it you really want to do?"

I was totally blank. What was it I really wanted to do?

"Don't know?" It was almost a taunt. I was fidgeting under his gaze. "Your sister knew what she wanted, so when the chance came, she could take it."

I opened my mouth, but he waved me quiet. "You, Sara Louise. Don't tell me no one ever gave you a chance. You don't need anything given to you. You can make your own chances. But first you have to know what you're after, my dear." His tone was softening.

"When I was younger I wanted to go to boarding school in Crisfield—"

"Too late for that now."

"I—this sounds silly—but I would like to see the mountains."

"That's easy enough. Couple of hundred miles west is all." He waited, expecting more.

"I might—" the ambition began to form along with the sentence. "I want to be a doctor."

"So?" He was leaning forward, staring warmly at me. "So what's to stop you?"

Any answer would have been an excuse to him, the one I gave, most of all. "I can't leave them," I said, knowing he wouldn't believe me.

18

Two days after my parents' return from New York, I came the closest I ever came to fighting with my mother. Children raised as I was did not fight with their parents. There was even a commandment to take care of it, number five: "The only one of the Ten Commandments with a promise attached." I can still hear the preacher's twang as he lectured us. "Honor thy father and thy mother, that thy days may be long upon the land which the Lord thy God giveth thee."

When my mother got off the ferry, there was something different about her. At first I thought it was the hat. Caroline had bought her a new hat for the wedding, and she had worn it on the trip home. It was pale blue felt with a wide rolled-up brim that went out from her face at a slant. There was charm, both in the color, which exactly matched her eyes, and in the angle, which made her face look dramatic instead of simply thin. I could tell by looking at her how beautiful the hat made her feel. She was radiant. My father beside her looked proud and a little awkward in his Sunday suit. The sleeves had never been quite long enough to cover his brown wrists, and his huge weathered hands stuck out rather like the pinchers on a number one Jimmy.

They seemed glad enough to see me, but I could tell that they weren't quite ready to let go of their time together. I carried one of the suitcases and lagged behind them in the narrow street. Occasionally, one or the other of them would turn and smile at me to say something like "Everything go all right?" but they walked closer together than they needed to, touching each other as they walked every few steps and then smiling into each other's faces. My teeth rattled, I was shivering so.

Grandma was standing in the doorway waiting for us. They patted her as they went in. She seemed to sense at once whatever it was going on between them. Without a word of greeting she rushed to her chair, snatched up her Bible, and pushed the pages roughly and impatiently until she found the place she wanted.

"'My son, give me thine heart, and let thine eyes observe my ways. For a whore is a deep ditch; and a strange woman is a narrow pit.'"

Momma's whole body shrank from the word "whore" but she recovered herself and went over to the umbrella stand where she carefully took the pins out of her hat. Her eyes steadily on her own image, she took off the hat, replaced the pins in the brim, and then patted her hair down with one hand. "There," she said, and taking one last look, turned from the mirror toward us. I was furious. Why didn't she scream? Grandma had no right—

"We'd best change," my father said and started up the stairs with the suitcases. She nodded and followed him up.

Grandma stood there, panting with frustration, all those words that she was bursting to say and no one but me to hear. Apparently, I would have to do. She glared at me and then began reading to herself as hastily as she could, searching, I suppose, for something she could fire at me and thus release her coiled spring.

"Here, Grandma," I said, my voice dripping molasses. "Let me help you." I'd been preparing for this moment for months. "Read it, here. Proverbs twenty-five, twenty-four." I flipped over and stuck my finger on the verse that I had memorized gleefully. "'It is better,'" I recited piously, "'to live in a corner of the housetop than in a house with a contentious woman.'" I smiled as sweetly as ever I knew how.

She snatched her Bible out from under my hand, slammed it shut, and holding it in both hands whacked me on the side of the head so hard that it was all I could do to keep from crying out. But at the same time I was glad that she hit me. Even while she stood there grinning at my surprise and pain, I felt a kind of satisfaction. I was deserving of punishment. I knew that. Even if I was not quite clear what I deserved it for.

But the incident didn't help Grandma. She was at my mother all the time now, following three steps behind her as she swept or cleaned, carrying the black Bible and reading and reciting to her. My father, meanwhile, seemed less than anxious to get the *Portia Sue* out on the Bay again. He spent several precious days happily tinkering with his engine, wasting lovely, almost warm, oyster weather. Couldn't he see how badly I needed to get away from that awful house? Couldn't he see that being cooped up with Grandma when she was going full throttle was driving me to the brink of insanity?

And my mother didn't help. Every waking moment was poisoned by Grandma's hatred, but my mother, head slightly bent as though heading into the wind, kept her silent course around the house with only a murmured word or two when a reply seemed necessary and could be given without risking further rancor. It would have been easier for me if she'd screamed or wept, but she didn't.

She did, however, propose that we wash the windows, a job we had done quite thoroughly at the end of the crab season. As I opened my mouth to protest, I saw her face and realized how much she needed to be outside the house, though she would never say so. I fetched the buckets of warm water and ammonia. We scrubbed and wiped in blessed silence for nearly a half hour. Through the porch window where I was working, I could see Grandma, poking anxiously about the living room. She wouldn't dare step out because of her arthritis, but it was clear that our peculiar behavior was disturbing to her. Watching her pinched face, I went through a spectrum of emotions. First a kind perverted pride that my meek mother had bested the old woman, if only for an afternoon. Then a sort of nagging guilt that I should take such pleasure in my grandmother's discomfort. I could not forget that only the week before I had been touched by her childish griefs. This shifted to a growing anger that my clever, gentle, beautiful mother should be so unjustly persecuted, which was transformed, heaven knows how, into a fury against my mother for allowing herself to be so treated.

I moved my bucket and chair to the side of the house where she was standing on her chair, scrubbing and humming happily. "I don't understand it!" The words burst out unplanned.

"What, Louise?"

"You were smart. You went to college. You were good-looking. Why did you ever come here?"

She had a way of never seeming surprised by her children's questions. She smiled, not at me, but at some memory within herself. "Oh, I don't know," she said. "I was a bit of a romantic. I wanted to get away from what I thought of as a very conventional small town and try my wings." She laughed. "My first idea was to go to France."

"France?" I might not surprise her, but she could certainly surprise me.

"Paris, to be precise." She shook her head as she wrung out her rag over the bucket beside her on the chair. "It just shows how conventional I was. Everyone in my college generation wanted to go to Paris and write a novel."

"You wanted to go to Paris and write a novel?"

"Poetry, actually. I had published a few little things in college."

"You published poetry?"

"It's not as grand as it sounds. I promise you. Anyhow, my father wouldn't consider Paris. I didn't have the heart to defy him. My mother had just died." She added the last as though it explained her renunciation of Paris.

"You came to Rass instead of going to *Paris*?"

"It seemed romantic—" She began scrubbing again as she talked. "An isolated island in need of a schoolteacher. I felt—" She was laughing at herself. "I felt like one of the pioneer woman, coming here. Besides—" She turned and looked at me, smiling at my incomprehension. "I had some notion that I would find myself here, as a poet, of course, but it wasn't just that."

The anger was returning. There was no good reason for me to be angry but my body was filled with it, the way it used to be when Caroline was home. "And did you find yourself here on this little island?" The question was coated with sarcasm.

She chose to ignore my tone. "I found very quickly," she scratched at something with her fingernail as she spoke, "I found there was nothing much to find."

I exploded. It was as though she had directly insulted me by speaking so slightingly of herself. "Why? Why did you throw yourself away?" I flung my rag into the bucket, sloshing gray ammonia water all over my ankles. Then I jumped from my chair and wrung out the rag as though it were someone's neck. "You had every chance in the world and you threw it all away for that—" and I jabbed my wrenched rag toward Grandma's face watching us petulantly from behind the glass.

"Please, Louise."

I turned so that I would not see either of their faces, a sob rising from deep inside me. I pounded on the side of the house to stop the tears, smashing out each syllable. "God in heaven, what a stupid waste."

She climbed off her chair and came over to me where I stood, leaning against the clapboard, shaking with tears of anger, grief—who knew what or for whom? She came round where I could see her, her arms halfway stretched out as though she would have liked to embrace me but dared not. I jumped aside. Did I think her touch would taint me? Somehow infect me with the weakness I perceived in her? "You could have done anything, been anything you wanted."

"But I am what I wanted to be," she said, letting her arms fall to her sides. "I chose. No one made me become what I am."

"That's sickening," I said.

"I'm not ashamed of what I have made of my life."

"Well, just don't try to make me like you are," I said.

She smiled. "I can promise you I won't."

"I'm not going to rot here like Grandma. I'm going to get off this island and do something." I waited for her to stop me, but she just stood there. "You're not going to stop me, either."

"I wouldn't stop you," she said. "I didn't stop Caroline, and I certainly won't stop you."

"Oh, Caroline. Caroline's different. Everything's always been for Caroline. Caroline the delicate, the gifted, the beautiful. Of course, we must all sacrifice our lives to give her greatness to the world!"

Did I see her flinch, ever so slightly? "What do you want us to do for you, Louise?"

"Let me go. Let me leave!"

"Of course you may leave. You never said before you wanted to leave."

And, oh, my blessed, she was right. All my dreams of leaving, but beneath them I was afraid to go. I had clung to them, to Rass, yes, even to my grandmother, afraid that if I loosened my fingers an iota, I would find myself once more cold and clean in a forgotten basket.

"I chose the island," she said. "I chose to leave my own people and build a life for myself somewhere else. I certainly wouldn't deny you that same choice. But," and her eyes held me if her arms did not, "oh, Louise, we will miss you, your father and I."

I wanted so to believe her. "Will you really?" I asked. "As much as you miss Caroline?"

"More," she said, reaching up and ever so lightly smoothing my hair with her fingertips.

I did not press her to explain. I was too grateful for that one word that allowed me at last to leave the island and begin to build myself as a soul, separate from the long, long shadow of my twin.

19

Every spring a waterman starts out with brand clean crab pots. Crabs are particular critters, and they won't step into your little wire house if your bait is rank or your wire rusty and clogged with sea growth. But throw down a nice shiny pot with a bait box full of alewife that's just barely short of fresh, and they'll come swimming in the downstairs door, and before they know it they're snug in the upstairs and on the way to market.

That's the way I started out that spring. Shiny as a new crab pot, all set to capture the world. At my mother's suggestion, I wrote the county supervisor who had graded my high school exams, and he was happy to recommend me for a scholarship at the University of Maryland. My first thought was to stay home and help with the crabs until September. My father brushed the offer aside. I think my parents were afraid that if I didn't go at once, I'd lose my nerve. I wasn't worried about that, but I was eager to go, so I took off for College Park in April and got a room near the campus, waiting tables to pay my way until the summer session when I was able to move into the dormitory and begin my studies.

One day in the spring of my sophomore year, I found a note in my box directing me to see my advisor. It was a crisp, blue day that made me feel as I walked across the quadrangle that out near Rass the crabs were beginning to move. The air was fresh with the smell of new growth, and I went into that building and up to that office humming with the pure joy of being alive. I had forgotten that life, like a crab pot, catches a lot of trash you haven't bargained for.

"Miss Bradshaw." He cleaned his pipe, knocking it about the ashtray until I was ready to offer to clean it for him. "Miss Bradshaw. So."

He coughed and then elaborately refilled and lit his pipe.

"Yes, sir?"

He took a puff before going on. "I see you are doing well in your courses."

"Yes, sir."

"I suppose you are considering medicine."

"Yes, sir. That's why I'm in premed."

"I see." He puffed and sucked a bit. "You're serious about this? I would think that a good-looking young woman like you—"

"Yes, sir, I'm sure."

"Have you thought about nursing?"

"No, sir. I want to be a doctor."

When he saw how determined I was, he stopped fooling with his pipe. He wished it were different, he said, but with all the returning veterans, the chances of a girl, "even a bright girl like you" getting into medical school were practically nonexistent. He urged me to switch to nursing at the end of the semester.

A sea nettle hitting me in the face couldn't have stung worse. For a few days I was desolate, but then I decided that if you can't catch crabs where you are, you move your pots. I transferred to the University of Kentucky and into the nursing school, which had a good course in midwifery. I would become a nurse-midwife, spend a few years in the mountains where doctors were scarce, and then use my experience to persuade the government to send me to medical school on a public health scholarship.

When I was about ready to graduate, a list of Appalachian communities asking for nurse-midwives was posted on the student bulletin board. From the neat, double-spaced list, the name "Truitt" jumped out at me. When I was told the village was in a valley completely surrounded by mountains, the nearest hospital a two-hour drive over terrible roads, I was delighted. It seemed exactly the place for me to work for two or three years, see all the mountains I ever wanted to see, and then, armed with a bit of money and a lot of experience, to batter my way into medical school.

A mountain-locked valley is more like an island than anything else I know. Our water is the Appalachian wilderness, our boats, the army surplus jeeps we count on to navigate our washboard roads and the hairpin curves across the mountains. There are a few trucks, freely loaned about in good weather to any valley farmer who must take his pigs or calves to market. The rest of us seldom leave the valley.

The school is larger than the one on Rass, not only because there are twice the number of families, but because people here, even more than islanders, tend to count their wealth in children. There is a one-room Presbyterian Church, built of native stone, to which a preacher comes every three weeks when the road is passable. And every fourth Sunday, God and the weather willing, a Catholic priest says mass in the schoolhouse. There are no mines open in our pocket of western Virginia now, but the Polish and Lithuanian miners who were brought down from Pennsylvania two generations ago stayed and turned their hands to digging fields and cutting pastures out of the hillsides. They are still considered outsiders by the tough Scotch-Irish who have farmed the rocks of the valley floor for nearly two hundred years.

The most pressing health problem is one never encountered on Rass. On Saturday night, five or six of the valley men get blind drunk and beat their wives and children. In the Protestant homes I am told it is a Catholic problem, and in the Catholic homes, a Protestant. The truth, of course, is that the ailment crosses denominational lines. Perhaps it is the fault of the mountains, glowering above us, delaying sunrise and hastening the night. They are as awesome and beautiful as the open water, but the valley people do not seem to notice. Nor are they grateful for the game and timber that the mountains so generously provide. Most of them only see the ungiving soil from which a man must wrestle his subsistence and the barriers that shut him out from the world. These men struggle against their mountains. On Rass men followed the water. There is a difference.

Although the valley people are slow to accept outsiders, they did not hesitate to come to me. They needed my skill.

"Nurse?" An old ruddy-faced farmer was at my door in the middle of the night. "Nurse, would you be kind enough to see to my Betsy? She's having a bad go of it."

I dressed and went with him to his farm to deliver what I thought was a baby. To my amazement, he drove straight past the house to the barn. Betsy was his cow, but neither of us would have been prouder of that outsized calf had it been a child.

I came to wonder if every disease of man and beast had simply waited for my arrival to invade the valley. My little house, which was also the clinic, was usually jammed, and often there was a jeep waiting at the door to take me to examine a child or a cow or a woman in labor.

The first time I saw Joseph Wojtkiewicz (what my grandmother would have done to that name!), the first time I saw him to know who he was, that is, he arrived in his jeep late one night to ask me to come and treat his son, Stephen. Like most of the valley men, he seemed ill at ease with me, his only conversation during the ride was about the boy who had a severe earache and a fever of 105, which had made his father afraid to bring him out in the cold night air to the clinic.

The Wojtkiewicz house was a neatly built log cabin with four small rooms. There were three children, the six-year-old patient, and his two sisters, Mary and Anna, who were eight and five. The mother had been dead for several years.

The county had sent me an assortment of drugs including a little penicillin, so I was able to give the child a shot. Then an alcohol rubdown to bring the fever down a bit until the drug had time to do its work, a little warm oil to soothe the ear, a word or two to commend bravery, and I was ready to go.

I had repacked my bag and was heading for the door when I realized the boy's father had made coffee for me. It seemed rude not to drink it, so I sat opposite him at his kitchen table, my face set in my most professional smile, mouthing reassurance and unnecessary directions for the child's care.

I became increasingly aware that the man was staring at me, not impolitely, but as though he were studying an unknown specimen. At last he said, "Where do you come from?"

"The University of Kentucky," I said. I prided myself on never letting remarks made by patients or their families surprise me.

"No, no," he said. "Not school. Where do you really come from?"

I began to tell him quite matter-of-factly about Rass, where it was, what it looked like, slipping into a picture of how it had been. I hadn't returned to the island since entering nursing school except for two funerals, my grandmother's and the Captain's. Now as I described the marsh as it was when I was a child, I could almost feel the wind on my arms, and hear the geese baying like a pack of hounds as they flew over. No one on the mainland had ever invited me to talk about home before, and the longer I talked, the more I wanted to talk, churning with happiness and homesickness at the same time.

The little girls had come into the kitchen and were leaning on either side of their father's chair, listening with the same dark-eyed intensity. Joseph put an arm around each of them, absently stroking the black curls of Anna who was on his right.

At last I stopped, a little shy for having talked so much. I even apologized.

"No, no," he said. "I asked because I wanted to know. I knew there was something different about you. I kept wondering ever since you came. Why would a woman like you, who could have anything she wanted, come to a place like this? Now I understand." He left off stroking his daughter's hair and leaned forward, his big hands open as though he needed their help to explain his meaning. "God in heaven,"—I thought at first it was an oath, it had been so long since I'd heard the expression used in any other way—"God in heaven's been raising you for this valley from the day you were born."

I was furious. He didn't know anything about me or the day I was born or he'd never say such a foolish thing, sitting there so piously at his kitchen table, sounding for all the world like a Methodist preacher.

But then, oh, my blessed, he smiled. I guess from

that moment I knew I was going to marry Joseph Wojtkiewicz—God, pope, three motherless children, unspellable surname and all. For when he smiled, he looked like the kind of man who would sing to the oysters.

20

It is far simpler to be married to a Catholic than anyone from my Methodist past would believe. I am quite willing for the children, his, of course, but also ours as they come along, to be raised in the Catholic faith. The priest frets about me when we meet, but he's only around once a month, and Joseph himself has never suggested that I ought to turn Catholic or even religious. My parents showed their approval by making the long trip from Rass to attend our schoolhouse wedding. I will always be glad that my father and Joseph met each other that once, because this year, on the second of October, my father went to sleep in his chair after a day of crabbing and never woke up.

Caroline called me from New York. I couldn't remember ever having heard her cry aloud before, and there she was weeping for the benefit of the entire Truitt village party line. I was unreasonably irritated. She and Call were going down at once and would stay through the funeral. It seemed wrong that she should be able to go and not me. I was the child who had fished his crab floats and culled his oysters, but I was so far along in my ninth month that I knew better than anyone how crazy it would be to try such a trip; so Joseph went in my place and got back to the farm four days before our son was born.

We thought he might bring Momma back with him then, but Caroline was making her New Haven debut as Musetta in *La Bohème* on the twenty-first. Our parents had planned to go before my father's death, so Caroline and Call begged her to return with them and stay on through the opening. Since she would be coming to live with us soon, it seemed the right thing for her to do. Joseph did not plead my condition. He was already learning midwifery, and I think my mother understood that he would have been disappointed not to deliver our child himself.

I suppose every mother is reduced to idiocy when describing her firstborn, but, oh, he is a beauty—large and dark like his father, but with the bright blue eyes of the Bradshaws. I swear from his cry that he will be a singer and from his huge hands that he will follow the water, which makes his father laugh aloud and tease me about our son setting sail on the trickle of a stream that crosses our pasture.

The older children adore him, and, as for the valley people, it doesn't matter how often I explain that we named the baby for my father, they are all sure that Truitt is their namesake. Their need for me made them accept me into their lives, but now I feel that they are taking me into their hearts as well.

My work did not, could not, end with my marriage to Joseph and his children or even with the birth of Truitt. There is no one else to care for the valley. The hospital remains two hours away, and the road is impassable for much of the winter.

This year our winter came early. In November I was watching over two pregnancies, one of which I worried about. The mother is a thin, often-beaten girl of about eighteen. From the size of her, I quickly suspected twins and urged her and her husband to go to the hospital in Staunton or Harrisonburg for the delivery.

Despite his bouts of drunkenness, the young husband is well-meaning. He would have taken her, I believe, had there been any money at all. But how could I urge them to make the trip when the hospital might well reject her? And without money where could they stay in the city until the babies actually came? I counted the days and measured her progress as best I could and then sent word to a doctor in Staunton that I would need help with the birth. But it snowed twenty inches the day before Essie went into labor, so when they called me, I went alone.

The first twin, a nearly six-pound boy, came fairly easily, despite Essie's slender frame, but the second did not follow as I thought it should. I had begun to fear for it, when I realized that it was very small, but in a breach position. I reached in and turned the twin so that she was delivered head first, but blue as death. Before I even cut the cord, I put my mouth down and breathed into her tiny one. Her chest, smaller than my fist, shuddered, and she gave a cry, but so weak, so like a parting, that I was near despair.

"Is it all right?" Essie asked.

"Small," I said and busied myself cutting and tying off the cord. How cold she was. It sent painful shivers up my arms. I called the grandmother, who had been taking care of the boy, to get me blankets and see to the afterbirth.

I swathed the child tightly and held her against my body. It was like cuddling a stone. I almost ran from the bedroom. What was I to do? They must give me an incubator if they expected me to care for newborn babies in this godforsaken place.

The kitchen was slightly warmer than the bedroom. I went over to the enormous iron stove. A remnant of a fire was banked in the far corner under the stove top. I put my hand on the stove and found it comfortingly warm. I grabbed an iron pot, stuffed it with all the dishrags and towels I could reach with one hand, lay the baby in it, and set it in the oven door. Then I pulled up a kitchen stool and sat there with my hand on the baby's body and watched. It may have been hours. I was too intent to keep track, but, at length, a sort of pinkness invaded the translucent blue skin of her cheek.

"Nurse?" I jumped at the sound. The young father had come into the kitchen. "Nurse, should I go for the priest?" His eyes widened at the sight of the nurse cooking his baby in the oven, but, rather than protest, he repeated his question about fetching the priest.

"How could you on these roads?" I'm sure I sounded impatient. I wanted to be left in peace to guard my baby.

"Should I do it myself?" he asked, apparently alarmed by whatever it was he was suggesting. "Or you could."

"Oh, do be quiet."

"But, Nurse, it must be baptized before it dies."

"She won't die!"

He flinched. I'm sure he found me terrifying. "But, if it did—"

"She will not die." But to keep him quiet and get

rid of him, I poured water out of the cold teakettle onto my hand and reached into the oven, placing my hand on the blur of dark hair. "What is her name?"

He shook his head in bewilderment. Apparently, everything was left for me to do. Susan. Susan was the name of a saint, wasn't it? Well, if not, they could have the priest fix it later. "Essie Susan," I said, "I baptize you in the name of the Father and of the Son and of the Holy Ghost. Amen." Under my hand the tiny head stirred.

The father crossed himself, nodded a scared-rabbit kind of thank you, and hurried out to report the sacrament to his wife. Soon the grandmother was in the kitchen.

"Thank you, Nurse. We're grateful to you."

"Where is the other twin?" I asked, suddenly stricken. I had forgotten him. In my anxiety for his sister, I had completely forgotten him. "Where have you put him?"

"In the basket." She looked at me, puzzled. "He's sleeping."

"You should hold him," I said. "Hold him as much as you can. Or let his mother hold him."

She started for the door. "Nurse. Should I baptize him as well?"

"Oh, yes," I said. "Baptize him and then let Essie nurse him."

My own breasts were swollen with milk for Truitt.

I knew his father would bring him to me soon, but there was plenty. I took my baby out of the oven and held her mouth to catch the milk, which began to flow of its own accord. A perfect tongue, smaller than a newborn kitten's, reached out for the drops of milk on her lips. Then the little mouth rooted against my breast until she had found the nipple for herself.

Hours later, walking home, my boots crunching on the snow, I bent my head backward to drink in the crystal stars. And clearly, as though the voice came from just behind me, I heard a melody so sweet and pure that I had to hold myself to keep from shattering:

I wonder as I wander out under the sky . . .

ABOUT THE AUTHOR

Katherine Paterson's works have received wide acclaim. Among them are *Bridge to Terabithia*, winner of the 1978 Newbery Medal; *The Great Gilly Hopkins*, a Newbery Honor Book and winner of the 1979 National Book Award; and *The Master Puppeteer*, awarded the 1977 National Book Award.

Katherine Paterson was born in China, the daughter of missionary parents, and spent part of her childhood there. She was educated in both China and the United States, graduating from King College, in Bristol, Tennessee, and later receiving her master's degree in English Bible from the Presbyterian School of Christian Education in Richmond, Virginia. She lived in Japan for four years, working for two of those years as a Christian Education Assistant to a group of eleven pastors in rural Japan.

Her four children and their friends have provided her with some of the subject matter for her sharply observant stories of family life. She lives with her family in Barre, Vermont.